BARE BONES

KATHY REICHS

SCRIBNER

NEW YORK   LONDON   TORONTO   SYDNEY   SINGAPORE

SCRIBNER
1230 Avenue of the Americas
New York, NY 10020

SCRIBNER and design are trademarks of Macmillan Library Reference USA, Inc.,
used under license by Simon & Schuster, the publisher of this work.

For information regarding special discounts for bulk purchases,
please contact Simon & Schuster Special Sales at 1-800-456-6798
or *business@simonandschuster.com*

DESIGNED BY ERICH HOBBING

Text set in Stempel Garamond

Manufactured in the United States of America

3   5   7   9   10   8   6   4   2

Library of Congress Cataloging-in-Publication Data
Reichs, Kathy.
Bare bones/Kathy Reichs.
p. cm.
1. Brennan, Temperance (Fictitious character)—Fiction. 2. Forensic anthropology—
Fiction. 3. Women anthropologists—Fiction. 4. Endangered species—Fiction.
5. Smuggling—Fiction. 6. North Carolina—Fiction. I. Title.

PS3568.E476345B375 2003
813'.54—dc21
2003040725

ISBN 0-7432-3346-8

Dedicated to all those fighting to protect our precious wildlife, especially:

The United States Fish and Wildlife Service
The World Wildlife Foundation
The Animals Asia Foundation

ACKNOWLEDGMENTS

I WISH TO EXPRESS GRATITUDE TO CAPTAIN JOHN GALLAGHER (retired); to Detective John Appel, Guilford County, North Carolina, Sheriff's Department (retired); to Detective Chris Dozier, Charlotte-Mecklenburg Police Department; and, especially, to Ira J. Rimson, P.E., for help with the Cessna/drug scenario.

Many of those working to protect endangered wildlife gave generously of their time and expertise. Special thanks to Bonnie C. Yates, forensics specialist, Morphology/Mammals Team Leader, and Ken Goddard, director, Clark R. Bavin National Fish and Wildlife Forensics Laboratory; to Lori Brown, investigative assistant, and Tom Bennett, resident agent in charge, United States Fish and Wildlife Service; and to Agent Howard Phelps, Carolyn Simmons, and the staff at the Pocosin Lakes National Wildlife Refuge. You are on the front lines, battling to save what we can't afford to lose. Your efforts are appreciated.

David M. Bird, Ph.D., McGill University, provided information on threatened bird species. Randy Pearce, DDS, and James W. Williams, J.D., shared their knowledge of the Melungeons of Tennessee. Eric Buel, Ph.D., director, Vermont Forensics Laboratory, coached me on amelogenin. Michael Baden, M.D., and Claude Pothel, M.D., enlightened me on the details of diatoms and death by drowning.

Captain Barry Faile, Lancaster County Sheriff's Department, and Michael Morris, Lancaster County coroner, were patient with my questions. Michael Sullivan, M.D., welcomed me at the Mecklenburg County Medical Examiner facility. Terry Pitts, D.Min., NCFD, offered suggestions on funeral home basements. Judy H. Morgan, GRI, kept me accurate on Charlotte real estate and geography.

I appreciate the continued support of Chancellor James Woodward of the University of North Carolina–Charlotte. *Merci* to André Lau-

ACKNOWLEDGMENTS

zon, M.D., chef de service, and to all of my colleagues at the Labora-toire de Sciences Judiciaires et de Médecine Légale.

A thousand thanks to Jim Junot for answers to a million questions.

Thanks to Paul Reichs for comments on the manuscript, and to the whole ragtag beach bunch for title suggestions and other minutiae.

My incredibly patient and brilliant editor, Susanne Kirk, took a rough piece of work and made it flow.

A special thanks to my supersonic agent, Jennifer Rudolph Walsh. You delivered Wyatt Z. the same day I delivered *Bare Bones.* It was a very good year.

BARE
BONES

As I was packaging what remained of the dead baby, the man I would kill was burning pavement north toward Charlotte.

I didn't know that at the time. I'd never heard the man's name, knew nothing of the grisly game in which he was a player.

At that moment I was focused on what I would say to Gideon Banks. How would I break the news that his grandchild was dead, his youngest daughter on the run?

My brain cells had been bickering all morning. You're a forensic anthropologist, the logic guys would say. Visiting the family is not your responsibility. The medical examiner will report your findings. The homicide detective will deliver the news. A phone call.

All valid points, the conscience guys would counter. But this case is different. You *know* Gideon Banks.

I felt a deep sadness as I tucked the tiny bundle of bones into its container, fastened the lid, and wrote a file number across the plastic. So little to examine. Such a short life.

As I secured the tub in an evidence locker, the memory cells floated an image of Gideon Banks. Wrinkled brown face, fuzzy gray hair, voice like ripping duct tape.

Expand the image.

A small man in a plaid flannel shirt arcing a string mop across a tile floor.

The memory cells had been offering the same image all morning. Though I'd tried to conjure up others, this one kept reappearing.

Gideon Banks and I had worked together at the University of North Carolina at Charlotte for almost two decades until his retirement three years back. I'd periodically thanked him for keeping my office and lab clean, given him birthday cards and a small gift each Christmas. I knew he was conscientious, polite, deeply religious, and devoted to his kids.

And he kept the corridors spotless.

That was it. Beyond the workplace, our lives did not connect.

Until Tamela Banks placed her newborn in a woodstove and vanished.

Crossing to my office, I booted up my laptop and spread my notes across the desktop. I'd barely begun my report when a form filled the open doorway.

"A home visit really is above and beyond."

I hit "save" and looked up.

The Mecklenburg County medical examiner was wearing green surgical scrubs. A stain on his right shoulder mimicked the shape of Massachusetts in dull red.

"I don't mind." Like I didn't mind suppurating boils on my buttocks. "I'll be glad to speak to him."

Tim Larabee might have been handsome were it not for his addiction to running. The daily marathon training had wizened his body, thinned his hair, and leatherized his face. The perpetual tan seemed to gather in the hollows of his cheeks, and to pool around eyes set way too deep. Eyes that were now crimped with concern.

"Next to God and the Baptist church, family has been the cornerstone of Gideon Banks's life," I said. "This will shake him."

"Perhaps it's not as bad as it seems."

I gave Larabee the Look. We'd had this conversation an hour earlier.

"All right." He raised a sinewy hand. "It seems bad. I'm sure Mr. Banks will appreciate the personal input. Who's driving you?"

"Skinny Slidell."

"Your lucky day."

"I wanted to go alone, but Slidell refused to take no for an answer."

"Not Skinny?" Mock surprise.

"I think Skinny's hoping for some kind of lifetime achievement award."

"I think Skinny's hoping to get laid."

I pegged a pen at him. He batted it down.

"Watch yourself."

Larabee withdrew. I heard the autopsy room door click open, then shut.

I checked my watch. Three forty-two. Slidell would be here in twenty minutes. The brain cells did a collective cringe. On Skinny there was cerebral agreement.

I shut the computer down and leaned back in my chair.

What would I say to Gideon Banks?

Bad luck, Mr. Banks. Looks like your youngest gave birth, wrapped the tyke in a blanket, and used him as kindling.

Good, Brennan.

Wham-o! The visual cells sent up a new mental image. Banks pulling a Kodak print from a cracked leather wallet. Six brown faces. Close haircuts for the boys, pigtails for the girls. All with teeth too big for the smiles.

Zoom out.

The old man beaming over the photo, adamant that each child would go to college.

Did they?

No idea.

I slipped off my lab coat and hung it on the hook behind my door.

If the Banks kids had attended UNC–Charlotte while I was on the faculty, they'd shown little interest in anthropology. I'd met only one. Reggie, a son midrange in the offspring chronology, had taken my human evolution course.

The memory cells offered a gangly kid in a baseball cap, brim low over razor-blade brows. Last row in the lecture hall. A intellect, C+ effort.

How long ago? Fifteen years? Eighteen?

I'd worked with a lot of students back then. In those days my research focused on the ancient dead, and I'd taught several undergraduate classes. Bioarchaeology. Osteology. Primate ecology.

One morning an anthro grad showed up at my lab. A homicide detective with the Charlotte-Mecklenburg PD, she'd brought bones recovered from a shallow grave. Could her former prof determine if the remains were those of a missing child?

I could. They were.

That case was my first encounter with coroner work. Today the only seminar I teach is in forensic anthropology, and I commute between Charlotte and Montreal serving as forensic anthropologist to each jurisdiction.

The geography had been difficult when I'd taught full-time, requiring complex choreography within the academic calendar. Now, save for the duration of that single seminar, I shift as needed. A few weeks north, a few weeks south, longer when casework or court testimony requires.

North Carolina and Quebec? Long story.

My academic colleagues call what I do "applied." Using my knowledge of bones, I tease details from cadavers and skeletons, or parts thereof, too compromised for autopsy. I give names to the skeletal, the decomposed, the mummified, the burned, and the mutilated, who might otherwise go to anonymous graves. For some, I determine the manner and time of their passing.

With Tamela's baby there'd been but a cup of charred fragments. A newborn is chump change to a woodstove.

Mr. Banks, I'm so sorry to have to tell you, but—

My cell phone sounded.

"Yo, Doc. I'm parked out front." Skinny Slidell. Of the twenty-four detectives in the Charlotte-Mecklenburg PD Felony Investigative Bureau/Homicide Unit, perhaps my least favorite.

"Be right there."

I'd been in Charlotte several weeks when an informant's tip led to the shocking discovery in the woodstove. The bones had come to me. Slidell and his partner had caught the case as a homicide. They'd tossed the scene, tracked down witnesses, taken statements. Everything led to Tamela Banks.

I shouldered my purse and laptop and headed out. In passing, I stuck my head into the autopsy room. Larabee looked up from his gunshot victim and waggled a gloved finger in warning.

My reply was an exaggerated eye roll.

The Mecklenburg County Medical Examiner facility occupies one end of a featureless brick shoebox that entered life as a Sears Garden Center. The other end of the shoebox houses satellite offices of the Charlotte-Mecklenburg Police Department. Devoid of architectural charm save a slight rounding of the edges, the building is surrounded by enough asphalt to pave Rhode Island.

As I exited the double glass doors, my nostrils drank in an olfactory cocktail of exhaust, smog, and hot pavement. Heat radiated from the building walls, and from the brick steps connecting it to a small tentacle of the parking lot.

Hot town. Summer in the city.

A black woman sat in the vacant lot across College Street, back to a sycamore, elephant legs stretched full length on the grass. The woman was fanning herself with a newspaper, animatedly arguing some point with a nonexistent adversary.

A man in a Hornets jersey was muscling a shopping cart up the sidewalk in the direction of the county services building. He stopped just past the woman, wiped his forehead with the crook of his arm, and checked his cargo of plastic bags.

Noticing my gaze, the cart man waved. I waved back.

Slidell's Ford Taurus idled at the bottom of the stairs, AC blasting, tinted windows full up. Descending, I opened the back door, shoved aside file folders, a pair of golf shoes stuffed with audiotapes, two Burger King bags, and a squeeze tube of suntan lotion, and wedged my computer into the newly created space.

Erskine "Skinny" Slidell undoubtedly thought of himself as "old school," though God alone knew what institution would claim him. With his knockoff Ray-Bans, Camel breath, and four-letter speech, Slidell was an unwittingly self-created caricature of a Hollywood cop. People told me he was good at his job. I found it hard to believe.

At the moment of my approach Dirty Harry was checking his lower incisors in the rearview mirror, lips curled back in a monkey-fear grimace.

Hearing the rear door open, Slidell jumped, and his hand shot to the mirror. As I slid into the passenger seat, he was fine-tuning the rearview with the diligence of an astronaut adjusting Hubble.

"Doc." Slidell kept his faux Ray-Bans pointed at the mirror.

"Detective." I nodded, placed my purse at my feet, and closed the door.

At last satisfied with the angle of reflection, Slidell abandoned the mirror, shifted into gear, crossed the lot, and shot across College onto Phifer.

We rode in silence. Though the temperature in the car was thirty degrees lower than that outside, the air was thick with its own blend of odors. Old Whoppers and fries. Sweat. Bain de Soleil. The bamboo mat on which Slidell parked his ample backside.

Skinny Slidell himself. The man smelled and looked like an "after" shot for an antismoking poster. During the decade and a half I'd been consulting for the Mecklenburg County ME, I'd had the pleasure of working with Slidell on several occasions. Each had been a trip to Aggravation Row. This case promised to be another.

The Bankses' home was in the Cherry neighborhood, just southeast of I-277, Charlotte's version of an inner beltway. Cherry, unlike many inner-city *quartiers,* had not enjoyed the renaissance experienced in recent years by Dilworth and Elizabeth to the west and north. While those neighborhoods had integrated and yuppified, Cherry's fortunes had headed south. But the community held true to its ethnic roots. It started out black and remained so today.

Within minutes Slidell passed an Autobell car wash, turned left off Independence Boulevard onto a narrow street, then right onto another. Oaks and magnolias thirty, forty, a hundred years old threw shadows onto modest frame and brick houses. Laundry hung limp on clotheslines. Sprinklers ticked and whirred, or lay silent at the ends of garden hoses. Bicycles and Big Wheels dotted yards and walkways.

Slidell pulled to the curb halfway up the block, and jabbed a thumb at a small bungalow with dormer windows jutting from the roof. The siding was brown, the trim white.

"Beats the hell outta that rat's nest where the kid got fried. Thought I'd catch scabies tossing that dump."

"Scabies is caused by mites." My voice was chillier than the car interior.

"Exactly. You wouldn't have believed that shithole."

"You should have worn gloves."

"You got that right. And a respirator. These people—"

"What people would that be, Detective?"

"Some folks live like pigs."

"Gideon Banks is a hardworking, decent man who raised six children largely on his own."

"Wife beat feet?"

"Melba Banks died of breast cancer ten years ago." There. I did know something about my coworker.

"Bum luck."

The radio crackled some message that was lost on me.

"Still don't excuse kids dropping their shorts with no regard for consequences. Get jammed up? No-o-o-o problem. Have an abortion."

Slidell killed the engine and turned the Ray-Bans on me.

"Or worse."

"There may be some explanation for Tamela Banks's actions."

I didn't really believe that, had spent all morning taking the opposite position with Tim Larabee. But Slidell was so irritating I found myself playing devil's advocate.

"Right. And the chamber of commerce will probably name her mother of the year."

"Have you met Tamela?" I asked, forcing my voice level.

"No. Have you?"

No. I ignored Slidell's question.

"Have you met any of the Banks family?"

"No, but I took statements from folks who were snorting lines in the next room while Tamela incinerated her kid." Slidell pocketed the keys. "*Excusez-moi* if I haven't dropped in for tea with the lady and her relations."

"You've never had to deal with any of the Banks kids because they were raised with good, solid values. Gideon Banks is as straitlaced as—"

"The mutt Tamela's screwing ain't close to straight up."

"The baby's father?"

"Unless Miss Hot Pants was entertaining while Daddy was dealing."

Easy! The man is a cockroach.

"Who is he?"

"His name is Darryl Tyree. Tamela was shacking up in Tyree's little piece of heaven out on South Tryon."

"Tyree sells drugs?"

"And we're not talking the Eckerd's pharmacy." Slidell hit the door handle and got out.

I bit back a response. *One hour. It's over.*

A stab of guilt. Over for me, but what about Gideon Banks? What about Tamela and her dead baby?

I joined Slidell on the sidewalk.

"Je-zus. It's hot enough to burn a polar bear's butt."

"It's August."

"I should be at the beach."

Yes, I thought. Under four tons of sand.

I followed Slidell up a narrow walk littered with fresh-mown grass to a small cement stoop. He pressed a thumb to a rusted button beside the front door, dug a hanky from his back pocket, and wiped his face.

No response.

Slidell knocked on a wooden portion of the screen door.

Nothing.

Slidell knocked again. His forehead glistened and his hair was separating into wet clumps.

"Police, Mr. Banks."

Slidell banged with the heel of his hand. The screen door rattled in its frame.

"Gideon Banks!"

Condensation dripped from a window AC to the left of the door. A lawn mower whined in the distance. Hip-hop drifted from somewhere up the block.

Slidell banged again. A dark crescent winked from his gray polyester armpit.

"Anyone home?"

The AC's compressor kicked on. A dog barked.

Slidell yanked the screen.

Whrrrrp!

Pounded on the wooden door.

Bam! Bam! Bam!

Released the screen. Barked his demand.

"Police! Anyone there?"

Across the street, a curtain flicked, dropped back into place.

Had I imagined it?

A drop of perspiration rolled down my back to join the others soaking my bra and waistband.

At that moment my cell phone rang.

I answered.

That call swept me into a vortex of events that ultimately led to my taking a life.

2

"Tempe Brennan."

"Pig pickin'!" My daughter gave a series of guttural snorts. "Barbecue!"

"Can't talk now, Katy."

I turned a shoulder to Slidell, pressing the cell phone tight to my ear to hear Katy over the static.

Slidell knocked again, this time with Gestapo force. "Mr. Banks!"

"I'll pick you up at noon tomorrow," Katy said.

"I know nothing about cigars," I said, speaking as softly as I could. Katy wanted me to accompany her to a picnic given by the owner of a cigar and pipe store. I had no idea why.

"You eat barbecue."

Bam! Bam! Bam! The screen door danced in its frame.

"Yes, bu—"

"You like bluegrass." Katy could be persistent.

At that moment the inner door opened and a woman scowled through the screen. Though he had an inch on her in height, the woman had Slidell hands down in poundage.

"Is Gideon Banks at home?" Slidell barked.

"Who askin'?"

"Katy, I've got to go," I whispered.

"Boyd's looking forward to this. There's something he wants to discuss with you." Boyd is my estranged husband's dog. Conversations with or about Boyd usually lead to trouble.

Slidell held his badge to the screen.

"Pick you up at noon?" My daughter could be as unrelenting as Skinny Slidell.

"All right," I hissed, punching the "end" button.

The woman studied the badge, arms akimbo like a prison guard.

I pocketed the phone.

The woman's eyes crawled from the badge to my companion, then to me.

"Daddy's sleepin'."

"I think it might be best to wake him," I jumped in, hoping to defuse Slidell.

"This about Tamela?"

"Yes."

"I'm Tamela's sister. Geneva. Like Switzerland." Her tone suggested she'd said that before.

Geneva backhanded the screen. This time the spring made a sound like piano keys.

Removing his shades, Slidell squeezed past her. I followed, into a small, dim living room. An archway opened onto a hall directly opposite our entry point. I could see a kitchen to the right with a closed door beyond, two closed doors to the left, a bath straight ahead at the end.

Six kids. I could only imagine the competition for shower and sink time.

Our hostess let the screen *whrrrrppp* to its frame, pushed the inner door shut, and turned to face us. Her skin was a deep, chocolate brown, the sclera of her eyes the pale yellow of pine nuts. I guessed her age to be mid-twenties.

"Geneva is a beautiful name," I said for lack of a better opening. "Have you been to Switzerland?"

Geneva looked at me a long time, face devoid of expression. Perspiration dotted the brow and temples from which her hair had been pulled straight back. The lone window unit apparently cooled another room.

"I get Daddy."

She tipped her head toward a worn couch on the right wall of the living room. Curtains framing the open window above hung limp with heat and humidity.

"Wanna sit." It was more a statement than a question.

"Thank you," I said.

Geneva waddled toward the archway, shorts bunching between her thighs. A small, stiff ponytail stuck straight out from the back of her head.

As Slidell and I took opposite ends of the couch, I heard a door open, then the tinny sound of a gospel station. Seconds later the music was truncated.

I looked around.

The decorating was nouveau Wal-Mart. Linoleum. Vinyl recliner. Oak-laminate coffee and end tables. Plastic palms.

But a loving hand was clearly present.

The frilled curtains behind us smelled of laundry detergent and Downy. A rip on my armrest had been carefully darned. Every surface gleamed.

Bookshelves and tabletops overflowed with framed photos and crudely made objets d'art. A garishly painted clay bird. A ceramic plate with the impression of a tiny hand, the name *Reggie* arching below. A box constructed of Popsicle sticks. Dozens of cheap trophies. Shoulder pads and helmets encased forever in gold-coated plastic. A jump shot. A cut at a fastball.

I surveyed the snapshots closest to me. Christmas mornings. Birthday parties. Athletic teams. Each memory was preserved in a dimestore frame.

Slidell picked up a throw pillow, raised his brows, set it back between us. *God is Love,* embroidered in blue and green. Melba's handiwork?

The sadness I'd been feeling all morning intensified as I thought of six children losing their mother. Of Tamela's doomed infant.

The pillow. The photos. The school and team memorabilia. Save for the portrait of a black Jesus hanging above the archway, I could have been sitting in my childhood home in Beverly, on the south side of Chicago. Beverly was shade trees, and PTA bake sales, and morning papers lying on the porch. Our tiny brick bungalow was my Green Gables, my Ponderosa, my starship *Enterprise* until the age of seven. Until despair over her infant son's death propelled my mother back to her beloved Carolina, husband and daughters following in her mournful wake.

I loved that house, felt loved and protected in it. I sensed those same feelings clinging to this place.

Slidell pulled out his hanky and mopped his face.

"Hope the old man scores the air-conditioned bedroom." Spoken through one side of his mouth. "With six kids, I suppose he'd be lucky just to score a bedroom."

I ignored him.

Heat magnified the smells inside the tiny house. Onions. Cooking oil. Wood polish. Whatever was used to scrub the linoleum.

Who scrubbed it? I wondered. Tamela? Geneva? Banks himself?

I studied the black Jesus. Same robe, same thorny crown, same open palms. Only the Afro and skin tones differed from the one that had hung over my mother's bed.

Slidell sighed audibly, hooked his collar with a finger, and pulled it from his neck.

I looked at the linoleum. A pebble pattern, gray and white.

Like the bones and ash from the woodstove.

What will I say?

At that moment a door opened. A gospel group singing "Going On in the Name of the Lord." The swish of padded soles on linoleum.

Gideon Banks looked smaller than I remembered, all bone and sinew. That was wrong, somehow. Backward. He should have seemed larger in his own space. King of the realm. Paterfamilias. Was my recall incorrect? Had age shriveled him? Or worry?

Banks hesitated in the archway, and his lids crimped behind their heavy lenses. Then he straightened, crossed to the recliner, and lowered himself, gnarled hands gripping the armrests.

Slidell leaned forward. I cut him off.

"Thank you for seeing us, Mr. Banks."

Banks nodded. He was wearing Hush Puppies slippers, gray work pants, and an orange bowling shirt. His arms looked like twigs sprouting from the sleeves.

"Your home is lovely."

"Thank you."

"Have you lived here long?"

"Forty-seven years come November."

"I couldn't help noticing your pictures." I indicated the photo collection. "You have a beautiful family."

"It's jus' Geneva and me here now. Geneva my second oldest. She hep me out. Tamela my youngest. She lef' a couple months ago."

In the corner of my eye I noticed Geneva move into the archway.

"I think you know why we're here, Mr. Banks." I was flailing about for a way to begin.

"Yes'm, I do. You lookin' for Tamela."

Slidell did some "get on with it" throat clearing.

"I'm very sorry to have to tell you, Mr. Banks, but material recovered from Tamela's living room stove—"

"Weren't Tamela's place," Banks broke in.

"The property was rented to one Darryl Tyree," Slidell said. "According to witnesses, your daughter'd been living with Mr. Tyree for approximately four months."

Banks's eyes never left my face. Eyes filled with pain.

"Weren't Tamela's place," Banks repeated. His tone wasn't angry or argumentative, more that of a man wanting the record correct.

My shirt felt sticky against my back, the cheap upholstery scratchy under my forearms. I took a deep breath, started again.

"Material recovered from the stove in that house included fragments of bone from a newborn baby."

My words seemed to catch him off guard. I heard a sharp intake of breath, and noticed his chin cock up a fraction.

"Tamela only seventeen. She a good girl."

"Yes, sir."

"She weren't with child."

"Yes, sir, she was."

"Who say that?"

"We have that information from more than one source." Slidell.

Banks considered a moment. Then, "Why you go looking in someone's stove?"

"An informant stated that an infant had been burned at that address. We investigate such reports."

Slidell didn't point out that the tip came from Harrison "Sonny" Pounder, a street-corner dopeman bargaining for favor after his recent bust.

"Who say that?"

"That's not important." Irritation sharpened Slidell's tone. "We need to know Tamela's whereabouts."

Banks pushed to his feet and shuffled to the nearest bookshelf. Easing back into the recliner, he handed me a photo.

I looked at the girl in the picture, acutely conscious of Banks's eyes on my face. And of his second oldest looming in the archway.

Tamela wore a short-skirted gold jumper with a black *W* on the front panel. She sat with one knee bent, one leg straight out behind her, hands on her hips, surrounded by a circle of gold and white pom-poms. Her smile was enormous, her eyes bright with happiness. Two barrettes sparkled in her short, curly hair.

"Your daughter was a cheerleader," I said.

"Yes'm."

"My daughter tried cheerleading when she was seven," I said. "Pop Warner football, for the little kids. Decided she preferred playing on the team to cheering."

"They all have their own mine, I guess."

"Yes, sir. They do."

Banks handed me a second photo, this one a Polaroid.

"That Mr. Darryl Tyree," Banks said.

Tamela stood beside a tall, thin man wearing gold chains around his neck and a black do-rag on his head. One spidery arm was draped over Tamela's shoulders. Though the girl was smiling, the fire was gone from her eyes. Her face looked drawn, her whole body tense.

I handed the photos back.

"Do you know where Tamela is, Mr. Banks?" I asked softly.

"Tamela a grown girl now. She say I can't axe."

Silence.

"If we can just talk to her, perhaps there's an explanation for all this."

More silence, longer this time.

"Are you acquainted with Mr. Tyree?" Slidell asked.

"Tamela gonna finish high school, same's Reggie, 'n' Harley, 'n' Jonah, 'n' Sammy. Din't have no problem with drugs or boys."

We let that hang a moment. When Banks didn't continue Slidell prodded.

"And then?"

"Then Darryl Tyree come along." Banks practically spit the name, the first sign of anger I'd seen. "'Fore long she forget her books, spend all her time moonin' over Tyree, worryin' when he gonna show up."

Banks looked from Slidell to me.

"She think I don't know, but I heard about Darryl Tyree. I tole her he weren't no fit company, tole her he weren't to be comin' round here no more."

"Is that when she moved out?" I asked.

Banks nodded.

"When did that happen?"

"Roun' Easter time. 'Bout four months back."

Banks's eyes glistened.

"I knew she had somethin' on her mine. I thought it was jus' Tyree. Sweet Jesus, I din't know she was with child."

"Did you know she was living with Mr. Tyree?"

"I didn't axe, Lord forgive me. But I figured she'd went over to his place."

"Do you have any idea why your daughter might have wanted to harm her baby?"

"No, ma'am. Tamela a good girl."

"Might Mr. Tyree have placed pressure on your daughter because he didn't want the child?"

"Weren't like that."

We all turned at the sound of Geneva's voice.

She gazed at us dully, in her shapeless blouse and terrible shorts.

"What do you mean?"

"Tamela tells me things, you know what I'm sayin'?"

"She confides in you?" I said.

"Yeah. Confides in me. Tells me things she can't tell Daddy."

"What she can't tell me?" Banks's voice sounded high and wheedly.

"Lots of stuff, Daddy. She couldn't talk to you about Darryl. You shouting at her, tryin' to get her to pray all the time."

"I got to be thinkin' 'bout her sou—"

"Did Tamela discuss her relationship with Darryl Tyree?" Slidell cut Banks off.

"Some."

"Did she tell you she was pregnant?"

"Yeah."

"When was that?"

Geneva shrugged. "Last winter."

Banks's shoulders slumped visibly.

"Do you know where your sister is?"

Geneva ignored Slidell's question.

"What d'you find in Darryl's woodstove?"

"Charred fragments of bone," I replied.

"You sure they from a baby?"

"Yes."

"Maybe that baby was born dead."

"There is always that possibility." I doubted the words even as I spoke them, but couldn't bear the look of sadness in Geneva's eyes. "That's why we have to locate Tamela and find out what really happened. Something other than murder could explain the baby's death. I very much hope that turns out to be true."

"Maybe the baby come too early."

"I'm an expert on bones, Geneva. I can recognize changes that take place in the skeleton of a developing fetus."

I reminded myself of the KISS principle. Keep It Simple, Stupid.

"Tamela's baby was full-term."

"What's that mean?"

"The pregnancy lasted the full thirty-seven weeks, or very close to it. Long enough that the baby should have survived."

"There could have been problems."

"There could have been."

"How d'you know that was Tamela's baby?"

Slidell jumped in, ticking off points on his sausage fingers.

"Number one, several witnesses have stated that your sister was pregnant. Two, the bones were found in a stove at *her* residence. And three, she and Tyree have disappeared."

"Could be someone else's baby."

"And I could be Mother Teresa, but I ain't."

Geneva turned back to me.

"What about that DNA stuff?"

"The fragments were too few and too badly burned for DNA testing."

Geneva showed no reaction.

"Do you know where your sister has gone, Miss Banks?" Slidell's tone was growing sharper.

"No."

"Is there anything you *can* tell us?" I asked.

"Just one thing."

Geneva looked from her father to me to Slidell. White woman. White cop. Bad choices.

Deciding the woman might be safer, she launched her bombshell in my direction.

3

As Slidell drove back to my car, I tried to quell my emotions, to remember that I was a professional.

I felt sadness for Tamela and her baby. Annoyance at Slidell's callous treatment of the Banks family. Anxiety over all I had to accomplish in the next two days.

I'd promised to spend Saturday with Katy, had company arriving on Sunday. Monday I was leaving on the first nonfamily vacation I'd allowed myself in years.

Don't get me wrong. I love my annual family trek to the beach. My sister, Harry, and my nephew Kit fly up from Houston, and all my estranged husband's Latvian relatives head east from Chicago. If no litigation is in process, Pete joins us for a few days. We rent a twelve-bedroom house near Nags Head, or Wilmington, or Charleston, or Beaufort, ride bikes, lie on the beach, watch *What About Bob?*, read novels, and reestablish extended-kin bonds. Beach week is a time of relaxed togetherness that is cherished by all.

This trip was going to be different.

Very different.

Again and again, I ran a mental checklist.

Reports. Laundry. Groceries. Cleaning. Packing. Birdie to Pete.

Sidebar. I hadn't heard from Pete in over a week. That was odd. Though we'd lived apart for several years, I usually saw or heard from him regularly. Our daughter, Katy. His dog, Boyd. My cat, Birdie. His

Illinois relatives. My Texas and Carolina relatives. Some common link usually threw us together every few days. Besides, I liked Pete, still enjoyed his company. I just couldn't be married to him.

I made a note to ask Katy if her dad had gone out of town. Or fallen in love.

Love.

Back to the list.

Hot waxing?

Oh, boy.

I added an item. Guest room sheets.

I'd never get it all done.

By the time Slidell dropped me in the ME parking lot, tension was hardening my neck muscles and sending tentacles of pain up the back of my head.

The heat that had built up in my Mazda didn't help. Nor did the uptown traffic.

Or was it downtown? Charlotteans have yet to agree on which way their city is turned.

Knowing it would be a late night, I detoured to La Paz, a Mexican restaurant at South End, for carryout enchiladas. Guacamole and extra sour cream for Birdie.

My home is referred to as the "coach house annex," or simply the "annex" by old-timers at Sharon Hall, a nineteenth-century manor-turned-condo-complex in the Myers Park neighborhood in southeast Charlotte. No one knows why the annex was built. It is a strange little outbuilding that doesn't appear on the estate's original plans. The hall is there. The coach house. The herb and formal gardens. No annex.

No matter. Though cramped, the place is perfect for me. Bedroom and bath up. Kitchen, dining room, parlor, guest room/study down. Twelve hundred square feet. What realtors call "cozy."

By six forty-five I was parked beside my patio.

The annex was blissfully quiet. Entering through the kitchen, I heard nothing but the hum of the Frigidaire and the soft ticking of Gran Brennan's mantel clock.

"Hey, Bird."

My cat did not appear.

"Birdie."

No cat.

Setting down my dinner, purse, and briefcase, I crossed to the refrigerator and popped a can of Diet Coke. When I turned, Birdie was stretching in the dining room doorway.

"Never miss the sound of a pop-top, do you, big guy?"

I went over and scratched his ears.

Birdie sat, shot a leg in the air, and began licking his genitals.

I knocked back a swig of Coke. Not Pinot, but it would do. My days of boogying with Pinot were over. Or Shiraz, or Heineken, or cheap Merlot. It had been a long struggle but that curtain was down for good.

Did I miss alcohol? Damn right. Sometimes so much I could taste and smell it in my sleep. What I didn't miss were the mornings after. The trembling hands, the dilated brain, the self-loathing, the anxiety over words and actions not remembered.

From now on, Coke. The real thing.

The rest of the evening I spent writing reports. Birdie hung in until the guacamole and sour cream ran out. Then he lay on the couch, paws in the air, and dozed.

In addition to Tamela Banks's baby, I'd examined three sets of remains since my return to Charlotte from Montreal. Each required a report.

A partially skeletonized corpse was discovered under a pile of tires at a dump in Gastonia. Female, white, twenty-seven to thirty-two years of age, five-foot-two to five-foot-five in height. Extensive dental work. Healed fractures of the nose, right maxilla, and jaw. Sharp instrument trauma on the anterior ribs and sternum. Defense wounds on the hands. Probable homicide.

A boater on Lake Norman had snagged a portion of an upper arm. Adult, probably white, probably male. Height five-foot-six to six feet.

A skull was found on the banks of Sugar Creek. Older adult, female, black, no teeth. Not recent. Probably a disturbed cemetery burial.

As I worked, my mind kept drifting back to the previous spring in Guatemala. I'd picture a stance. A face. A scar, sexy as hell. I'd feel a ripple of excitement, followed by a prick of anxiety. Was this upcoming beach trip such a good idea? I had to force myself to focus on the reports.

At one-fifteen I shut down the computer and dragged myself upstairs.

It wasn't until I was showered and lying in bed that I had time to consider Geneva Banks's statement.

"It wasn't Darryl's baby."

"What!" Slidell, Banks, and I had replied as one.

Geneva remumbled her shocker.

Whose?

No idea. Tamela had confided that the child she was carrying had not been fathered by Darryl Tyree. That was all Geneva knew.

Or would say.

A thousand questions jockeyed for position.

Did Geneva's information clear Tyree? Or did it render him even more suspect? Knowing the child was not his, had Tyree murdered it? Had he forced Tamela to kill her own baby?

Did Geneva have a valid point? Could the infant have been born dead? Had there been a genetic defect? An umbilical cord problem? Had Tamela, heartbroken, merely chosen the most expedient way and cremated the lifeless body in the woodstove? It was possible. Where had the baby been delivered?

I felt Birdie land on the bed, explore possibilities, then curl behind my knees.

My mind circled back to the upcoming beach junket. Could it lead anywhere? Did I want that? Was I looking for something meaningful, or merely hoping for rock-and-roll sex? God knows, I was horny enough. Was I capable of committing to another relationship? Could I trust again? Pete's betrayal had been so painful, the breakup of our marriage so agonizing, I wasn't sure.

Back to Tamela. Where was she? Had Tyree harmed her? Had they gone to ground together? Had Tamela run off with someone else?

As I drifted off, I had one final, disquieting thought.

Finding answers concerning Tamela was up to Skinny Slidell.

When I awoke, scarlet sun was slashing through the leaves of the magnolia outside my window. Birdie was gone.

I checked the clock. Six forty-three.

"No way," I mumbled, drawing knees to chest and burrowing deeper beneath the quilt.

A weight hit my back. I ignored it.

A tongue like a scouring brush scraped my cheek.

"Not now, Birdie."

Seconds later I felt a tug on my hair.

"Bird!"

A reprieve, then the tugging began again.

"Stop!"

More tugging.

I shot up and pointed a finger at his nose.

"Don't chew my hair!"

My cat regarded me with round, yellow eyes.

"All right."

Sighing dramatically, I threw back the covers and pulled on my summer uniform of shorts and a T.

I knew giving in was providing positive reinforcement, but I couldn't take it. It was the one trick that worked, and the little bugger knew it.

I cleaned up the guacamole Birdie had recycled onto the kitchen floor, ate a bowl of Grape-Nuts, then grazed through the *Observer* as I drank my coffee.

There'd been a pileup on I-77 following a late-night concert at Paramount's Carowinds theme park. Two dead, four critical. A man had been shotgunned in a front yard on Wilkinson Boulevard. A local humanitarian had been charged with cruelty to animals for crushing six kittens to death in his trash compactor. The city council was still wrangling over sites for a new sports arena.

Refolding the paper, I weighed my choices.

Laundry? Groceries? Vacuuming?

Screw it.

Refilling my coffee, I shifted to the den and spent the rest of the morning wrapping up reports.

Katy picked me up at exactly twelve noon.

Though an excellent student, gifted painter, carpenter, tap dancer, and comic, promptness is not a concept my daughter holds in high esteem.

Hmm.

Nor, to my knowledge, is the Southern rite known as the pig pickin'.

Though my daughter's official address remains Pete's house, where she grew up, Katy and I often spend time together when she is home from the University of Virginia in Charlottesville. We have gone to rock concerts, spas, tennis tournaments, golf outings, restaurants, bars, and movies together. Never has she proposed an outing involving smoked pork and bluegrass in a backyard.

Hmm.

Watching Katy cross my patio, I marveled, yet again, at how I could have produced such a remarkable creature. Though I'm not exactly last week's meat loaf, Katy is a stunner. With her wheat-blonde hair and jade-green eyes, she has the beauty that makes men arm-wrestle their buddies and perform swan dives from rickety piers.

It was another sultry August afternoon, the kind that brings back childhood summers. Where I grew up, movie theaters were air-conditioned, and houses and cars sweltered. Neither the bungalow in Chicago nor the rambling frame farmhouse to which we relocated in Charlotte was equipped with AC. For me, the sixties were an era of ceiling and window fans.

Hot, sticky weather reminds me of bus trips to the beach. Of tennis under relentless blue skies. Of afternoons at the pool. Of chasing fireflies while adults sipped tea on the back porch. I love the heat.

Nevertheless, Katy's VW could have used some AC. We drove with the windows down, hair flying wildly around our faces.

Boyd stood on the seat behind us, nose to the wind, eggplant tongue dangling from the side of his mouth. Seventy pounds of prickly brown fur. Every few minutes he'd change windows, flinging saliva on our hair as he whipped across the car.

The breeze did little more than circulate hot air, swirling the odor of dog from the backseat to the front.

"I feel like I'm riding in a clothes dryer," I said as we turned from Beatties Ford Road onto NC 73.

"I'll have the AC fixed."

"I'll give you the money."

"I'll take it."

"What exactly is this picnic?"

"The McCranies hold it every year for friends and regulars at the pipe shop."

"Why are *we* going?"

Katy rolled her eyes, a gesture she'd acquired at the age of three.

Though I am a gifted eye roller, my daughter is world-class. Katy is adept at adding subtle nuances of meaning I couldn't begin to master. This was a low-level I've-already-explained-this-to-you roll.

"Because picnics are fun," Katy said.

Boyd switched windows, stopping midway to lick suntan lotion from the side of my face. I pushed him aside and wiped my cheek.

"Why is it we have dogbreath with us?"

"Dad's out of town. Does that sign say Cowans Ford?"

"Nice segue." I checked the road sign. "Yes, it does."

I reflected for a moment on local history. Cowans Ford had been a river crossing used by the Catawba tribe in the 1600s, and later by the Cherokee. Davy Crockett had fought there during the French and Indian War.

In 1781 Patriot forces under General William Lee Davidson had fought Lord Cornwallis and his Redcoats there. Davidson died in the battle, thus lending his name to Mecklenburg County history.

In the early 1960s the Duke Power Company had dammed the Catawba River at Cowans Ford and created Lake Norman, which stretches almost thirty-four miles.

Today, Duke's McGuire Nuclear Power Plant, built to supplement the older hydroelectric plant, sits practically next to the General Davidson monument and the Cowans Ford Wildlife Refuge, a 2,250-acre nature preserve.

Wonder how the general feels about sharing his hallowed ground with a nuclear power plant?

Katy turned onto a two-lane narrower than the blacktop we were leaving. Pines and hardwoods crowded both shoulders.

"Boyd likes the country," Katy added.

"Boyd only likes things he can eat."

Katy glanced at a Xerox copy of a hand-drawn map, stuck it back behind the visor.

"Should be about three miles up on the right. It's an old farm."

We'd been traveling for almost an hour.

"The guy lives out here and owns a pipe store in Charlotte?" I asked.

"The original McCranie's is at Park Road Shopping Center."

"Sorry, I don't smoke pipes."

"They also have zillions of cigars."

"There's the problem. I haven't laid in this year's stock."

"I'm surprised you haven't heard of McCranie's. The place is a Charlotte institution. People just kind of gather there. Have for years. Mr. McCranie's retired now, but his sons have taken over the business. The one who lives out here works at their new shop in Cornelius."

"And?" Rising inflection.

"And what?" My daughter looked at me with innocent green eyes.

"Is he cute?"

"He's married."

Major-league eye roll.

"But he has a friend?" I probed.

"You got to have friends," she sang.

Boyd spotted a retriever in the bed of a pickup speeding in the opposite direction. *Rrrrppping,* he lunged from my side to Katy's, thrust his head as far out as the half-open glass would allow, and gave his best if-I-weren't-trapped-in-this-car growl.

"Sit," I ordered.

Boyd sat.

"Will I meet this friend?" I asked.

"Yes."

Within minutes parked vehicles crowded both shoulders. Katy pulled behind those on the right, killed the engine, and got out.

Boyd went berserk, racing from window to window, tongue sucking in and dropping out of his mouth.

Katy dug folding chairs from the trunk and handed them to me. Then she clipped a leash to Boyd's collar. The dog nearly dislocated her shoulder in his eagerness to join the party.

Perhaps a hundred people were gathered under enormous elms in the backyard, a grassy strip about twenty yards wide between woods and a yellow frame farmhouse. Some occupied lawn chairs, others milled about or stood in twos and threes, balancing paper plates and cans of beer.

Many wore athletic caps. Many smoked cigars.

A group of children played horseshoes outside a barn that hadn't seen paint since Cornwallis marched through. Others chased each other, or tossed balls and Frisbees back and forth.

A bluegrass band had set up between the house and barn, at the farthest point permitted by their extension cords. Despite the heat, all four wore suits and ties. The lead singer was whining out "White House Blues." Not Bill Monroe, but not bad.

A young man materialized as Katy and I were adding our chairs to a semicircle facing the bluegrass boys.

"Kater!"

Kater? It rhymed with "tater." I peeled my shirt from my sweaty back.

"Hey, Palmer."

Palmer? I wondered if his real name was Palmy.

"Mom, I'd like you to meet Palmer Cousins."

"Hey, Dr. Brennan."

Palmer whipped off his shades and shot out a hand. Though not tall, the young man had abundant black hair, blue eyes, and a smile like Tom Cruise's in *Risky Business*. He was almost disconcertingly good-looking.

"Tempe." I offered a hand.

Palmer's shake was a bone crusher.

"Katy's told me a lot about you."

"Really?" I looked at my daughter. She was looking at Palmer.

"Who's the pooch?"

"Boyd."

Palmer leaned over and scratched Boyd's ear. Boyd licked his face. Three slaps to the haunch, then Palmer was back at our level.

"Nice dog. Can I get you ladies a couple of brews?"

"I'll have one," Katy chirped. "Diet Coke for Mom. She's an alckie."

I shot my daughter a look that could have frozen boiling tar.

"Help yourself to chow." Palmer set off.

Hearing what he thought was a reference to his bloodline, Boyd shot forward, yanking the leash from Katy's hand, and began racing in circles around Palmer's legs.

Recovering his balance, Palmer turned, a look of uncertainty on his perfect face.

"He's OK off the leash?"

Katy nodded. "But watch him around food."

She retrieved the leash and unclipped it from the collar.

Palmer gave a thumbs-up.

Boyd raced in delighted circles.

Behind the main house, folding tables offered homemade concoctions in Tupperware tubs. Coleslaw. Potato salad. Baked beans. Greens.

One table was covered with disposable aluminum trays mounded with shredded pork. On the edge of the woods, wisps of smoke still floated from the giant cooker that had been going all night.

Another table held sweets. Another, salads.

"Shouldn't we have brought a dish?" I asked as we surveyed the Martha Stewart country-dining assemblage.

Katy pulled a bag of Fig Newtons from her purse and parked it on the dessert table.

I did some eye rolling of my own.

When Katy and I returned to our chairs the banjo player was doing "Rocky Top." Not Pete Seeger, but not bad.

For the next two hours a parade of folks stopped by to chat. It was like career day at the junior high. Lawyers. Pilots. Mechanics. A judge. Computer geeks. A former student, now a homemaker. I was surprised at the number of CMPD cops that I knew.

Several McCranies came over, welcoming us and expressing thanks for our coming. Palmer Cousins also came and went.

I learned that Palmer had been a fix-up through Lija, Katy's best friend since the fourth grade. I also learned that Lija, having completed a BA in sociology at the University of Georgia, was working in Charlotte as a paramedic.

Most important of all, I learned that Palmer was single, twenty-seven, a Wake Forest biology grad currently employed with the U. S. Fish and Wildlife Service at its field office in Columbia, South Carolina.

And a McCranie's regular when he was back home in Charlotte. The missing piece in why I was now munching on pulled pork in a clover field.

Boyd alternated between sleeping at our feet, racing with varying aggregates of children, and working the crowd, attaching himself to whoever looked like the easiest touch. He was in nap phase when a group of kids ran up requesting his company.

Boyd opened one eye, readjusted his chin on his paws. A girl of around ten wearing a purple Bible Girl cape and headgear waggled a cornmeal muffin. Boyd was off.

Watching them round the barn, I remembered Katy's words on the phone about Boyd wanting to have a conversation.

"What was it the chow wanted to discuss?"

"Oh, yeah. Dad's got a trial going in Asheville, so I've been taking care of Boyd." A thumbnail teased the edge of her Budweiser label. "He thinks he's going to be there another three weeks. But, um . . ." She dug a long tunnel in the wet paper. "Well, I think I'm going to move uptown for the rest of the summer."

"Uptown?"

"With Lija. She's got this really cool town house in Third Ward, and her new roommate can't occupy until September. And Dad's gone, anyway." The beer label was now effectively shredded. "So I thought it would be fun to, you know, just live down there for a few weeks. She's not going to charge me rent or anything."

"Just until school starts."

Katy was in her sixth and, by parental dictate, *last* undergraduate year at the University of Virginia.

"Of course."

"You're not thinking of dropping out."

The World Cup of eye rolls.

"Do you and Dad have the same scriptwriters?"

I could see where the conversation was going.

"Let me guess. You want me to take Boyd."

"Just until Dad gets back."

"I'm leaving for the beach on Monday."

"You're going to Anne's place on Sullivan's Island, right?"

"Yes." Wary.

"Boyd loves the beach."

"Boyd would love Auschwitz if they fed him."

"Anne wouldn't mind if you took him with you. And he'll keep you company so you won't be all alone."

"Boyd isn't welcome at the town house?"

"It isn't that he's unwelcome. Lija's landlor—"

From somewhere deep in the woods I heard Boyd's frantic barking. Seconds later, the barking was joined by a blood-chilling scream. Then another.

I BOLTED FROM MY CHAIR, HEART THUDDING IN MY CHEST.

The picnickers around me appeared as on split screen. Those on the house side of the bluegrass quartet continued their milling and chatting and eating, oblivious to whatever calamity might be unfolding in the woods. Those on the barn side formed a frozen tableau, mouths open, heads turned in the direction of the terrible sounds.

I raced toward the screams, weaving among lawn chairs and blankets and people. I could hear Katy and others close on my heels.

Boyd had never harmed a child, had never so much as growled at one. But it was hot. He was excited. Had some kid provoked or confused him? Had the dog suddenly turned?

Sweet Jesus.

My mind scanned images of mauling victims. I saw gaping slashes, severed scalps. Fear shot through me.

Rounding the barn, I spotted a break in the trees and veered off on a trickling dirt path. Branches and leaves tugged my hair and scratched the skin on my arms and legs.

The screams grew shriller, more strident. The spaces between disappeared and the cries blended together in a crescendo of fear and panic.

I ran on.

Suddenly, the shrieking stopped. The sound vacuum was more chilling than the shrieks.

Boyd's barking continued, frenzied and unrelenting.

The sweat went cold on my face.

Moments later I spotted three kids huddled behind an enormous hedge. Through a gap in the foliage I could see that the two girls were clutching each other. The boy had a hand on Bible Girl's shoulder.

The boy and the younger girl were staring at Boyd, expressions of fascination/repulsion distorting their features. Bible Girl had her eyes shut, clenched fists pressed to the lids. Every now and then her chest gave an involuntary heave.

Boyd was with them on the far side of the hedge, lunging forward then backpedaling, snapping at something a yard from the base of the growth. Every few seconds he'd point his nose skyward and let loose with a series of high-pitched barks. His hackles were engaged, giving him the look of an auburn wolf.

"You kids all right?" I gasped, pushing through the gap in the hedge.

Three solemn nods.

Katy and Palmer and one of the McCranie sons raced up behind me.

"Anyone hurt?" Katy panted.

Three head shakes. A tiny sob.

Bible Girl ran to McCranie, wrapped her arms around his waist, and collapsed against him. He began stroking the crooked part between her ponytails.

"It's OK, Sarah. You're fine."

McCranie looked up.

"My daughter's a little high-strung."

I shifted my attention to the chow.

And knew immediately what was happening.

"Boyd!"

Boyd whipped around. Seeing Katy and me, he loped forward, nudged my hand, then darted back to the hedge and reengaged.

"Stop!" I shouted, bending to relieve the stitch in my side.

When unconvinced of the wisdom of an order directed at him, Boyd rotates the long hairs that serve as his eyebrows. It's his way of asking "Are you crazy?"

Boyd turned and did that now.

"Boyd, sit!"

Boyd spun and resumed barking.

Sarah McCranie's arms tightened around her father. Her playmates watched me with saucer eyes.

I repeated my command.

Boyd twisted his head and did the eyebrow thing, this time with feeling: *Are you frigging nuts?*

"Boyd!" Keeping my left hand on my thigh, I leveled my right index finger at his snout.

Boyd canted his head, blew air out his nose, and sat.

"What's wrong with him?" Katy was panting as hard as I was.

"Dork Brain probably thinks he's discovered the lost colony from Roanoke."

Boyd turned back to the hedge, flattened his ears, and drew a long, low growl from deep in his chest.

"What?"

Ignoring my daughter's question, I picked my way through roots and undergrowth. When I drew close, Boyd shot to his feet and looked at me expectantly.

"Sit."

Boyd sat.

I squatted beside him.

Boyd rocketed up, tail rigid and trembling.

My heart sank.

Boyd's find was much larger than I'd expected. His last hit had been a squirrel, dead perhaps two or three days.

I looked at the chow. He returned my gaze, the large amount of white visible in each eye an indication of his agitation.

Refocusing on the mound at my feet, I began to share his apprehension. I picked up a stick and poked at the center. Plastic popped, then a stench like rotting meat rose from the leaves. Flies buzzed and darted, bodies iridescent in the sticky air.

Boyd, the self-taught cadaver dog, strikes again.

"Shit."

"What?"

I heard rustling as Katy worked her way toward the chow and me.

"What did he find?" My daughter squatted beside me, then bounced to her feet as though tied to a bungee. A hand flew to her mouth. Boyd danced around her legs.

"What the hell is it?"

Palmer joined us.

"Something's dead." After that masterful observation Palmer squeezed his nostrils with a thumb and forefinger. "Human?"

"I'm not sure." I pointed to semi-fleshed digits projecting from a tear Boyd had made in the plastic. "That's definitely not a dog or deer."

I probed the dimensions of the half-buried bag. "Not many other animals are this big."

I scraped back dirt and leaves and examined the soil below.

"No evidence of fur."

Boyd moved in for a sniff. I elbowed him back.

"Holy crap, Mom. Not at a picnic."

"I didn't will this here." I flapped a hand at Boyd's find.

"Are you going to have to do the whole ME bit?"

"This may be nothing. But on the outside chance it's *something*, the remains have to be recovered properly."

Katy groaned.

"Look, I don't like this any more than you do. I'm supposed to leave for the beach on Monday."

"This is so embarrassing. Why can't you be like other mothers? Why can't you just"—she looked at Palmer, then back to me—"bake cookies?"

"I prefer Fig Newtons," I snapped, rising to my feet. "Might be best to take the kids back," I said to Sarah's father.

"No!" the boy yelped. "It's a dead guy, right? We want to see you dig up the DOA." His face was flushed and glossy with perspiration. "We want to know who you like for the hit."

"Yeah!" The younger girl looked like Shirley Temple in pink denim coveralls. "We want to see the DOA!"

Inwardly cursing TV crime shows, I chose my words carefully.

"It would be most useful to the case if you'd collect your thoughts, talk over your observations, and then give a statement. Could you do that?"

The two looked at each other, eyes grown from saucers to platters.

"Yeah," said Shirley Temple, clapping chubby hands. "We'll give cool statements."

*   *   *

The crime scene truck arrived at four. Joe Hawkins, the MCME death investigator on call that weekend, showed up a few minutes later. By then most of the McCranies' guests had folded their blankets and chairs and departed.

So had Katy, Palmer, and Boyd.

Boyd's discovery lay beyond the hedge dividing the McCranies' property from the adjacent farm. According to Sarah's father, no one occupied the neighboring house, which belonged to someone named Foote. A quick check drew no response, so we brought in our equipment through its driveway and yard.

I explained the situation to Hawkins as two crime scene techs unloaded cameras, shovels, screens, and other equipment we'd need for processing.

"It may be an animal carcass," I said, feeling apprehensive about calling people out on a Saturday.

"Or it may be some guy's wife with an ax in her head." Hawkins pulled a body bag from his transport van. "Ain't our job to second-guess."

Joe Hawkins had been hauling stiffs since DiMaggio and Monroe married in '54, and was about to hit mandatory retirement age. He could tell some stories. Autopsies were performed in the basement of the jail back then, in a room equipped with little more than a table and sink. When North Carolina overhauled its death investigation system in the eighties, and the Mecklenburg County ME facility was moved to its current location, Hawkins took only one memento: an autographed portrait of Joltin' Joe. The picture still sat on the desk in his cubicle.

"But if we've got a bad one, *you'll* make the call to Doc Larabee. Deal?"

"Deal," I agreed.

Hawkins slammed the van's double doors. I couldn't help thinking how the job had molded the man's physiognomy. Cadaver thin, with dark circles under puffy eyes, bushy brows, and dyed black hair combed straight back from his face, Hawkins looked like a death investigator from central casting.

"Think we'll need lights?" asked one of the techs, a woman in her twenties with blotchy skin and granny glasses.

"Let's see how it goes."

"All set?"

I looked at Hawkins. He nodded.

"Let's do her," said granny glasses.

I led the team into the woods, and for the next two hours we photographed, cleared, bagged, and tagged according to ME protocol.

Not a leaf stirred. My hair bonded to my neck and forehead, and my clothes grew damp inside the Tyvek jumpsuit Hawkins had brought me. Despite liberal applications of Hawkins's Deep Woods, mosquitoes feasted on every millimeter of exposed flesh.

By five we had a pretty good idea of what we were facing.

A large black trash bag had been placed in a shallow grave, then covered with a layer of soil and leaves. Close to the ground surface, wind and erosion had taken their toll, finally exposing one corner of the bag. Boyd had accomplished the rest.

Beneath the first bag, we discovered a second. Though we left both sealed, except for such tears and holes as they already had, the odor oozing from the sacks was unmistakable. It was the sweet, fetid stench of decomposing flesh.

The fact that the remains appeared to be limited to their packaging sped our processing time. By six we'd removed the sacks, sealed them in body bags, and placed the bags in the ME van. After receiving assurances that granny glasses and her partner and I would be fine, Hawkins set off for the morgue.

An hour of screening turned up nothing from the surrounding or underlying soil.

By seven-thirty we'd packed the truck and were rolling toward town.

By nine I was in my shower, exhausted, discouraged, and wishing I'd chosen another profession.

Just when I thought I was catching up, two fifty-gallon Heftys had entered my life.

Damn!

And a seventy-pound chow.

Damn!

I lathered my hair for the third time and thought about the day to come and my visitor. Could I get through the bags before meeting him at baggage claim?

I pictured a face, and my stomach did a mini-flip.

Oh, boy.

Was this little rendezvous such a good idea? I hadn't seen the guy since we'd worked together in Guatemala. A vacation had seemed a good plan then. We'd both been under tremendous pressure. The place. The circumstances. The sadness of dealing with so much death.

I rinsed my hair.

The vacation that never was. The case was done. We were on our way. Before we'd reached La Aurora International, his pager had sounded. Off he'd gone, regretful, but obedient to the call of duty.

I pictured Katy's face at the picnic today, later at the site of Boyd's discovery. Was my daughter serious about the intensely captivating Palmer Cousins? Was she considering dropping out of school to be near him? For other reasons?

What was it about Palmer Cousins that bothered me? Was "the boy," as Katy would call him, just too damn good-looking? Was I growing so narrow-minded that I was starting to judge character by appearance?

No matter about Cousins. Katy was an adult now. She would do what she would do. I had no control over her life.

I soaped myself with almond-peppermint bath gel and reverted to worrying about Boyd's plastic sacks.

With a little luck, the contents would be animal bone. But what if that wasn't the case? What if Joe Hawkins's ax theory wasn't a joke?

In a heartbeat the water went tepid, then cold. I leaped out of the shower, wrapped one towel around my torso, another around my hair, and headed for bed.

Things will be fine, I told myself.

Wrong.

Things were going to get worse before they got worse.

5

Sunday morning. Time: seven thirty-seven. Temperature: seventy-four Fahrenheit. Humidity: eighty-one percent.

We were heading for a record. Seventeen straight days busting ninety degrees.

Entering the small vestibule of the MCME, I used my security card and passed Mrs. Flowers's command post. Even her absence was imposing. All objects and Post-it notes were equally spaced. Paper stacks were squared at the edges. No pens. No paper clips. No clutter. One personal photo, a cocker spaniel.

Monday through Friday, Mrs. Flowers screened visitors through the plate-glass window above her desk, blessing some with a buzz through the inner door, turning others away. She also typed reports, organized documents, and kept track of every shred of paper stored in the black file cabinets lining one side of the room.

Turning right past the cubicles used by the death investigators, I checked the board on the back wall where cases were entered daily in black Magic Marker.

Boyd's find was already there. MCME 437–02.

The place was exactly as I'd expected, deserted and eerily quiet.

What I hadn't expected was the fresh-brewed coffee on the kitchenette counter.

There is a merciful God, I thought, helping myself.

Or a merciful Joe Hawkins.

The DI appeared as I was unlocking my office.

"You're a saint," I said, raising my mug.

"Thought you might be here early."

During the recovery operation, I'd told Hawkins of my plans for a Monday escape to the beach.

"You'll be wanting yesterday's booty?"

"Please. And the Polaroid and the Nikon."

"X rays?"

"Yes."

"Main or stinky?"

"I'd better work in back."

The MCME facility has a pair of autopsy rooms, each with a single table. The smaller of the two has special ventilation for combating foul odors.

Decomps and floaters. My kind of cases.

Pulling a form from the mini-shelves behind my desk, I filled in a case number and wrote a brief description of the remains and the circumstances surrounding their arrival at the morgue. Then I went to the locker room, changed to surgical scrubs, and crossed to the stinky room.

The bags were waiting. So were the cameras and the items needed to accessorize my ensemble: paper apron and mask, plastic goggles, latex gloves.

Fetching.

I shot 35-millimeter prints, backups with the Polaroid, then asked Hawkins to X-ray both bags. I wanted no surprises.

Twenty minutes later he wheeled the bags back and snapped a half dozen plates onto a light box. We studied the gray-on-grayer jumble.

Bones mixed with a pebbly sediment. Nothing densely opaque.

"No metal," Hawkins said.

"That's good," I said.

"No teeth," Hawkins said.

"That's bad," I said.

"No skull."

"Nope," I agreed.

After donning my protective gear, sans goggles, I opened the twist tie and emptied the uppermost bag onto the table.

"Holy buckets. Those look like the real deal."

In all, there were eight semi-fleshed hands and feet, all truncated. I placed them in a plastic tub and asked for X rays. Hawkins carried them off, shaking his head and repeating his comment.

"Holy buckets."

Slowly, I spread the remaining bones as best I could. Some were free of soft tissue. Others were held together by leatherized tendon and muscle. Still others retained remnants of decomposing flesh.

Sometime in late Miocene, roughly seven million years ago, a line of primates began experimenting with upright posture. The locomotor shift required some anatomic tinkering, but in a few epochs most kinks had been ironed out. By the Pliocene, roughly two million years ago, hominids were running around waiting for someone to invent Birkenstocks.

The move to bipedalism had its downside, of course. Lower back pain. Difficult childbirth. The loss of a grasping big toe. But, all things considered, the adjustment to upright worked well. By the time *Homo erectus* cruised the landscape looking for mammoth, approximately one million years back, our ancestors had S-shaped spines, short, broad pelves, and heads sitting directly on top of their necks.

The bones I was viewing didn't fit that pattern. The hip blades were narrow and straight, the vertebrae chunky, with long, swooping spinous processes. The limb bones were short, thick, and molded in a way not seen in humans.

I drew a sigh of relief.

The victims in the bag had run on all fours.

Often bones delivered to me as "suspicious" turn out to be those of animals. Some are leftovers from Sunday dinner. Calf. Pig. Lamb. Turkey. Others are relics of last year's hunt. Deer. Moose. Duck. Some are the remains of farm animals or family pets. Felix. Rover. Bessie. Old Paint.

Boyd's find fell into none of those categories. But I had a hunch.

I began sorting. Right humeri. Left humeri. Right tibiae. Left tibiae. Ribs. Vertebrae. I was almost through when Hawkins arrived with the X rays.

One glance confirmed my suspicion.

Though the "hands" and "feet" looked jarringly human, skeletal differences were evident. Fused navicular and lunate bones in the hands. Deeply sculpted ends on the metatarsals and phalanges of the feet. Increasing digit length from the inside toward the outside.

I pointed out the latter trait.

"In a human foot, the second metatarsal is the longest. In a human hand, it's the second or third metacarpal. With bears, the fourth is the longest in both."

"Makes it look like the critter's reversed."

I indicated pads of soft tissue on the soles of the feet.

"A human foot would be more arched."

"So what is it, Doc?"

"Bear."

"Bear?"

"Bears, I should say. I've got at least three left femora. That means a minimum of three individuals."

"Where are the claws?"

"No claws, no distal phalanges, no fur. That means the bears were skinned."

Hawkins chewed on that thought for a while.

"And the heads?"

"Your guess is as good as mine."

I flipped off the light box and returned to the autopsy table.

"Bear hunting legal in this state?" Hawkins asked.

I peered at him over my mask.

"Your guess is as good as mine."

It took a couple of hours to sort, inventory, and photograph the contents of the first sack.

Conclusion: Bag one contains the partial remains of three *Ursus americanus*. Black bear. Species verification using Gilbert's *Mammalian Osteology* and Olsen's *Mammal Remains from Archaeological Sites*. Two adults and one juvenile represented. No heads, claws, distal phalanges, teeth, or outer integument present. No indicators of cause of death. Cut marks suggest skinning with a nonserrated double-edged blade, probably a hunting knife.

Between bags I took a break to phone US Airways.

Of course the flight was on time. Airlines operate to the nanosecond when the passenger or pickup is running late.

I looked at my watch. Eleven-twenty. If bag two held no surprises I could still make it to the airport on time.

I popped a can of Diet Coke and took a Quaker caramel-nut granola bar from a box I'd stashed in a kitchen cabinet. As I chewed I studied the Quaker pilgrim. He beamed at me with such a kindly smile. What could possibly go wrong?

Returning to the autopsy room, I glanced again at the X rays of bag two. Seeing nothing suspicious, I untied the knotted ends and upended the sack.

A soupy conglomerate of bone, sediment, and decomposing flesh oozed onto the stainless steel. A stench filled the air.

Readjusting my mask, I began poking through the mess.

More bear.

I lifted a smaller long bone that was clearly not bear. It felt light in my hand. I noted that the outer envelope of bone was thin, the marrow cavity disproportionately large.

Bird.

I began a triage.

Ursus.

Aves.

Time passed. My shoulders began to ache. At one point I heard a phone. Three rings, then silence. Either Hawkins had answered or the service had picked up.

When I'd separated by taxonomic affiliation, I started an inventory of the new bear bones. Again, there were no heads, claws, skin, or fur.

An hour later the bear count had risen to six.

I rolled that around in my head.

Was it legal to hunt black bears in North Carolina? Six seemed like a lot. Were there limits? Did these remains represent one slaughter, or were they the accumulation of multiple outings? The unevenness in decomposition supported that hypothesis.

Why had six headless carcasses been bundled in trash bags and buried in the woods? Had the bears been killed for their skins? Were their heads kept as trophies?

Was there a bear season? Had the hunting taken place during a legally approved period? When? It was hard to tell how long the animals had been dead. Until Boyd came along, the plastic had acted as an effective barrier to insects and other scavengers that hasten decomposition.

I was turning to the bird bones when voices floated in from the corridor. I stopped to listen.

Joe Hawkins. A male voice. Hawkins again.

Holding gloved hands in the air, I pushed the door with my bum and peeked out.

Hawkins and Tim Larabee were engaged in conversation outside the histology room. The ME looked agitated.

I was retreating when Larabee spotted me.

"Tempe. I'm glad to see you. I've been phoning your cell." He was wearing jeans and a tweedy golf shirt with black collar and trim. His hair was wet, as though he'd just showered.

"I don't bring my purse to an autopsy."

He looked past me to the table.

"That the stuff from out near Cowans Ford?"

"Yes."

"Animal?"

"Uh-huh."

"Good. I need your help on something else."

Oh, no.

"I got a call from the Davidson PD about an hour ago. A small plane went down just past one."

"Where?"

"East of Davidson, that spot where Mecklenburg County corners out to meet Cabarrus and Iredell."

"Tim, I'm pretty—"

"Plane slammed into a rock face, then fireballed."

"How many on board?"

"That's unclear."

"Can't Joe help you out?"

"If the victims are both burned and segmented, it'll take a trained eye to spot the pieces."

This couldn't be happening.

I checked my watch. Two-forty. Ninety minutes to touchdown.

Larabee was gazing at me with soulful eyes.

"I have to clean up and make a few phone calls."

Larabee reached out and squeezed my upper arm.

"I knew I could count on you."

Tell that to Detective Studpuppy, who'll be hailing a cab in an hour and a half. Alone.

I hoped I'd make it home before he was sound asleep.

6

At 4 P.M. THE TEMPERATURE WAS NINETY-SEVEN, THE HUMIDITY roughly the same. Slam dunk for the record keepers.

The crash site was almost an hour north of town, in the far northeastern corner of the county. Unlike the Lake Norman sector to the west, with its Sea-Doos and Hobie Cats, and J-32s, this part of Mecklenburg was corn and soybeans.

Joe Hawkins was already there when Larabee and I pulled up in his Land Rover. The DI was smoking a cigarillo, leaning against a quarter panel of the transport van.

"Where'd she go down?" I asked, slinging my backpack over a shoulder.

Hawkins pointed with a sideways gesture of his cigarillo.

"How far?" I was already perspiring.

"'Bout two hundred yards."

By the time our little trio traversed three cornfields, Larabee and Hawkins with the equipment locker, I with my pack, we were wheezy, itchy, and thoroughly soaked.

Though smaller than usual, the normal cast of players was present. Cops. Firemen. A journalist. Locals, viewing the proceedings like tourists on a double-decker.

Someone had run crime scene tape around the perimeter of the wreckage. Looking at it across the field, I was struck by how little there seemed to be.

Two fire trucks sat outside the yellow tape, scars of flattened cornstalks running up to their tires. They were at ease now, but I could see that a lot of water had been pumped onto the wreckage.

Not good news for locating and recovering charred bone.

A man in a Davidson PD uniform appeared to be in charge. A brass tag on his shirt said *Wade Gullet*.

Larabee and I introduced ourselves.

Officer Gullet was square-jawed, with black eyes, a sculpted nose, and salt-and-pepper hair. The leading-man type. Except that he stood about five-foot-two.

We took turns shaking.

"Glad you're here, Doc." Gullet nodded at me. "Docs."

The ME and I listened as Gullet summarized the known facts. His information went little beyond that which Larabee had provided outside the autopsy room.

"Landowner called in a report at one-nineteen. Said he looked out his living room window, saw a plane acting funny."

"Acting funny?" I asked.

"Flying low, dipping from side to side."

Looking over Gullet's head, I estimated the height of the rock outcrop at the far end of the field. It couldn't have exceeded two hundred feet. I could see red and blue smears maybe five yards below the peak. A trail of scorched and burned vegetation led from the impact point to the wreckage below.

"Guy heard an explosion, ran outside, saw smoke rising from his north forty. When he got here the plane was down and burning. Farmer—"

Gullet consulted a small spiral notepad.

"—Michalowski saw no signs of life, so he hotfooted it home to call 911."

"Any idea how many were on board?" Larabee asked.

"Looks like a four-seater, so I'm thinking less than a six-pack."

Gullet apparently wanted to compete with Slidell for movie cop work.

Flipping the cover with a one-handed motion, Gullet slid the spiral into his breast pocket.

"The dispatcher has notified the FAA or the NTSB, or whatever feds need contacting. Between my crew and the fire boys, I think we can handle the scene here. Just tell me what you need on your end, Doc."

I'd noticed a pair of ambulances parked on the shoulder where we'd pulled up.

"You've notified a trauma center?"

"Alerted CMC down in Charlotte. Paramedics and I took a peek once the fire was under control." Gullet gave a half shake of the head. "There's no one sucking air in that mess."

As Larabee started explaining how we'd proceed, I snuck a look at my watch. Four-twenty. Visitor ETA at my condo.

I hoped he'd gotten my message saying I'd be late. I hoped he'd found a taxi. I hoped he'd spotted the key I'd asked Katy to tape to the kitchen door.

I hoped Katy had taped the key to the kitchen door.

Relax, Brennan. If there's a problem he'll phone.

I unhooked and checked my cell phone. No signal.

Damn.

"Ready for a look-see?" Gullet was saying to Larabee.

"No hot spots?"

"Fire's out."

"Lead on."

Hating my job at that moment, I followed Gullet and Larabee through the cornrows and under the police tape to the edge of the wreckage.

Up close, the plane looked better than it had from a distance. Though accordioned and burned, the fuselage was largely intact. Around it lay scorched and twisted pieces of wing, melted plastic, and a constellation of unrecognizable rubble. Tiny cubes of glass sparkled like phosphorous in the afternoon sun.

"Ahoy!"

At the sound of the voice, we all turned.

A woman in khakis, boots, and dark blue shirt and cap was striding toward us. Big yellow letters above her brim announced the arrival of the National Transportation Safety Board.

"Sorry it's so late. I got the first available flight."

Draping a camcorder strap around her neck, the woman offered a hand.

"Sheila Jansen, air safety investigator."

We took turns shaking. Jansen's grip was anaconda strong.

Jansen removed her cap and ran a forearm across her face. Without the hat she looked like a milk commercial, all blonde and healthy and lousy with vitality.

"It's hotter here than in Miami."

We all agreed it was hot.

"Everything as it was, Officer?" Jansen asked, squinting through the viewfinder of a small digital camera.

"Except for dousing the flames." Gullet.

"Survivors?"

"No one's reported in to us."

"How many inside?" Jansen kept clicking away, moving a few feet left and a few feet right to capture the scene from different angles.

"At least one."

"Your officers walked the area?"

"Yes."

"Give me a minute?" Jansen raised the camcorder.

Larabee gave a go-ahead gesture with one hand.

We watched her circle the wreckage, shooting stills and video. Then she photographed the rock face and the surrounding fields. Fifteen minutes later Jansen rejoined us.

"The plane's a Cessna-210. The pilot's in place, there's a passenger in back."

"Why in back?" I asked.

"The right front seat's not there."

"Why?"

"Good question."

"Any idea who owns the plane?" Larabee asked.

"Now that I have the tail registration number I can run a trace."

"Where'd it take off?"

"That could be a tough one. Once you come up with the pilot's name I can interview family and friends. In the meantime, I'll check whether radar had tracking on the flight. Of course, if it was only a VFR flight, radar won't have an identifier and it'll be harder than crap to trace the plane's course."

"VFR?" I asked.

"Sorry. Pilots are rated as instrument flight rule or visual flight rule. IFR pilots can fly in all kinds of weather and use instruments to navigate.

"VFR pilots don't use instruments. They can't fly above the cloud line or within five hundred feet of the ceiling on overcast or cloudy days. VFR pilots navigate using landmarks on the ground."

"Good job, Sky King," Gullet snorted.

I ignored him.

"Don't pilots have to file flight plans?"

"Yes, if an aircraft takes off from a GA airport under ATC. That's new since nine-eleven."

Investigator Jansen had more acronyms than alphabet soup.

"GA airport?" I asked. I knew ATC was air traffic control.

"Category-A general aviation airport. And the plane must fly within specific restrictions, especially if the GA airport is close to a major city."

"Are passenger manifests required?"

"No."

We all stared at the wreckage. Larabee spoke first.

"So this baby may have been out on its own?"

"The coke and ganja boys aren't big on regulations *or* flight plans, GA airport or not. They tend to take off from remote locations and fly below radar control. My guess is we're looking at a drug run gone bad, and there won't be any flight plan."

"Gonna call in the Feebs and the DEA?" Gullet asked.

"Depends on what I discover out there." Jansen waggled the digital. "Let me get a few close-ups. Then you can start bringing out the dead."

For the next three hours that's just what we did.

While Larabee and I struggled with the victims, Jansen scrambled around shooting digital images, running her camcorder, sketching diagrams, and recording her thoughts on a pocket Dictaphone.

Hawkins stood by the cockpit, handing up equipment and taking pictures.

Gullet drifted in and out, offering bottled water and asking questions.

Others came and went throughout the rest of that sweaty, buggy afternoon and evening. I hardly noticed, so absorbed was I with the task at hand.

The pilot was burned beyond recognition, skin blackened, hair gone, eyelids shriveled into half-moons. An amorphous glob joined his abdomen to the yoke, effectively soldering the body in place.

"What is that?" asked Gullet on one of his periodic visits.

"Probably the guy's liver," Larabee replied, working to free the charred tissue.

It was the last question from Officer Gullet.

A peculiar black residue speckled the cockpit. Though I'd worked small plane crashes, I'd never seen anything like it.

"Any idea what this flaky stuff is?" I asked Larabee.

"Nope," he said, attention focused on extricating the pilot.

Once disengaged, the corpse was zipped into a body bag and placed on a collapsible gurney. A uniformed officer helped Hawkins carry it to the MCME transport vehicle.

Before turning to the passenger, Larabee called a break to enter observations on his own Dictaphone.

Jumping to the ground, I pulled off my mask, tugged up the sleeve on my jumpsuit, and glanced at my watch. For the zillionth time.

Five past seven.

I checked my cell phone.

Still no service. God bless the country.

"One down," said Larabee, slipping the recorder into a pocket inside his jumpsuit.

"You won't need my help with the pilot."

"Nope," Larabee agreed.

Not so for the pax.

When a rapidly moving object, like a car or plane, stops suddenly, those inside who are not securely fastened become what biomechanics call "near-flung objects." Each object within the larger object continues at the same speed at which it was traveling until coming to its own sudden stop.

In a Cessna, that ain't good.

Unlike the pilot, the passenger hadn't been belted. I could see hair and bone shards on the windshield frame where his head had come to its sudden stop.

The skull had suffered massive comminutive fracturing on impact. The fire had done the rest.

I felt plate tectonics in my stomach as I looked from the charred and headless torso to the grisly mess lying around it.

Cicadas droned in the distance, their mechanical whining like an anguished wail on the breathless air.

After a moment of serious self-pity, I replaced my mask, eased into the cockpit, climbed to the back, and began sifting bone fragments from their matrix of debris and brain matter, most of which had ricocheted backward after hitting the windshield frame.

The cornfield and its occupants receded. The cicadas faded. Now and then I heard voices, a radio, a distant siren.

As Larabee worked on the passenger's body, I rummaged for the remnants of his shattered head.

Teeth. Orbital rim. A chunk of jaw. Every fragment coated with flaky black gunk.

While the pilot had been speckled, the passenger was totally encrusted. I had no idea what the substance could be.

As I filled a container, Hawkins replaced it with an empty one.

At one point I heard workers setting up a portable generator and lights.

The plane reeked of charred flesh and airplane fuel. Soot filled the air, turning the cramped space into a miniature Dust Bowl. My back and knees ached. Again and again I shifted, fruitlessly searching for more comfortable positions.

I willed my body temperature down by calling up cool images in my mind.

A swimming pool. The smell of chlorine. The roughness of the boardwalk on the soles of my feet. The shock of cold on that first plunge.

The beach. Waves on my ankles. Wind on my face. Cool, salty sand against my cheek. A blast of AC on Coppertone skin.

Popsicles.

Ice cubes popping in lemonade.

We finished as the last pink tendrils of day slipped below the horizon.

Hawkins made a final trip to the van. Larabee and I stripped off our jumpsuits and packed the equipment locker. At the blacktop I turned for a closing look.

Dusk had drained all color from the landscape. Summer night was taking over, painting cornstalks, cliff, and trees in shades of gray and black.

At center stage, the doomed plane and its responders, glowing under the portable lights like some macabre performance of Shakespeare in a cornfield.

A Midsummer Night's Nightmare.

I was so exhausted I slept most of the way home.

"Do you want to swing by the office to pick up your car?" Larabee asked.

"Take me home."

That was the extent of the conversation.

An hour later Larabee deposited me beside my patio.

"See you tomorrow?"

"Yes."

Of course. I have no life.

I got out and slammed the door.

The kitchen was dark.

Lights in the study?

I tiptoed to the side of the annex and peeked around the corner.

Dark.

Upstairs?

Ditto.

"Good," I mumbled, feeling stupid. "I hope he's not here."

I let myself into the kitchen.

"Hello?"

Not a sound.

"Bird?"

No cat.

Dumping my pack on the floor, I unlaced and pulled off my boots, then opened the door and set them outside.

"Birdie?"

Nope.

I walked to the study and flipped the wall switch.

And felt my mouth open in dismay.

I was filthy, exhausted, and light-years past niceness.

"What the hell are *you* doing here?"

7

RYAN OPENED ONE VERY BLUE EYE.

"Is that all you ever say to me?"

"I'm talking to him."

I pointed a sooty finger at Boyd.

The dog was flopped at one end of the couch, paws dangling over the edge. Ryan lay propped at the other end, legs extended, ankles crossed on top of the chow.

Neither wore shoes.

On hearing my voice Boyd sat bolt upright.

I moved the finger.

Boyd slunk to the floor. Ryan's size-twelves dropped to the cushion.

"Furniture infraction?" Both blue eyes were open now.

"I take it you found the key?"

"No problemo."

"How did chowbreath get here, and why did he permit you to just waltz in?"

Boyd and Ryan looked at each other.

"I've been calling him Hooch. Saw it in a movie. Thought it fit him."

Boyd's ears shot up.

"Who let *Hooch* in, and why did Hooch let you in?"

"Hooch remembers me from the TransSouth disaster up in Bryson City."

I'd forgotten. When his partner was killed transporting a prisoner from Georgia to Montreal, Ryan had been invited to help the NTSB with the crash investigation. He and Boyd had met at that time, in the Carolina mountains.

"How did *Hooch* get in here?"

"Your daughter brought him."

Boyd wedged his snout under Ryan's hand.

"Nice kid."

Nice ambush, I thought, fighting back a smile. Katy figured a guest couldn't refuse the dog.

"Nice dog."

Ryan scratched Boyd behind the ears, swiveled his feet to the floor, and gave me a once-over. The corners of his mouth twitched upward.

"Nice look."

My clothes were filthy, my nails caked with mud and soot. My hair was sweaty-wet and matted, my cheeks fiery from a zillion insect bites. I smelled of corn, airplane fuel, and charred flesh.

How would my sister Harry describe me? Rode hard and put away wet.

But I was not in the mood for a fashion critique.

"I've been scraping up fried brain matter, Ryan. You wouldn't look like a Dior ad either."

Boyd regarded me but kept his thoughts to himself.

"Have you eaten?"

"The event wasn't catered."

Hearing my tone, Boyd jammed his snout back under Ryan's hand.

"Hooch and I were thinking about pizza."

Boyd wagged his tail at the sound of his new nickname. Or at the mention of pizza.

"His name's Boyd."

"Why don't you go upstairs and clean up some. Boyd and I'll see what we can rustle up."

Rustle up?

Born in Nova Scotia, Ryan has lived his entire adult life in the province of Quebec. Though he's traveled extensively, his view of American culture is typically Canadian. Rednecks. Gangsters. Cowboys. Now and then he tries to impress me with his *Gunsmoke* lingo. I hoped he wasn't about to do that now.

"I'll be a few minutes," I said.

"Take your time."

Good. No "podna" or "ma'am" tacked on for effect.

It came as I was trudging up the stairs.

"—Miz Kitty."

Another sudsy, steamy bathroom session to cleanse body and soul of the smell of death. Lavender shower gel, juniper shampoo, rosemary-mint conditioner. I was going through a lot of aromatic plants of late.

Soaping up, I thought about the man downstairs.

Andrew Ryan, lieutenant-détective, Section de Crimes contre la Personne, Sûreté du Québec.

Ryan and I had worked together for nearly a decade, homicide detective and forensic anthropologist. As specialists within our respective agencies headquartered in Montreal, the Quebec coroner's bureau and the Quebec provincial police, we'd investigated serial killers, outlaw biker gangs, doomsday cults, and common criminals. I'd do the vics. He'd do the legwork. Always strictly professional.

Over the years I'd heard stories about Ryan's past. Bikes, booze, binges closed out on drunk-tank floors. The near-fatal attack by a biker with the shattered neck of a twelve-ounce Bud. The slow recovery. The defection to the good guys. Ryan's rise within the provincial police.

I'd also heard tales about Ryan's present. Station-house stud. Babe meister.

Irrelevant. I had a steadfast rule against workplace romances.

But Ryan isn't good at following rules. He pressed, I resisted. Less than two years back, at last accepting the fact that Pete and I were better off as friends than spouses, I'd agreed to date him.

Date?

Jesus. I sounded like my mother.

I squeezed more lavender onto my scrunchy and lathered again.

What term did one use for singles over forty?

Go out? Court? Woo?

Moot point. Before anything got off the ground, Ryan disappeared undercover. Following his reemergence, we'd tried a few dinners, movies, and bowling encounters, but never got to the wooing part.

I pictured Ryan. Tall, lanky, eyes bluer than a Carolina sky.

Something flipped in my stomach.

Woo!

Maybe I wasn't as tired as I thought.

Last spring, at the close of an emotionally difficult time in Guatemala, I'd finally decided to take the plunge. I'd agreed to vacation with Ryan.

What could go wrong at the beach?

I never found out. Ryan's pager beeped while en route to the Guatemala City airport, and instead of Cozumel, we flew to Montreal. Ryan returned to surveillance in Drummondville. I went back to bones at the lab.

Woo-us interruptus.

I rinsed.

Now Detective Don Juan had his buns parked on the couch in my study.

Nice buns.

Flip.

Tight. With all the curves in the right places.

Major flip.

I twisted the handle, hopped out of the shower, and groped for a towel. The steam was so thick it obscured the mirror.

Good thing, I thought, picturing the handiwork of the mosquitoes and gnats.

I slipped into my ratty old terry-cloth robe, a gift from Harry upon completion of my Ph.D. at Northwestern. Torn sleeve. Coffee stains. It is the comfort food of my garment collection.

Birdie was curled on my bed.

"Hey, Bird."

If cats could look reproachful, Birdie was doing it.

I sat next to him and ran a hand along his back.

"I didn't invite the chow."

Birdie said nothing.

"What do you think of the other guy?"

Birdie curled both paws under his breast and gave me his Sphinx look.

"Think I should pull out the string bikinis?"

I lay back next to the cat.

"Or hit the Victoria's Secret stash?"

Victoria's Secret knockoffs, actually, from Guatemala. I'd found them in a lingerie store, and bought the mother lode for the beach trip that never was. Those items were still in their Vic-like pink bag, tags in place.

I closed my eyes to think about it.

The sun was again cutting through the magnolia, throwing warm slashes across my face.

I smelled bacon and heard activity in my kitchen.

A moment of confusion, then recollection.

My eyes flew open.

I was in a fetal curl on top of the spread, Gran's afghan over me.

I checked the clock.

Eight twenty-two.

I groaned.

Rolling from the bed, I pulled on jeans and a T and ran a brush through my hair. Sleeping on it wet had flattened the right side, pooched the left into a demi-pompadour.

I tried water. Hopeless. I looked like Little Richard with hat hair.

Terrific.

I was halfway down the stairs when I thought about breath.

Back up to brush.

Boyd greeted me at the bottom step, eyes shining like a junkie's on crack. I scratched his ear. He shot back to the kitchen.

Ryan was at the stove. He wore jeans. Just jeans. Slung low.

Oh, boy.

"Good morning," I said, for lack of a more clever opener.

Ryan turned, fork in hand.

"Good morning, princess."

"Listen, I'm sorr—"

"Coffee?"

"Please."

He filled a mug and handed it to me. Boyd gamboled about the kitchen, high on the smell of frying fat. Birdie remained upstairs, radiating resentment.

"I must have bee—"

"Hooch and I had a hankerin' for bacon and eggs."

Hankerin'?

"Sit," said Ryan, pointing his fork at the table.

I sat. Boyd sat.

Realizing his mistake, the chow stood, eyes fixed on the bacon Ryan was transferring to a paper towel.

"Did you find a pillow and blanket?"

"Yes, ma'am."

I took a sip of my coffee. It was good.

"Good coffee."

"Thank ya, ma'am."

No doubt about it. This was going to be a cowboy day.

"Where did you get the bacon and eggs?"

"Hooch and I went for a run. Hit the Harris-Tooter. Weird name for a grocery store."

"It's Harris-Teeter."

"Right. Makes more sense for product recognition."

I noticed an empty pizza box on the counter.

"I'm really sorry about flaking out last night."

"You were exhausted. You crashed. No big deal."

Ryan gave Boyd a strip of bacon, turned, and locked his baby blues onto mine. Slowly, he raised and lowered both brows.

"Not what I had in mind, of course."

Oh, boy.

I tucked hair behind my ears with both hands. The right side stayed.

"I'm afraid I have to work today."

"Hooch and I expected that. We've made plans."

Ryan was cracking eggs into a frying pan, tossing shells into the sink with a jump-shot wrist move.

"But we could use some wheels."

"Drop me off, you can have my car."

I didn't ask about the plans.

As we ate, I described the crash scene. Ryan agreed that it sounded like drug traffickers. He, too, had no idea about the odd black residue.

"NTSB investigator didn't know?"

I shook my head.

"Larabee'll autopsy the pilot, but he's asked me to deal with the passenger's head."

Boyd pawed my knee. When I didn't respond he shifted to Ryan.

Over second, then third cups of coffee, Ryan and I discussed mutual friends, his family, things we would do when I returned to Montreal at the end of the summer. The conversation was light and frivolous, a million miles from decomposing bears and a shattered Cessna. I found myself grinning for no reason. I wanted to stay, make ham and mustard and pickle sandwiches, watch old movies, and meander wherever the day might take us.

But I couldn't.

Reaching out, I pressed my palm to Ryan's cheek.

"I really am glad you're here," I said, smiling a smile with giggles behind it.

"I'm glad I'm here, too," said Ryan.

"I have a few animal bones to finish up, but that shouldn't take any time at all. We can leave for the beach tomorrow."

I finished my coffee, pictured the shards of skull I'd extricated from the charred fuselage. My cupcake smile drooped noticeably.

"Wednesday at the latest."

Ryan gave Boyd the last strip of bacon.

"The ocean is everlasting," he said.

So, it would turn out, was the parade of corpses.

8

Ryan couldn't drop me off. I had no car.

I called Katy. She arrived within minutes to taxi us downtown, cheerful about the early-morning errand.

Yeah. Right.

The air was hot and humid, the NPR weatherman negative on the subject of a temperature break. Ryan looked overdressed in his jeans, socks, loafers, and chopped-sleeve sweatshirt.

At the MCME I handed Ryan my keys. Across College, a kid in an extra-large Carolina Panthers jersey and crotch-hangers headed in the direction of the county services building, bouncing a basketball to a rhythm he was hearing from his headphones.

Though my mood was gloomy, I couldn't help but smile. In my youth jeans had to be tight enough to cause arteriosclerosis. This kid's drawers would accommodate a party of three.

Watching Katy then Ryan drive off, my smile collapsed. I didn't know where my daughter was going, or what plans Ryan shared with my estranged husband's dog, but I wished I were heading out, too.

Anywhere but here.

A morgue is not a happy place. Visitors do not come for pleasant diversion.

I know that.

Every day greed, passion, carelessness, stupidity, personal self-loathing, encounters with evil, and plain bad luck send otherwise healthy people rolling in with their toes up. Every day those left behind are sucker punched by the suddenness of unexpected death.

Weekends produce a bumper crop, so Mondays are the worst.

I know that, too.

Still, Monday mornings bum me out.

When I came through the outer door, Mrs. Flowers waved a chubby hand and buzzed me from the lobby into the reception area.

Joe Hawkins was in his cubicle speaking to a woman who looked like she might have worked at a truck-stop counter. Her clothes and face were baggy. She could have been forty or sixty.

The woman listened, eyes glazed and distant, fingers working a wadded tissue. She wasn't really hearing Hawkins. She was getting her first glimpse of life without the person whose corpse she'd just viewed.

I caught Hawkins's eye, motioned him to stay at his task.

The board showed three cases logged since yesterday. Busy Sunday for Charlotte. The pilot and passenger had checked in as MCME 438–02 and 439–02.

Larabee already had the pilot on the main autopsy room table. When I peeked in he was examining the burned skin through a hand-held magnifier.

"Any word on who we have here?" I asked.

"Nothing yet."

"Prints or dentals?"

"Fingers are too far gone on this one. But most of the teeth are intact. Looks like he might have seen a dentist at some point in this millennium or the last. He definitely saw his tattoo artist. Check out the artwork."

Larabee offered the lens.

The man's lower back must have been protected from the flames by contact with the seat. Across it writhed the south end of a snake, taloned and winged. Red flames danced through the coils and around the edges of Mr. Serpent.

"Recognize the design?" I asked.

"No. But someone should."

"Guy looks white."

Larabee sponged upward on the tattoo. More snake emerged from the soot, like a message on a Burger King scratch-and-win. The skin between the scales was pasty white.

"Yeah," he agreed, "but check this out."

Snugging a hand under the pilot's shoulder, Larabee eased the man up. I leaned in.

Black patches clung to the man's chest like tiny charred leeches.

"That's the same stuff that's all over the passenger," I said.

Larabee let the pilot's shoulder drop to the table.

"Yep."

"Any idea what it is?" I asked.

"Not a clue."

I told Larabee I'd be working in the other room.

"Joe's got the X rays up on the box," he said.

I opened a case file, changed to scrubs, got a small cart, and walked to the cooler. When I pulled the handle on the stainless-steel door, a malodorous whoosh of charred and refrigerated flesh blasted my nostrils.

The gurneys were parked in two neat rows. Seven empty. Four occupied.

I checked the tags on the body bag zippers.

MCME 437–02. *Ursus* and company.

MCME 415–02. Unknown black male. We called him Billy in recognition of the site of his discovery, off the Billy Graham Parkway. Billy was a toothless old man who'd died under a blanket of newspapers, alone and unwanted. In three weeks no one had come forward to claim him. Larabee was giving Billy until the end of the month.

MCME 440–02. Earl Darnell Boggs. DOB 12/14/48. I assumed the unfortunate Mr. Boggs went with the lady in Joe Hawkins's cubicle.

MCME 439–02. Unknown. The passenger.

I unzipped the pouch.

The body was as I remembered, headless, charred, upper limbs curled into the pugilist pose. The hands were shriveled claws. There would be no prints on this one either.

Hawkins had centered my plastic tubs in a clump above the passenger's shoulders, as though trying to simulate the shattered head. Transferring the tubs, I rezipped the bag and wheeled the cart to the small autopsy room.

The X rays glowed black and white like the test patterns in the olden days of television. The second film showed two metallic objects mingled with teeth and chunks of jaw. One object looked like a fleur-de-lis, the other like Oklahoma.

Good. The passenger had also seen a dentist.

I gloved, spread a sheet across the table, and emptied container two. It took several minutes to locate and remove the two loose dental restorations. After sealing those items in a vial, I picked out all jaw and tooth fragments, placed them on a tray, and set it aside.

Then I turned to the skull.

There would be no reconstruction for this guy. The fire damage was too severe.

Teasing off charred flesh and flaky black gunk, I began working my way through the jigsaw puzzle of cranial architecture.

A segment of frontal bone rolled down into a pair of prominent brow ridges. Occipital pieces showed bulbous mastoids and the largest neck muscle attachment I'd ever seen. The back of the guy's head must have bulged like a golf ball.

The rear-seat passenger had definitely been male. Not that useful. Larabee would nail that during his post.

On to age.

Taking two steps to the right, I studied the tray of dental fragments.

Like plants, teeth send roots into their sockets long after the crowns have sprouted through the gums. By twenty-five, the garden is in full bloom, and the third molars, or wisdom teeth, are complete to their tips. That's a wrap, dentally speaking. From that point on, it's dental breakdown.

Though the passenger's enamel was either missing or too crumbly to evaluate, every viewable root was complete. I'd need X rays to observe those hidden in the sockets.

I returned to the cranial wreckage.

As with dentition, skulls come with some assembly required. At birth, the twenty-two bones are in place, but unglued. They meet along squiggly lines called sutures. In adulthood, the squiggles fill in, until the vault forms a rigid sphere.

Generally, the more birthday candles, the smoother the squiggles.

By stripping blackened scalp from the cranial fragments, I was able to view portions of suture from the crown, back, and base of the head.

The basilar squiggle was fused. Most others were open. Only the sagittal, which runs from front to back across the top of the head, showed any bony bridging.

Though vault closure is notoriously variable, this pattern suggested a young adult.

On to ancestry.

Race is a tough call at any time. With a shattered skull it's a bitch.

The upper third of one nasal bone remained in place on the large frontal fragment. Its slope downward from the midline was acute, giving the nasal bridge a high, angled shape, like a church steeple.

I swapped the piece of forehead for a chunk of midface.

The nasal opening was narrow, with a rolled lower edge and a tiny spike at the midway point. The bone between the bottom of the nose and the upper-tooth row dropped straight down when viewed from the side. The cheekbones ballooned out in wide, sweeping arcs.

The steepled nasal bridge, sharp inferior nasal border, and nonprojecting lower face suggested European ancestry.

The flaring zygomatics, or cheekbones, suggested Asian or Native American ancestry.

Great.

Back to the dentition.

Only one front tooth retained a partial crown. I turned it over. The back was slightly ridged at the point where the enamel met the gum line.

I was staring at the incisor when Joe Hawkins poked his head through the door.

"You look stumped."

I held out my hand.

"I'm not sure it's shoveled, but there's something weird there."

Joe looked at the tooth.

"If you say so, Doc."

Shoveling refers to a U-shaped rimming on the tongue side of the center four teeth. Shoveled incisors are usually indicative of Asian or Native American ancestry.

I returned the tooth to the tray and requested X rays of the jaw fragments.

I checked the time. One-forty.

No wonder I was starving.

Stripping off gloves and mask, I washed with antibacterial soap and threw a lab coat over my scrubs. Then I went to my office and washed down a granola bar with a can of Diet Coke.

As I ate, I scanned my phone messages.

A journalist from the *Charlotte Observer.*

Skinny Slidell. Something about the Banks baby case.

Sheila Jansen. She'd called early. The NTSB works hard.

The fourth pink slip caught my attention.

Geneva Banks.

I tried the Bankses' number. No answer.

I tried Jansen.

Her voice mail invited a message.

I left one.

I stopped back into the main autopsy room. The passenger lay where the pilot had been, and Larabee had just made his second Y incision of the day.

I walked over and looked at the body. Though gender was clear, age and race were not. Those aspects would have to be determined skeletally.

I explained the discrepancy in racial features. Larabee said he'd spotted nothing useful in the body.

I asked for the pubic symphyses, the portions of the pelvis where the two halves meet in front, and the sternal ends of the third through fifth ribs to tighten my age estimate. Larabee said he'd send them over.

Larabee told me he'd talked with Jansen. The NTSB investigator would be dropping by in the late afternoon. Neither Geneva Banks nor Skinny Slidell had phoned him.

When I returned to the stinky room, Hawkins had popped the dental X rays onto the light boxes.

The roots of the left canine and second molar, and of both wisdom teeth, were visible in various jaw fragments. While the canine and M-2 were complete to their tips, the M-3s were not quite over the plate.

Dentally, the passenger looked eighteen to twenty-five.

Race was still a crapshoot.

Back to the zygomatic arch.

Yep. Mongoloid-looking cheeks.

Back to the maxilla and frontal.

Yep. Caucasoid-looking nose.

As I was staring at the frontal bone, an irregularity on the nasal caught my eye. I carried the fragment to the scope and adjusted focus.

Under magnification the irregularity looked circular and more porous than the surrounding bone. The edges of the circle were clearly defined.

A puzzling lesion, unlike usual findings in nasal bones. I had no idea what it meant.

I spent the next hour mining fragments, stripping flesh, and recording observations. Though I found no other signs of disease, I decided to request X rays of the rest of the skeleton. The nasal lesion looked active, suggesting a chronic condition of some sort.

At three-thirty, Hawkins delivered the ribs and pubes. He promised to take a full set of films when Larabee finished with the passenger's body.

I was placing the pubes and ribs in a solution of hot water and Spic and Span when Larabee entered, followed by Sheila Jansen. Today the NTSB investigator wore black jeans and a sleeveless red shirt.

Hours of exposure had numbed me to the smell of the passenger's unrefrigerated head, now decomposing on my table. My greasy, soot-stained gloves and scrubs undoubtedly added to the room's bouquet.

Jansen's lips and nostrils tightened. Her expression went opaque as she attempted to regain control of her face.

"Time to swap stories?" I asked, peeling off mask and gloves and tossing them into a biohazard container.

Jansen nodded.

"Why don't I meet you two in the conference room?"

"Good idea," Larabee said.

When I joined them, the ME was going over his findings.

"—multiple traumatic injuries."

"Soot in the airways?" Jansen asked.

"No."

"That makes sense," Jansen said. "When the plane slammed the cliff face, the fuel tanks ruptured. There was immediate ignition and fireball. I figure both victims died on impact."

"External burning was severe, but I didn't find a lot of deep-tissue destruction." Larabee.

"After impact gravity took over and the fuel cascaded down the cliff face," Jansen explained.

In my mind's eye I saw the trail of burned vegetation.

"So the victims were exposed to the fireball effect of the explosion, but the burning wouldn't have lasted very long."

"That fits," Larabee said.

"Both bodies show evidence of a black residue," I said, settling into a chair. "Especially the passenger."

"I found the same stuff all over the cockpit. I've sent a sample off for testing."

"We're screening for alcohol, amphetamines, methamphetamines, barbiturates, cannabinoids, opiates," Larabee said. "If these guys were flying high, we'll catch it."

"You're calling them guys." Jansen.

"Pilot was a white male, probably in his thirties, five-eight to five-ten, lots of dental work, great tattoo."

Jansen was nodding as she wrote it all down.

"Passenger was also male. Taller. With his head, that is." He turned to me. "Tempe?"

"Probably early twenties," I said.

"Racial background?" Jansen asked.

"Yes."

She looked up.

"I'm working on it."

"Any unique identifiers?"

"At least two fillings." I pictured the nasal. "And he had something going on with his nose. I'll let you know on that, too."

"My turn." Jansen flipped pages in her notebook. "The plane was registered to one Richard Donald Dorton. Ricky Don to his friends."

"Age?" I asked.

"Fifty-two. But Dorton wasn't flying yesterday. He's riding out the heat wave at Grandfather Mountain. Claims he left the Cessna safe and sound at a private airstrip near Concord."

"Did anyone see the plane take off?" I asked.

"No."

"Flight plan?"

"No."

"And no one spotted it in flight."

"No."

"Do you know why it crashed?"

"Pilot flew it into a rock face."

We let that hang a moment.

"Who is Ricky Don Dorton?" I asked.

"Ricky Don Dorton owns two strip joints, the Club of Jacks and the Heart of Queens, both in Kannapolis. That's a mill town just north of here, right?"

Nods all around.

"Ricky Don supplied sleaze for gentlemen of every lifestyle."

"Man's a poet." Larabee.

"Man's a lizard." Jansen. "But a rich lizard. The Cessna-210's just one of his many toys."

"Are tits and ass that profitable?" I asked.

Jansen gave a beats-me shrug.

"Could it be that Ricky Don is also in the import business?" I asked.

"That thought has crossed the minds of local law enforcement. They've had Dorton under surveillance for some time."

"Let me guess," I said. "Ricky Don doesn't hang with the Baptist choir."

Larabee clapped me on the shoulder. "She's good, isn't she?"

Jansen smiled. "One problem. The plane was clean."

"No drugs?"

"Nothing so far."

We all stood.

I asked one last question.

"Why would a grown man call himself Ricky Don?" It sounded like one of Harry's Texas saloons.

"Perhaps he doesn't want to appear pretentious."

"I see," I said.

I didn't.

It was four-thirty by the time Jansen left. I wanted to go home, take another long shower, tap into the Victoria's Secret knockoff reserve, and spend the evening with Ryan.

But I also wanted to split for the beach first thing in the morning.

And I had bear bones in the cooler.

If annoying tasks are avoidable, I am a world-class procrastinator.

I advance mail from pile to pile, then chuck it when the deadline or opportunity has passed. I wait out snow until it melts. I coexist with dandelions and weeds. My garden relies on rain.

Conversely, unfinished but ultimately unavoidable chores hang over my head like guillotine blades. All through school I submitted papers in advance of due dates. I never pulled an all-nighter. I pay bills on time. I can't rest until the inescapable is put to bed.

I phoned Ryan's cell. Four rings, then his voice requested a message in French then in English.

"Get cooking, slick. I'll be home by seven."

Hanging up, I questioned the wisdom of my phrasing. I was referring to steak and potatoes. Ryan might take it to mean something else.

I tried Geneva Banks. Still no answer.

I considered Skinny Slidell.

Avoidable.

Returning to the autopsy room, I tied on a new paper apron, changed the soaking solution for the pubes and ribs, and packed up the remains of the passenger's skull. Then I went to the cooler, reunited the tubs with their headless owner, and rolled out The Three Bears.

Only a portion of one bag remained unexamined. How long could it take?

Untwisting the plastic, I dumped the contents onto the table.

The large bones took ten minutes. All bear.

I was laying down the last tibia when something crawled into my peripheral vision. I turned to the mound of smaller material I'd scooped into a pile by my left elbow.

My eyes went to an object that had rolled free.

My heart plunged.

I poked through the pile, teased free another.

My fingers curled into fists and my head flopped forward like a Dalí clock.

9

I DREW A DEEP BREATH, OPENED MY EYES, AND REEXAMINED THE
two small bones. One was cuboid with a hooklike process. The other
resembled a miniature, half-carved bust.

Neither had anything to do with *Ursus.*

Damn!

My heart was in free fall.

Scooping the carpals onto my glove, I sought out Larabee. He was
in his office.

I held out the bones.

He glanced at them, then up at me.

"A hamate and a capitate," I said.

"From the Goldilocks gang?"

I nodded.

"Paw?"

"Hand."

His face skewed into a frown.

"Human?"

"Very."

"You're sure?"

I did not reply.

"Damn!" Larabee tossed his pen onto the desk.

"My thought precisely."

He leaned back in his chair.

"Damn it to blue blazes!"

"I'll go with that, too."

"We'll have to haul ass back out there."

"Yes."

"If that"—he jabbed a thumb at my upturned palm—"hand is recent, whoever did the burying might rethink his arrangement."

"Could be searching for a shovel as we speak."

"Tomorrow?"

I nodded.

Larabee reached for the phone. "Could it be an old unmarked grave?"

"Anything's possible."

I didn't believe it.

Joe Hawkins dropped me at the annex.

Ryan was stretched out watching an *I Love Lucy* rerun. His day had obviously included shopping, for he now featured plaid shorts and a T-shirt that proclaimed BEER: NOT JUST FOR BREAKFAST ANYMORE. Though his face was tanned, his legs were the color of uncooked perch.

Boyd was dozing at his end of the couch.

The coffee table held a dead Heineken and a cereal bowl containing a half-dozen chips. An empty bowl sat on the floor.

Four eyes scanned me when I appeared in the doorway. Birdie was sulking out of sight.

Boyd slunk to the floor.

"Bonjour, Madam La Docteure."

I allowed my pack and purse to slide from my shoulder.

"Rough day?" Ryan asked.

I nodded, smiled. "Hope yours was better."

"Hooch and I went to Kings Mountain."

"The national park?"

"The Yanks kicked some serious British butt there, right, podna?" He scratched Boyd's ear. Boyd laid his chin on Ryan's chest.

While I was up to my elbows in putrid flesh, these two were strolling down history lane. At least someone had enjoyed the day.

Ryan palmed chips into his mouth. Boyd's eyes followed his hand.

"Hooch kicked some serious squirrel butt."

I crossed to the couch. Ryan drew back his feet, and I dropped into the spot Boyd had vacated.

Boyd sniffed Ryan's chip bowl. I nudged him and he turned and gave me the eyebrows.

Lucy and Ethel were hiding in a closet, trying to change out of work clothes. Lucy was cautioning Ethel not to tell Ricky.

"Why doesn't she just get a job?" Ryan asked.

"Ricky won't let her."

I thought about Ricky Don Dorton.

"Turns out the Cessna belongs to a local bar owner who's probably running drugs on the side."

"Who's that?"

"Doesn't matter." I wanted no comments on the naming preferences of my Dixie brethren. "The plane was clean and the owner wasn't flying."

"The fine citizen's aircraft was stolen."

"Yep."

"I hate it when that happens to me."

I cuffed Ryan on the chest and gave him the spare-me face.

"Who was on board?"

"Don't know. The NTSB investigator is liaising with the cops. They'll check their missing persons, then run our descriptors through NCIC."

Ryan fought back a smile.

"But you already know that." I scratched at a mosquito bite on my elbow. "I've got some bad news."

Boyd shifted his chin to my knee.

"Remember the animal bones I mentioned?"

"I do."

"Rin Tin Tin here actually discovered them. They were buried on farmland out in the county. I was pretty sure the stuff was animal, but I brought it in to the ME office just in case. I spent most of Sunday going through it."

Lucy was on her bum. Ethel was trying to pull the coveralls over Lucy's shoes.

"And?" Ryan coaxed.

"Today I found a pair of human hand bones."

"Mixed in with Smokey."

I nodded.

"So tomorrow's going to be another special day."

"Unfortunately. Look, I'm really sorry. You know I would much rather be with you."

"And Hooch." Ryan flicked his eyes to the dog, then back to me.

"And Hooch." I patted Boyd's head. "By the way, I really do appreciate you looking after him."

Ryan raised palms and eyebrows in a gesture of *c'est la vie.*

"If Hooch has unearthed a homicide, you don't want the perp relocating his vic."

Boyd transferred back to Ryan.

"No," I agreed, with an enthusiasm I reserve for Pap smears and rectals.

"You gotta do what you gotta do."

"Right."

Ryan was, of course. Nevertheless I felt trapped, stuck in town like a moth on a pest strip.

I leaned forward, arched my back, and rotated my head. Things crunched in my neck.

Ryan sat up and scootched close.

"Turn."

I did.

Ryan began kneading my shoulders with strong, circular movements. I closed my eyes.

"Mmm."

"Too hard?"

"Hm uhm." I hadn't realized how tense I was.

Ryan ran a thumb along the inner edge of each shoulder blade.

A tiny groan curled up from my throat. I cut it off.

Ryan's thumbs moved to the base of my skull.

Ohgod.

Up the back of my head.

Ohmygod.

Back down, across my shoulders, and along the muscles to either side of my spine.

Full groan.

Seconds later the hands withdrew, and I felt the couch cushion change shape.

"Here's a plan."

I opened my eyes.

Ryan was leaning back, fingers laced behind his head. The chip bowl was empty. Boyd had crumbs on the side of his mouth.

"I'm buying you dinner."

"No argument. Where?"

"Your town, your choice."

An hour later Ryan and I were munching bruschetta at Toscana. The night was Hollywood-summertime perfect, the moon a full O overhead.

Toscana is an Italian eatery hidden in Specialty Shops on the Park, an enclave of cafés, spas, and boutiques at which Charlotte's elite sip Silver Oak Cabernet, get wrapped in mud, and purchase bandannas for their dogs.

While the establishments are a bit *too* special for my budget, I do enjoy Toscana, especially in the outdoor dining months. It and Volare are my favorites of the Italian places, and are roughly equidistant from Sharon Hall. Tonight I chose Toscana.

Ryan and I sat at a small wrought-iron table in the restaurant's cobbled courtyard. Behind us, a fountain tinkled softly. To our left, a couple debated the mountains versus the beach. A female threesome on our right compared golf handicaps.

Ryan sported tan Dockers and a crisp cotton shirt the exact cornflower blue of his eyes. His face was tan from the Kings Mountain outing, his hair still shower wet.

He looked good.

Very good.

I wasn't chopped liver myself.

Man-eater black linen sundress. Strap sandals. Guatemalan Victoria's most secret thong.

The last few days had served up too many corpses and too much death. I'd made a decision. Like my neckline, I was taking the plunge.

"Does everyone in North Carolina play golf?" Ryan asked, as a white-shirted waiter handed us menus the size of legal briefs.

"It's state law."

The waiter inquired as to our cocktail preferences. Ryan asked for a Sam Adams. I ordered Perrier with lemon. Barely masking his disappointment, the waiter withdrew.

"Do you?"

I looked at Ryan. He dragged his gaze from my chest to my eyes.

"Play golf."

"I've had a few lessons."

In truth, I hadn't swung a club in years. Golf was Pete's thing. When I left my husband, I left the game. My handicap was probably a forty-two.

The woman to our right was claiming six strokes.

"Would you like to hit a few balls?" I asked.

Since Pete and I had never legally terminated our marriage, technically I was still a spouse and could use the facilities at Carmel Country Club.

Why *hadn't* I done the paperwork? I wondered for the zillionth time. Pete and I had been separated for years. Why not cut the cord and move on?

Was it a cord?

Not the time, Brennan.

"Could be fun," Ryan said, reaching across the table to place his hand on mine.

Definitely not the time.

"Of course, Hooch wouldn't like being left out."

"His name is Boyd." My voice sounded as though I'd inhaled helium.

"Hooch must learn to enjoy the serenity of his own inner beauty. Maybe you could get him started on yoga."

"I'll mention that to Pete."

The waiter returned with our drinks, explained the menu. Ryan ordered the sea bass. I went for the veal Marsala, carefully leaving my palm on the table.

When the waiter departed, Ryan's hand came back to mine. His face showed a mixture of concern and confusion.

"You're not nervous about tomorrow, are you?"

"No," I scoffed.

Really, no.

"You seem tense."

"I'm just disappointed about the beach."

Ryan tiptoed his fingertips up my arm.

"I've been waiting these many years to see you in a string bikini."

The fingers spidered back down.

"We *will* get to the beach."

If goose bumps can burn, mine did.

I cleared my throat.

"There are scores of unmarked graves on these old farms. Those hand bones have probably been underground since Cornwallis crossed Cowans Ford."

At that moment the waiter placed salads between us.

We switched gears during dinner, talking about everything but ourselves and our work. Not a word about bones. No reference to tomorrow.

No reference to later tonight.

It was after eleven by the time we'd finished coffee and tiramisu.

Hooch/Boyd greeted us at the door of the annex. When I unpegged his leash, the chow yelped and bounded around the kitchen.

"Hooch does appreciate the small things," Ryan said.

Again, I pointed out that the dog's name was Boyd.

"And he's flexible," Ryan added.

The night smelled of petunias and mown grass. A light breeze ruffled the periwinkle. A million crickets performed a summer symphony in the round.

Boyd led us from tree to tree, tail and nose working double-time, now and then flushing a bird or squirrel. Every few seconds he'd loop back, as though reminding us to stay focused on him.

I wasn't. My mind was in countdown to plunge.

Back home, Boyd went straight to his bowl, guzzled water, blew air like a baleen, and flopped on the floor.

I hung up the leash and locked the door. As I set the alarm, I felt the warmth of Ryan's body inches from mine.

With one hand Ryan took my wrist and turned me to him. With the other he reached up and flicked off the light. I smelled Irish Spring and cotton tinged with male sweat.

Pressing close, Ryan raised my hand and laid it against his cheek.

I looked up. His face was swallowed in shadow.

Ryan brought my other hand up. My fingertips felt the features I'd known for a decade. Cheekbones, a corner of his mouth, the angle of his jaw.

Ryan stroked my hair. His fingers slithered down the sides of my neck, moved across my shoulders.

Outside, my wind chime tinkled gaily.

Ryan's hands glided over the curves of my waist, my hipbones.

A strange sensation flooded my brain, like something remembered from a distant dream.

Ryan's lips brushed mine.

I drew in my breath. No. It drew in of its own accord.

Ryan kissed me hard on the mouth.

I kissed back.

Let go, every cell in my brain commanded.

My arms went around Ryan's neck. I drew him to me, heart racing like some wild, frightened thing.

Ryan's hands moved to my back. I felt my zipper slide down. His hands rose, eased the straps from my shoulders. I lowered my arms.

Black linen pooled at my feet.

All the sadness and frustration and unfulfilled desire of the past few days evaporated in that instant. The kitchen receded. The earth. The cosmos.

My fingers sought the buttons on the cornflower shirt.

10

Palmer Cousins, Katy, and I were in Montreal, sipping cappuccinos at an outdoor café. Across the way a street busker was playing the spoons.

Palmer was describing a yoga class to which participants brought their dogs.

Instead of clacking, the spoons began shrilling in the busker's hands. The noise grew louder and louder until I couldn't understand what my daughter's friend was saying.

I opened my eyes.

And looked at the back of Ryan's head.

And felt like a kid who'd given it up on prom night.

Turning onto my side, I groped for the phone.

"—lo?" Groggy.

"Tim Larabee."

I felt Ryan roll over behind me.

"Sorry to wake you." The ME didn't sound all that sorry.

Scooping me by the waist, Ryan tucked my bum into the angle formed by his hips and thighs. My breath came out with a soft "Hmff."

"You OK?"

"Cat."

I squinted at the clock. My thong obscured the digits.

"Time?" Monosyllables were all I could handle.

"Six."

Ryan molded our bodies together like spoons.

"Did you get my message?" Larabee asked.

A protrusion was forming where the bowl of Ryan's spoon met the handle.

"Message?"

"I called around eight last night."

"I was out." And too busy getting nooky to check my voice mail.

"I couldn't score a dog to save my life. Your chow zeroed in on those bear bones, so I figure he must have a nose for rot. Thought maybe you could bring him along today."

The protrusion was growing, severely hampering my ability to concentrate.

"Boyd's not cadaver trained."

"Better than nothing."

Larabee had never met Boyd.

"By the way, Sheila Jansen got a match on the Cessna pilot."

I sat up, raised my knees, and pulled the quilt to my chin.

"That was quick."

"Harvey Edward Pearce."

"Dentals?"

"Plus the snake tattoo. Harvey Pearce is a thirty-eight-year-old white male from Columbia, North Carolina, out near the Outer Banks. Popped right up on the NCIC search."

"Pearce's only been dead since Sunday. Why were his identifiers in the system?"

"Seems Harvey's ex wasn't real patient about child support. Hubby skipped a payment, the little woman reported him missing."

"And Harvey missed a few."

"You've got it. Eventually the locals got wise to the bogus missing person reports, but not before Harvey's personal stats were well known to the law."

Ryan tried to draw me back to him. I pointed a finger and scrunched my face into an exaggerated frown, as I would with Boyd.

"Where exactly is Columbia?"

"About half an hour west of Manteo on US 64."

"Dare County?"

"Tyrrell County. See you in an hour at the farm. Bring the dog."

Clicking off, I faced the first problem of the day.

I could bolt from the room naked. Or I could take the quilt, leaving Ryan to fend for himself.

I was opting for a bare-ass sprint when Ryan's arm snaked around my waist. I looked down at him.

His eyes were fixed on my face. Amazing eyes. In the pale gray of dawn they looked almost cobalt.

"Ma'am?"

"Yes?" Tentative.

"I respect you with my whole heart and my whole soul, ma'am." Somber as an evangelical preacher.

I drummed my fingers on his chest. "You're not half bad yourself, cowboy."

We shared a laugh.

Ryan tipped his head at the phone. "Sheriff rounding up a posse?"

I lowered my voice, CIA style. "If I told you that, I might have to kill you."

Ryan nodded knowingly.

"Could you and the boys use an extra hand?"

"Seems we could. But they've only requested Boyd."

He feigned disappointment. Then, "Could you put in a word, ma'am?"

I finger-drummed his chest again.

"Have you other talents, gunslinger?"

"This boy can shoot straight as a yard of pump water."

Where did he get this stuff?

"But are you good at recovery?"

Ryan lifted the quilt.

I took a peek. Oh, yeah.

"I'll see what I can do."

"I'm beholden, ma'am. In the meantime, how about I hep you out in the shower?"

"One condition."

"Anything you say, ma'am."

"Loose the Chester bit."

We *both* sprinted naked to the bathroom.

* * *

Two hours later I was heading toward the Cowans Ford bridge. Ryan was beside me. Boyd was doing his bird dog routine in back. My car's AC was whirring at "max." I hoped I would recognize the turnoff.

Noting the high ceiling and clear sky, I pictured Harvey Pearce and wondered why the man had augered into a visible rock face on a sunny Sunday afternoon.

I pictured the macabre black residue coating Pearce and his passenger, and wondered again what that substance could be.

I also wondered about the passenger's parentage. And about his odd nasal lesion.

"What are you thinking?" Ryan pushed Boyd's snout from his ear. Boyd shot to the window behind me.

"I thought men hated to be asked that question."

"I'm not like other guys."

"Really." I cocked an eyebrow.

"I know the names of at least eight colors."

"And?"

"I don't kill my own meat."

"Hmm."

"Thinking about last night?" Ryan flashed his eyebrows. I think he was picking the schtick up from Boyd.

"Something happen last night?" I asked.

"Or tonight?" Ryan gave me the have-I-ever-got-something-in-mind-for-you look.

Yes! I thought.

"I was thinking about the Cessna crash," I said.

"What troubles you, buttercup?"

"The passenger was in back."

"Why was that? No upgrades?"

"There was no right front seat. He flew forward on impact. Why wasn't he buckled in?"

"Didn't want to wrinkle his leisure suit?"

I ignored that.

"And where was the right front seat?"

"Blasted out on impact?"

"I didn't see it among the wreckage." I spotted the turnoff and made a left. "Neither Jansen nor Gullet mentioned one."

"Gullet?"

"Davidson PD. The local cop on the scene."

"Could the seat have been removed for repairs?"

"I suppose that's a possibility. The plane wasn't new."

I described the black gunk. Ryan thought a moment.

"Don't you people call yourselves tarheels?"

For the rest of the trip I listened only to Public Radio.

When I pulled up at the farm adjoining McCranies', vehicles clogged one side of the road. This time the assemblage included Tim Larabee's Land Rover, a police cruiser, the CMPD crime scene truck, and the MCME transport van.

Two kids watched from the opposite shoulder, spindly legs hanging from cutoff jeans, fishing gear strapped to their bikes. Not bad as far as gawkers go. But it was still early, just past eight. Others would arrive once our little army was spotted. Passersby, the neighbors, perhaps the media, all salivating for a glimpse of the misfortune of others.

Larabee was standing on the lawn with Joe Hawkins, two CMPD uniforms, one black, one white, and the pair of crime scene unit techs who'd helped recover the bear bones.

Someone had made a Krispy Kreme run. Everyone but the black cop held a Styrofoam cup and a doughnut.

Boyd leaped up, nearly knocking himself unconscious against the roof when Ryan and I left him in the backseat. Righting himself, he stuck his snout through the six inches of open window and began licking the exterior glass in a circular pattern. His yips followed us to the little circle beside the blacktop.

After introductions, during which I simply identified Ryan as a visiting police colleague from Montreal, Larabee laid out the plan. Officers Salt and Pepper looked hot and bored, seeming curious only about Ryan.

"This property is supposed to be abandoned, but the officers are going to look around to see if they can interest anyone in their warrant."

Officer Salt shifted his feet, finished the last of his chocolate with sprinkles. Officer Pepper folded his arms across his chest. The muscles looked the size and strength of banyan roots.

"Once the officers give the go-ahead, we'll cruise the dog around, get his thoughts on the place."

"His name is Boyd," I said.

"Boyd sociable?" asked the CSU tech with the granny specs.

"Offer him a doughnut, you've got a buddy for life."

Red sun flashed off a lens as she turned to look at the chow.

"Boyd hits, we dig," Larabee went on. "We find any human remains our anthropologist here determines to be suspicious, the warrant says we can toss the place. Everyone OK with that?"

Nods all around.

Ten minutes later the cops were back.

"No signs of life in the house. Outbuildings are empty," said Officer Salt.

"Place has the charm of a hazardous waste dump," said Officer Pepper. "Watch yourselves."

"OK," Larabee said to me. "You three take the western half." He raised his chin at Hawkins. "We'll take the east."

"And we'll be in Scotland afore ye," sang Ryan.

Larabee and Hawkins looked at him.

"He's Canadian," I said.

"Boyd hits, give a holler," said Larabee, handing me a radio.

I nodded and went to leash the chow, who was bursting with eagerness to serve.

The farm wasn't really a farm. My herb garden produces a higher yield of edibles.

The crop here was kudzu.

North Carolina. We're mountains. We're beaches. We're dogwoods, azaleas, and rhododendron.

And we're up to our asses in kudzu.

Pueraria lobata is native to China and Japan, where it's used as a source of hay and forage, and for control of soil erosion. In 1876 some horticultural genius decided to bring kudzu to the United States, thinking the vine would make a great ornamental.

The legume took one look at the Southern states and said, "Hot diggity!"

In Charlotte, you can sit on your porch on summer nights and hear the kudzu edge forward. My friend Anne claims she once set out a marker. In twenty-four hours the runners on her banister had advanced two inches.

Kudzu covered the rusted chain-link fence at the back of the property. It slithered along power lines, swallowed trees and bushes, and blanketed the house and its outbuildings.

Boyd didn't care. He dragged me from vine-draped oak to magnolia to pump house to well, sniffing and wagging as he had at the annex.

Other than the depression left behind by the bear bones, nothing got a rise but the chipmunks and squirrels.

Boyd of the Baskervilles.

By eleven the mosquitoes had drained so much blood I was starting to think "transfusion." Boyd's tongue was barely clearing the ground, and Ryan and I had said "fuck" a thousand times each.

Fat, leaden clouds were drifting in overhead and the day was turning dark and sluggish. An anemic little breeze carried the threat of rain.

"This is pointless," I said, wiping the side of my face on the shoulder of my T-shirt.

Ryan didn't disagree.

"Except where we went digging for bear by the McCranie hedge, dogbreath hasn't so much as stiffened a whisker."

"He liked that sneak swoop-and-sniff of your tush." Ryan addressed Boyd. "Didn't think I was watching, did you, Hooch?"

Boyd looked at Ryan, went back to licking a rock.

"Ryan, we need to do something."

"We are doing something."

I cocked an eyebrow.

"We're sweating."

Katy would have been proud of the eye roll.

"And doing a damn fine job of it, considering this heat."

"Let's stroll Boyd past the hedge one more time, remind him what we're looking for, then make a final sweep and call it a day."

I put my hand down and Boyd licked it.

"Sounds like a plan," said Ryan.

I wrapped the leash around my palm and yanked. Boyd looked up and twirled the eyebrow hairs, as though questioning the sanity of another sortie.

"I think he's getting bored," Ryan said.

"We'll find him a squirrel."

When Ryan and I set off, Boyd fell into step. We were weaving through the outbuildings at the back of the house, when the chow went into his "sniff-squirt-and-cover" routine.

Moseying up to a kudzu-shrouded shack, Boyd snuffled the earth, lifted a leg, took two forward steps, then kicked out with both back feet. Tail wagging, he repeated the maneuver, working his way along the foundation.

Sniff. Lift. Squirt. Step, step. Kick, kick.

Sniff. Lift. Squirt. Step, step. Kick, kick.

"Good rhythm," said Ryan.

"Pure ballet."

I was about to tug Boyd from the shed when his muscle tonus changed. His head and ears shot forward and his belly sucked up.

One beat.

Snout to the ground.

Another beat.

Muscles rigid, Boyd inhaled then exhaled through his nostrils, sending dead vegetation spiraling outward.

Then the dog went absolutely, utterly still.

A heartbeat. A lifetime.

Boyd's ears flattened, his hackles rose, and an eerie sound crawled from his throat, more keening than growl.

The hairs on my neck went vertical. I'd heard it before.

Before I could speak, Boyd exploded. Lips curled, teeth gleaming, the keening gave way to frenzied barking.

"Easy, Boyd!"

The chow lunged forward and backward, delivering his threat from every angle.

I tightened my grip and braced both feet.

"Can you hold him?" I asked.

Without a word, Ryan took the leash.

Heart pounding, I circled the shed, searching for a door.

The radio crackled. Larabee said something.

I found the entrance on the south side, away from the house. Gingerly brushing back spiderwebs, I pulled on the handle.

The door wouldn't budge.

I looked up and down along the frame. Two nails held the door in place. They looked new compared with the dry, flaky wood around them.

Boyd's frenzy continued. Ryan held tight to the leash, calling "Hooch," then "Boyd" to calm him.

Unfolding my Swiss army knife, I gouged out one nail, then the other.

Larabee's voice sounded small and tinny on the radio, as though emanating from some alien star system.

I depressed the button and reported my position.

When I tried again, the door creaked open, and a fetid, earthy smell drifted out, like dead plants and garbage left too long in the sun. Flies buzzed in agitation.

Cupping a hand across my mouth and nose, I peered in.

Flies danced in threads of light slicing in through gaps in the boards. Slowly, my eyes adjusted to the dim interior.

"Perfect," I said. "Picture fucking perfect."

11

I WAS STARING INTO A PRIVY.

At one time *chez toilette* offered state-of-the-art comfort in human waste disposal technology: insect control, toilet paper, a spiffy one-seater with a flip-top lid.

All that was gone now. What remained were dried and shriveled pest strips, a rusted flyswatter, two nails driven into a board at sitting height, a pile of splintered wood, and a chipped and flaking wooden pink oval.

A pit approximately two feet square yawned through an opening in the floorboards at the far end of the shack.

The stench was familiar, bringing to mind privies in summer camps, national parks, and Third World villages. This one smelled sweeter, softer, somehow.

My mind added a string of expletives to those Ryan and I had floated during our walkabout with Boyd.

"Crap!" I said aloud for emphasis.

Not three months earlier I'd been up to my elbows investigating debris in a septic tank. I'd vowed never to slog through feces again.

Now this.

"Crap! Crap! Crap!"

"Not very ladylike."

Larabee craned over my shoulder. I stepped aside. Behind us Boyd continued his frenzy and Ryan continued his attempts to calm him.

"But entirely apropos." I slapped a mosquito that was lunching on my arm.

Larabee stuck his head into the privy, pulled it back quickly.

"Could be Boyd was just rocked by the smell."

I scowled at Larabee's back.

"Could be. But you're going to want to check it out," I said. "Make sure no one's been pissing on Jimmy Hoffa."

"No one's been pissing on anyone in here for some time." Larabee let the door bang shut. "The grand-finale whiz probably took place during the Eisenhower years."

"Something's going bad in that pit."

"Yep."

"Suggestions?" I backhanded gnats from my face.

"Backhoe," he said.

"Can we take a look in the house first, try to estimate when Farmer John splurged for the indoor pipes?"

"Find me one human bone, I'll have CSU shooting close-ups under the sink."

A metacarpal came up with the seventh scoop.

Joe Hawkins, Ryan, and I had been working the privy for three hours. Bucketful by bucketful, the pit was giving up its treasure.

That treasure consisted of shards of broken glass and china, scraps of paper, chunks of plastic, rusted utensils, animal bones, and gallons of deep, black organic matrix.

The backhoe operator would scoop, deposit, and wait. Hawkins would triage bones to one pile, household debris to another. Ryan would transport buckets of compost to my screen. I'd sieve and rummage.

We were growing optimistic. The skeletal part of the treasure looked strictly nonhuman and purely culinary. And, unlike Boyd's discovery at the McCranie hedge, the privy bones were devoid of tissue.

These animals had been dead a long time.

The metacarpal turned up at 3:07 P.M.

I stared at it, searching for something to allow me doubt.

There was no doubt. The bone had been part of a thumb. A thumb that could hitchhike, twirl spaghetti, play trumpet, write a sonnet.

I gave in and closed my eyes.

Hearing footsteps, I opened them. Larabee was circling the pile of wreckage that until hours earlier had been the outhouse.

"How's Boyd doing?" I asked.

"Enjoying a cool one on the front lawn. The chow's not bad company."

Seeing my face his smile evaporated.

"Find something?"

I brought my hand up and positioned the metacarpal next to the base of my thumb.

"Damn."

Ryan and Hawkins joined us at the screen.

"Damn." Ryan echoed Larabee.

Hawkins said nothing.

The backhoe operator put a boot heel on the control panel, leaned back, and gulped bottled water.

"Now what?" Larabee asked.

"The digger's got a delicate touch," I said. "And the pit conforms pretty well to the shape of the shovel. I think we can keep going like this. Whatever's in there isn't likely to be damaged."

"I thought you hated backhoes?"

"This guy's good."

We all glanced at the operator. He looked like he could possibly be less interested. But only with the aid of serious pharmaceuticals.

Thunder rumbled in the distance. The sky was now dark and menacing.

"How much longer?" Larabee asked.

"I've started seeing sterile subsoil in the last few scoops. We're close to the bottom."

"OK," Larabee said. "I'll turn CSU loose on the house."

He straightened.

"And Tim?" I said.

"Yeah?"

"This may be a good time to get homicide on board."

We finished as drops began sputtering from the sky.

I raised my chin, thankful for the cool wetness on my face.

I was exhausted and incredulous. So much work, and just when I most wanted to be free.

Gran would have been unsympathetic. Born on the auld sod and educated by nuns, the old lady had a unique perspective on sex, particularly sex not sanctioned by the parish priest.

No marriage, no whoopie. In her eighty-nine years on earth, she'd never budged from that position, and to my knowledge, had never condoned exceptions.

Wrapping my arms around my waist, I watched Ryan bundle the animal bones into a Hefty bag.

I watched Hawkins seal the human remains in a plastic tub, pull a body tracking form from a zip valise, and start filling in data.

Address where decedent was picked up.

OK. We had that.

Decedent's name. Age. Race. Sex. Date of death.

All those lines remained blank.

Body condition.

Skeletal.

To be precise, a skull and mandible, three cervical vertebrae, and bones comprising the better part of a right and left hand.

We'd screened and rescreened, but that's all that turned up.

Hawkins matched the number on the tag to the number on the form, then dropped the tag into the plastic container.

I looked around. A human being had been killed in this place. The victim's head and hands had been severed and thrown into the privy, the body dumped elsewhere.

Or had the killing occurred at another location, the head and hands brought to the privy for disposal?

Either case was a common pattern. Ditch the head, ditch the hands. No dentals. No fingerprints.

But on a farm in rural Mecklenburg County?

I closed my eyes and let rain fall on my face.

Who was this victim?

How long had the body parts been in the privy?

Where was the rest of the corpse?

Why had two of the hand bones been buried with bears? Was the slaughter of the animals related to the killing of the human?

"Ready?"

Ryan's voice snapped me back.

"What?"

"Everything's loaded."

When we circled to the front of the property, I could see that a white Taurus had joined the cars and vans on the shoulder. A large man was emerging from the driver's side, a cigarette dangling from the corner of his mouth.

A tall, lanky man was unfolding from the passenger seat, feet splayed, long, bony fingers braced against the door frame.

Larabee exchanged a few words with the men as he and Hawkins passed them on the way to their vehicles.

"Great," I muttered under my breath.

"What?" Ryan asked.

"You're about to meet Tweedledum and Tweedledee."

"That's not very charitable."

"Rinaldi's OK Slidell wouldn't make the cut for *Jerry Springer.*"

Skinny Slidell exhaled a stream of smoke, flicked the butt, then he and his partner started toward us.

While Slidell lumbered, Rinaldi seemed to move by fits and starts. Standing six-foot-four and carrying just a little over 160, the man looked like a stilt walker dressed by Hugo Boss.

Skinny Slidell and Eddie Rinaldi had partnered for nineteen years. No one on the force could understand the attraction.

Slidell was sloppy. Rinaldi was neat. Slidell mainlined cholesterol. Rinaldi ate tofu. Slidell was beach music and rock-and-roll oldies. Rinaldi was strictly opera. Slidell's fashion sense ran toward the blue-light special. Rinaldi's suits were custom-made.

Go figure.

"Hey, Doc," said Slidell, yanking a wadded hanky from his back pocket.

I returned the greeting.

"Ain't so much the heat as the humility, eh?" He ran the yellowed swatch across his brow, jammed it home with the backs of his fingers.

"The rain should cool things down."

"Good Lord willin'."

The skin on Slidell's face looked like it had been stretched forward hard then allowed to drop. It hung in crescents below his cheeks and eyes, and drooped from the border of his jaw.

"Dr. Brennan." Rinaldi's hair was wiry thin on top, and stood out from his scalp like that of one of the characters in "Peanuts." I could never remember. Was that Linus or Pigpen? Though Rinaldi's jacket was off, his tie was meticulously knotted.

I introduced Ryan. As the men shook, Boyd ambled over and sniffed Slidell's crotch.

"Boyd!" Grabbing his collar, I yanked the dog back.

"Whoa, girl." Slidell bent and roughed Boyd's ears. The back of his shirt was soaked in the shape of a T.

"His name's Boyd," I said.

"No news on the Banks case," Slidell said. "Little mama's still AWOL."

Slidell straightened.

"So you found yourself a stiff in the crapper."

Slidell's face remained flaccid as I described the remains. At one point I thought I saw a flicker in Rinaldi's eyes, but it came and went so quickly, I couldn't be sure.

"Let me get this straight." Slidell sounded skeptical. "You think the bones you found in the grave come from one of the hands you found in the dumper."

"I see no reason to think otherwise. Everything is consistent and there are no duplications."

"How'd these bones get out of the dumper and in with the bears?"

"That sounds like a question for a detective."

"Any clue when the vic was chucked in?" Slidell.

I shook my head.

"Any impression on gender?" Rinaldi asked.

I'd made a quick evaluation. Though the skull was large, all sex indicators were annoyingly intermediate. Nothing robust, nothing gracile.

"No."

"Race?"

"White. But I'll have to verify that."

"How confident do you feel?"

"Pretty confident. The nasal opening is narrow, the bridge steepled, the cheekbones tight to the face. The skull looks classically European."

"Age?"

"Skeletal maturation is complete in the fingers, the teeth show little wear, the cranial sutures minimal closure."

Rinaldi pulled a leather-bound notepad from his shirt pocket.

"Meaning?"

"Adult."

Rinaldi jotted it down.

"There is one other little thing."

Both men looked at me.

"There are two bullet holes in the back of the head. Small caliber. Probably a twenty-two."

"Cute, saving that for last," said Slidell. "Don't suppose you found a smoking gun?"

"Nope. No gun. No bullets. Nothing for ballistics."

"Why's Larabee cutting free?" Slidell tipped his head toward the parked cars.

"He's giving a talk tonight."

Rinaldi underlined something in his notes and slid the pen into its slot.

"Shall we go inside?" he asked.

"I'll be there in a minute."

I stood, listening to rain tick the magnolia leaves overhead, unconsciously putting off the inevitable. Though the scientist in me wanted to know whom we'd pulled from the privy, another part of me wanted to turn away, to take no part in the dissection of another murder.

Friends often ask, "How can you constantly deal with the remains of death? Doesn't that debase life? Make brutal death commonplace?"

I shrug off the queries with a stock response about media. Everyone knows about violent death, I say. The public reads about the stabbings, the shootings, the airline disasters. People hear the statistics, watch the footage, follow the trials on Court TV. The only difference? I see the carnage closer up.

That's what I say. But the truth is, I think a lot about death. I can be fairly philosophical about the hard cases who do each other in as part of doing business. But I can never avoid the sense of pity for the young and the weak who simply happened to get in the way of some psychopath listening to voices from another planet, or some druggie in need of fifty dollars for a fix, or for the genuinely innocent who through no fault of their own happened to be in the wrong place at the wrong time and were subsumed by events of which they had no understanding.

My friends interpret my reluctance to discuss my work as stoicism, or professional ethics, or even as a desire to spare their sensitivities. That's not it. It's more a concern for me than them. At the end of the day, I need to leave those cadavers cold and silent on their stainless steel. I need to not think about them. I need to read a book, or see a movie, or discuss politics or art. I need to reestablish perspective and remind myself that life offers much more than violence and mayhem.

But with certain cases, the emotional fire wall is harder to maintain. With certain cases, my mind loops back to the pure horror of it, no matter what rationalizations I make.

As I watched Slidell and Rinaldi walk toward the house, a tiny voice sounded in my head.

Be careful, it whispered. This may be one of the rough ones.

The wind kicked up, agitating the dried magnolia leaves and blossoms at our feet and whipping the kudzu into undulating green waves.

Boyd danced around my legs, looking from me to the house, then back again.

"What?"

The dog whined.

"You wimp."

Boyd'll take on a rottweiler without batting an eye, but storms scare him silly.

"We going in?" Ryan asked.

"We're going in!" I replied in a Walter Mitty contralto.

I bolted for the house. Ryan followed. Boyd overtook us.

As I bounded onto the porch, the screen door opened and Slidell's face appeared in the gap. He'd abandoned the cigarette and was now chewing on a wooden toothpick. Before speaking, he rolled the toothpick with his thumb and index finger.

"You're gonna shit your Calvin Klein's when you see what's in here."

12

THE TEMPERATURE IN THE HOUSE WAS WELL OVER A HUNDRED. The air was stale and moldy, with that no-one's-lived-here-in-a-long-time smell.

"Upstairs," said Slidell. He and Rinaldi disappeared through a double doorway straight ahead, then I heard boots moving around overhead.

The porch overhang, kudzu, dirt-crusted screens and windows, and the impending storm limited the interior light to subterranean levels.

I found it hard to breathe, hard to see. From nowhere, a cloud of foreboding engulfed me, and something menacing tapped at the back of my thoughts.

I sucked in my breath.

Ryan's hand brushed my shoulder. I reached up, but already it was gone.

Slowly, my eyes adjusted. I appraised my surroundings.

We were in a living room.

Red shag carpet with navy flecks. Faux-pine paneling. Early American couch and chair. Wooden arms and legs. Red-and-blue-plaid upholstery. Cushions littered with candy wrappers, cotton stuffing, mouse droppings.

Above the sofa, a flea market print of Paris in springtime, *Le Tour Eiffel* all out of proportion to the street below. Carved wall shelf overflowing with glass animals. More figurines parading across a wooden cornice above the windows.

Collapsible TV trays, the kind with plastic tops and metal legs. Soft drink and beer cans. More cans on the carpet. Cheetos and corn chip bags. A Pringles canister.

I enlarged my scan.

Dining room dead ahead through a double doorway. Round maple table with four captain's chairs. Red-and-blue ruffled seat pads. Upended basket of plastic flowers. Junk food packaging. Empty cans and bottles. Stairs rising steeply off to the right.

Beyond the dining room table was a swinging door identical to one that had separated my grandmother's dining room from her kitchen. Beveled wood. Clear plastic panel at hand level.

Adult hand level. Gran had spent hours wiping grape jelly, pudding, and little prints from the paint below.

Again, my nerves buzzed with an ill-formed sense of apprehension.

Through the swinging door came the sound of cabinets being opened and closed.

Boyd put his forepaws on the couch and sniffed a Kit Kat wrapper. I pulled him back.

Ryan spoke first.

"I'd say the last decorating order was placed around the time that latrine was dug."

"But someone tried." I gestured around the room. "The art. The glass animals. The red-and-blue motif."

"Nice." Ryan nodded false appreciation. "Patriotic."

"The point is, someone cared about the place. Then it went to shit. Why?"

Boyd oozed back to the couch, mouth open, tongue dangling.

"I'm going to take the dog out where he'll be cooler," I said.

Boyd offered only token objection.

When I returned, Ryan had disappeared.

Stepping gingerly, I crossed the dining room and pushed the swinging door with my elbow.

The kitchen was typical of old farmhouses. Appliances and workspace spread for miles along the right-hand wall, the centerpiece a white porcelain sink below the room's single window. Kelvinator at the far end. Coldspot at the near end. Formica countertop at waist level. Worn wooden cabinets above and below.

To move from stove to sink or from sink to refrigerator required actual walking. The place was massive compared with my kitchen at the annex.

Two doors opened from the left-hand wall. One onto a pantry. One onto a basement stairway.

A chrome-and-Formica table occupied the middle of the room. Around it were six chrome chairs with red plastic seats.

The table, chairs, and every surface in the room were coated with black fingerprint powder. The granny glasses–wearing tech was shooting close-ups of prints on the refrigerator door.

"Think tank's upstairs," she said, without looking up from the camera.

I returned to the dining room and climbed to the second floor.

A quick survey revealed three bedrooms. The remaining footage was given over to the glorious modern WC. Like the first-floor motif, the bathroom fixtures looked circa 1954.

Ryan, Slidell, Rinaldi, and the male CSU tech were in the northeast bedroom. All four were focused on something on the dresser. All four looked up when I appeared in the doorway.

Slidell hitched his pants and switched the toothpick to the other corner of his mouth.

"Nice, eh? Kinda Green Acres Gone Trailer Park."

"What's up?" I asked.

Slidell swept a hand over the dresser, Vanna White displaying a game show prize.

Entering the room was like walking into a moldy greenhouse. Violets, now brown with age, covered the wallpaper, the fabric on an overstuffed chair, the curtains hanging limp at each window.

A framed picture lay against one baseboard, a cropped magazine shot of a nosegay of violets. The picture's glass was cracked, its corners off their ninety-degree angle.

Crossing to the bureau, I glanced at the focus of everyone's attention.

And felt the buzz electrify in my chest.

I raised my eyes, not comprehending.

"What's up is your baby killer," said Slidell. "Take another gander."

I didn't need a second look. I recognized the object. What I didn't understand was its meaning. How had it come to be in this dreadful room with its terrible flowers?

My eyes dropped back to the white plastic rectangle.

Tamela Banks stared from the lower left corner, curly black hair outlined by a red square. Across the top of the card a blue banner declared *State of North Carolina*. Beside the banner, red letters on white stated *DMV*.

I looked up.

"Where did you find this?"

"Under the bed," said the CSU tech.

"With enough crud to make a bioterrorist pee his shorts." Slidell.

"Why would Tamela Banks's driver's license be in this house?"

"She must have come here with that hump, Tyree."

"Why?" I repeated myself. This wasn't making sense.

The CSU tech excused himself, returned to processing the next room.

Slidell pointed his toothpick at Rinaldi.

"Gosh, what do you think, Detective? Think it could have something to do with the two kilos of blow we found in the basement?"

I looked at Rinaldi.

He nodded.

"Maybe Tamela lost the license," I groped. "Maybe it was stolen."

Slidell pooched out his lips and rolled the toothpick. Looking for gonadal camaraderie, he turned to Ryan.

"What do you think, Lieutenant? Either of those theories ring true to you?"

Ryan shrugged. "If the queen invited Camilla to that Golden Jubilee concert, anything's possible."

Slidell's left eye twitched as a drop of sweat rolled into it.

"Did you run a history on this place?" I asked.

Another toothpick repositioning, then Slidell pulled a notebook from his back pocket.

"Until recently, the property didn't change hands that much."

Slidell read his notes. We all waited.

"Place belonged to Sander Foote from 1956 until 1986. Sander got it from his daddy, Romulus, who got it from his daddy, Romulus, blah,

blah, blah." Slidell rotated a hand. "String of Romulus Sanderses on the tax records prior to fifty-six. Not really relevant to current events."

"No," I agreed impatiently.

"When Foote died in eighty-six, the farm went to his widow, Dorothy Jessica Harrelson Oxidine Pounder Foote." Slidell looked up. "Lady was the marrying kind."

Back to his notes.

"Dorothy was the third Mrs. F. She and Foote married late, had no kids. He was seventy-two, she was forty-nine. But here's where the story gets interesting."

I wanted to shake Slidell to make him go faster.

"The widow didn't really inherit the farm. Foote's will allowed Dorothy, and her son by a previous marriage, to live on the place until her death. After that, the kid could stay until he was thirty years old."

Slidell shook his head. "This Foote must have been some kind of fruit bat."

"Because he wanted his wife's son to have a home until the boy was established?" I kept my voice calm.

The wind picked up. Leaves thrashed the window screen.

"After that?" Ryan asked.

"After that, the place goes to Foote's daughter by his first marriage."

Something rolled across the lawn with a hollow, thunking sound.

"Dorothy Foote is dead?" I asked.

"Five years ago." Slidell closed the notebook and returned it to his pocket.

"Has her son turned thirty?"

"No."

"Does he live here?"

"Technically, yes."

"Technically?"

"The little sleaze rents the place out to turn a few bucks."

"Can he do that under the terms of the will?"

"Couple years back Foote's daughter hired a lawyer to look into that. Guy couldn't find any way to get the kid tossed. Kid does everything under the table, so there's no record of money changing hands. Daughter lives in Boston, never comes to God's little acre here. Place isn't worth that much. Kid's twenty-seven." Slidell shrugged. "Guess she decided to wait it out."

"What's Dorothy's son's name?" I asked.

Slidell smiled. There was no humor in it.

"Harrison Pounder."

Where had I heard that name?

"You remember him, Doc."

I did. From where?

"We discussed Mr. Pounder just last week." Toothpick. "And it wasn't because the squirrel's appearing on our new career leaflet for police recruits."

Pounder. Pounder.

"Harrison 'Sonny' Pounder," Rinaldi supplied.

Recollection sluiced through my brain.

"Sonny Pounder?" I asked, incredulous.

"Mama Foote's baby boy," Slidell said.

"Who's Sonny Pounder?" Ryan asked.

"Sonny Pounder's a dime-a-dozen, low-life dirtbag who'd sell his mama to the Taliban for the right price." Slidell.

Ryan turned to me.

"Pounder's the dealer who traded the tip about Tamela Banks's baby."

Thunder cracked.

"Why didn't you know this was Pounder's place?" I asked.

"When dealing with authorities, Mr. Pounder prefers listing his city address. Legally, this farm is deeded to Mama," Rinaldi said.

Another peal of thunder. A low wail from the porch.

"Tamela may have come here with Tyree, but that doesn't mean she dealt dope or killed her baby." My reasoning sounded weak, even to me.

In the yard, a door banged, banged again.

"Are you going to talk to Pounder?" I asked Slidell.

The hound-dog eyes settled on mine.

"I'm not a moron, Doc."

Yes, you are, I thought.

At that moment, the storm broke.

Ryan, Boyd, and I sat on the porch until the squall played itself out. The wind flapped our clothes and blew warm rain across our faces. It felt wonderful.

Boyd was less enthused about the raw power of nature. He lay at my side, head thrust into the triangle of space below my crooked knees. It was a tactic on which Birdie often relied. If I can't see you, you can't see me. Ergo, I am safe.

By six the shower had dwindled to a slow, steady drizzle. Though Slidell, Rinaldi, and the CSU techs continued their search of the house, there was nothing more Ryan and I could do.

As a precaution, I trotted Boyd around every floor a couple of times. Nothing caught his interest.

I told Slidell we were taking off. He said he'd call me in the morning.

Happy day.

When I let Boyd into the backseat, he circled, curled with his chin on his hind paws, and gave a loud sigh.

Ryan and I got in.

"Hooch is probably not looking at a career as a narcotics dog."

"No," I agreed.

On his first circuit Boyd had sniffed the two bags of cocaine, wagged once, and continued prancing around the basement. On his second visit, he'd ignored them.

"But he's a pistol with carrion."

I reached back and Boyd licked my hand.

On the way home I swung by the MCME to pick up a laptop power cord I'd left behind. While I went inside, Boyd and Ryan played the chow's single idea of a game: Ryan stood stationary in the parking lot and Boyd ran circles around him.

As I was leaving the building, Sheila Jansen swung in, got out of her car, and crossed to me.

"You're here late," I said.

"Got some news, so I came by on the chance I might catch you here." She did not comment on my appearance. I did not offer.

Boyd abandoned Ryan and shot to Jansen to try the crotch schtick. The NTSB agent cut him off with a double-handed ear scratch. Ryan ambled over and I made introductions. Boyd began orbiting the three of us.

"Looks like the drug theory's right on," Jansen said. "When we rolled the Cessna, damned if the right front door hadn't been fitted with another, smaller door inside."

"I don't understand."

"A hole was cut in the right front door, then covered by a small flap hinged at the bottom to swing down inside the plane."

"Like a one-way doggy door?"

"Exactly. The modification wouldn't have been obvious to a casual observer."

"Why?"

"To allow air drops."

I pictured the two kilos of blow we'd just left behind.

"Of illegal drugs."

"You've got it."

"To a pickup crew waiting with a car on the ground."

"Bingo."

"Why go to all the trouble of modifying the plane? Why not simply open the door and shove the stuff out?"

"Stall speed for a C-210 is around sixty-four miles per hour. That's the minimum they could fly at drop time. It's tough to push something out at that speed. Think about holding open your car door while going down the highway at sixty-five."

"Right."

"Here's the scenario I'm liking. The right front seat's been removed for access to the modified door. The passenger is in back. The product is in the small cargo compartment behind the passenger. Are you picturing this?"

"Yes."

"Pearce—"

She flicked her eyes to Ryan. I nodded. She turned to him. "That's the pilot."

Ryan nodded.

"Pearce is using the rock face as his landmark. He spots the cliff, gives the signal, the passenger unbuckles, reaches back, and starts shoving product from the plane."

"Coke?" Ryan asked.

"Probably. You couldn't get enough weed into a C-210 to make the run worth your while. Though I've seen it done."

"Wouldn't a fall from that height cause the packets of coke to explode?" I asked.

"That's why they're using parachutes."

"Parachutes?"

"Small cargo chutes they could have purchased in a surplus store. The locals are checking that out. Anyway, the coke is bundled inside heavy plastic sheeting, padded with bubble wrap, and bound with enough duct tape to cover my aunt Lilly's ass. Auntie was a big girl."

"Sounds like my great-aunt Cornelia," Ryan said. "Good eater."

Jansen glanced at Ryan, turned back at me.

"Go on," I said.

"Each bundle is attached to a chute with more duct tape and a cinch strap. The chute is wrapped around the bundle, and a twenty-foot polypropylene line is overwrapped around the chute to hold it tight around the bundle. You with me?"

"Yes."

"Pearce gives the word. The pax secures the loose end of the line to something inside the aircraft, opens the doggy door, and shoves the bundle out. As the bundle tumbles, the rope unwraps, the chute is pulled free and deploys, and the snort drifts to earth, sweet as a songbird."

Boyd nipped Ryan's calf. Ryan clapped at him. The dog leaped backward and resumed looping.

"So what went wrong?" I asked.

"How's this. They're flying low over the drop area, close to stall speed, things are hunky-dory, then the last bundle streams back toward the tail. The chute or bundle gets tangled in the rudder or elevator, the pilot can't steer, loses control. Hello, rock face."

"Explains why Pearce was belted and his passenger wasn't."

I pictured the two burned corpses, each coated with the crispy black residue.

"These chutes are made of lightweight nylon, right?"

"Yes."

"How about this. The last chute deploys prematurely, inside the plane. It envelops the passenger. He struggles. Pearce reaches over, tries to disentangle him, loses control, flies into the rock face. Fireball."

"Explains the black residue. Fried parachute." Jansen was with me.

"But this is still all conjecture," I said.

"Not really," Jansen said.

I waited.

"Couple of kids made an interesting discovery yesterday morning."

"THREE KIDS WERE RUNNING THEIR DOGS IN A FIELD EAST OF THE crash site early Monday, spotted what they thought was a ghost flapping around on Grandpa's old tobacco barn."

An image. A pilot's corpse, parachute rising and falling with the wind. Ryan voiced my thought.

"*Lord of the Flies,*" he said.

"Perfect analogy," Jansen said. "Having pondered the situation over Nehi and Moon Pies, our little geniuses decided to do some sleuthing. When their beastie turned out to be a parachuted packet of white powder, they voted to stash the booty while considering further action."

"That action included a broader search," I guessed.

"They found three more packets of blow in the woods. Knowing about the Cessna, and being *Cops* and *CSI* regulars, they figured good fortune had befallen them."

"They called 911 to inquire about a reward."

"Phoned around ten this morning. The Charlotte-Mecklenburg PD contacted the parents, and an open discussion ensued. Bottom line: the kids had four bundles of snort and four parachutes squirreled away in Gramp's shed."

"You're sure it's cocaine?" I asked.

"The stuff will have to be tested. But, yeah, I'd bet my ass it's coke."

"Why would the pilot's pickup crew leave the stuff behind?"

"Access to the location is by one narrow, winding road. They probably watched the Cessna go down, figured if they lingered they'd meet emergency responders on their way out. Opting for freedom over fortune, they hauled ass."

That made sense.

"According to our scenario, the last chute opened prematurely," I said. "Why?"

"Could have been just lousy luck. Or the blowout could have been caused by an airstream."

"How so?"

"The army airborne has had deaths over the years from parachutes inflating accidentally while the jumper stands in the door. The reserve chute is worn in front, and the whipping airstream sometimes gets inside and rips the pack open, dragging the chute and the jumper out the door prematurely."

"Opening the doggy door would have caused an airstream to whip around inside the cabin?" Ryan asked.

"It's possible," Jansen said.

"But they'd successfully launched four chutes. Why a screwup with the fifth?" I asked.

"Maybe the last bundle was lighter. Maybe the pax didn't get the chute wrapped fast enough. Maybe the pilot made a sudden maneuver with the plane."

"Maybe," I said.

"The snort was packed in one-foot-square bundles. That was a pretty tight fit for the doggy door. Maybe the last bundle got jammed and the chute blew before they could knock it free," Ryan suggested.

"Wouldn't that leave one bundle in the plane?" I asked.

"Or under it." Jansen hesitated a microsecond. "I did find something."

"Another packet of drugs?" I asked.

"Hardly a packet. Mostly ash and melted plastic."

"Underneath the wreckage?"

"Yeah."

"Ash from what?"

"I'm not sure. But the stuff doesn't whisper nose candy to me."

"Is a mixed payload common?"

"As a wino with a muscatel buzz."

* * *

When we arrived at the annex Boyd went straight to his bowl.

Ryan won the toss on which I insisted. Bad idea. While he showered I checked my messages.

Harry.

Katy.

A UNCC colleague.

One hang-up.

I tried Lija's town house. A male voice answered, said my daughter was out, but that she was expected shortly. The voice did not identify itself.

I left a message, clicked off.

"And who the hell are you?" I asked the handset. "The intensely engaging Palmer Cousins?" And why didn't you say so? Are you living at Lija's town house, too? I didn't want to think about it.

Boyd looked up, went back to eating.

I tried my colleague. He had a question about a graduate thesis that I could not answer.

Having inhaled every nasty brown nugget in the bowl, Boyd flopped onto his side.

To call Harry, or not to call Harry?

My sister doesn't grasp the concept of the short conversation. Besides, Harry can smell sex over a phone line, and I didn't want to discuss my recent adventures. Hearing footfalls on the stairs, I laid the phone on the table.

Ryan appeared with Birdie pressed to his chest. The cat's forepaws and chin rested on his shoulder.

When I reached out, Birdie turned his head.

"Aw, come on, Bird."

Two unblinking eyes swung my way.

"You're a fraud, Birdie." I stroked the cat's head. "You're not even trying to get away."

Birdie's chin went up, and I scratched his throat.

"If he wanted down," I said to Ryan, "he'd be doing this pushy-paw thing on your chest."

"I found him on the bed."

Hearing Ryan's voice, Boyd scrambled to his feet, tags jangling, toenails scrabbling for purchase on the wooden floor.

Birdie rocketed off Ryan's chest like a shuttle at Canaveral.

"There's beer in the fridge," I said. "Paper's in the den. I won't be long."

When I returned, Ryan was at the kitchen table, *Observer* open to the sports section. He'd finished a Sam Adams and started on a second. Boyd's chin was on his knee.

When I entered, both looked up.

"Of all the gin joints, in all the towns in all the world, she had to walk into mine," Ryan played Bogey to the dog.

"Thanks, Rick."

"Your daughter called."

"Oh?" I was surprised Ryan had answered my phone.

"The thing was lying here, it rang, I answered by reflex. Sorry."

"Did she say why she was calling?"

"I didn't realize who it was. I told her you were showering. She said it wasn't important, gave her name, and hung up."

So Katy and I both had some 'splaining to do.

Ryan and I drove to the Selwyn Pub, a tiny tavern just a few blocks from Sharon Hall. To the uninitiated, the brick bungalow looks like a private home, small for Myers Park, but not intolerable.

Other than a nondescript sign, the only indication that the place is a bar is the assemblage of cars parked where the lawn should be. When I turned in, Ryan looked puzzled, but said nothing.

Patrons descend on the Selwyn Pub in two shifts. Early evenings it's free-range professionals knocking back brews before a game, a date, or dinner with June and Wally and the Beaver.

Later, as the developers and lawyers and accountants head out, students from Queens College pour in. Silk, gabardine, and Italian leather yield to denim, cotton, and hemp sandals. The Benzes, Beemers, and SUVs give way to Hondas, Chevys, and cheaper SUVs.

Ryan and I arrived in the lull at shift change. I'd been in good spirits after my shower, a bit down over Tamela's baby and the privy find, but buoyed by Ryan's presence. Sad-happy. But crossing the pub courtyard, I felt a gloom settling over me.

I loved having Ryan here, was having a terrific time with him. Why the sadness? No idea. I tried to push the darkness aside.

Most of the regulars had gone, and only a few tables and barstools were occupied. Feeling less sociable by the minute, I led Ryan to the pub's single booth.

I ordered a cheeseburger and fries. Ryan chose the evening's special from a handwritten blackboard above the fireplace: barbecue and fries.

Diet Coke for me. Pilsner Urquell for Ryan.

As we waited, Ryan and I rehashed our conversation with Sheila Jansen.

"Who owns the Cessna?" Ryan asked.

"A man named Ricky Don Dorton."

Ryan's draft and my Coke arrived. Ryan flashed the waitress a giant Pepsi smile. She beamed him a Jumbo Super Deluxe. My downward spiral gathered speed.

"Any chance I could have my burger medium rare?" I interrupted the dental exchange.

"Sure." Sister Pepsi turned to Ryan. "You all right with Eastern?"

"Just fine."

After smiling the waitress back to the kitchen, Ryan turned to me.

"What's geography got to do with barbecue?"

"The barbecue from down east is made with a vinegar-mustard-based sauce. Western Carolina sauce relies more on the tomato."

"That reminds me. What's 'swite tay'?"

"What?"

"Servers keep offering it to me."

Swite tay? I rolled the phrase around.

"Sweet tea, Ryan. Iced tea with sugar."

"Learning a foreign language is a bitch. OK. Back to Mr. Dorton. When we first spoke of him you said the gentleman was saddened by the theft of his aircraft."

"Devastated."

"And surprised."

"Dumbfounded."

"Who is Ricky Don Dorton?"

The waitress delivered our food. Ryan asked for mayo. We both looked at him.

"For the fries," he explained.

The waitress turned to me. I shrugged.

When she'd gone, I pounded ketchup onto my fries, transferred the lettuce, pickle, and tomato from the plate to my burger, and added condiments.

"I told you. Dorton owns a couple of strip clubs in Kannapolis, just north of Charlotte."

I took a bite. The ground beef was somewhere between scorched and vaporized. I took a swig of Coke. It was Coke. Not Diet Coke.

My mood was darkening by the nanosecond.

"The police have been watching Dorton on and off for a few years, but they've never been able to nail him with anything."

The waitress presented Ryan with a tiny corrugated cup of mayonnaise and more teeth than a coping saw.

"Thanks," he said.

"Anytime," she said.

I felt my eyes roll toward my frontal lobe.

"They think Mr. Dorton's lifestyle exceeds his earning power?" Ryan asked, dipping a fry into the mayo.

"Apparently the man's got a lot of toys."

"Dorton's back under surveillance?"

"If Ricky Don so much as spits on a sidewalk, he's busted."

I upended the ketchup, pounded, returned the bottle to the table with a loud crack.

We ate in silence for several minutes. Then Ryan's hand slipped over mine.

"What's bugging you?"

"Nothing."

"Tell me."

I looked up. Deep concern in the cornflower eyes. I looked down.

"It's nothing."

"Talk to me, cupcake."

I knew where this was going and I didn't like it.

"What is it?" Ryan probed.

Easy one. I didn't like feeling depressed by my work. I didn't like feeling cheated because of a postponed vacation. I didn't like feeling jealous over an innocent flirtation with an anonymous waitress. I didn't like feeling that I had to answer to my daughter. I didn't like feeling left out of her life.

I didn't like feeling I was not in control.

Control. That was always my problem. Tempe had to be in control. That was the sole insight I'd gained from my single experience with analysis.

I didn't like analysis, didn't like admitting I needed outside help.

And I didn't like talking about my feelings. Ever. Not with a psychologist. Not with a priest. Not with Yoda. Not with Ryan. I wanted to slide from the booth and forget this conversation.

As if in betrayal, a lone tear headed south from one eye. Embarrassed, I backhanded my cheek.

"Done?"

I nodded.

Ryan paid the check.

The parking lot held two SUVs and my Mazda. Ryan leaned against the driver's door, pulled me to him, and tilted my face upward with both hands.

"Talk."

I tried to lower my chin.

"Let's jus—"

"Does this have to do with last night?"

"No. Last night was . . ." My voice trailed off.

"Was what?"

God, I hated this.

"Fine." Skyrockets and the *William Tell* Overture.

Ryan ran a thumb under each of my eyes.

"Then why the tears?"

OK, buster. You want feelings?

I took a deep breath and unloaded.

"Some sick son of a bitch torched a newborn. Some other prick's been slaughtering wildlife like it was mold under the sink. Two guys wasted themselves on a rock face while in the act of boosting the Colombian economy. And some poor bastard got his brains blown out, and his head and hands lobbed into a shithouse."

My chest gave a series of tiny heaves.

"I don't know, Ryan. Sometimes I think goodness and charity are racing toward extinction faster than the condor or the black rhino."

Tears were now flowing.

"Greed and callousness are winning out, Ryan. Love and kindness and human compassion are becoming just a few more entries on the list of endangered species."

Ryan pulled me close. Wrapping my arms around him, I wept on his chest.

The lovemaking was slower, gentler that night. Cellos and a triangle, not drums and a crash cymbal.

Afterward, Ryan stroked my hair as I lay with my cheek nestled in the hollow beneath his collarbone.

Drifting off, I felt Birdie hop onto the bed and curl behind me. The clock ticked softly. Ryan's heart thudded with a peaceful, steady rhythm. Though perhaps not happy, I felt secure.

It was the last I'd feel safe for a long, long time.

14

I LOOKED AT THE CLOCK. FOUR TWENTY-THREE. BIRDIE WAS GONE.
Ryan was snoring softly beside me.

I'd been dreaming about Tamela Banks. I lay there a minute, trying
to reassemble fragmented images.

Gideon Banks. Geneva. Katy. A baby. A pit.

My dreams are usually a piece of cake. My mind takes recent events
and weaves them into nocturnal mosaics. No subliminal puzzlers. No
Freudian brainteasers.

So what the hell was this dream all about?

Guilt over my failure to return Geneva Banks's call?

I'd tried.

Twice.

Guilt for not telling my daughter about Ryan?

Katy had met him when she dropped Boyd off.

Met him, yes.

Fear for Tamela? Sadness over her baby?

Then my mind was off and running.

Why was Tamela Banks's driver's license at a farm belonging to
Sonny Pounder, a man recently busted for dealing drugs? Had Tamela
gone there with Darryl Tyree? Did the cocaine belong to Tyree? To
Pounder? Why had it been left in the basement?

Where was Tamela?

Where was Darryl Tyree?

A sudden terrible thought.

Could the victim in the privy be Tamela Banks? Had Darryl Tyree killed her out of fear she'd reveal what had happened to the baby? Out of anger that the child wasn't his?

But that was impossible. The bones in the privy were devoid of flesh. Tamela's baby was found only a week ago.

But when had the infant died?

I recapped what I knew about timing.

Tamela told her sister about the pregnancy last winter. She left her father's home sometime around Easter. Witnesses reported she'd been living with Tyree in a South Tryon Street house for four months.

The baby could have been born in July, or even late June. When had Tamela last been seen? Could she have died several weeks ago? Could the highly organic environment in the privy have hastened decomposition?

If not Tamela, who was the privy victim? Why was he there? Who had shot him?

I thought the skull looked male, but *was* it a he?

Where was Darryl Tyree? Could I be wrong about the skull looking Caucasian? Could we have pulled Tyree's head and hands from the pit?

Had I really seen a reaction in Rinaldi's eyes? Had the head and hands triggered some recollection? If so, why keep it to himself?

Slidell's question was a good one. How had two of the privy pit hand bones ended up in a shallow grave with bears and birds?

Who had killed all of those animals?

If the privy remains were not Tamela's, could she have suffered the same fate as that victim?

Questions looped and spun in my head.

From the privy pit farm, my mind traveled west across the county to a cornfield crash site. I pictured Harvey Pearce and his anonymous passenger, their corpses encased in crispy black shrouds.

Who was Pearce's passenger? What was the strange lesion on his nasal bone?

Jansen found charred matter under the Cessna. Was it more cocaine, or some other illegal drug? Something else entirely?

What was the relationship of the men in the Cessna to Ricky Don Dorton? Had Pearce and his passenger stolen Dorton's plane, or were the three part of a drug trafficking ring? The doggy door and the missing seat seemed inconsistent with a recently stolen plane.

I turned my head on the pillow.

Was I making a mistake with Ryan? Could this work? If not, could we hold on to the friendship we had? To an outsider, our constant bantering might look like hostility. That was our way. Sparring. Teasing. Jousting. But underneath lay respect and affection. If it turned out we couldn't be lovers, could we once again be colleagues and friends?

Did I want to be a couple? Could I really yield my long-fought-for independence? Would I have to?

Did Ryan want a committed relationship? Was he capable of monogamy? Was he capable of monogamy with me? Could I again believe in it?

It was a relief when day finally dawned. In the gathering light I watched familiar objects take shape in my room. The conch shell I'd collected on the beach at Kitty Hawk two summers back. The champagne glass into which I tossed my earrings. The framed pictures of Katy. The *kabawil* I'd purchased in Guatemala.

And the unfamiliar.

Ryan's face was darker than usual, tanned from his days at Kings Mountain and the farm. The early light lay golden on his skin.

"What?" Ryan caught me gazing at him.

I stared into his eyes. No matter how often I experienced it, the intensity of the blue always surprised me.

I shook my head.

Ryan raised up on an elbow.

"You look tense."

I wanted to say what was on my mind, to form forbidden words, ask prohibited questions. I held back.

"It's scary stuff."

"Yes," I agreed.

What's scary, Andrew Ryan? You? Me? A baby in a woodstove? A HydroShok to the head?

"I'm really sorry about the beach." Safer ground.

Ryan broke into a grin. "I've got two weeks. We'll get there."

I nodded.

Ryan threw back the covers.

"I think today it's the Queen City."

*   *   *

Ryan and I swung by Starbucks, then he dropped me at the MCME office. Immediately upon arriving, I phoned Geneva Banks. Again, I got no answer.

A prick of apprehension. Neither Geneva nor her father worked outside the home. Where were they? Why wasn't someone picking up?

I was dialing Rinaldi when he and his partner walked into my office.

"How's it going?" I asked, replacing the receiver.

"Good."

"Good."

We gave each other prefab smiles.

"Have you spoken to Geneva or Gideon Banks recently?"

Slidell and Rinaldi exchanged glances.

"Geneva phoned Monday," I said. "I returned her call, but got no answer. I just tried again. Still no answer."

Rinaldi glanced down at his loafers. Slidell looked at me flatly.

Cold fingers wrapped around my heart.

"This is the part where you tell me they're dead, right?"

Slidell answered with one word.

"Gone."

"What do you mean, gone?"

"Splitsville. Vamoosed. In the wind. We're here to see if you might know something, you and Geneva being girlfriends and all."

I looked from Slidell to his partner.

"The shades are drawn, and the place is secured tighter than a nuclear reactor. A neighbor saw the Bankses' car pull out early Monday. No sign of them since."

"Were they alone?"

"The neighbor wasn't sure, but thought she saw someone in the backseat."

"What are you doing about it?"

Rinaldi adjusted his tie, carefully centering the top flap over the bottom.

"We're looking for them."

"Have you spoken to the other Banks kids?"

"Yes."

I turned back to Slidell.

"If this Tyree's the scumbag you say he is, Geneva and her father could be in danger."

"Uh-huh."

I swallowed.

"Tamela and her family could already be dead."

"You're preaching to the choir, Doc. Far as I'm concerned, the faster we haul their asses to the bag, the better."

"You're kidding, right?"

"Ever heard of aiding and abetting?"

"Gideon Banks is in his seventies, for God's sake. Geneva probably has the IQ of parsley."

"How about obstructing justice, or accessory after the fact?"

"After *what* fact?" I wasn't believing this.

"Let's start with infantalcide." Slidell.

"The word is 'infanticide,'" I snapped.

Slidell put a fist on each hip and leaned back, stretching his lower shirt buttons to their tensile limits.

"You wouldn't have any idea as to the whereabouts of these folks, now, would you, Doc?"

"I wouldn't tell you if I did."

Slidell's hands dropped and his head came forward. We glared across my desk, baboons challenging for first dibs at the watering hole.

"Let's talk about this other situation," said Rinaldi.

As if on cue, a cell phone rang. Slidell scooped his out of a pocket. "Slidell."

He listened a moment, then stepped into the hall.

I looked Rinaldi straight in the eye.

"When I was describing what we found in that privy yesterday, something clicked for you."

"What makes you say that?"

"Something in your eyes."

Rinaldi tugged his shirt cuffs from underneath his jacket and smoothed them against his wrists.

"Have you completed your examination of the skull and hand bones?"

"It tops my agenda."

The fluorescents hummed overhead. Slidell's voice drifted in from the hall.

"Who is this Darryl Tyree?" I asked.

"A pimp, a drug dealer, and a pornographer. Although I'm not sure that's the order Mr. Tyree uses on his résumé. Let me know what you decide about the skull."

Rinaldi started toward the door just as Joe Hawkins appeared in it. Both men stopped. Hawkins reached past Rinaldi and handed me a large brown envelope.

I thanked him. Hawkins withdrew.

Rinaldi did a slow turn and rolled his eyes in his partner's direction.

"Skinny can be a bit gruff. But he's a good cop. Don't worry, Dr. Brennan. We'll find the Bankses."

At that moment Slidell stuck his head through the door.

"Looks like Green Acres ain't the crime scene for the privy vic."

Rinaldi and I waited for him to continue.

"CSU shined a LumaLite around the place this morning." Though Slidell smiled, the corners of his mouth stayed flat. "No blood. Dark as a mall on Christmas Day."

When Rinaldi and Slidell had gone, I took Hawkins's envelope to the stinky room and began popping X rays onto the light boxes.

Each film inspired a fresh title for Slidell.

Dork.

Prick.

One-syllable appellations worked best. Unless a corner slipped and the film needed readjustment.

Asshole.

Dickhead.

Plate by plate, I worked my way through the passenger's infrastructure. Ribs, vertebrae, pelvis, arm, leg, breast, and collarbone.

Other than massive deceleration trauma, the skeleton looked perfectly normal.

Until I popped up the last four plates.

I was staring at the passenger's hands and feet when Larabee came up behind me. For a full ten seconds neither of us spoke.

Larabee broke the silence.

"Jesus Christ in a blooming pear tree. I hope that's not what I think it is."

I STARED INTO THE PATTERN OF GRAYS AND WHITES RADIATING from the X ray. Beside me, Larabee did the same.

"Could you see involvement when you examined the nasal bones?" the ME asked.

"One lesion."

"Active?"

"Yes."

I heard Larabee's soles squeak on the tile, his palms rub up and down on his upper arms.

"Are you thinking leprosy?" he asked.

"Sure looks like it."

"How the hell does someone get leprosy in North Carolina?"

The question hung in the air as I dug through layers at the back of my mind.

Graduate school. Systematics of bone pathology.

A: anatomical distribution.

I pointed the tip of my pen at the finger and toe bones.

"Other than the nasals, the process seems to be restricted to the bones of the hands and feet, especially the proximal and middle phalanges."

Larabee agreed.

B: osseous modification. Abnormal size, shape, bone loss, bone formation.

"I see three types of change."

I pointed to a punched-out-looking circle. "Some lesions look round and cystic, like the one on the nasal."

I indicated a honeycombed pattern in the index finger.

"There's lacelike coarsening in some phalanges."

I moved my pen to a phalange whose shape had altered from that of a dumbbell to that of a sharpened pencil.

"Resorption in one."

"Looks like classic radiology textbook leprosy to me," said Larabee.

"Did you pick up hints of anything elsewhere in the body?"

Larabee turned both palms up and shrugged in a "not really" gesture. "A couple of enlarged lymph nodes, but they didn't strike me as any big deal. The lungs were hamburger, so I couldn't really see much."

"With lepromatous leprosy, the most obvious skin lesions would have been on the face."

"Yeah. And this guy didn't have one."

Back to my hindbrain.

No macroscopically observable changes in soft tissue.

Diffuse spotty rarefaction, cortical thinning, penciling of at least one phalange.

Down through the mental strata.

Neoplasias. Deficiency diseases. Metabolic. Infectious. Autoimmune.

Slow, benign course.

Hands and feet.

Young adult.

"But you can bet your ass I'll take a close look at the histo when the slides are ready."

Larabee's words hardly registered as I thumbed through possible diagnoses. Leprosy. Tuberculosis. Spina ventosa. Osteochondromatosis.

"Don't phone Father Damien yet," I said, clicking off the light boxes. "I'm going to do some digging."

"In the meantime, I'll take another look at what's left of this guy's skin and lymph nodes." Larabee wagged his head. "Sure would help if he had a face."

I'd barely settled at my desk when the phone rang. It was Sheila Jansen.

"I was right. It wasn't coke burned onto the underbelly of that Cessna."

"What was it?"

"That has yet to be determined. But the stuff wasn't blow. Any progress on the passenger?"

"We're working on it."

I didn't mention our suspicion about the man's health. Better to wait until we were sure.

"Discovered a bit more about Ricky Don Dorton," Jansen said.

I waited.

"Seems Ricky Don got into a slight misunderstanding with the United States Marine Corps back in the early seventies, did some brig time, got the boot."

"Drugs?"

"Corporal Dorton decided to send a little hash home as a memento of his time in Southeast Asia."

"There's an original thought."

"Actually, his scheme was pretty ingenious. Dorton was assigned to casualty affairs in Vietnam. He'd slip drugs into coffins in the mortuary in Da Nang, then an associate would remove them on arrival Stateside, before the serviceman's body was processed on to the family. Dorton was probably working with someone he'd met during his tour, someone who knew the morgue routine."

"Clever." Jesus. "Cold, but clever."

"Except Corporal Einstein got nailed the last week of his tour."

"Bad timing."

"Dorton disappeared for a while after his release. Next we see him, he's back in Sneedville running field trips for the Grizzly Woodsman Fishing Camp."

"Grizzly Woodsman? Is that one of those outfits that helps accountants from Akron reel in the bass of their dreams?"

"Yeah. Guess the GED education and dishonorable discharge limited Ricky Don's options with the big Wall Street firms. But not his aspirations. Two years as an angling coach, and Dorton opens his own operation. Wilderness Quest."

"You don't suppose Ricky Don got some product across before the Corps discovered his little export scheme?"

"Nah. Fine citizen probably set aside a little from every paycheck, worked a civilian job on weekends, that sort of thing. Anyway, by the mid-eighties, Dorton switched from hip waders to pinstripes. In addition to the fishing camp he owns a sporting goods store in Morristown, Tennessee, and the two entertainment palaces in Kannapolis."

"A respected businessman," I said.

"And Ricky Don's military experience taught him well. If Dorton's into something illegal, he operates from a distance now. Stays so cool the cops can't make him flinch."

Something moved in the sludge at the back of my brain.

"Did you say Dorton's from Sneedville?"

"Yeah."

"Tennessee?"

"Yeah. Mama Dorton and about a trillion kin still live there."

The sludge thought rolled over, sluggish and lazy.

"Any chance Dorton's a Melungeon?"

"How did you guess that?"

"Is he?"

"Sure is. I'm impressed. Until yesterday I'd never heard of Melungeons." Jansen may have picked up on something in my voice. "That trigger a line of thought?"

"Just a hunch. Could be nothing."

"You know how to reach me."

I sat a moment when we'd disconnected.

Dig.

Upper layers. Recent deposits.

American Academy of Forensic Sciences. Scientific session.

What year? What city?

I turned to the AAFS programs on my shelf.

Within ten minutes I found what I was looking for. Twelve years back. A graduate student presentation on disease frequencies among Melungeon populations.

As I read the abstract, the sludge thought lumbered to its feet and slowly took form.

"Sarcoidosis."

When Larabee looked up, his desk lamp threw shadows across the lines in his face.

"That would take us back to lymph nodes, lungs, and skin."

"Approximately fourteen percent of sarcoidosis cases show

skeletal involvement, mostly in the short bones of the hands and feet."

I laid a pathology textbook on the desk in front of him. Larabee read a moment, then leaned back, chin on palm. His expression told me he was unconvinced.

"Most cases of sarcoidosis are asymptomatic. The disease pursues a slow, benign course, usually with spontaneous healing. People don't even know they have it."

"Until they get an X ray for some other reason," he said.

"Exactly."

"Like being dead."

I ignored that.

"Sarcoidosis primarily affects young adults," I said.

"And is most evident radiographically in the lungs."

"You said the lungs were hamburger."

"Sarcoidosis is mainly seen among African-Americans."

"There's a high incidence among Melungeons."

Larabee looked at me as though I'd said Olmec warriors.

"It all fits. There's an Anatolian bump on the back of the passenger's head and modified shoveling on his incisors. His cheekbones are flaring, otherwise the guy looks like Charlton Heston."

"Refresh me on Melungeons."

"They're fairly dark-skinned people with European-looking features. Some have an Asian eye fold."

"Living where?"

"Most are in the mountains of Kentucky, Virginia, West Virginia, and North Carolina."

"Who are they?"

"Survivors of the lost colony of Roanoke, Portuguese shipwrecks, the lost tribes of Israel, Phoenician seamen. You can take your pick of theories."

"What's the current favorite?"

"Descendants of Spanish and Portuguese colonists who abandoned the settlement of Santa Elena in South Carolina during the late sixteenth century. Supposedly these folks mingled with the Powhatans, the Catawbas, the Cherokees, and a number of other tribes. There may even have been some input from Moorish and Turkish galley slaves and from Portuguese and Spanish prisoners left on Roanoke Island in 1586."

"Left by whom?"

"Sir Francis Drake."

"Who do *Melungeons* think they are?"

"They claim to be variously of Portuguese, Turkish, Moorish, Arabic, and Jewish origin mixed with Native Americans."

"Any evidence to support that?"

"When first encountered back in the sixteen hundreds they were living in cabins, speaking broken English, and described themselves as 'Portyghee.'"

Larabee made a give-me-more gesture with his hand.

"A recent gene-frequency study showed no significant differences between Melungeon populations in Tennessee and Virginia and populations in Spain, Portugal, North Africa, Malta, Cyprus, Iran, Iraq, and the Levant."

Larabee shook his head. "How do you remember stuff like that?"

"I don't. I just looked it up. There are lots of Melungeon Web sites."

"Why is this relevant?"

"There's a large population of Melungeons living near Sneedville, Tennessee."

"And?"

"Remember Ricky Don Dorton?"

"The owner of the Cessna."

"Dorton's from Sneedville, Tennessee."

"That works."

"Thought it might."

"Give Sheila Jansen a call. I'll get on the horn to Sneedville."

I'd just completed my call to the NTSB agent when Slidell and Rinaldi made their second appearance of the day.

"Ever hear of a man named J. J. Wyatt?" Rinaldi asked.

I shook my head.

"Looks like Wyatt was on Darryl Tyree's speed dialer."

"Meaning Tyree called Wyatt frequently?"

Rinaldi nodded. "From his cell phone."

"Recently?"

"The final three calls were placed just before seven last Sunday morning."

"To?"

"Wyatt's cell phone." Slidell face looked poached with heat.

"Which was located where?" I asked.

"Most likely in Wyatt's hand." Slidell mopped his brow.

I was biting back a reply when Larabee joined us wearing a smile wider than a lean face such as his could support.

"Guys," the ME said to Slidell and Rinaldi, "you are in the presence of genius."

Larabee did a half-bow in my direction, then waggled a slip of paper in the air.

"Jason Jack Wyatt."

Absolute quiet crammed my little office.

Puzzled by our nonreaction, Larabee looked from Slidell to Rinaldi to me.

"What?"

Slidell spoke first.

"What about Jason Jack Wyatt, Doc?"

"Twenty-four-year-old male Melungeon from Sneedville, Tennessee. Wyatt was reported missing three days ago by a worried grandma."

Larabee glanced up from his notes.

"Granny says young J.J. suffered from 'the arthrity' in his hands and feet. Dental records are in transit, and it looks good for a match on the Cessna passenger."

No one said a word.

"Ready for the best part?"

Three nods.

"Grandma's name is Effie Opal Dorton Cumbo."

Larabee's impossibly wide smile broadened.

"J. J. Wyatt and Ricky Don Dorton are Tennessee kissin' cousins."

16

Thirty seconds passed before anyone spoke.

Rinaldi stared at the ceiling. Slidell studied his shoes. Both looked like they were doing complicated math in their heads.

Knowing he was out of the loop, but not knowing why, Larabee waited us out, the smile gone. His slack face looked like it had spent a lifetime baking in an oven.

I started the dialogue by holding up an index finger.

"Jason Jack Wyatt might be the passenger on the Cessna."

"The Cessna was owned by Ricky Don Dorton," Rinaldi said.

I added a finger.

"Wyatt was Dorton's cousin," Slidell offered.

Ring man.

"Darryl Tyree made frequent calls to Wyatt, including three on the morning the Cessna crashed." Rinaldi.

Pinky.

"Having off-loaded at least four kilos of blow." Slidell.

My thumb went up.

"Tyree is a dealer," Rinaldi said, "whose girlfriend has recently gone missing."

I started on a second hand.

"Having offed her own kid." Slidell.

"Maybe," I said.

"Two members of Tamela's family are also missing." Rinaldi ignored our exchange about the baby.

My second middle finger went up.

"And sweet cheeks' license turned up in a house with two kilos of snort and a dead guy in the privy." Slidell.

Ring man number two.

"A house in the possession of Sonny Pounder, a low-level dealer who snitched to the cops about Tamela's baby."

Pinky number two.

"A house with bears interred in the yard," I added, dropping both hands.

Slidell tendered an emphatic expletive.

I suggested one of my own.

A phone rang in Larabee's office.

"You're going to fill me in on all of this," the ME said to me, then shot out the door.

Rinaldi reached into an inside pocket, withdrew a Ziploc baggie, and tossed it onto my desk.

"CSU found this stashed with the cocaine. Thought it might mean something to you."

Before reaching for the bag I glanced at Rinaldi.

"Trace analysis has already gone over it."

Unzipping the seal, I studied the contents.

"Feathers?"

"Very unusual feathers." Rinaldi.

"I know nothing about feathers."

Slidell shrugged. "You were all over Yogi and his friends, Doc."

"That's bone. These are feathers."

Rinaldi withdrew an eight-inch plume and twirled it. Even under fluorescent light the blues looked rich and iridescent.

"It's no song sparrow," he said.

"I'm not following this," I said.

"Why would someone hide avian plumage with illegal drugs?"

"Maybe the feathers were already in the basement and the coke was accidentally parked on top of them."

"Maybe." Rinaldi replaced the feather.

I flashed on the bear bones.

"Actually, there was some kind of bird mixed in with the bears."

"Tell me more."

"That's all I know."

"Identifying the species might not hurt."

"You need an ornithologist."

"Know any?"

"I can make a few calls." I gave Rinaldi a look that had talons. "But first let's talk headless bodies."

Rinaldi's arms folded across Brooks Brothers linen.

"I don't like being kept in the dark, Detective."

"And we don't like woolly thinking, Doc." Slidell.

I turned to him.

"Is there something you're not sharing?"

"Nothing gained by a lot of pointless wheel spinning." Slidell scowled at me.

I scowled back.

"When we've verified what we're looking at, we'll pass it on." Slidell.

Rinaldi picked at a callus on his thumb. Between the spiky hairs, his scalp looked pale and shiny.

Larabee's voice drifted down from his office.

Slidell held my look. I wondered if he could hang on to it with my boot up his ass.

Rinaldi broke the silence.

"I see no harm in including Dr. Brennan in our thinking."

Slidell's eyes rolled to his partner, snapped back to me.

"What the hell." Slidell sighed. "No skin off my nose."

"Three, four years back. I can't precisely recall. An inquiry came across my desk."

"About a body with no head or hands."

Rinaldi nodded.

"Where?"

"South Carolina."

"It's a big state."

"Fort Mill. Gaffney. Chester." Rinaldi flapped a long, bony hand. "Nothing is centralized down there, it's hard to backtrack."

Unlike the Tarheel State, South Carolina relies on a coroner system, with practitioners operating independently in each county. Coroners are elected. A nurse, a funeral director, a cemetery owner. Few are trained in medicine, fewer still in forensic pathology. Autopsies are farmed out to local doctors.

"Most South Carolina coroners don't have the facilities to keep a corpse very long."

"Got that damn straight," Slidell snorted. "Gave Michael Jordan's daddy, what, three days before they smoked him?"

Slidell had the tact of a sledgehammer. But he was right.

"I've sent out a query," Rinaldi said. "I hope to hear back by the end of the day."

"Was this headless, handless body in good shape?"

"As I recall, the remains were skeletonized. But it wasn't relevant to anything we were investigating at the time, so I didn't take much notice."

"Black or white?"

Rinaldi raised then dropped his shoulders.

"Male or female?"

"Definitely," Rinaldi said.

When the detectives had gone I phoned the university. A colleague could look at the feathers the following day.

Next I went to the cooler and rolled out the gurney with the animal remains. I packaged everything that looked like bird, and placed the bundle in a sack with Rinaldi's baggie of feathers.

Exchanging the animal gurney for that holding the privy remains, I spent the next several hours doing as thorough an analysis as possible.

My initial impressions changed little, though I was able to be more precise on the age estimate.

Race: white.

Age: twenty-five to forty years.

Sex: roll the dice.

When I returned to my office, Ryan was leafing through a copy of *Creative Loafing*, Nikes resting on the edge of my desk. He was wearing the same luau shirt and shorts he'd had on that morning and a Winston Cup cap. He looked like Hawaii Five-O does NASCAR.

"Have a good day?"

"Latta Plantation then Freedom Park."

"Didn't know you were such a history buff."

"Hooch can't get enough of the stuff."

"Where is he?"

"The call of Alpo overpowered the call of the wild."

"Surprised he let you out on your own."

"When last seen, man's best friend was investigating the contents of an Oreo bag."

"Chocolate is bad for dogs."

"We discussed that. Hooch thought he could handle it."

"If Hooch guessed wrong, you're cleaning the carpet."

"Making progress with privy man?"

"Apt segue." Tossing the privy case folder onto my desk, I dropped into my chair. "I just finished."

"That took a while," Ryan said.

"Toody and Muldoon came by twice today."

"Slidell and his partner?"

I nodded.

"Aren't you kind of hard on the guy?"

"Slidell probably needs instructions to make ice cubes."

"Is he really that stupid?"

I thought about that.

Slidell was not actually stupid. Not in the way that a fern is stupid. Or a wood frog. Slidell was just Slidell.

"Probably not. But he's off the bell curves for uncouth and annoying."

"What did they want?"

I told Ryan about Jason Jack Wyatt and the cell phone link to Darryl Tyree.

"The boyfriend of the lady with the dead baby?"

I nodded.

"Curiouser and curiouser."

"Here's another flash. Rinaldi remembers a headless, handless body inquiry a few years back. He and Slidell are tracking it down."

"Descriptors match your privy guy?"

"Rinaldi's recollection is a bit vague."

"*Is* yours a guy?"

"I think so."

Ryan raised his brows in a question.

"There's not a single cranial feature that's definitive for gender. I ran every measurement possible through the Fordisc 2.0 program."

"Let me guess. The skull falls into the overlap range."

I nodded. "Though closer to the male than the female end."

"Ditto for measurements on the hand bones?"

"Yes."

"What's your gut feeling?"

"Male."

"A young-adult white person who probably used the little boys' room. That's not a bad start."

"With lousy teeth."

"Oh?"

"Lots of decay. At least on the teeth we recovered."

"Missed a few?"

"Yeah."

"Shitty job."

"How did I know you would say that?"

"Any dental work?"

I shook my head. "The victim was not a believer in regular checkups."

"Anything else?"

"Maybe some slight bone demineralization."

"I think you've made an excellent start, Dr. Brennan."

"Rinaldi also had feathers."

"Doesn't seem like his style."

"They turned up with the coke in the cellar."

"What kind of feathers?"

"He wants me to find out."

"Do you know any big birdbrains?"

"I know you, cowboy."

Ryan made a pistol with his hand and pointed it at me.

"Ready for another field trip tomorrow?"

"Hee-haw."

This time the finger made a lasso.

We were passing Mrs. Flowers's desk when the phone rang. She answered, then flapped a hand in my direction.

I waited while she spoke, then placed the call on hold.

"It's Detective Slidell."

I felt a sigh elbowing up my chest, but resisted the impulse toward melodramatics.

Mrs. Flowers smiled at me, then at Ryan. When he grinned back, a pink spot blossomed on each of her cheeks.

"He sounds like the cat that swallowed the canary."

"Not a pretty picture." Ryan winked.

Mrs. Flowers giggled, and her cheeks went raspberry.

"Do you want to take it?"

Like I wanted Ebola.

I reached for the receiver.

17

"L<small>ANCASTER</small>."

"Lancaster who?"

"South Carolina."

I heard cellophane crinkle, then the sound of chewing.

"That's about forty minutes south of Charlotte."

"Uh-huh. Straight down five twenty-one."

Pause.

"What *about* Lancaster, South Carolina?"

"Skeleton." Garbled through what sounded like caramel and peanuts.

"Three"—crinkle—"years back."

Slidell was in Snickers mode. My grip tightened on the receiver.

"Hikers."

A lot of crinkling, and a comment I couldn't make out.

"Park."

"Hikers found a headless, handless skeleton in a park near Lancaster?" I prompted.

"Yep."

A click, as though Slidell were picking a tooth with a thumbnail.

"Were the remains ID'ed?"

"Nope."

"What happened to them?"

"Packed up and shipped to Columbia."

"To Wally Cagle?"

"He the anthropologist down there?"

"Yes."

"Stubby little fruit fly, goatee looks like a mallard's arse?"

"Walter Cagle is a highly qualified, board-certified forensic anthropologist." It took an effort to keep my voice level. "You haven't answered my question."

"Probably."

"What does that mean?"

"Fine citizens of Lancaster County elected themselves a new coroner two years back. New kid claims his predecessor didn't keep real good records."

"Who circulated the query?"

"Sheriff."

"What does he say?"

"Says talk to the former coroner. Sheriff's new, too."

"Have you done that?"

"Tough order. Guy's dead."

I was gripping the receiver so tightly the plastic was making small popping sounds.

"Does the current coroner have any information on the case?"

"Unknown. Partial skeleton with animal damage."

"That's it?"

"That's what's in the original police report. Nothin' else in the file."

"Is someone checking with Dr. Cagle?"

"Yeah."

"Are you pulling up missing persons for an ID on the privy skull?"

"Hard to do with nothing to go on."

Slidell had a point.

"White male, twenty-five to forty. Bad teeth, four restorations." I kept my voice even.

Mrs. Flowers's fingers were flying over her keyboard. Now and then she'd glance up at Ryan. He'd smile, and the color in her cheeks would deepen.

"That helps."

"But don't rule out a female if everything else works."

"The hell are you saying? Don't a person got to be one or the other?"

"Yes. One does."

I looked at Ryan. He grinned.

"I'll keep my cell turned on," I said to Slidell. "Call me when you know something."

Normally my refrigerator contains leftover carryout, frozen dinners, condiments, coffee beans, Diet Coke, and milk, with a smattering of slimed-out produce in the bins. That night it was uncharacteristically full.

When I opened the door, a Vidalia onion dropped to the floor and rolled to a stop against Boyd's haunch. The chow sniffed, licked, then relocated himself under the table.

"Been foraging?" I asked.

"Hooch pointed me to the Fresh Market."

Boyd's ears rose, but his chin stayed on his paws.

I picked up a package wrapped in butcher paper.

"You know how to cook swordfish?"

Ryan held out both arms.

"I am a son of Nova Scotia."

"Uh-huh. Would you like a Sam Adams?"

"Generations of my people have made their living from the sea."

I really could love this guy, I thought.

"Your parents were born in Dublin, trained in medicine in London," I said.

"They ate a lot of fish."

I handed him the beer.

"Thanks."

He twisted off the lid and took a long swig.

"Why don't you—"

"I know," I interrupted. "Why don't I take a shower while you and Hooch rustle up some vittles."

Ryan winked at Boyd.

Boyd wagged at Ryan.

"OK."

That's not how it went.

I'd just lathered my hair when the shower door opened. I felt cool air, then a warm body.

Fingers began massaging my scalp.

I pressed into Ryan.

"Have you started the fish?" I asked, without opening my eyes.

"No."

"Good."

We were cuddled on the couch when the phone rang.

It was Katy.

"What's up?"

"Just finished dinner."

"Now?"

I looked at the mantel clock. Ten-thirty.

"Some things, uh, came up."

"You need to ease back, Mom. Take some time for yourself."

"Um."

"Are you still working on Boyd's big score?"

"Boyd's big score may actually turn out to be something."

"Such as?"

"I found human bones mixed in with the animal remains."

"You're kidding."

Ryan tickled behind my ear. I brushed his hand away.

"I'm not kidding. Anyway, where have you been hiding out?"

"Subbing at Dad's firm while the receptionist is on vacation. It is so boring."

She gave the "so" at least three syllables.

"What do they have you doing?"

Ryan blew air onto the nape of my neck.

"Licking envelopes and answering the phone. 'Bialystock und Bloom. Bialystock und Bloom.'" She imitated the Swedish receptionist from *The Producers*.

"Not bad."

"Lija and I thought we'd throw a dinner party."

"That sounds like fun."

Ryan unwrapped his arm from my shoulders, stood, and waggled his coffee cup. I shook my head and mouthed "no thanks."

"Is someone else there?"

"Who do you plan to invite?"

Short pause.

"When I called, some guy answered your phone."

Slightly shorter pause.

"That guy's staying with you, isn't he? That's why you sound funny. You're playing tonsil tennis with the studmuffin from Montreal."

"Are you talking about Andrew Ryan?"

"You know exactly who I'm talking about." Sudden recollection. "Wait a minute. It's been bugging me, but I just figured out who that is. I met that guy when I visited you in Montreal and some serial killer tried to reconfigure your larynx with a chain."

"Katy—"

"Anyway, *le monsieur* was there when I dropped Boyd off. Whoooo, Mom. That guy's a player."

I heard her shout across the apartment.

"My mom's shacking up with a gendarme."

"Katy!"

Muffled comment.

"Oh, yeah. This dude makes Harrison Ford look like Freddy Geek-meister."

More muffled commentary.

Katy spoke into the phone.

"Lija says keep him."

Again, a voice in the distance.

"Good idea." Katy reengaged. "Lija says bring him to the party."

"When is this gala?"

"Tomorrow night. We thought it might be fun to dress up."

I looked at Ryan. After our shower, the studmuffin had swapped the luau shirt and shorts for cutoffs, tank, and flip-flops.

"What time?"

At nine-seventeen the next morning Ryan and I entered an office on the third floor of the McEniry Building at UNCC. Though not large, the room was sunny and bright, with a colorful throw rug overlying the institutional wall-to-wall. Woven in primary colors, stylized nests formed an outer border, and a long-legged heron took flight in the center.

Floor-to-ceiling shelves filled the wall to the left. Those to the right held dozens of aviary prints and photos. Brilliant, dull, tropical, arctic, predatory, flightless. The variety in beaks and plumage was astonishing.

Carved and sculpted birds perched on the desk and filing cabinets, and peeked from atop and between shelved books. Tapestry bird pillows rested on the window ledge. A parrot marionette hung from the ceiling in one corner.

The place looked as though someone had hired an ornithologist, then consulted a "Birds Я Us" catalog to equip the office with what were thought to be exemplary furnishings.

Actually, Rachel had done it herself. One of the foremost ornithologists in the country, Rachel Mendelson was passionate about her science. She lived, breathed, slept, dressed, and probably dreamed birds. Her home, like her office, was resplendent with feathered subjects, both living and inanimate. On each visit I expected a shrike or a spoonbill to swoop in, settle in the recliner, and begin hogging the remote.

A window filled the upper half of the wall opposite the door. The blinds were half open, allowing a partial view of Van Landingham Glen. The rhododendron forest shimmered like a mirage in the midmorning heat.

A desk sat squarely in front of the window. Two chairs faced it, standard-issue metal with upholstered seats. One held a stuffed puffin, the other a pelican.

The desk chair looked like something designed for astronauts with orthopedic complaints. It held Dr. Rachel Mendelson.

Barely.

She looked up when we entered, but didn't rise.

"Good morning," Rachel said, then sneezed twice. Her head double-dipped, and her topknot bobbed.

"Sorry we're late," I said when Rachel had recovered. "Traffic was terrible on Harris Boulevard."

"That's why I'm always on the road by first light." Even her voice was birdlike, with an odd, chirpy quality to it.

Rachel pulled a tissue from a painted owl holder, and blew her nose loudly.

"Sorry. Allergies."

She wadded the tissue, tossed it into something below the desk, and lumbered to her feet.

It wasn't much of a lumber, since Rachel stood only five feet tall. But what the woman lacked in height she made up for in breadth.

And color. Today Rachel was wearing lime green and turquoise. Lots of it.

For as long as I'd known Rachel, she had struggled with her weight. Diet after diet had enthused then failed her. Five years back she'd tried a regimen of veggies and canned shakes and dropped to 180, her all-time postpubescent best.

But try as she might, nothing lasted. By some bizarre chromosomal trick, Rachel's set point seemed stuck at 227.

As though to compensate, her double helices granted Rachel thick, auburn hair, and the most beautiful skin I have ever seen.

And a heart big enough to accommodate a Radio City Music Hall Rockettes finale.

"*Bonjour, Monsieur Ryan.*" Rachel extended a chubby hand.

Ryan kissed the back of her fingers.

"*Bonjour, madame. Parlez-vous français?*"

"*Un petit peu.* My grandparents were *québecois.*"

"*Excellent.*"

Rachel's eyes swung to me. Her brows rose and her lips rounded into a tiny O.

"Just say 'down, boy,'" I said.

Ryan released her hand.

"Down, boy." Rachel made a palms-down movement with both hands. "And girl."

We all sat.

Ryan pointed to a metal sculpture atop a pile of exam books. "Nice duck."

"It's a grebe," Rachel corrected.

"You can put this visit on his bill." Ryan.

"You know, I've never heard that one before." Rachel could be as deadpan as Ryan. "Now. What's this about a dead bird?"

Keeping details to a minimum, I explained the situation.

"I'm not top-drawer with bones, but I'm crackerjack with feathers. Let's go into my lab."

If Rachel's office held a few dozen genera of birds, her lab was home to the entire Linnaean lineup. Kestrels. Shrikes. Moorhens. Condors. Hummingbirds. Penguins. There was even a stuffed kiwi in a glass-fronted cabinet at the far end.

Rachel led us to a black-topped worktable and I spread the bones on it. Raising half-moon glasses from her bosom to her nose, she poked through the assemblage.

"Looks like Psittacidae."

"I thought so, too," said Ryan.

Rachel did not look up.

"Parrot family. Cockatoos, macaws, loris, lovebirds, parakeets."

"I had a pip of a parakeet when I was a kid," said Ryan.

"Did you?" said Rachel.

"Named him Pip."

Rachel glanced at me, and the chains on her half-moons swung in unison.

I pointed to my temple and shook my head.

Returning her attention to the table, Rachel selected the breastbone and gave it an appraising look.

"Probably a macaw of some sort. Too bad we don't have the skull."

A flashback. Larabee speaking of the headless passenger.

"Too small for a hyacinth's. Too big for a red-shouldered."

Rachel turned the sternum over and over in her hands, than laid it on the table.

"Let's see the feathers."

I unzipped the baggie and shook out the contents. Rachel's eyes dropped back to the table.

If a woman can lock up, Rachel did it. For several seconds not a molecule of her being moved. Then, reverently, she reached out and picked up one feather.

"Oh, my."

"What?"

Rachel gaped at me like I'd just pulled a nickel from her ear.

"Where did you get these?"

I repeated my explanation about the farmhouse basement.

"How long were they down there?"

"I don't know."

Rachel carried the feather to a work counter, pulled two strands from it, placed them on a glass slide, dropped liquid onto them, poked and repositioned them with the tip of a needle, blotted, and added a cover slip. Then she settled her ample buttocks on a round, backless stool, fiddled and adjusted, and peered through a microscope.

Seconds passed. A minute. Two.

"Oh, my."

Rachel rose, waddled to a bank of long, wooden drawers, and withdrew a flat, rectangular box. Returning to the scope she removed the slide she had just prepared, selected one from the box, and viewed the latter.

Puzzled, Ryan and I exchanged glances.

Rachel followed the first reference slide with another from the box, then went back to the slide made from Rinaldi's feather.

"I wish I had a comparison scope," she said, exchanging Rinaldi's feather for a third reference slide. "But I don't."

When Rachel finally looked up her face was flushed and her eyes were wide with excitement.

18

"*Cyanopsitta spixii.*" Hushed, like a zealot speaking the name of her god.

"That's some kind of parrot?" Ryan asked.

"Not just any parrot." Rachel pressed both palms to her chest. "The world's rarest parrot. Probably the world's rarest bird."

The crossed hands rose and fell with the lime-turquoise bosom.

"Oh, my."

"Would you like water?" I asked.

Rachel fluttered agitated fingers.

"It's a macaw, actually." Slipping off her half-moons, she let them drop to the end of their chain.

"A macaw is a type of parrot?"

"Yes." She lifted the feather from beside the scope and stroked it lovingly. "This is from the tail of a Spix's macaw."

"Do you have a stuffed specimen?" Ryan asked.

"Certainly not." She slid from her stool. "Thanks to habitat destruction and the cage-bird trade, there aren't any more. I'm lucky to have the reference slides for the feathers."

"What is it you look at?" I asked.

"Oh, my. Well, let me see." She thought a moment, going through her own KISS abridgment. "Feathers have shafts out of which grow barbs. The barbs have mini-barbs, called barbules, connected by structures called nodes. In addition to the overall morphology and color of the feather, I look at the shape, size, pigmentation, density, and distribution of those nodes."

Rachel went to one of the shelves above the drawers and returned with a large brown volume. After checking the index, she opened and laid the book flat.

"That"—she tapped a photo with a pudgy finger—"is a Spix's."

The bird had a cobalt blue body and pale head. The legs were dark, the eye gray, the beak black and less hooked than I'd expected.

"How big were they?"

"Fifty-five, sixty centimeters. Not the largest, not the smallest of the macaws."

"Where did they hang out?" Ryan.

"The arid interior of east-central Brazil. Northern Bahia province, mostly."

"The species is no more? They are an ex-species?"

I caught Ryan's Monty Python reference. Rachel did not.

"The last surviving wild Spix's disappeared in October of 2000," she said.

"That's a known fact?" I asked.

She nodded. "That bird's story is very poignant. Would you like to hear it?"

Ryan was getting that look.

My eyes crimped in warning.

Ryan's lips pressed together.

"Very much," I said.

"Recognizing the Spix's macaw's perilous status, in 1985 Birdlife International decided to census the species in its only known habitat."

"In Brazil."

"Yes. Depressingly, the total count came to five."

"That's not good," I said.

"No. And the situation went downhill from there. By the end of the decade the number of sightings had fallen to zero. In 1990, Tony Juniper, one of the world's top parrot experts, went to Brazil to determine whether the Spix's truly was extinct in the wild. After six weeks of scouring Bahia by four-wheel drive, questioning every farmer, schoolboy, padre, and poacher he met, Juniper located a single male living in a cactus on a riverbank near the town of Curaça."

"Where's that?" Ryan asked, flipping through the macaws.

"About thirteen hundred miles north of Rio." With a tight smile, Rachel retrieved and closed her book.

I did some quick math. "The Spix's lived on by itself for ten years after the initial sighting?"

"That bird became an international cause célèbre. For a decade, teams of scientists and an entire Brazilian village recorded its every move."

"Poor guy." Ryan.

"And they didn't just watch," Rachel said. "The situation turned into an ornithological soap opera. Believing the Spix's genes were too precious to waste, conservationists decided the male needed a mate. But macaws bond for life and this little guy already had a spouse, a bright green Illiger's macaw."

"Birdie miscegenation." Ryan.

"Sort of." Rachel answered Ryan, then gave me a puzzled look. "Though the couple never cohabitated. The Spix's lived on a facheiro cactus, the Illiger's in a hollow tree trunk. They'd fly together during the day, then at sundown the male Spix's would drop the female Illiger's off at her tree and return to his cactus."

"Sometimes a man needs a place of his own." Ryan.

Two vertical lines puckered Rachel's brow, but she continued.

"In 1995 researchers released a female Spix's into the male's territory, hoping the two would bond and reproduce."

"Uh-oh. The proverbial other woman."

Rachel ignored that.

"The female Spix's courted the male, and he responded."

"Divorce court?"

"The three birds flew together for a month."

"Ménage à trois."

"Is he always like this?" Rachel asked me.

"Yes. Then what happened?"

"The Spix's female disappeared, and the odd couple returned to its previous domestic arrangement."

Rachel glanced at Ryan to see if he'd appreciated her witticism.

"Was hubby the sloppy one or neat one?" he asked.

Rachel made an odd, giggling sound through her nose. *Sni. Sni. Sni.*

"What happened to the Spix's female?" I asked.

"She had a run-in with power lines."

"Ouch." Ryan winced.

"Next, researchers tried all kinds of manipulations with the Illiger's eggs, finally swapping live Illiger hatchlings for the dead hybrid embryos the female was incubating."

"What happened?"

"The Brady Bunch." *Sni. Sni. Sni.*

"The pair turned out to be good parents," I guessed.

Rachel nodded.

"And here's the surprising part. Although the chicks were completely Illiger's genetically, the young developed voices identical to Dad's."

"That's amazing," I said.

"Researchers were planning to slip captive-bred Spix's hatchlings into the nest when the big guy disappeared."

"The lovebirds were still a couple?" Ryan.

"We're talking about macaws. Lovebirds are *Agapornis.*" A little Rachel bird humor.

"So there are still some Spix's alive in captivity?" I asked.

Rachel sniffed to show her disdain.

"Approximately sixty exist in private collections."

"Where?"

"On a commercial bird farm in the Philippines, on the estate of a Qatari sheikh, and in a private aviary in northern Switzerland. I think there's one at the São Paulo zoo, and several at a parrot park in the Canary Islands."

"The owners are qualified ornithologists?"

"There's not a biology degree among them."

"Is that legal?"

"Unfortunately, yes. The birds are considered private property, so the owners can do what they like with them. But the Spix's macaw has been an Appendix One species under CITES since 1975."

Random particles of an idea began to form in my head.

"CITES?"

"The Convention on International Trade in Endangered Species. Appendix One species are considered endangered, and commercial trade in wild specimens is permitted only in exceptional circumstances."

The particles started to coalesce.

"Is there a market for live Spix's?"

"The Spix's was already rare in the eighteenth century because it was so highly valued by collectors." She virtually spat the last word. "Today, a live Spix's could bring a hundred thousand dollars or more from a well-heeled buyer."

Like matter, an idea exploded into being.

I couldn't wait to phone Slidell.

There was no need. My cell rang as I was turning from campus onto University Boulevard. It was Slidell.

"Talked with the Lancaster County sheriff."

"What did he have?"

"Mostly holes."

"Meaning?"

Ryan reached out and reduced the volume of his Hawksley Workman and the Wolves CD to background.

"No one knows nothing much."

That was not what I wanted to hear.

"The bones did go down to your buddy Cagle."

"You contacted him?"

"Ever try getting an academic on the horn in August?"

"Did you try his home?"

"His home. His office. His lab. Thinking about setting up a séance with his dead granny."

Slidell spoke to someone else, came back to me.

"Department secretary finally hooked me up with his top-secret, tell-you-and-I'll-have-to-kill-you cell phone number. Guy sounded like he was wearing fuchsia tights."

"And?"

"Walter"—Slidell gave the name a three-note trill—"was excavating on some island off Beaufort, South Carolina. Said he'd get hold of his grad student to read him the Lancaster report as soon as he finished digging up some dead Indian."

"That was nice of him."

"Yeah. I'm thinking of mailing him some chocolate chips."

"Did you run the descriptors through NCIC?"

"Not sure about sex, not sure about time of death. No dentals, tattoos, prints, height, weight. I'd get a printout the length of Soldier Field."

Slidell was right. Based on what we knew, a national database search of missing persons would be pointless. I changed tacks.

"Ryan and I just met with an ornithologist. Your feathers come from a bird that's been extinct in the wild since 2000."

"How'd they get into Pounder's basement?"

"Good question."

"Got a good answer?"

"These birds can go for a hundred thousand dollars."

"You're shitting me. Who'd pay a hundred grand for a bird?"

"People with more money than brains."

"That legal?"

"Not if the bird is wild."

"You're thinking black market?"

"Could explain why the feathers were hidden with the coke."

"Doesn't Tweetie have to be chirping to bring the bucks?"

"It could have died in transport."

"So the mope saves the feathers thinking they might be worth something."

"And buries the carcass with the other animals he's slaughtered."

"The bear bones?"

"That's what I'm thinking."

"Thought you said they were garden-variety black bears."

"I did."

"That an endangered species?"

"No."

A moment of empty air.

"Doesn't hang," Slidell said.

"Why so many bears?"

"Where's the money?"

That had been Ryan's question, too.

"I'm not sure, but I intend to find out."

And I knew just whom I was going to ask.

19

For the first day in almost a week, there was no need to go to the MCME. I'd done what I could with the privy remains, the Cessna passenger, and the bears. Slidell could get the feathers personally if he needed them quickly.

Over grilled cheese sandwiches at Pike's Soda Shop, Ryan and I discussed the wisdom of leaving for the beach. We decided it was better to hold off for a few days than to be yanked back to Charlotte.

We also discussed my suspicions concerning the illegal trade in wildlife. Ryan agreed my theory posed a possibility given the feathers found with the cocaine, and the large number of black bears buried at the farm. Neither he nor I had any idea how the bears figured in, nor what the link was among the farm, Tamela Banks and Darryl Tyree, the privy victim, and the Cessna's owner, pilot, and passenger, though there was clearly a cocaine connection to Tyree.

After an hors d'oeuvre run to Dean & DeLuca's at Phillips Place, we returned to the annex. While Ryan changed into running gear, I phoned Mrs. Flowers.

Wally Cagle, the forensic anthropologist who'd done the headless, handless skeleton from Lancaster County, had called. She gave me the number.

Next I checked my voice mail messages.

Katy.

Harry.

Harry's son, Kit, warning that his mother would be calling.

Harry.

Harry.

Pierre LaManche, the chef de service for the medicolegal section at the crime lab in Montreal. An informant had led police to a woman buried seven years in a sandpit. The case was not urgent, but he wanted me to know that an anthropological analysis was required.

My arrangement with the Laboratoire de Sciences Judiciaires et de Médecine Légale was that I would rotate through the lab on a monthly basis, doing all cases for which my expertise had been requested, and that I would return immediately should a critical investigation, disaster, or subpoena demand my presence. I wondered if the sandpit case could wait until my planned return to Montreal at the end of the summer.

Two hang-ups.

Knowing the Harry-Kit-Harry-Harry sequence meant my sister and twenty-something nephew were arguing, I put that conversation off.

As I disconnected, man and his best friend entered the kitchen, Boyd trailing like a shark on a blood scent. Ryan wore running shorts, a sweatband, and a T that suggested PERFORM RANDOM ACTS OF KINDNESS AND SENSELESS BEAUTY.

"Nice shirt," I said.

"Half the proceeds went toward saving the Karner Blue."

"What's a Karner Blue?"

"Butterfly." Ryan unpegged the leash. The chow went berserk. "It's in trouble and the salesperson was deeply concerned."

Smiling, I waved the two off and dialed my daughter.

She requested hors d'ouevres for the evening's soiree. I told her I had purchased stuffed mushrooms and cheese sticks.

She asked if I was bringing the French Foreign Legion. I told her I'd be accompanied.

I called Montreal. LaManche had departed the lab for an afternoon of administrative meetings. I left a message about my scheduled return date.

I hadn't seen Harry since the family beach trip in early July. Knowing this would be a long one, I got a Diet Coke from the refrigerator and dialed my sister's number.

The fight concerned my sister's latest boyfriend, a massage thera-
pist from Galveston. Thirty minutes later I understood the issue.

Kit didn't like him. Harry did.

I was dialing Wally Cagle when a series of beeps indicated another
caller was trying to reach me. I clicked over.

"Checked your e-mail, Dr. Brennan?" The voice was high and war-
bly, like an electronic doll's.

Tiny hairs rose on the nape of my neck.

"Who is this?"

"I know where you are. I know all about you."

Annoyance alternated with anger. And fear. I searched for a snappy
response, found none, repeated myself.

"Who is this?"

"The face in the glass."

My eyes flew to the window.

"The dust bunny under your bed." Singsong. "The beastie in the
closet."

Unconsciously, I drifted to the wall and pressed my back to it.

"Welcome." The child-voice mimicked AOL. "You've got mail."

The line went dead.

I stood rigid, clutching the phone.

This case? Some other case? A random nut?

I jumped when the ringer sounded in my hand. The caller-ID window indicated a private number.

My finger sought the "connect" button. Slowly, I raised the receiver
to my ear.

"Hello?" A man's voice.

I waited, breath still frozen in my throat.

"Ye-ho? Someone there?"

High-pitched Boston accent.

Walter Cagle.

Slow exhale.

"Hey, Wally."

"That you, Tempe?"

"It's me."

"You all right, princess?" Wally called most women he liked
"princess." Some were offended. Some weren't. I saved my ire for big-
ger issues.

"I'm fine."

"You sound edgy."

"I've just had an odd call."

"Not bad news, I hope."

"Probably just a crank." Dear God, what if it wasn't?

"Guy wanted to see you in hip waders and a Dale Evans bra?"

"Something like that."

A tap at the window. My eyes whipped back up.

A chickadee was perched on the bird feeder. As it dipped for seed, the feeder rocked gently against the glass.

I closed my eyes and steadied my voice.

"Listen, I'm glad you called. Did Detective Slidell fill you in on what's going on?"

"He said you needed information on an old case."

"A partial skeleton, found near Lancaster about three years back."

"I remember it. No skull. No hand bones. Coroner should have my report on file."

"That coroner is dead. The current coroner has nothing but the original police report, which is useless."

"Doesn't surprise me." Deep sigh. "Guy struck me as one notch above simpleminded. A teensy notch."

"Do you mind discussing your findings?"

"Of course not, princess. Case went nowhere, as I recall."

"We think we may have found the head and hands up here in Mecklenburg County."

"No kidding."

The line was silent a moment. I could picture Wally crossing his legs, kicking one foot, composing his thoughts.

"I'm down in Beaufort, but I called my lab, had a graduate student read me the highlights from my report. It was a complete skeleton lacking the head, mandible, first three cervical vertebrae, and all hand bones."

Pause.

"Well preserved, devoid of soft tissue and odor, some bleaching. Extensive animal damage. Time since death at least one year, probably longer."

Wally was summarizing in speech as he might have on paper. Or perhaps he was reading from notes he'd jotted during the call with his student.

"Male. Thirty years old, plus or minus five years. Age based on ribs and pubic symphyses. Or at least on what was left of them."

Pause.

"Caucasoid."

Pause.

"Height seventy-three inches, plus or minus. Can't remember that exactly. Muscle attachments slight."

"Any evidence of trauma?" I asked.

"Just postmortem. Animal damage. Cut marks on the third cervical vertebra suggestive of decapitation by a sharp instrument with a nonserrated blade. That's about it."

"Did you have any feel for the case at the time?"

"A tall white boy pissed somebody off. That somebody killed him and whacked off his head and hands. That in accord with what you're seeing?"

"Pretty much."

I looked out my window. The trees around my patio shimmered in the heat. My heartbeat had returned to normal. Concentrating on Cagle's narrative, I'd nearly forgotten the prior call.

"I had a tough time determining sex with this skull. Didn't fall on either side of the line," I said.

"I had the same problem," Cagle said. "Sheriff's deputies recovered no clothes or personal effects. Dogs and raccoons used the body as carryout for a goodly period of time. Pelvis was badly chewed, so were the ends of the long bones. Had to calculate stature from one relatively complete fibula. Except for that height estimate, I saw zilch with regard to sex."

"There are tall women," I said.

"Look at professional basketball," Cagle agreed. "Anyway, I thought I had a tall male, but wasn't one hundred percent sure. So when I sent a femoral sample off for DNA profiling, I requested an amelogenin test."

"And?"

"Two bands."

"Male." I said it more to myself than to Cagle.

"X and a Y, holding hands."

"The state lab agreed to do a blind DNA?"

"Of course not. The sheriff's query turned up a missing person as a possible match. DNA said otherwise."

"What happened to the skeleton?"

"I shipped it back to Lancaster when I mailed my report. Coroner sent me a receipt."

"Do you remember his name?"

"Snow. Murray P. Snow. Probably held the bones a week then torched them."

"Did you take pictures?" I asked.

"They're on file in my lab at the university."

I thought a moment.

"Is there any way you could scan the images and transmit them to me electronically?"

"No problem, princess. I'll be back in Columbia by late this afternoon. I'll do it toot sweet, and fax you a copy of the report."

I thanked him, disconnected, and went straight to my computer. Though Cagle's call had distracted me for a time, I was anxious to see what kind of e-mail stalker wanted to be my chat buddy.

What kind of psychopath knew my home phone number.

The flag on my inbox was straight up. A cheery voice told me I had mail.

Barely breathing, I double-clicked the icon.

Forty-three e-mails.

I scrolled downward.

And my heartbeat ratcheted up.

Twenty-four messages had been sent by someone using the screen name Grim Reaper. Each file carried an attachment. Each subject line held the same message in bold caps: **BACK OFF!**

I recoiled from the monitor.

Breathe in.

Out.

In.

My hand shook as I double-clicked one of the Grim Reaper subject bars.

The message window was blank. The attachment was a numbered graphics file, 1.jpg. Download time was estimated at less than a minute.

I hit "download."

AOL asked if I knew the sender.

Good point.

I went to the member directory. No profile on Grim Reaper.

Back to the e-mail.

A moment of hesitation.

I had to know.

I clicked "yes," told the download manager to save.

Slowly, an image unfolded down the screen. My face, a hash-marked circle superimposed.

My subconscious knew instantly as my conscious mind moved toward comprehension.

My left hand flew to my mouth.

I was viewing myself through the scope of a high-powered rifle.

For a moment I could only stare.

Seriously frightened now, I closed that e-mail and opened another.

2.jpg.

Myself, leaving a Starbucks. This time the scope was trained on my back.

3.jpg.

Myself, leaving the MCME facility, bull's-eye on my forehead.

Morbidly fascinated, I had to see more.

8.jpg.

A picture of Ryan and me leaving the McEniry Building at UNCC.

12.jpg.

Boyd, exiting my kitchen door.

18.jpg.

Myself, entering Pike's Soda Shop.

Breathing hard and starting to sweat, I opened another.

22.jpg.

The sweat went cold on my skin and I shivered.

Katy sat reading on what I guessed to be Lija's front porch swing. She was wearing shorts and a tank top I'd purchased at the Gap. One bare foot was lazily pushing against the railing.

A rifle was aimed at her head.

20

At the sound of the door, I flew to the kitchen.

Boyd was guzzling from his bowl.

Ryan was digging water from the refrigerator. I watched him straighten, uncap the bottle, throw back his head, and drink. His skin glistened. Strong, ropy muscles rippled in his arm, neck, and back.

Seeing him calmed me.

Needing a male presence to calm me annoyed me.

I shoved both feelings aside.

"Good run?" I asked, attempting a conversational tone.

Ryan turned.

One look told him all was not well.

"What's up?"

"When you've showered I'd like you to look at something." Though I tried for steady, my voice shook.

"What's happened, babe?"

"I'd rather show you."

Ryan set down the water, crossed to me, and took both my hands in his.

"You OK?"

"I'm OK."

Long, probing look.

"Hold on to that thought."

While Ryan was upstairs I viewed the rest of the e-mails. The settings varied. The theme did not. Every one was a threat.

Ryan was back in ten minutes, smelling of Irish Spring and Mennen Speed Stick. Kissing the top of my head, he took the chair beside mine.

I described the phone call, took him through the e-mails.

Ryan's face hardened as he viewed the images. Now and then a jaw muscle bulged, relaxed.

After we'd finished, he held me close. When he spoke, his voice sounded strange, harder, somehow.

"As long as I'm drawing breath no one will ever hurt you or your daughter, Tempe. I promise you that." His tone grew softer, his words more clipped. "I swear. For you. And for me." He stroked my hair. "I want you in my life, Tempe Brennan."

I did not trust myself to answer. Confusion, delight, and surprise were now tangoing with the anger and fear.

Ryan squeezed, then released me, and asked to see the images again.

Having no desire for a third run-through, I yielded my place and went to replenish Boyd's bowl. When I returned, Ryan fixed me with fierce blue eyes.

"There was a multicar wreck here recently?"

"Last Friday night."

"One of the injured just died?"

"No idea." I hadn't expected a current events quiz.

"Do you have this week's papers?"

"In the pantry."

"Get them."

"Are you going to let me in on your Black Dahlia moment, or am I going to have to guess?"

I was feeling anxious. Anxious makes me churlish.

"Please get the papers." Ryan's voice held no trace of humor.

I dug the week's *Observers* from the recycle box and returned to the study.

The wreck victim died Tuesday night at Mercy Hospital. She was headmistress at a private high school, so her death made Wednesday's headline.

Ryan opened the 2.jpg e-mail. An *Observer* box sat to the right of the Starbucks door. Placing the curser on it, he zoomed in. Though fuzzy, the words were legible.

FOURTH CRASH VICTIM DIES

I was holding the same headline in my hand.

Ryan spoke first.

"Assuming the photos were scanned in order, the first two were taken Wednesday morning. That's yesterday. We went to Starbucks yesterday."

I felt my flesh crawl.

"Jesus Christ, Ryan." I threw the paper on the sofa. "Some nutcase has been stalking me with his Nikon Cool Pics. Who cares exactly *when* the damn things were taken?"

I couldn't stand still. I began pacing.

"Knowing when the photos started may provide a clue about motive."

I stopped. He was right.

"Why yesterday?" he asked.

I thought back over the past few days.

"Take your pick. On Friday I told Gideon Banks his daughter had killed her baby. On Saturday I excavated bear soup. On Sunday I scraped two guys out of a Cessna."

"Dorton was ID'ed as the plane's owner on Monday."

"Right," I agreed. "Pearce was ID'ed as the pilot on Tuesday. That's also when we tossed the Foote farm."

"Wasn't the Cessna's payload also discovered that day?"

"The coke was found on Monday, reported on Tuesday."

"Makes me think somehow Dorton's behind this. He gives the word on Monday or Tuesday. One of his henchmen starts clicking away on Wednesday."

"Maybe. What about this. Slidell and Rinaldi were already looking at Darryl Tyree last week for the death of the Banks baby. By Wednesday they knew that Tyree and Jason Jack Wyatt were telephone buddies."

"The Cessna passenger."

I nodded.

"Tyree could have sent the e-mails."

I thought about the warning in each subject line.

"Back off from *what*?" I asked.

"Dogging Tyree?" Ryan threw out.

I made a face. "Slidell and Rinaldi are after Tyree. Why threaten me?"

"You're the one who examined the baby. You're the one pressing to find Tamela and her family."

"Maybe." I wasn't persuaded. How hard was I really pressing?

"Maybe it's the privy victim," Ryan suggested. "Maybe someone thinks you're getting too close on that."

"Slidell didn't talk to Lancaster County until Wednesday. According to your reasoning, this scumbag was already following me around by then."

"What about the feathers?"

"We didn't learn about the Spix's until this morning."

Boyd joined us. Ryan reached out and scratched his ear.

"We excavated the privy on Tuesday," he said.

"Hardly anyone knew what we were looking for or what we found." I counted on my fingers. "Larabee, Hawkins, Slidell, Rinaldi, the CSU techs, and the backhoe operator."

Boyd swiveled and nudged my hand. I stroked him absently.

"I should call Slidell."

"Yes."

Ryan stood and wrapped his arms around me. I pressed my cheek to his chest. The tension in his body was palpable.

When Ryan spoke his chin tapped the crown of my head.

"Whatever twisted mutant did this doesn't realize the world of hurt that's about to befall him."

Charlotte is neighborhoods. Elizabeth. Myers Park. Dillworth. Plaza-Midwood. Most cling to the past like Boston biddies gripping the genealogy charts that identify them as Daughters of the American Revolution. Zoning is enforced. Trees are protected. Nontraditional architecture, if not banned outright by a homeowners' ordinance, is viewed with disapproval by obdurate residents.

But that times-of-yore grip has slipped uptown, where the theme is concrete, glass, and steel. Those same Charlotteans who sip martinis on magnolia-shaded patios in the evening take pride in their city's skyscraper core during the working day. In fact, it is the preservationists who are on the run uptown.

One circle out from the nerve center lie four wards, three of which have undergone modernization in recent decades.

Though not exactly Williamsburg, Fourth Ward is the city's version of an historic district. The neighborhood is whimsical Victorians, tasteful brick condos and town homes, narrow streets with towering shade trees. There is even a faux colonial tavern.

In First and Third Wards there was no pretense at historic preservation. During the eighties and nineties, the old was bulldozed for the new, and run-down bungalows, shabby repair shops, and seedy diners gave way to the modern multiuse concept. Offices and homes above, specialty shops below. Condos, apartments, and lofts proliferated, all with views of man-made ponds, and names like Clarkson Green, Cedar Mills, Skyline Terrace, Tivoli.

Lija's town house was in Third Ward's Elm Ridge, tucked between Frazier Park and the Carolina Panthers practice fields. The complex consisted of double rows of two-story duplexes facing each other across grassy courtyards. Each unit featured a wide front porch with a swing or rockers, bird feeders and hanging ferns optional.

In the early dusk, Elm Ridge looked like a pastel rainbow. In my mind I heard the architectural planning session. Charleston yellow. Savannah peach. Birmingham buff.

Lija's was the last unit in the eastern row of the middle pair. Miami melon with Key West holly-berry shutters.

Ryan and I climbed to the porch and I rang the bell. The doormat stated HI, I'M MAT!

As we waited my eyes were drawn to the swing, and my heart seemed to drop to my toes. My gaze darted left then right. Was the stalker out there, even now, watching us?

Sensing my apprehension, Ryan squeezed my hand. I squeezed back, forced my lips into an upward arc. I would give Katy a heads-up when I had her alone, but I would not transmit the full extent of my fear to her.

My daughter hugged me, stated approval of my look, the black linen number with a slapdash iron job. Then her eyes went to Ryan.

My date had chosen an ensemble of ecru pants, blue blazer, pale yellow shirt, and yellow and navy polka-dot tie.

And high-top sneakers. Red.

With an almost imperceptible cocking of one eyebrow, Katy smiled at Ryan and relieved him of the hors d'ouevres. Then she led us inside and introduced us to the other guests, Lija's current boyfriend, Brandon Salamone, a woman named Willow, and a man named Cotton.

And the irresistibly handsome Palmer Cousins.

Cousins's outfit suggested whole colonies of homeless mulberry worms. Silk tie. Silk shirt. Silk trousers and jacket with modest input from merino sheep.

Katy offered wine and beer, excused herself, returned and again offered wine and beer, then asked in a whisper that I join her in the kitchen.

A black lump lay in a broiler pan on the stovetop. The room smelled like the inside of a barbecue kettle.

Lija was working at something in the sink. She turned when we entered, threw up both hands, returned to her task.

To say she looked tense would be like saying Enron's accountants did some rounding up.

"I think we burned the roast," Katy said.

"We didn't burn it," Lija snapped. "It caught on fire. There's a difference."

"Can you do something with it?" Katy asked.

The roast didn't look burned. Burned would have been an improvement. It looked incinerated.

I jabbed it with a fork. Briquettelike chunks snapped off and rolled to the pan.

"The roast is toast."

"Great." Lija yanked the drain plug. Water rushed down the pipes.

"What are you doing?" I asked her back.

"Thawing chicken." She sounded close to tears.

I crossed to the sink and poked the rock she was holding.

Lija replaced the plug and turned on the tap.

At the rate she was going, her Pick-of-the-Chix would defrost in several decades.

I checked the pantry.

Spices. SpaghettiOs. Kraft dinner. Campbell's soup. Olive oil. Balsamic vinegar. Six boxes of linguine.

"How close is the nearest store?"

"Five minutes."

Lija turned, poultry in hand.

"Do you have garlic?" I asked.

Two nods.

"Parsley?"

Nods.

"We've got a primo salad in the refrigerator." Lija smiled tremu-lously.

I sent Katy for canned clams and frozen garlic bread.

While my daughter raced to the market, Lija served appetizers, and I boiled water and chopped. When Katy returned, I browned garlic in the olive oil, added fresh parsley, the clams, and oregano, and let the sauce simmer while the pasta cooked.

Thirty minutes later Katy and Lija were fielding compliments on their linguine vognole.

Nothing. Really. Family recipe.

Throughout the meal Palmer Cousins seemed distracted, con-tributing little to the conversation. Each time I turned toward him, his eyes flicked sideways.

Was it my imagination, or was I being evaluated? As a conversa-tionalist? A potential mother-in-law? A person?

Was I being paranoid?

When Katy urged us to the living room for coffee, I settled on the couch next to Cousins.

"How are things at the U.S. Fish and Wildlife Service?" Cousins and I had talked briefly about his job while at the McCranies' picnic. Tonight I intended to probe deeper.

"Not too bad," Cousins replied. "Hookin' 'em and bookin' 'em in the fight for wildlife."

"As I recall, you told me you're stationed in Columbia?"

"Good memory." Cousins pointed a finger at me.

"Is it a large operation?"

"I'm pretty much it." Self-deprecating smile.

"Does the FWS have many field offices in the Carolinas?"

"Washington, Raleigh, and Asheville in North Carolina, Columbia and Charleston in South Carolina. The RAC in Raleigh oversees everything."

"Resident agent in charge?"

Cousins nodded.

"Raleigh is the only operation that isn't one-man." Boyish grin. "Or one-woman. The forensics lab is also up there."

"Didn't know we had one."

"The Rollins Diagnostic Laboratory. It's associated with the Department of Agriculture."

"Isn't there a national fish and wildlife lab?"

"Clark Bavin, out in Ashland, Oregon. It's the only forensics lab on the planet dedicated exclusively to wildlife. They do cases from all over the world."

"How many agents does the FWS have?"

"At full staff, two hundred and forty, but with cutbacks the number's down to a couple hundred and dropping."

"How long have you been an agent?"

Ryan was stacking dishes at the table behind us. I could tell he was listening.

"Six years. Spent the first couple in Tennessee following my training."

"Do you prefer Columbia?"

"It's closer to Charlotte." Cousins gave my daughter a little finger wave.

"Would you mind talking shop a minute?"

The perfect eyebrows rose ever so slightly.

"Not at all."

"I'm aware illegal wildlife is big business. How big?"

"I've read estimates of ten to twenty billion dollars a year. That's third only to the illegal trade in drugs and arms."

I was stunned.

Ryan settled into a chair on the far side of the steamer-trunk coffee table.

"Is there much black market trade in exotic birds?" I asked.

"I suppose. If something is rare, people will buy it." Despite the practiced nonchalance, Cousins looked uncomfortable. "But as far as I'm concerned, the biggest problem right now is overexploitation."

"Of?"

"Sea turtles are a good example. U.S. turtles are sold by the tons overseas. The other big problem comes from the bush-meat market."

"Bush meat?"

"Giant cane rats and duikers from Africa. Lizards-on-a-stick from

Asia. Those are reptiles that are slit along the belly and spread like big lollipops. Smoked pygmy lorises, roasted pangolin scales."

Cousins must have interpreted the revulsion on my face as confusion.

"The pangolin is also called the scaly anteater. The scales are sold as a cure for syphilis."

"People import these things for medicinal use?" Ryan asked.

"Could be anything. Take the turtles. Sea turtle shells are used for jewelry, the meat and eggs go to restaurants and bakeries, whole carapaces are used as wall mounts."

"What about bears?" I asked.

Cousins's chin tilted up a fraction of an inch.

"Don't know much about bears."

"The Carolinas have large populations, don't they?"

"Yes."

"Is poaching a problem?" Ryan asked.

Silken shrug. "Wouldn't think so."

"Has the service ever investigated that?" I asked.

"Beats me."

Lija's boyfriend joined us and posed a question about the merits of man-to-man versus zone defense. Cousins's attention veered to that conversation.

So much for bear poaching.

On the way home I solicited Ryan's reaction to Cousins's comments.

"Odd that a wildlife agent in the Carolinas would know nothing about bears."

"Yes," I agreed.

"You don't like the guy, do you?" Ryan asked.

"I never said I didn't like him."

No reply.

"Is it that obvious?" I asked after a few moments.

"I'm learning to read you."

"It isn't that I don't like him," I said defensively. What then? "It's that I don't like not knowing if I don't like him."

Ryan opted not to touch that.

"He makes me uneasy," I added.

As we arrived at the annex, Ryan made another unsettling observation.

"Maybe your uneasiness isn't totally off base, Mom."

I shot Ryan a look that was wasted in the dark.

"You told me Boyd made his big score during that cigar store picnic."

"Katy was thrilled."

"That's where you first met Cousins."

"Yes."

"He saw Boyd's find."

"Yes."

"That means at least one more person was at least partially privy to the situation at the Foote farm. No pun intended."

Again my heart went into free fall.

"Palmer Cousins."

21

THE EASTERN HORIZON STARTS OOZING GRAY AROUND FIVE-
thirty in August in Piedmont North Carolina. By six the sun is heading uphill.

I awoke at first ooze, watched dawn define the objects on my
dresser, nightstand, chair, and walls.

Ryan was sprawled on his stomach beside me. Birdie lay curled in
the crook of my knees.

I lasted in bed until half past six.

Birdie blinked when I slipped from under the covers. He stood and
arched as I collected my panties from the lampshade. I heard paws
thump carpet as I tiptoed from the room.

The refrigerator hummed to me while I made coffee. Outside,
birds exchanged the morning's avian gossip.

Moving as quietly as possible, I poured and drank a glass of orange
juice, then collected Boyd's leash and went to the study.

The chow was stretched full length on the sofa, left foreleg upright
against the seat back, right extended across his head.

Boyd the Protector.

"Boyd," I whispered.

The dog went from flat on his side to four on the floor without
seeming to move through any intermediary stage.

"Here, boy."

No eye contact.

"Boyd."

The chow rolled his eyes up at me but didn't budge.

"Walk?"

Boyd held steady, a picture of skepticism.

I dangled the leash.

No go.

"I'm not upset about the couch."

Boyd dropped his head, looked up, and did a demi-twirl with each eyebrow.

"Really."

Boyd's ears pricked forward and his head canted.

"Come on." I uncoiled the leash.

Realizing it was not a trap, and that a walk was actually afoot, Boyd raced around the sofa, ran back to me and jumped up with his forepaws on my chest, dropped, spun, jumped up again, and began lapping my cheek.

"Don't push it," I said, clipping the leash to his collar.

A fine mist floated among the trees and shrubs at Sharon Hall. Though I felt reassured by the presence of a seventy-pound chow, I was still filled with a formless apprehension as we moved about the grounds, kept watching for a flash, or the flicker of light on a camera lens.

Four squirrels and twenty minutes later, Boyd and I were back at the annex. Ryan was at the kitchen table, full mug of coffee and unopened *Observer* in front of him. He smiled when we entered, but I saw something in his eyes, like the shadow of a cloud passing over waves.

Boyd trotted to the table, placed his chin on Ryan's knee, and looked up with the expectation of bacon. Ryan patted his head.

I poured myself coffee and joined them.

"Hey," I said.

Ryan leaned forward and kissed me on the mouth.

"Hey." Taking both my hands, he looked into my eyes. It was not a happy look.

"What's happened?" I asked, fear pricking my stomach.

"My sister called."

I waited.

"My niece has been hospitalized."

"I'm so sorry." I squeezed his hands. "An accident?"

"No." Ryan's jaw muscles bulged. "Danielle did it on purpose."

I could think of nothing to say.

"My sister is pretty fragmented. Crises are not her forte."

Ryan's Adam's apple rose and fell.

"Motherhood is not her forte."

Though curious to know what had happened, I didn't push. Ryan would tell the story in his own way.

"Danielle's had problems with substance abuse in the past, but she's never done anything like this."

Boyd licked Ryan's pants leg. The refrigerator hummed on.

"Why the hell—" Shaking his head, Ryan let the question die on the air.

"Your niece may be crying out for attention." The words sounded clichéd as I said them. Spoken solace is not my forte.

"That poor kid doesn't know what attention is."

Boyd nudged Ryan's knee. Ryan did not respond.

"When is your flight?" I asked.

Ryan blew air through his lips and slumped back in his chair.

"I'm not going anywhere while some brain-fried psycho's got you in his viewfinder."

"You have to go." I couldn't bear the thought of his leaving, but wouldn't let on.

"No way."

"I'm a big girl."

"It wouldn't feel right."

"Your niece and sister need you."

"And you don't?"

"I've outwitted the bad guys before."

"You're saying you don't need me around?"

"No, handsome. I don't need you around." I reached out and stroked his cheek. His hand rose and made a strange, faltering movement. "I *want* you around. But that's my problem. Right now your family needs you."

Ryan's whole body radiated tension.

I looked at my watch. Seven thirty-five.

God, why now? As I picked up the phone to dial US Airways, I realized how very much I wanted him to stay.

*   *   *

Ryan's flight departed at nine-twenty. Boyd looked deeply wounded as we left him at the annex.

From the airport, I went directly to the MCME. No fax had arrived from Cagle. Settling in my office, I looked up the number, and phoned the FWS field office in Raleigh.

A female voice informed me that the resident agent in charge was Hershey Zamzow.

Zamzow came on after a brief hold.

I explained who I was.

"No need for introductions, Doc. I know who you are. Hot down there as it is up here?"

"Yes, sir."

The temperature at nine had been eighty-two.

"What can I do for you this fine summer morning?"

I told him about the Spix's feathers, and asked if there was any local black market trade in exotic birds.

"A huge amount of wildlife flows through the Southeast from the Southern Hemisphere. Snakes, lizards, birds. You name it. If a species is rare, some pissant with mush for brains will want it. Hell, the Southeast is one big poachers' paradise."

"How are live animals smuggled into the country?"

"All sorts of clever ways. They're drugged and stuffed into poster tubes. They're hidden inside elasticized vests." Zamzow didn't try to conceal his disgust. "And the mortality rate is astronomical. Think about it. You taken a flight lately that ran on time? How clever do you think these cretins are at calculating the amount of oxygen in a concealed storage space?

"But getting back to your feathers, birds are a popular sideline for South American cocaine smugglers. Guy scores a few parrots from the village poacher, runs them up to the States with his next shipment of blow. Birds live, he turns a nice profit. Birds die, he's out beer money for the week."

"What about bears?" I asked.

"*Ursus americanus.* No need for smuggling. Got black bears right here in the Carolinas. Handful of young bears are trapped each year for 'bear baiting'—that's bear fighting for the unenlightened. Genteel entertainment for the red of neck. Used to be a market for live bears, but with zoo populations skyrocketing, that's pretty much dried up."

"Are there a lot of bears in North Carolina?"

"Not as many as there ought to be."

"Why is that?"

"Habitat destruction and poaching."

"There's a season when bears are hunted legally?"

"Yes, ma'am. Varies by county, but mostly in the fall and early winter. Some South Carolina counties distinguish between hunting stationary and hunting with dogs."

"Tell me about the poaching."

"My favorite topic." His voice sounded bitter. "Illegal killing of black bears was made a misdemeanor by the Lacy Act in 1901, a felony in 1981. But that doesn't stop the poachers. In season, hunters take the whole bear, use the meat and fur. Out of season, poachers take the parts they want and leave the carcasses to rot."

"Where does most bear poaching take place?"

"Ten, twenty years ago it was pretty much restricted to the mountains. Nowadays coastal animals are getting hit just as hard. But it's not just a Carolina problem. There are less than half a million bears left in North America. Every year hundreds of carcasses turn up intact except for the paws and gallbladders."

"Gallbladders?" I couldn't mask my shock.

"Hell of a black market. In traditional Asian medicine, bear gall ranks right up there with rhino horn, ginseng, and deer musk. Bear bile is thought to cure fever, convulsions, swelling, eye pain, heart disease, hangover, you name it. And the meat ain't chopped liver, either. Some Asian cultures view bear paw soup as a real delicacy. A bowl can sell for as much as fifteen hundred bucks in certain restaurants. Off the menu, of course."

"What are the main markets for bear galls?"

"South Korea ranks number one, since the native supply is nonexistent. Hong Kong, China, and Japan aren't far behind."

I took a moment to digest all that.

"And bear hunting is legal in season in North Carolina?"

"As in many states, yes. But selling animal body parts, including gallbladders, heads, hides, claws, and teeth, is illegal. Few years back, Congress considered legislation aimed at halting the trade in bear organs. Didn't pass."

Before I could comment, he went on.

KATHY REICHS

"Look at Virginia. State has about four thousand bears. Officials estimate six hundred to nine hundred are killed legally every year, but have no numbers as to how many are poached. Busted a ring up there not long ago, seized about three hundred gallbladders and arrested twenty-five people."

"How?" I was so repulsed I could hardly form questions.

"Hunters tipped officials to poaching in and around Shenandoah National Park. Agents ultimately infiltrated the ring, posed as middlemen, accompanied poachers on hunts, that sort of thing. I worked a similar sting up in Graham County about ten years back."

"Not the Joyce Kilmer Memorial Forest?"

"The very same. The trees may be lovely, but the bears are profit."

The line hummed as Zamzow sorted through recollections.

"One couple up there had been in business seventeen years. Jackie Jo and Bobby Ray Jackson. What pieces of work they were. Claimed to sell three hundred galls annually to customers up and down the eastern seaboard. Claimed they got their galls from hunt clubs, farmers, and by their own hunting and trapping."

Zamzow was on a roll.

"Some of these poachers are as blatant as Seventh Avenue hookers. Leave a business card at a hunting lodge saying you want to buy bear gall, they'll phone you right back."

Ricky Don Dorton. Wilderness Quest. Cocaine. Bears. Exotic birds. Random particles of thought were again seeking each other's company in my head.

"How do these rings operate?"

"Nothing complex. Contact is made by a poacher via word of mouth or a phone call to a buyer. The buyer meets the poacher in a parking lot, maybe at an isolated location, and the transaction is made. Poacher gets thirty-five, maybe fifty bucks for each gall, middleman gets seventy-five to a hundred. Street value skyrockets in Asia."

"Where do the galls leave the country?"

"A lot traffics through Maine, since that's one of the few states where it's legal to sell black bear galls to Asia. But, again, it's illegal to sell bear parts killed in North Carolina in *any* state. Lately Atlanta's become a big gateway."

"How are the galls preserved?"

« 176 »

"Poacher freezes them intact ASAP outta the bear."

"And then?"

"He turns them over to his Asian contact. Since freshness determines value, most galls are dried in the destination city. But not always. Some Asian contacts do their drying in the United States so they can transport larger quantities. A gall is about the size of a human fist and weighs less than a pound. Drying shrinks it to a third that size."

"How is it done?"

"Nothing high-tech. The gall is tied with monofilament line and hung over a low heat. Slow drying is important. If a gall is dried too fast, the bile is ruined."

"How are they smuggled out?"

"Again, no mind-bender. Most are transported in carry-on luggage. If the galls are spotted on a security scanner, the carrier claims he's bringing dried fruit to his mama. Some grind the galls up and put them in whiskey."

"Less risky than smuggling drugs," I said.

"And very lucrative. A single preserved gall usually brings about five thousand dollars in Korea, but prize galls have sold for as much as ten thousand. That's U.S greenbacks we're talking."

I was stunned.

"Ever hear of CITES?" Zamzow asked.

"Convention on International Trade in Endangered Species." That was the second reference in as many days.

"Bear galls have been classified under Appendix Two."

"There are bears in Asia. Why come all the way to North America for gall?"

"All five Asian bear species, the sun, sloth, Asiatic black, brown, and giant panda are threatened. Only fifty thousand bears are thought to be left in the wild in Asia, from India all the way across to China and down into Southeast Asia."

"Because of the demand for bile."

"With the exception of the giant panda, bears are the only mammals that produce significant amounts of ursodeoxycholic acid, or UCDA."

"That's what people are paying thousands of dollars for?"

"That's it." Zamzow snorted in disdain. "At least twenty-eight different forms of packaged medicines purporting to contain bear bile are legally available in China. Singapore has banned the sale of products extracted from bears, but shops still sell bear bile pills, powder, crystals, ointments, and whole dried galls. Crap like bear bile wine, shampoo, and soap hit the market every day. You can find them in Chinatowns across the United States."

Disgust tightened my stomach.

"Can't bears be raised domestically?"

"China began bear farming in the eighties. It's almost worse. Animals are crammed into tiny cages and milked through holes cut into their abdomens. Their teeth and claws may be filed down. Sometimes their paws are even chopped off. Once the animals stop producing bile, they're killed for their galls."

"Can't UCDA be produced synthetically?"

"Yes. And many botanic alternatives exist."

"But people want the real thing."

"You've got it. Popular thinking is that artificial UCDA isn't as effective as the natural form. Which is ass backwards. The amount of natural UCDA in a bear gall can vary from zero to thirty-three percent, hardly a reliable source of the drug."

"Long-held cultural beliefs die hard."

"Phrased like an anthropologist. Speaking of which, why are you interested in Spix's macaws and black bears?"

I sorted through the events of the past week. What to share? What to hold back?

Tamela Banks and Darryl Tyree?

Possibly unrelated. Confidential.

Ricky Don Dorton and the Cessna crash?

Ditto.

Yesterday's cyber threats?

Probably irrelevant.

I told Zamzow about the findings at the Foote farm, excluding only the part about Tamela Banks's license. I also told him about the Lancaster County skeleton.

For a full thirty seconds I listened to nothing.

"Are you still there?" I asked, thinking we'd been disconnected.

"I'm here."

I heard him swallow.

"You at the ME office?"

"Yes."

"You'll be working awhile?"

"Yes." Where the hell was this going?

"I'll be there in three hours."

ZAMZOW ARRIVED JUST PAST NOON. HE WAS A HEAVYSET MAN, probably in his forties, with thick, bristly hair cropped very short. His skin was pasty, his eyes the identical ginger of his hair and freckles, giving him a pale, monochromatic appearance, like someone who'd been born and lived his whole life in a cave.

Seating himself in the chair opposite my desk, Zamzow got straight to the point.

"This may be nothing, but I was going to be passing on my way to the Pee Dee Wildlife Refuge in Anson County this morning, so I thought I'd divert over to Charlotte and lay it on you in person."

I said nothing, completely at a loss as to what was of such importance that Zamzow felt it needed a face-to-face.

"Five years back, two FWS agents disappeared. One worked out of my office, the other was in North Carolina on temporary assignment."

"Tell me about them." I felt a shiver of excitement ripple down my spine.

Zamzow drew a photo from a shirt pocket and laid it on my desk. In it, a young man leaned against a stone bridge. His arms were folded and he was smiling. On his shirt I could see the same badge and shoulder patch that Zamzow was wearing.

I flipped the picture. *Brian Aiker, Raleigh, 9/27/1998* had been handwritten on the back.

"The agent's name was Brian Aiker," Zamzow said.

"Age?" I asked.

"Thirty-two. Aiker had been with us three years when he went missing. Nice fellow."

"Height?"

"Tall guy. I'd say six-one, six-two."

"He was white," I said, flipping back to the front of the photo.

"Yeah."

"And the visiting agent?"

"Charlotte Grant Cobb. Odd duck, but a good officer. Cobb was with the service more than ten years."

"Do you have a picture?"

Zamzow shook his head. "Cobb didn't like being photographed. But I can request her file if you think it's warranted. The service has a photo ID of every agent."

"Cobb is female?"

"Yeah. White, I'd say mid-thirties."

"What was she working?"

"Operation FDR. Sea turtles."

"FDR?"

Zamzow shrugged one shoulder. "Franklin wore a lot of turtle-necks. I didn't pick the label. Anyway, think your unknown could be Aiker or Cobb?"

"Cobb's out. DNA from the Lancaster bones came up male. But there could be a link. Was Aiker working the sting with Cobb?"

"Not officially, though I know he spent time with her."

"Tell me what happened."

"Not much to tell. Six, seven years ago we were tipped about poachers trucking turtles up to Charlotte from the coast, transfer-ring them on to buyers in New York and D.C. Service sent Cobb to try to infiltrate the ring. Figured a female might get inside quicker."

"How?"

"The usual. Cobb was hanging around places the suspects fre-quented. Bars, restaurants, some gym."

"She was living in Charlotte?"

"Had an apartment. One of those month-to-month deals."

"How was it going?"

"No idea. Cobb didn't report to me." Zamzow snorted. "And the lady wasn't what you'd call the social type. When she was in Raleigh, Cobb pretty much kept to herself. Guess it's tough being under- cover in this business."

"Or being female."

"Could be."

"Did Cobb and Aiker disappear at the same time?"

"Aiker failed to show up one Monday in December. I remember. It was cold as hell. We phoned for two days, eventually busted into his apartment. No sign of him."

Zamzow looked as though he hadn't spoken of Aiker in a long time, but had returned to the man many times in his thoughts.

"When we backtracked, last anyone had seen him was the previous Friday. We thought he might have gone through ice somewhere. Checked rivers, dredged ponds, that sort of thing. Nothing. Never found Aiker or his car."

"Any signs he planned on leaving? Emptied bank accounts? Miss- ing prescription medications?"

Zamzow shook his head. "Aiker ordered two hundred dollars' worth of fishing tackle over the Net the week before he disappeared. Left fourteen grand in a savings account at First Union."

"Doesn't sound like a man intending to take off. What about Cobb?"

"Cobb's disappearance was harder to nail down. According to neighbors she stayed to herself, kept odd hours, often disappeared for days at a stretch. Landlord was persuaded to open the apartment a week after Aiker disappeared. Looked like Cobb had been gone awhile."

I thought a moment.

"Were Aiker and Cobb an item?"

Zamzow frowned. "There was talk. Aiker made several trips to Charlotte while Cobb was here. Records showed they talked on the phone, but that could have been business."

I kept my voice level to mask my excitement.

"The skeleton I examined is tall, white, and male. From what you tell me, Aiker's age fits and so does the time frame. Sounds like it could be your missing agent."

"As I recall, the Raleigh PD got dental records on both Aiker and Cobb. Never needed them."

I was so eager to talk to Slidell I nearly hustled Zamzow out of my office. But I had one more topic to broach.

"Do you know an agent named Palmer Cousins?"

Zamzow shifted in his chair.

"Met him."

I waited for him to elaborate. When he didn't, I asked, "Your impression?"

"Young."

"And?"

"Young."

"I talked to Cousins the other night, asked about bear poaching in the Carolinas. He seemed to know very little."

Zamzow looked me straight in the eye. "Your point?"

"He knew nothing about the smuggling of exotic birds."

Zamzow checked his watch. Then, "Don't know Cousins myself, but the man attracts his share of admirers."

I found the comment odd, but didn't pursue it.

"Good luck to you, Doc."

Zamzow stood.

I stood.

As he turned to go, I picked up the photo of Brian Aiker. "May I keep this?"

Zamzow nodded. "Don't be a stranger."

With that, he was gone.

Staring at the chair Zamzow had vacated, I wondered what had just happened. Throughout our conversation, the RAC had been friendly and candid. At the mention of Palmer Cousins, the man closed up like an armadillo poked with a stick.

Was Zamzow holding ranks, refusing to speak badly of a fellow officer? Did he know something about Katy's friend that he was unwilling to share? Was he simply unacquainted with the man?

Tim Larabee interrupted my thoughts.

"Where's your little pal?"

"If you mean Detective Ryan, he flew back to Montreal."

"Too bad. He's good for your complexion."

A hand rose to my cheek.

"Gotcha." Larabee made a finger pistol and fired it at me.

"You're so hilarious, Hawkins may have to roll a gurney in here when I die laughing."

I told him what I'd learned from Wally Cagle about the Lancaster skeleton, and about my conversations with Hershey Zamzow.

"I'll call Raleigh. See if someone can drive Aiker's dental records down," Larabee said.

"Good."

"Could be a breakthrough day. Jansen called. Slidell called. Tea party in half an hour."

"Do they have news?"

Larabee checked, then tapped his watch.

"Main ballroom in thirty minutes. Dress is casual."

The corners of Larabee's mouth curled upward.

"Your hair's got a gleam to it, too."

My eyes rolled so far back I thought they might never return.

When Larabee moved on, I checked again with Mrs. Flowers. Still no fax from Cagle.

I gathered and glanced through my message slips.

Jansen.

Slidell.

Cagle.

I tried Cagle's cell. No answer.

A crime reporter with the *Charlotte Observer* had called.

A colleague at UNC-Greensboro.

I tried Cagle again. He still wasn't picking up.

I looked at my watch.

Showtime.

Placing the pink slips in the middle of my blotter, I headed for the conference room.

Larabee and Jansen were discussing the merits of the Panthers versus the Dolphins. The NTSB investigator was dressed in jeans, sandals, and a tan cotton tank from Old Navy. Her short blonde hair looked like it had just been blow-dried.

Slidell and Rinaldi arrived as Jansen and I were shaking hands.

Rinaldi was in blue blazer, gray chinos, and a turquoise and lemon Jerry Garcia tie.

Slidell was in shirtsleeves. His neckwear looked like something one got from a Kmart bargain table after the good ones had already been picked.

While the others coffeed up, I helped myself to a Diet Coke.

"Who goes first?" I asked when we'd all taken seats.

Larabee waved a palm in my direction.

I repeated what I'd told the ME about the Lancaster remains, described how I'd gotten the details from Wally Cagle, and explained the skeleton's possible link to the privy head and hands. I outlined what I'd learned from Hershey Zamzow and Rachel Mendelson concerning bear poaching and about the illegal trade in rare and endangered species. Finally, I dropped my bombshell about the missing wildlife agents Brian Aiker and Charlotte Grant Cobb.

As I spoke, Rinaldi took notes on his designer pad. Slidell listened, legs thrust forward, thumbs tucked into his belt.

For several seconds, no one said a word. Then Jansen slapped the table.

"Yes!"

Slidell's eyes crawled to her.

"Yes," she repeated.

Unzipping a leather case, Jansen withdrew several papers, laid them on the table, ran her finger down the middle of one, stopped, and read aloud.

"'The charred substance from the underbelly of the Cessna contained the alkaloids hydrastine, berberine, canadine, and berberastine.'"

"That make Ovaltine?" Slidell asked.

"That makes goldenseal," Jansen said.

We all waited for her to go on.

Jansen flipped to another paper.

"*Hydrastis canadensis.* Goldenseal. The roots and rhizomes are thought to have medicinal properties because of the hydrastine and berberine. Cherokee Indians used goldenseal as an antiseptic and to treat snakebite. Iroquois used it to treat whooping cough, pneumonia, digestive disorders. Early pioneers used it as an eyewash, and for sore throats, mouth sores. Commercial demand for goldenseal began around the time of the Civil War"—Jansen looked up from her notes—"and it's now a top-selling herb in North America."

"Used for what?" Larabee's disdain of herbal medicines came through in his tone.

Jansen went back to her printout.

"Nasal congestion, mouth sores, eye and ear infections, as a topical antiseptic, laxative, anti-inflammatory, take your pick. Some people think goldenseal boosts the immune system and increases the effectiveness of other medicinal herbs. Some think it can induce abortion."

Larabee *sheeshed* air through his lips.

Jansen looked up to see if we were with her.

"I got on the Net, did a little research."

She selected a third printout.

"There's been such intensive harvesting for both the domestic and international markets that goldenseal is now in trouble. Of the twenty-seven states reporting native patches, seventeen consider the plant imperiled. Its wholesale value has increased more than six hundred percent in the last decade."

"Call the posy police." Slidell.

"Does goldenseal grow in North Carolina?" I asked.

"Yes, but only in a few places. Goldenseal Hollow, for example, deep in the mountains in Jackson County."

"Is it considered endangered in North Carolina?"

"Yes. And because of that status a permit is required to cultivate or propagate the plant within the state. Ever hear of CITES?"

"Yes." Three for three.

"You need a CITES permit to export cultivated or wild-collected goldenseal roots or parts of roots. To get a permit you need to show that your roots, rhizomes, and seeds came from legally acquired parental stock and that the plants were cultivated for four years or more without augmentation from the wild."

"So it's difficult to obtain a supply of living roots with which to start plantations in this country?" Rinaldi asked.

"Very."

"Is there a black market for goldenseal?" I asked.

"There is a black market for all herbs found in the North Carolina mountains, including goldenseal. So much so that a special five-agency task force has been set up in Appalachia."

"Sweet God in heaven, there really is a veggie squad." Slidell pooched out his cheeks and wagged his head, like one of those dogs in an auto rear window.

"The task force is made up of agents from the National Park Service, U.S. Forestry Service, North Carolina Department of Agriculture, North Carolina Wildlife Service, and U.S. Fish and Wildlife Service. It's headed by the U.S. Attorney's Office."

The group went mute as each of us tried to integrate Jansen's report with my findings. Slidell broke the silence.

"Some mope was dealing snort out of the Foote farm. We know that 'cause we found product in the basement. You're saying the place was also used for trafficking dead animals?"

"I'm suggesting it's a possibility," I said.

"As a sideline to the coke?"

"Yes," I said coolly. "And the bird was probably alive."

"And this Agent Aiker might have been closing in," said Rinaldi.

"Maybe," I said.

"So the perp gets spooked, kills Aiker, dumps his head and hands in the privy, and hauls his body to Lancaster County?" Slidell sounded unconvinced.

"We'll know when we get the dental records," I said.

Slidell turned to Jansen.

"Your Cessna was also flying a cargo of snort. Snort's heavy time. You get nailed, you do a long stretch inside. Why bother with herbs?"

"Entrepreneurial sideline."

"Like Brennan's birds."

I didn't bother to comment.

"Yes," Jansen said.

"Why goldenseal? Why not ginseng, or something grows you hair or perks up your pecker?"

Jansen looked at Slidell like she might have eyed a dead spider in her cat's litter.

"Goldenseal makes more sense."

"Why's that?"

"Some people think it masks certain drugs in your urine."

"Does it?"

"Does a line of coke turn you into a rock star?"

Jansen and Slidell locked eyes. For a few seconds neither spoke. Then Slidell rethumbed his waistband.

"We've been grilling Pounder."

"And?"

"Maroon's got the brains of a carp. We're still liking Tyree or Dorton."

"Might have to rethink that."

The five of us turned as one. Joe Hawkins was standing in the doorway.

"You'd better come see this."

23

W<small>E</small> FOLLOWED H<small>AWKINS DOWN THE CORRIDOR AND AROUND</small> the corner to the intake bay, where a gurney had been rolled onto the weigh-in scale. The pouch it held showed a very large bulge.

Wordlessly, Hawkins unzipped the body bag and laid back the flap. Like a class on a field trip, we leaned in.

Gran called it fay, claimed prescience as a family trait. I call it deductive reasoning.

Perhaps it was Hawkins's demeanor. Perhaps it was the image I'd conjured in my mind. Though we'd never met, I knew I was staring at Ricky Don Dorton.

The man's skin was the color of old leather, creased by vertical lines beside his eyes and ears and at the corners of his mouth. The cheeks were high and broad, the nose wide, the hair dead black and combed straight back. Irregular, yellowed teeth peeked from purple, death-slacked lips.

Ricky Don Dorton had died bare-chested. I could see two gold chains in the folds of his neck, and the Marine Corps emblem on his right upper arm, the words SEMPER FI circling below.

Larabee scanned the police report.

"Well, well. Mr. Richard Donald Dorton."

"Son of a bitch." Slidell spoke for us all.

Larabee handed the paper to me. I stepped close to Jansen so we could read together.

Larabee asked Hawkins, "You just bring him in?"

Hawkins nodded.

According to the report, Ricky Don was found dead in his bed in an uptown motel.

"Dorton checked in with a woman around one-thirty A.M.," Hawkins said. "Desk clerk said they both looked hammered. Maid found the body about eight this morning. Knocked, got no answer, figured the room had been vacated. Poor thing's probably looking through the want ads even as we speak."

"Who caught the case?" Slidell asked.

"Sherrill and Bucks."

"Narco."

"Room held enough pharmaceuticals and hypodermics to stock a Third World clinic," said Hawkins.

"Suppose Dorton's midnight companion was Sister Mary Innocent working to save his soul?" Slidell asked.

"Desk clerk suspected the woman was a hooker," said Hawkins. "Thought Dorton had been there before. Same deal. Late-night check-in. Floozy date."

"Get hopped. Get lucky. Get a room." Larabee.

"Guess Ricky Don's luck ran out." Slidell tossed the report onto the body bag.

I watched the paper slip to the gurney and settle against Ricky Don's pricey gold neckwear.

Before his departure, Ryan extracted a promise that I would discuss the previous day's e-mails with Slidell or Rinaldi. Though my anxiety had diminished considerably overnight, my nerves were still on edge. I was inclined to view the messages as the work of some warped cyber-moron, but had promised myself not to let fear alter my life. Business as usual. But I agreed with Ryan on one point.

If the threat was real, Katy was also at risk.

I'd tried to caution my daughter on the night of her party, but Katy's reaction had been to scoff at the e-mails. When I'd persisted, she'd become annoyed, told me my job was making me paranoid.

Twenty-something, bulletproof, and immortal. Like mother, like daughter.

In the privacy of my office, I described the pictures of Boyd, Katy, and myself. I acknowledged yesterday's terror, today's continuing uneasiness.

Rinaldi spoke first.

"You have no idea who this Grim Reaper is?"

I shook my head.

"What Ryan and I could make out from the AOL tracking information was that the messages were sent to my mailbox at UNCC through a couple of re-mailers, then forwarded from the university to my AOL address."

"That last part your doing?"

"Yes. I have all my e-mail forwarded." I shook my head. "You'll never trace the original sender."

"It can be done," Rinaldi said. "But it isn't easy."

"The pictures began on Wednesday morning?" Slidell asked.

I nodded. "Probably taken with a digital camera."

"So there's no way to track prints through a film processing company." Slidell.

"And the call was probably placed at a pay phone." Rinaldi. "Would you like us to order surveillance for you?"

"Do you think that's warranted?"

I had expected indifference, perhaps impatience. The sincerity of their responses was unsettling.

"We'll step up patrols past your place."

"Thank you."

"How about your kid's crib?" Slidell.

I saw Katy, relaxed and unaware on a front porch swing.

"Stepped up patrols would be good."

"Done."

When they'd gone I checked again with Mrs. Flowers. Still no fax from Cagle. She assured me she would deliver the report the second it finished printing.

Returning to my office, I tried to concentrate on a backlog of mail and paperwork. Thirty minutes later, the phone rang. I nearly knocked my soda to the floor snatching up the receiver.

It was Mrs. Flowers.

Cagle's fax with the Lancaster skeletal report had not arrived, but Brian Aiker's dental records had. Dr. Larabee had requested my presence in the main autopsy room.

When I arrived, the ME was arranging radiographs on two light boxes, each set consisting of twelve tiny films showing teeth in the upper and lower jaws. Joe Hawkins had taken one series on the privy skull and jaw. Brian Aiker's dentist had provided the other.

One look was enough.

"Don't think we'll need a forensic dentist for this one," Larabee said.

"Nope," I agreed.

Brian Aiker's X rays showed crowns and posts in two upper and two lower molars, clear evidence of root canal work.

The privy skull X rays showed none.

Wally Cagle's report did not arrive on Friday. Nor did it come on Saturday. Or Sunday.

Twice each day I visited the MCME. Twice each day I called Cagle at his office, his home, and on his cell.

Never an answer.

Twice each day I checked my e-mail for the scanned images.

Bad news and good news.

No photos from Cagle.

No photos from the Grim Reaper.

I spent the weekend wondering about the Lancaster bones. If the skull and postcranial remains belonged to the same person, it wasn't Brian Aiker. Who was it?

Did the privy skull really go with Cagle's skeleton? I'd been so sure, but it was just instinct. I had no hard data. Could we actually have two unknowns?

What had happened to Brian Aiker? To Charlotte Grant Cobb?

I also pondered the whereabouts of Tamela Banks and her family. The Bankses were unsophisticated people. How could they simply disappear? Why would they do so?

On Saturday morning I made a quick visit to the Bankses' home. The shades were still drawn. A pile of newspapers lay on the porch. No one answered my rings or knocking.

Ryan phoned daily, updating me on the condition of his sister and niece. Things were not sunny in Halifax.

I told Ryan about Ricky Don Dorton's demise, about my discussions with Hershey Zamzow concerning bear poaching and the missing wildlife agents, and about Jansen's goldenseal findings. He asked if I'd reported the Grim Reaper e-mails to Slidell or Rinaldi. I assured him that I had, and that they were increasing surveillance of my place and Lija's town house.

Each time we disconnected, the annex felt oddly empty. Ryan was gone, his belongings, his smell, his laugh, his cooking. Though he'd only been in my home a short time, his presence had filled the place. I missed him. A lot. Much more than I ever would have imagined.

Otherwise, I puttered, as my mother would call it. Runs and walks with Boyd. Talks with Birdie. Hair conditioning. Eyebrow plucking. Plant watering. Always with an eye to my back. An ear to the air for strange noises.

Saturday Katy talked me into a late-night soiree at Amos's to listen to a band named Weekend Excursion. The group was punchy, talented, and powerful enough to be picked up by instruments in deserts listening for signs of life in space. The crowd stood and listened, enthralled. At one point I screamed a question into Katy's ear.

"Doesn't anyone dance?"

"A few geeks might."

The old ABBA song "Dancing Queen" ran through my head.

Times change.

After Amos's, we had nightcaps one door over at a pub called the Gin Mill. Perrier and lime for me, a Grey Goose martini for Katy. Straight up. Dirty. With extra olives. My daughter was definitely a big girl now.

On Sunday we did manicure-pedicure mother-daughter bonding, then hit golf balls on the driving range at Carmel Country Club.

Katy had been a star on the Carmel swim team, semi-swimming her first lane rope-clinging freestyle at age four. She'd grown up on Carmel's golf courses and tennis courts, hunted Easter eggs, and watched Fourth of July fireworks on its lawns.

Pete and I had feasted on Carmel buffets, danced under the twirling New Year's Eve globes, drunk champagne, admired the ice sculptures. Many of our closest friendships had been formed at the club.

Though I remained legally married, entitling me to use of all facilities, it felt strange to be there, like revisiting a vaguely remembered place. The people I saw were like visions in a dream, familiar yet distant.

That evening Katy and I ordered pizza and watched *Meet the Parents*. I didn't ask if there was significance to her movie selection. Nor did I query the weekend whereabouts of Palmer Cousins.

Monday morning I rose early and checked my e-mail.

Still no photos from Cagle or messages from the Grim Reaper.

After spinning Boyd around the block, I headed to the MCME, confident that the Cagle report would be on my desk.

No fax.

By nine-thirty I'd called Cagle four times at each of his numbers. The professor still didn't answer.

When the phone rang at ten I nearly burst from my skin.

"Guess you heard."

"Heard what?"

Slidell picked up on the disappointment in my voice.

"What? You were expecting a call from Sting?"

"I was hoping it was Wally Cagle."

"You still waiting on that report?"

"Yes." I twisted the spirals of the cord around my finger. "It's odd. Cagle said he'd fax it on Thursday."

"Walter?" Slidell drew the name into three syllables.

"That was four days ago."

"Maybe the guy hurt himself pulling up his tights."

"Have you considered a support group for homophobics?"

"Look, way I see it, men are men and women are women, and everyone should sleep in the tent he was born with. You start crossing lines, no one's going to know where to buy their undies."

I didn't point out the number of metaphoric lines Slidell had just crossed.

"Cagle was also going to scan photos of the bones and send them by e-mail," I said.

"Jesus in a fish market, everything's e-mail these days. If you ask me, e-mail's some kinda voodoo witchcraft."

I heard Slidell's chair groan under the strain of his buttocks.

"If Aiker's out, what about the other one?"

"Different tent."

"What?"

"The other FWS agent was female."

"Maybe you got it wrong with the bones."

Not bad, Skinny.

"That's possible for the privy remains, but not for the Lancaster skeleton."

"Why's that?"

"Cagle sent a bone sample for DNA testing. Amelogenin came back male."

"Here we go again. The black arts."

I let him listen to silence for a while.

"You still there?"

"Do you want me to explain amelogenin, or do you prefer to remain in the nineteenth century?"

"Keep it short."

"You've heard of DNA?"

"I'm not a total cretin."

Questionable.

"Amelogenin is actually a locus for tooth pulp."

"Locus?"

"A place on the DNA molecule that codes for a specific trait."

"What the hell's tooth pulp got to do with sex?"

"Nothing. But in females, the left side of the gene contains a small deletion of nonessential DNA, and produces a shorter product when amplified by PCR."

"So this pulp locus shows length variation between the sexes."

"Exactly." I was incredulous that Slidell had grasped this so quickly. "Do you understand sex chromosomes?"

"Girls got two X's, boys got an X and a Y. That's what I'm saying. Nature throws the dice, you stick with the toss."

The metaphor thickened.

"When the amelogenin region is analyzed," I went on, "a female, having two X chromosomes, will show one band. A male, having both an X and a Y chromosome, will show two bands, one the same size as the female and one slightly larger."

"And Cagle's bones came up male."

"Yes."

"And your skull is male."

"Probably."

"Probably?"

"My gut feeling is yes, but there's nothing definitive about it."

"Genderwise."

"Genderwise."

"But it's not Aiker."

"Not if we have the right dental records."

"But the skeleton could be."

"Not if it goes with the privy skull."

"And you think it does."

"It sounds like a fit. But I haven't seen photos or the original bones."

"Any reason Cagle might have changed his mind, started avoiding your calls?"

"He was very cooperative when we talked."

Now the empty air was of Slidell's choosing.

"You game for a little spin down to Columbia?"

"I'll be waiting on the steps."

24

Fifteen minutes after leaving the MCME, Slidell and I were crossing into South Carolina. To either side of I-77 lay a border sprawl of low-end shops, restaurants, and entertainment emporia, a Carolina version of Nogales or Tijuana.

Paramount's Carowinds. Outlet Market Place. Frugal MacDougal's Discount Liquors. Heritage USA, abandoned now, but once a mecca for Jim and Tammy Faye's PTL faithful intent on God, vacation, and bargain basement clothes. Opinions varied as to whether PTL had stood for Praise the Lord or Pass the Loot.

Rinaldi had opted for a trip to Sneedville, Tennessee, to do some digging on Ricky Don Dorton and Jason Jack Wyatt. Rinaldi also planned to run a background check on the pilot, Harvey Pearce, and was intent on a meaningful conversation with Sonny Pounder.

Jansen had headed back to Miami.

Slidell had spoken little since picking me up, preferring the sputter of his radio to the sound of my voice. I suspected his coolness derived from my homophobia crack.

OK by me, Skinny.

We were soon rolling between heavily wooded, kudzu-draped hills. Slidell alternated between drumming the steering wheel and patting his shirt pocket. I knew he needed nicotine, but I needed O_2. Through a lot of sighing and throat clearing and drumming and patting, I refused to give the go-ahead to light up.

We passed the exits for Fort Mill and Rock Hill, later Highway 9 cutting east to Lancaster. I thought of Cagle's headless skeleton, wondered what we would find at his lab.

I also thought of Andrew Ryan, of times we'd been rolling toward a crime scene or body dump together. Slidell or Ryan? Who would I rather be with? No contest there.

The University of South Carolina system has eight campuses, with the mothership parked squarely in the heart of the state capital. Perhaps the Palmetto State founders were xenophobic. Perhaps funds were limited. Perhaps they simply preferred to have their offspring educated in their own backyard.

Or perhaps they foresaw the bacchanalian rite of spring break at Myrtle Beach, and tried reaching across the centuries to discourage a very different type of hajj.

In Columbia, Slidell took Bull Street and turned left at the edge of campus. Failing to locate a spot in the visitor-metered parking area, he pulled into a faculty lot and cut the engine.

"Some egghead gets me ticketed, I'll tell him to stick it up his PHD." Slidell pocketed the keys. "You know what those letters stand for, don't you, Doc?"

Though I indicated no interest, Slidell provided his definition.

"Piled higher and deeper."

Exiting the Taurus was brutal. The sun was white-hot, the pavement rippling as we crossed Pendelton Street. Overhead, leaves hung motionless, like damp nappies on clotheslines on a windless day.

The USC anthropology facilities were located in a dishwater-blond building named Hamilton College. Built in 1943 to spur the war effort, Hamilton now looked like it could use some spurring of its own.

Slidell and I located the departmental office and presented ourselves to the secretary/receptionist. Dragging her eyes from a computer screen, the woman regarded us through Dame Edna glasses. She was in her fifties, with a mulberry mushroom on her forehead and hair piled higher than a Texas deb's.

Slidell asked for Cagle.

The deb informed him that the professor was not in.

When had she last seen him?

A week ago Friday.

Had Cagle been on campus since?

Possible, though their paths hadn't crossed. Cagle's mailbox had been emptied the immediate past Friday. She hadn't seen him then or since.

Slidell asked the location of Cagle's office.

Third floor. Entrance was impossible without written permission.

Slidell asked the location of Cagle's lab.

Second floor. The deb reiterated the point about written permission.

Slidell flashed his badge.

The deb studied Slidell's shield, lipstick crawling into the wrinkles radiating from her tightly clamped lips. If she noticed the words "Charlotte-Mecklenburg," she didn't let on. She turned a shoulder, dialed a number, waited, disconnected, dialed again, waited again, hung up. Sighing theatrically, she rose, walked to a filing cabinet, opened the top drawer, unhooked one of several dozen keys, and checked its tag.

Keeping several steps ahead to minimize opportunity for conversation, our reluctant hostess led us to the second floor, down a tiled corridor, and around a corner to a wooden door with a frosted-glass window. The words HUMAN IDENTIFICATION LABORATORY were stenciled on the glass in bold, black letters.

"What exactly is it you need?" The deb ran a thumb back and forth across the small round key tag.

"Last Thursday Dr. Cagle promised he'd send me a case report and photos," I said. "I haven't received them. I can't reach him by phone and it's quite urgent."

"Dr. Cagle's been in the field all summer, only comes in on weekends. Y'all sure he intended to do it right away?"

"Absolutely."

Two creases puckered the mulberry mushroom. "Man's usually very predictable and very reliable."

The deb hunched her whole body when she turned the key, as though revelation of the wrist movement might constitute a security breach. Straightening, she swung the door inward, and pointed a lacquered nail at me.

"Don't disturb any of Dr. Cagle's things." It came out "thangs." "Some are official police evidence." It came out "poe-lice."

"We'll be very careful," I said.

"Check with me on your way out."

Drilling us each with a look, the deb marched off down the corridor.

"Broad missed her calling in the SS," Slidell said, moving past me through the open door.

Cagle's lab was an earlier-era version of mine at UNCC. More solid, outfitted with oak and marble, not molded plastic and painted metal.

I did a quick scan.

Worktables. Sinks. Microscopes. Light boxes. Copy stand. Ventilator hood. Hanging skeleton. Refrigerator. Computer.

Slidell tipped his head toward a wall of floor-to-ceiling storage cabinets.

"What do you suppose that meatball keeps locked up in there?"

"Bones."

"Jay-zus Kee-rist."

While Slidell went through the unlocked cupboards above the work counters, I checked the room's single desk. Its top was bare save for a blotter.

A file drawer on the left held forms of various types. Archaeological survey sheets. Burial inventories. Blank bone quizzes. Audiovisual requisitions.

The long middle drawer contained the usual assortment of pens, plastic-headed tacks, paper clips, rubber bands, stamps, and coins.

Nothing extraordinary.

Except that everything was organized into separate boxes, slots, and niches, each labeled and spotlessly clean. Inside the compartments, every item was aligned with geometric precision.

"Fastidious little wanker." Slidell had come up behind me.

I checked the right two drawers. Stationery. Envelopes. Printer paper. Labels. Post-its.

Same ordinary supplies. Same anal tidiness.

"Your desk look like that?" Slidell asked.

"No." I'd once found a dead goldfish in my desk drawer. Solved the mystery of its disappearance the previous spring.

"Mine sure don't."

Being familiar with Slidell's car, I didn't want to imagine the state of his desk.

"Any sign of the report?"

I shook my head.

Slidell moved on to the lower-counter drawers, and I began on the file cabinets to the left of the desk. One held class materials. The other was filled with forensic case reports.

Bingo!

Across the room, Slidell banged a drawer home.

"I've gotta get some air."

"Fine."

I said nothing about the files. Better to have Slidell outside smoking than breathing down my neck.

The dossiers were organized chronologically. Twenty-three dated to the year Cagle had examined the Lancaster skeleton. I found two for the proper month, but none for a headless body.

I checked the preceding and following years, then scanned the tab on every folder.

The report wasn't there.

Slidell returned after ten minutes, smelling of Camels, armpits, and sweaty hair cream.

"I found Cagle's case files."

"Oh, yeah?"

Slidell leaned over me, breathing cigarette breath.

"The Lancaster report isn't with the others."

"Suppose Wally-boy misplaced it?" Slidell asked.

"Doesn't seem likely, but keep looking."

Slidell went back to banging drawers.

I returned to the desk and surveyed the bulletin board. Like Mrs. Flowers, Wally Cagle insisted on equidistant spacing and ninety-degree angles.

A postcard sent by someone named Gene. Polaroids taken at an archaeological dig. Three pictures of a cat. A printout of names followed by four-digit university extensions.

The center of the board held a handwritten list of tasks followed by a column of dates. Those up through Thursday had been crossed out.

"Look at this," I said.

Slidell joined me at the desk.

I pointed to an item among Cagle's uncompleted tasks: *Pull photos and report for Brennan.*

"He uses a ruler to cross things out? Jesus, this guy's one tight spitter."

"That's not the point. Even though the secretary didn't see him, Cagle's been here as recently as last Thursday. Does the fact the item is *not* crossed off mean he never pulled the file? Or did he pull it, then forget?"

"Looks like Wally-boy never took a dump without itemizing and crossing it off."

"Maybe he was interrupted."

"Maybe."

"Maybe someone else took the file."

"Who?" Slidell's voice dripped skepticism.

"I don't know."

"Who even knew the damn thing existed?"

"Cagle's graduate student," I snapped. Slidell's attitude was making me churlish. "He read parts to Cagle over the phone."

"Maybe Cagle took the stuff to a home computer."

"Maybe."

"But he never sent you the report."

Good, Skinny. State the obvious.

"Or the photos."

"Nothing."

Slidell hitched his belt. It slid back into the groove below his spare tire.

"So where the hell are they?"

"An astute question."

"And where the hell is the good professor?"

"And another."

I was starting to get a bad feeling about Cagle's safety.

My gaze fell on the computer and its flatbed scanner. The setup looked like it might have been purchased when the Monkees were big.

Slidell watched me walk over and press the "on" button. As the CPU dragged through a boot, the Texas deb receptionist appeared in the doorway.

"What is it you think you're doing?"

"I located Dr. Cagle's case files, but the one in question is missing."

"So you think you're going to use his computer?"

"It might tell us if the photos were ever scanned."

As if on cue, the CPU beeped and the monitor flashed a password request.

"Do you have it?" I asked the deb.

"I could never give out a password." She sounded as though I'd asked for her bank card PIN. "Besides, I don't know it."

"Does anyone else use this computer?"

"Gene Rudin."

"Dr. Cagle's graduate student?"

The deb nodded. Not a hair moved.

"Gene's off to Florida until the start of fall term. Left Friday."

A long, lacquered finger pointed at the computer.

"But that scanner won't run. I've had a work order in to computer services for at least two weeks now."

Slidell and I exchanged glances. Now what?

"Did Dr. Cagle ask you to send any faxes last week?" I asked.

The lacquered hands vanished in an arm fold across her chest, a hip shifted, and one sandaled foot came forward. The toes were the same brilliant red as the fingers.

"I've already told you, I didn't see Dr. Cagle last week. And besides, do you know how many faculty I'm responsible for? Or how many grads and undergrads and booksellers and visitors and whatever trail through my office?" I guessed Slidell and I fell under the "whatever" heading. "Hells bells, I do half the student advising around here."

"That can't be easy," I said.

"Faculty faxing is *not* in my job description."

"You must get a lot of visitors."

"We get our share."

"Did Dr. Cagle have any unusual callers last week?"

"That would not be for me to say."

What the hell did that mean?

"Did Dr. Cagle have *any* visitors last week?"

There was a long pause as she chose her words.

"I may not agree with Dr. Cagle's alternative lifestyle"—she pronounced it as two words: "alter native"—"but he's a fine man, and I don't question his associations."

"Someone came to see Cagle?" Slidell asked gruffly.

One deb eyebrow shot up. "There's no need to be a grumpy pants, Detective."

Slidell opened his mouth. I cut him off.

"You were unfamiliar with Dr. Cagle's visitor?"

The deb nodded.

"What did he want?"

"The man asked for Dr. Cagle. I informed him the professor was out of town." The deb shrugged one freckled shoulder. "He left."

"Can you describe the guy?" Slidell.

"Short. Had black hair. Lots of it. Real shiny and thick."

"Age?"

"Wasn't no spring chicken, I'll tell you that."

"Glasses? Facial hair?" Slidell's tone was sharp.

"Don't get snippy with me, Detective."

The deb unfolded her arms and flicked at a nonexistent speck on her skirt, her way of allowing Slidell to cool his interrogatory heels.

"No mustache or beard, nothing like that."

"Can you remember anything else about the man?" I asked.

"He wore funny sunglasses, so I couldn't see his eyes."

"What *did* you see when you looked at his face?" Slidell glared at her.

"Myself." The deb slapped a key on the desktop. "That's for the wall cupboards. Check with me when you leave the building."

Slidell and I spent the next forty minutes searching every remaining cabinet, drawer, and shelf in the place. We found nothing related to the Lancaster case, and nothing to indicate where Cagle had gone.

Frustrated, I returned to the desk and idly ran my fingertips under the blotter's plastic edging.

Nothing.

I lifted a corner and peeked underneath.

A single card lay on the desktop under the blotter. I picked it up.

The logo resembled a police badge. I was about to read the printed information when the deb receptionist reappeared in the door, breathless from running up the stairs.

"I just talked with Dr. Cagle's housemate."

An agitated hand fanned the air in front of her face.

"Dr. Cagle's in intensive care on life support."

Laying both hands on her chest, the deb looked from me to Slidell and back, mascara-rimmed eyes wide with alarm.

"Sweet Lord Jesus. The doctors don't think he'll last out the day."

C AGLE LIVED IN A SMALL BRICK BUNGALOW IN A NEIGHBORHOOD of small brick bungalows a short drive from Hamilton College. The trim was lilac, and four straight-backed lilac rockers sat in perfect alignment on the broad front porch. The lawn was mown, every border edged with military precision.

An ancient live oak shaded the right half of the property, its roots crawling below the earth's surface like giant, serpentine fingers clinging for support. Jumbles of brightly colored annuals elbowed for room in beds along the walkway and porch foundation. As we approached the house, the odor of petunias, marigolds, and fresh paint sweetened the hot, humid air.

Climbing the steps, Slidell jabbed a thumb at a green metal holder attached to the house. Someone had coiled the garden hose in perfectly matched loops.

"Guess we got the right place."

The bell was answered within seconds. The man was younger than I expected, with black hair that had been gelled, spiked, and gathered from his forehead with an elastic headband. I guessed his age as mid-thirties, his weight at 140.

"You are the officers from Charlotte?"

Not bothering to correct him, Slidell merely held up his badge.

"Lawrence Looper." Looper stepped back. "Come in."

We entered a small foyer with a covered radiator to the left, sliding wooden doors straight ahead, and an open archway to the right. Looper led us through the archway into a living room with throw rugs on a polished oak floor and Pottery Barn furnishings. A wood-bladed fan turned lazily overhead.

"Please." Looper extended a manicured hand. "Do sit. Can I get either of you a cool beverage?"

Declining, Slidell and I seated ourselves on opposite ends of the sofa. The room smelled of artificial floral deodorizer from a plug-in-the-socket dispenser.

Looper lifted a footstool, placed it against the wall, considered the arrangement, repositioned the stool.

Beside me I heard Slidell puff air through his lips. I gave him a warning look. He rolled both eyes and his head.

Feng shui restored, Looper returned and took the chair opposite us.

"Wow. Dolores is really cross with me. I suppose she has a right to be."

"That'd be Miss Southern Charm over at the university." Slidell.

"Hmm. I should have called her after Wally's collapse, but . . ." Looper flexed an ankle, causing his flip-flop to make small popping sounds ". . . I didn't."

"And why is that?" Slidell's voice had that edge.

"I don't like Dolores."

"And why is that?"

Looper looked Slidell straight in the eye. "She doesn't like me."

The ankle flicked several times.

"And Wally never wants anyone to know when he isn't feeling well. He has . . ." Looper hesitated ". . . complaints." *Pop. Pop. Pop.* "The man likes to keep the state of his health private, so I didn't broadcast that he'd taken ill. I thought he'd prefer it that way."

Pop. Pop.

"But when you two showed up, and Dolores called, well, I couldn't lie about it." Looper put three extra *I*'s in the word "lie." "That would have been pointless."

"Please tell us what happened," I said.

"There isn't much to tell. I came home Thursday night and found Wally curled up on the bathroom floor."

A hand came up, and a finger pointed through a second archway at right angles to the one through which we'd entered the living room.

"In there. He was having trouble breathing, and his face was flushed, and he could hardly speak, but I did get out of him that he felt tightness in his chest. That scared me to death. And I could see that he'd thrown up."

The hand fluttered to Looper's chest.

"I got him into the car, which, let me tell you, wasn't easy with his legs all shaky and him moaning that he was going to die."

I wondered why Looper hadn't called for an ambulance, but I didn't ask him.

"When we got to the ER, he just stopped breathing."

We waited for Looper to go on. He didn't.

"They placed him on a respirator?" I prompted.

"Hmm. Wally started breathing on his own, but he wouldn't wake up. Still won't."

"Was it a heart attack?" I asked softly.

"I suppose so. The doctors don't really want to tell me much." *Pop. Pop.* "I'm not family, you know."

Overhead, the fan hummed softly. The artificial bouquet was beginning to cloy.

"Wally and I have been together a long time. I really hope he's going to pull through." Looper's eyes had reddened around the rims.

"I hope so, too. He's a fine man."

Brilliant, Brennan.

Looper laced his fingers, and one thumb began picking at the other.

"I suppose I should phone his sister, but they aren't close. And I keep thinking that any minute he's going to wake up and ask for his pipe and everything will be fine."

Looper recrossed his legs, and gave the flip-flop a few flicks.

"Why is it you're here?"

"I spoke to Dr. Cagle by phone on Thursday," I said. "He promised to send me a case report and photos. I never received them, and Detective Slidell and I wondered if perhaps he'd brought the materials home, intending to work here."

"He did sometimes work here on his laptop. But I haven't noticed anything in the house."

"A folder? An envelope?"

Looper shook his head.

"A briefcase?"

"Wally does usually carry a briefcase. That and his precious laptop."

Pop. Pop. "He doesn't keep a desktop computer here." Looper rose. "I'll look around his room."

Slidell lumbered to his feet and held out a hand.

"How 'bout I have a peek at the prof's wheels while you two check out his crib."

"Whatever." Suit-yourself shrug.

Looper produced a set of keys, then turned and walked toward the back of the house. I followed. Slidell exited through the front door.

Cagle's bedroom was ICU clean and OCD neat. Big surprise.

The search took five minutes. I saw no sign of a file or photos in Cagle's dresser or desk drawers, closet, or under his bed. There was nowhere else to look. Frustrated, I trailed Looper back to the living room.

"Let me understand this," Looper said, tucking one foot under him as he resumed his seat. "You spoke to Wally on Thursday?"

"Yes," I replied. "He was in Beaufort."

"Was he driving up just to send you this report thing?"

"He said he was heading home anyway."

"Hmmm."

Slidell rejoined us, shaking his head.

"Does that surprise you, Mr. Looper?" I asked.

"During the summer, Wally never returned to Columbia on Thursday. He always stayed at the dig until Friday. That's why I was so surprised to find him here."

"You have no idea why he might have been coming back early?"

Looper pulled the foot out, crossed his legs, and popped the flip-flop several times, the ankle-flexing more agitated than before.

"I was out of town all week, myself."

"Why was that?" Slidell.

"I'm in sales."

"What is it you sell, Mr. Looper?"

"Pumps. The hydraulic kind, not the ones you wear on your feet."

If this was an attempt at humor, Looper's delivery was beyond dry.

"I wasn't supposed to get back until Friday, but my appointments wrapped up earlier than I'd expected."

"Landed the big one?" Slidell.

"Actually, no."

"Do you have any guess as to why Wally might have cut short his workweek in Beaufort?" I asked.

Though one shoulder rose in a nonchalant shrug, Looper's face tensed visibly.

"We're here in regard to a murder investigation, Mr. Looper," I prompted.

Deep sigh.

"Wally may have been planning a rendezvous."

Deeper sigh.

"A tryst." Shoulder. "Behind my back."

There was a long silence. Even Slidell was shrewd enough not to break it.

"Wally met with someone. They didn't know I saw them together, but I did. In a coffee shop near campus two Fridays ago."

"And?" Slidell.

"There are certain things you just *know*." Looper inspected his bare toes.

"Know?" Slidell's voice was like razor wire.

Looper's gaze came up and locked on Slidell's.

"It didn't look like a business meeting."

"Were the two of them holdin—"

"Can you describe the man?" I cut Slidell off.

Looper sniffed, and his brows arced upward.

"Pretty."

"Could you be more specific?"

"Hunky build, salon tan."

"Tall?"

"No."

"Glasses? Facial hair? Tattoos?"

Continuous head shake.

"Hair?"

"Hugh Grant with a black dye job." Sniff. "Looked like he was done up for a *GQ* shoot."

Looper gave an eye roll that made Katy look like a tenderfoot, recrossed his legs, and went back to picking at his thumb.

"You didn't know this person?"

Head shake.

"Have you and Dr. Cagle been having difficulties?" I asked gently.

Slidell *sheeshed* air through his lips. I ignored him.

Looper shrugged and popped the flip-flop. "Some. Nothing ghastly."

"Is there any chance at all that Dr. Cagle might be able to speak to us? To communicate?"

Looper rose, walked to a credenza, picked up and dialed a phone. After a pause he asked about Cagle's condition, listened, thanked the other party, said he'd be by shortly, and disconnected.

Keeping his back to Slidell, Looper ran his right palm across each cheek, and breathed deeply. Then he squared his shoulders, wiped his hand on his cutoffs, and turned.

"He's still comatose."

Slidell's face registered nothing.

"What hospital?"

Looper bristled slightly.

"Palmetto Health Richland. He's in cardiac intensive care. His doctor's name is Kenneth MacMillan."

Slidell moved toward the door. I rose and approached Looper.

"Are you going to be all right?"

Looper nodded.

Digging a card from my purse, I scribbled my name and cell phone number, handed it to him, and squeezed his hand.

"If you come across the missing file, please let me know. And please call when Dr. Cagle wakes up."

Looper looked down at the card, flicked a glance at Slidell, came back to me.

"I will definitely call *you*."

He turned to Slidell.

"You have a really special day."

Looper's left hand still gripped the phone so tightly his wrist cords bulged like the live oak's roots.

Slidell lit up as soon as we hit the sidewalk. At the Taurus, I opened my door and waited out his Camel moment.

"Think there's any point to swinging by the hospital?" I asked.

Slidell flicked his butt, ground it with the ball of one foot.

"Can't hurt." Blotting his forehead with one wrist, he yanked open the driver's side door and jammed himself behind the wheel.

Slidell was right. It didn't hurt. Nor did it help. Walter Cagle was as dead to the world as Looper reported.

His doctor could offer no explanation. Cagle's vital signs had stabilized and his heart showed no damage. His white count, EEG, and EKG were normal. The man simply wasn't waking up.

We'd barely left the hospital when Slidell started in.

"Sounds like trouble in queen city."

I did not reply.

"The princess thinks the contessa was getting his weenie stroked behind his back."

Nope.

"And he don't like the fact that the whistling gypsy lover is a looker."

Catching the look on my face, Slidell fell silent. It didn't last.

"Suppose Looper and that Gestapo secretary are describing the same squirrel?"

"It's possible."

"Think Cagle was seeing this guy on the side?"

"Looper may have imagined the romantic angle. It could have been anything."

"Such as?"

I'd been asking myself that same question.

"Such as a potential student."

"Gestapo Gert said the guy asking for Cagle wasn't a kid."

"Adults enroll in college courses."

"Someone interested in a program would have left a message at the department office."

True.

"A workman of some sort."

"Why meet the guy in a coffee shop?" Slidell asked.

"An insurance salesman."

"Ditto."

"Walter Cagle is a grown man."

Slidell snorted. "Squirrel probably vacations at the Y."

Slidell's homophobia was getting on my nerves.

"There are any number of persons with whom Walter Cagle might have shared a cup of coffee."

"A pretty boy with drop-dead good looks that nobody close to the guy ever laid eyes on?"

"A lot of men fit that description," I snapped.

"Yeah?"

"Yeah."

"Real men?"

"Ball busters!"

"You know any?"

"My daughter's boyfriend," I shot back without thinking.

"You sure he's a boy?" Slidell patted his hair, flopped one wrist, snorted at his own joke.

Closing my eyes, I chose lyrics in my head. The Eagles. "Take It Easy."

We drove out of Columbia, four o'clock sun flickering through the trees like light off a pinwheel. I felt so hostile toward Slidell I didn't speak the entire way to Charlotte. When he lit up, I merely lowered my window, continued processing the events of the day in my mind.

Why had I thrown out that reference to Palmer Cousins? Was it merely a knee-jerk reaction to Slidell's wheedling, or was my subconscious seeing something that I was missing?

Did I distrust Palmer Cousins? Honest reply: yes.

Why? Because he was dating my daughter? Because of his seeming lack of knowledge of his own profession? Because he was handsome and lived in Columbia?

Who had Cagle met in the coffee shop? Who had visited the anthropology department? Was either man involved in the disappearance of Cagle's report? Was either responsible for Cagle's collapse? Were Looper and Dolores describing the same man?

Always, I came back to the same question.

Where was that report?

I vowed to find out.

My vow paid off sooner than I'd expected.

26

I T WAS FIVE-THIRTY WHEN SLIDELL DROPPED ME AT THE MCME.
Tim Larabee was on his way out.

"What's the word on Ricky Don?" I asked.

"No signs of trauma. Looks like an overdose, but we'll have to wait
for the tox report."

"Find signs of chronic use?"

"Yes. Course, that doesn't mean someone didn't nudge him over
last Friday."

I summarized my trip to Columbia with Slidell.

"Where'd you say this Cagle lives?"

I told him.

"Looper took him to Richland Hospital?"

"Yeah."

"Odd, since Baptist is right there at Sumter and Taylor."

"Richland isn't the closest hospital?"

"No."

"Maybe Looper didn't know that."

"Maybe." Larabee wagged his head. "Folks is dropping like flies, ma
dear."

"I'm going to phone Lancaster County, see if I can shake something loose on Cagle's report."

"Go, girl." Larabee pushed open the glass door and was gone.

Seated at my desk, I looked up the number and dialed.

"Lancaster County Sheriff's Department."

After introducing myself, I asked for the person in charge.

"Chief Deputy Roe is unavailable at the moment."

I gave a two-sentence synopsis of the potential Foote farm privy–Lancaster County skeletal connection, and of my problems in obtaining a copy of the anthropology report, and asked if anyone else could help me.

"Let me see if one of the investigating officers is in."

Pause. Several clicks, then a female voice.

"Terry Woolsey."

I repeated my spiel.

"The guy that caught that one has moved on. You'll have to talk with Chief Deputy Roe."

"Are you familiar with the case?"

"I remember it. Headless skeleton, turned up over at the state park about three years back."

"I understand there was a different sheriff then."

"Hal Cobber. Lost the election, retired to Florida."

"The coroner was Murray Snow?"

"Yes." Guarded.

"Did you know Mr. Snow?"

"Dr. Snow. He was an obstetrician. The position of coroner isn't full-time down here."

"Who is the current coroner?"

"James Park."

"Another doctor?"

"Park owns a funeral home. Bit of local irony. Snow brought folks into the world. Park sends 'em out."

It sounded like a joke that had been told a few times.

"Is Park an easy guy to work with?"

"He does his job."

"Any reason he'd be holding back on that anthropology report?"

"None he shared with me."

What the hell. Try the sisters-in-arms approach.

"Right." Moment of poignant hesitation. "Listen, I'm working with Detectives Slidell and Rinaldi up here in Charlotte," I said, frustration tinging my voice ever so slightly. "I'll be honest, Detective Woolsey. I don't think these guys are really keeping me in the loop."

"What's your point?"

So much for sisterhood.

"It doesn't seem likely that Dr. Cagle's report would just vanish from the system."

"Shit happens."

"You ever encountered that problem on a case?"

She ignored my question.

"Surely this anthropologist kept records. Why not ask him for his copy?"

"I did. Cagle's had some sort of medical crisis and his file and photos have gone missing."

"What sort of medical crisis?"

I explained about Cagle's collapse and subsequent coma.

There was a long pause, squad room noises in the background.

"And this dossier had been removed from his files?"

"Looks that way."

I heard her take several breaths, then rattling sounds, as though she was switching the receiver from one hand to the other.

"Can you meet me tomorrow?" Scratchy, as though her lips were now closer to the mouthpiece.

"Sure." I tried to keep the surprise from my voice. "Headquarters is on Pageland Road, right?"

"Don't come here."

Another, shorter pause while we both thought that over.

"You know the Coffee Cup, near where Morehead passes under I-77?"

"Of course." Everyone in Charlotte knew the Coffee Cup.

"I've got some business up your way tomorrow. Meet me at eight."

"I'll be at the counter."

When we'd disconnected, I sat for a full five minutes.

First Zamzow and now Woolsey. What could the detective have to say that couldn't be said in Lancaster?

When I got home, Boyd and Birdie were asleep in the den, dog on the couch, cat burrowed into a hidey-hole on a bookshelf behind my desk.

Hearing footsteps, Boyd oozed to the floor, lowered his head, and looked up at me, tongue dangling from between his lower front teeth.

"Hey, big guy." I clapped my hands and squatted.

Boyd bounded over, placed both paws on my shoulders, and lunged forward to lick my face. The force of his enthusiasm knocked me to my bum. Rolling to my stomach, I threw both arms over my head. Boyd sprinted three circles around me, then attempted to resume the saliva facial.

When I sat up, Birdie was looking at us with as much disapproval as a cat face can register. Then he stood, arched, dropped to the floor, and disappeared into the hall.

"Listen, Boyd."

Boyd froze a nanosecond, hopped back, and made another loop.

"Look at me. I'm out of shape. You saw Ryan. What did you think?"

Boyd ran another lap.

"You're right. Exercise."

Scrambling to my feet, I climbed to my bedroom and changed into running gear. When I returned to the kitchen and unpegged Boyd's leash, the chow went berserk.

"Sit."

Boyd attempted a sudden stop, lost his balance, and slid into a table leg.

I did my short route up Radcliffe, over to Freedom Park, a loop around the lake, then back down Queens Road West. Boyd padded along, now and then suggesting stops at points that held particular canine allure.

We ran through a late-August afternoon of young mothers pushing toddlers in strollers, of old men walking old dogs, of kids throwing Frisbees and footballs and riding on bikes.

The hot, heavy day made me acutely aware of sound. I heard leaves whispering in the slight breeze. A child's swing moving back and forth in the park. A lone frog. Geese overhead. A siren.

Though I stayed vigilant, I saw no sign of a cameraman, heard no shutter click. I was grateful for Boyd's company.

By the time we got back to Sharon Hall I was soaked with sweat and my heart rate was somewhere in the seven hundreds. Boyd's tongue hung from the side of his mouth like a thin slice of flank steak.

To cool down I allowed Boyd to sniff the grounds at his pace. The chow trotted from bush to tree to flower bed, perfecting his sniff-squirt-and-cover routine, now and then stopping for more in-depth snuffling and peeing.

In keeping with my new fitness campaign, dinner consisted of a large salad, fresh produce courtesy of Andrew Ryan. Boyd had brown nuggets.

By ten I was starving. I'd just dug yogurt, carrots, and celery from the fridge when the phone rang.

"Still think I'm the most handsome, intelligent, and exciting man on the planet?"

"You're dazzling, Ryan."

The sound of his voice perked my spirits. Grinning like a kid, I took a bite of carrot.

"What are you eating?"

"Carrots."

"Since when do you eat raw veggies?"

"Carrots are good for you."

"Really?"

"Good for the eyes."

"If carrots are so good for the eyes, how come I see so many dead rabbits on the road?"

"Is your niece OK?"

"Nothing's OK. This kid and her mother make the Osbourne family look normal."

"I'm sorry."

"But it's not hopeless. I think they're listening. Shouldn't be but a couple more days here. I've been thinking of putting in for a third week of vacation."

"Oh?" My grin now sent sparkles into the air.

Boyd carried a mouthful of nuggets from his bowl and dropped them on my foot.

"I've got some unfinished business in Charlotte."

"Really?" I shook my foot. The slimed-out nuggets slid to the floor. Boyd ate them.

"*Personal* business."

My stomach was too grossed out by the nuggets to flip. But it took notice of the comment.

"How's Hooch?"

"He's fine."

"Any developments on the privy bones?"

I described my sortie to Columbia.

"*¡Caramba!* A road trip with Skinny."

"The man is a Neanderthal."

"See any dead rabbits?"

"The anthropology department secretary said Cagle had a visitor she didn't know, short guy with dark hair. Looper also spotted Cagle with a stranger."

"Same description?"

"Roughly. Though Looper emphasized the fact that the guy was gorgeous. Saw him as competition."

"That happens to me a lot."

"The secretary didn't indicate Cagle's visitor was particularly good-looking."

"Beauty is in the eye of the beholder."

"I think her eye might have picked that up."

"The doctors are stumped about Cagle's collapse?"

"Apparently."

I told Ryan about my conversation with Terry Woolsey, and about the meeting scheduled for the following morning.

"She's a detective, so I'm sure she's legit."

"We're all sages and saints."

"I have no idea what she wants."

"An idea can be a dangerous thing."

"It's odd, Ryan."

"It's odd."

"Don't patronize me."

"I know what I'd rather do to you."

A stomach cartwheel.

"Have you received any more threatening e-mails?"

"No."

"They still got stepped-up patrols past your place?"

"Yes. And past Lija's town house."

"Good."

"I'm starting to think Dorton was behind the whole thing."

"Why?"

"Ricky Don turns up dead, the e-mails stop."

"Maybe. Maybe someone took Dorton out."

"Thanks for the reassurance."

"I want you to be careful."

"I hadn't thought of that."

"You can be a real pain in the ass, Brennan."

"I work at it."

"Hooch getting enough attention?"

"We had a nice, long run this afternoon."

"It was fifty-two degrees in Halifax today."

"It was ninety-four degrees in Charlotte today."

"Miss me, Miz Temperance?"

Here we go.

"Some."

"Admit it, darlin'. This hombre is your dream come true."

"You've stumbled upon my fantasy, Ryan. Men in chaps."

"Happy trails."

After disconnecting, I called Katy.

No answer.

I left a message.

Boyd, Birdie, and I watched the last few innings of a Braves-Cubs game. I finished the carrots, Boyd gnawed a rawhide bone, and Birdie lapped at the yogurt. At some point the two of them switched. Atlanta kicked ass.

Dog, cat, and Miz Temperance were down and out by eleven.

CHARLOTTE HAS MANY INSTITUTIONS DEVOTED TO THE PRESER-
vation and veneration of beauty. The Mint Museum of Art. Spirit
Square. The McGill Rose Garden. Hooters.

The intersection of Morehead and Clarkson does not make that list.
Though just a few blocks from the trendy, yuppie ghetto, this sliver of
Third Ward has yet to experience a similar rebirth, and highway over-
passes, aging warehouses, cracked pavements, and peeling billboards
remain the overriding architectural theme.

No matter. Business booms at the Coffee Cup.

Every morning and noon black and white professionals, government
workers, blue-collar laborers, lawyers, judges, bankers, and realtors are
packed shoulder to elbow. It ain't the ambience. It's the cookin'—
down-home food that will warm, then eventually stop your heart.

The Coffee Cup has been owned by a loosely affiliated group of
black cooks for decades. Breakfast never changes: eggs, grits, fatback,
deep-fried salmon patties, liver mush, and the usual bacon, ham, hot-
cakes, and biscuits. At lunch the cooks are a bit more flexible. The day's
menu is posted on two or three blackboards: stew meat, pig's feet,
country steak, ribs, chicken that's fried, baked, or served with
dumplings. Vegetables include collard greens, pinto beans, cabbage,
broccoli casserole, squash and onions, creamed potatoes, and black-eyed
peas. At lunch there's corn bread in addition to biscuits.

You'd never catch Jenny Craig or Fergie dining at the Cup.

I arrived at seven-fifty. The lot was overflowing, so I parked on the street.

Worming through those patrons waiting inside the door, I noticed that every table was full. I scanned the counter. Seven men. One woman. Tiny. Short brown hair. Heavy bangs. Fortyish.

I walked over and introduced myself. When Woolsey looked up, two turquoise and silver earrings swayed with the movement.

As we exchanged introductions, a place opened up two stools down. The intervening men shifted over. Patches over their pockets identified them as Gary and Calvin.

Thanking Gary and Calvin, I sat. A black woman moved toward me, pencil poised over pad. Screw the diet. I ordered fried eggs, biscuits, and a salmon patty.

Woolsey's plate was empty save for a mound of grits topped by a lake of butter the size of Erie.

"Not fond of grits?" I asked.

"I keep trying," she said.

The waitress returned, poured coffee into a thick white mug, and placed it in front of me. Then she held the pot over Woolsey's cup, put a hand on one hip, and raised her brows. Woolsey nodded. The coffee flowed.

While I ate, Woolsey provided what background she deemed appropriate. She'd been a detective in Lancaster for seven years, before that, a uniform with the Pensacola, Florida, PD. Moved north for personal reasons. The personal reasons married someone else.

When I'd finished breakfast, we took coffee refills.

"Tell me the whole story," Woolsey said, without preamble.

Sensing this was a woman who did not fancy equivocation, I did. Woodstove. Bears. Cessna. Privy. Cocaine. Macaw. Missing fish and wildlife service agents. Headless skeleton. Cagle report.

Woolsey alternated between sipping and stirring her coffee. She didn't speak until I'd finished.

"So you think the skull and hands you found in the Mecklenburg County, North Carolina, privy go with the bones we found at the state park in Lancaster County, South Carolina."

"Yes. But the Lancaster County remains were destroyed, and I haven't been able to read the anthropology report or view the photos."

"But if you're right, the John Doe is *not* this FWS agent."

"Brian Aiker. Yes. His dentals exclude the skull."

"But if the skull and hands are *not* a match to the skeleton, our Lancaster unknown could still be Brian Aiker."

"Yes."

"In which case you guys would still have an unknown."

"Yes."

"Who could possibly turn out to be the mother of the dead baby or her boyfriend."

"Tamela Banks or Darryl Tyree. Very unlikely, but yes."

"Who might have been involved in trafficking drugs, bear galls, and endangered bird species."

"Yes."

"Out of this abandoned farm where the bears and the skull turned up."

"Yes."

"And these dealers might have been business associates of two guys who crashed a Cessna while dumping coke."

"Harvey Pearce and Jason Jack Wyatt."

"Who might have been working for some cracker who owns strip joints and wilderness camps."

"Ricky Don Dorton."

"Who turned up dead in a Charlotte flophouse."

"Yes. Look, I'm just trying to put the pieces together."

"Don't get defensive. Tell me about Cagle."

I did.

Woolsey lay down her spoon.

"What I have to say is for your ears only. Understood?"

I nodded.

"Murray Snow was a good man. Married, three kids, great father. Never thought about leaving his wife." She took a breath. "He and I were involved at the time of his death."

"How old was he?"

"Forty-eight. Found unconscious in his office. Flatlined almost immediately at the ER."

"Was there an autopsy?"

Woolsey shook her head.

"Murray's family has a history of cardiac problems. Brother died at fifty-four, father at fifty-two, grandfather at forty-seven.

Everyone assumed Murray had had the big one. Body was released and embalmed within twenty-four hours. James Park handled everything."

"The funeral operator who replaced Snow as coroner?"

Woolsey nodded.

"It's not really that unusual for Lancaster County. Murray had a bum ticker, his wife was pretty hysterical, and the family wanted things wrapped up as quickly as possible."

"And there was no coroner."

She snorted a laugh. "Right."

"Seems pretty fast."

"Pretty damn fast."

Woolsey's eyes shifted up the counter, then returned to me.

"Something didn't ring true to me. Or maybe I was just feeling guilty. Or lonely. I'm not sure why, but I dropped by the ER, asked if there was anything I could send for tox screening. Sure enough, they'd drawn blood and still had the sample."

Woolsey paused while the waitress refilled Calvin's mug.

"Tests indicated Snow had large quantities of ephedrine in his system."

I waited.

"Murray suffered from allergies. I mean *suffered*. But he was a doctor with a sketchy heart. The man wouldn't touch anything with ephedrine. I tried to talk him into an over-the-counter sinus medication once. He was adamant."

"Ephedrine is bad for people with weak hearts?"

Woolsey nodded. "Hypertension, angina, thyroid problems, heart disease. Murray knew that."

Leaning toward me, she lowered her voice.

"Murray was looking into something shortly before his death."

"What?"

"I don't know. He started to tell me once, stopped, and never talked about it again. Two months later he died."

Something I couldn't define eclipsed her face.

"I think it involved that headless set of bones."

"Why didn't you open an investigation?"

"I tried. No one took me seriously. Everyone expected Murray to die young of a heart attack. He did. No mystery. End of story."

"The ephedrine?"

"Everyone also knew about his allergies. Sheriff didn't want to hear a conspiracy theory."

"That's what he called it?"

"Said next I'd be talking about grassy knolls and second shooters."

Before I could speak, my cell phone warbled. I checked the number.

"It's Detective Slidell."

Woolsey snatched the tickets tucked under our plates.

"I'll get this and meet you outside."

"Thanks."

Winding through the tables behind Woolsey, I clicked on.

"That you, Doc?" I could barely hear Slidell.

"Hold on."

Woolsey queued up at the register. I stepped out to the parking lot. The morning was hot and breathless, the clouds gauzy wisps against a dazzling blue sky.

"That you, Doc?" Slidell repeated.

"Yes." He was expecting Oprah Winfrey on my cell phone?

"Rinaldi had a pretty good day yesterday."

"I'm listening."

"He may be putting some flesh on those bare bones of yours. Get it? Bare bones? Bear bones?"

"I get it."

"Turns out Jason Jack Wyatt, our mysterious passenger, spent a lot of time stalking and trapping. Gramma over in Sneedville puts him one notch above the Crocodile Hunter. Only, get this. J.J.'s specialty was bear. A city slicker booked into Wilderness Quest, laid down a thousand clams, J.J. scored him a bear for his trophy wall."

A car pulled up and a black couple got out. The woman wore a tight red miniskirt, pink blouse, black hose, and stiletto heels. Flesh bulged from every place her clothing allowed a gap. The man had well-muscled arms and legs, but a belly that was yielding to a love of fatback and grits.

As Slidell talked, I watched the couple enter the Cup.

"Nothin' illegal, of course," I said.

"Of course not. And the other Sneedville young'un could have been president of the chamber of commerce, were it not for the Lord calling him home so soon."

"Ricky Don."

"The Donald Trump of Sneedville."

"The grandmother admitted the two knew each other?"

"Ricky Don gave his gifted but less fortunate cousin seasonal work at the Wilderness Quest hunting camp. Also sent him on errands from time to time."

"Errands?"

"Seems J.J.'s job involved terrific travel benefits."

"Ricky Don's plane."

"Also made long car trips."

"Think Wyatt was boosting drugs for Ricky Don?"

"Could explain the blow we found in his cabin."

"No kidding."

"Would I kid you?"

"Rinaldi got a warrant?"

"He would have, of course. But Gramma insisted on a look-see to make sure no one was messing with J.J.'s posessions since his passing. She asked Rinaldi to carry her on over there in his automobile."

"I'll be damned."

"So J.J. the bear slayer might have been muling for Ricky Don Dorton and dealing a little gall on the side."

"Granny know anything about little J.J.'s phone calls to Darryl Tyree?"

"Nope."

"Sonny Pounder talking yet?"

"Remains mute as a dead cat."

"What's the word on the pilot?"

"We're still digging on Harvey Pearce."

A tall man in cornrows, gold chains, and overpriced designer sunglasses approached the door just as Woolsey started through it. Something about him looked familiar.

The man stepped back, allowed Woolsey to pass, slid the shades down his nose, and followed the progress of her buttocks.

Slidell was saying something, but I wasn't listening.

Where had I seen that face?

My brain struggled toward pattern recognition.

In person? In a photo? Recently? In the distant past?

Slidell was still talking, his voice tinny through the cell phone.

Seeing my expression, Woolsey turned back toward the Cup. The man had disappeared inside.

"What?"

I held up a finger.

"Hel-lo?" Realizing he'd lost it, Slidell was trying to regain my attention.

I was about to disconnect and return to the restaurant when the man reappeared, white paper bag in one hand, keys in the other. Crossing to a black Lexus, he opened the rear door, placed the food on the seat, and slammed the door.

Before sliding behind the wheel, the man turned in our direction.

No shades. Full frontal view.

I studied the features.

Remove the cornrows and curly little pigtails.

Synapse!

The temperature seemed to drop. The day compressed around me.

"Holy shit!"

"What?" Slidell.

"What?" Woolsey.

"Can you follow that guy?" I asked Woolsey, pointing the phone at the Lexus.

"The guy with the cornrows?"

I nodded.

She nodded back.

We bolted for her car.

28

"Brennan!"

I clicked my seat belt and braced against the dash as Woolsey made a U-ey and gunned it up Clarkson.

"What the hell's happening?"

Slidell's voice had the agitated sound of someone in jammies calling out to things going bump in the night.

I put the phone to my ear.

"I just spotted Darryl Tyree."

"How do you know it's Tyree?"

"I recognized him from Gideon Banks's Polaroid."

"Where?"

"Picking up takeout at the Coffee Cup."

"That way," I said to Woolsey, pointing up Morehead.

"What do you think you're doing?" Slidell.

"Tailing him."

The wheels screeched softly as Woolsey whipped left onto Morehead, ignoring the sign prohibiting such a turn. I could see the black Lexus a block and a half up. Tyree didn't respect traffic controls, either.

"Don't tip him that we're following," I said to Woolsey.

She gave me a "thanks for the advice" look and focused on her driving, hands clamped at ten and two o'clock on the wheel.

"Jesus H. Christ. Are you crazy?" Slidell bellowed.

"He may lead us to Tamela Banks."

"Stay the fuck away from Tyree. That Looney Tune'll cap you without breaking a sweat."

"He won't know we're on him."

"Where are you?"

I braced as Woolsey made another turn.

"Freedom Drive."

I heard Slidell call out to Rinaldi. Then his voice went jumpy, as though he were jogging.

"Jee-zus, Brennan. Why can't you and your friends just go to the mall."

I didn't favor that with a reply.

"I want you to pull over right now. Leave this to detectives."

"I'm with a detective."

"Who?"

"Terry Woolsey. She's got a badge and everything. Visiting us from South Carolina."

"You can be a real pain in the ass, Brennan."

"You are not alone in that opinion."

I heard doors slam, then an engine turn over.

"Give me your position."

"We're heading east on Tuckaseegee," I said. "Wait."

Seeing brake lights, Woolsey slowed to drop back. Tyree made a right. Woolsey sped up and made the turn. Tyree was making a left at the next intersection.

Woolsey raced up the block and rounded the corner. Tyree was turning right at the end of the block.

Woolsey shot ahead and made the turn. This time the Lexus was nowhere in sight.

"Shit!" Simultaneous.

"What?" Slidell.

We were in a neighborhood of meandering streets and dead-end cul-de-sacs. I'd been lost in such residential labyrinths many times.

Woolsey accelerated to the mouth of a small street entering from the left.

No Lexus.

As Woolsey sped up the block, I checked driveways and parked cars.

No Lexus.

At the next intersection we both looked left then right.

"There!" I said.

The Lexus was parked two-thirds of the way down on the right. Woolsey made the turn and slid to the curb.

"—the fuck are you?" Slidell sounded apoplectic.

I put the phone to my ear and gave him the address.

"Don't do anything! Nothing! Not a goddamn thing!" Slidell shrieked.

"OK if I order out for Chinese? Maybe have some spring rolls delivered to the car?"

With a click of my thumb, I cut off the explosion.

"Your friend's got some thoughts on our coming here?" Woolsey asked, eyes sweeping the street.

"He'll warm to the idea."

"He a tad rigid?"

"Skinny's nickname doesn't come from the size of his shorts."

I took in my surroundings.

Save for a slab of plywood nailed here and there, the houses looked like they'd gone through few changes since their construction sometime during the Great Depression. Paint was peeling, rust and dry rot were running a footrace.

"Your boy's probably not here for a Rotary meeting," Woolsey remarked.

"Probably not."

"Who is he?"

I explained that Tyree was the drug dealer linked to Tamela, her baby, and her missing family.

"I can't help thinking everything's related," I said. "I have no proof, but my gut feeling is that Tamela holds the key to the whole situation."

Woolsey nodded, eyes roving, assessing.

A man emerged from a house two doors over from the one Tyree had entered. He wore a do-rag and a black silk shirt flapping open over a dingy white T. Next came a woman in hip-hugging jeans, her belly hanging out like a large, brown melon. Both looked like they could use a stretch at Betty Ford.

I glanced at my watch. Seven minutes since I'd cut Slidell off.

A rusted-out Ford Tempo rolled past us, slowed opposite Tyree's Lexus, then accelerated and disappeared around the far corner.

"Think we've been noticed?" I asked.

Woolsey shrugged, then reached out and jacked up the AC. Cold air blasted from the blower.

Time check. Eight minutes since I'd disconnected with Slidell.

A group of black teens, all with baggy pants, back-turned visors, and gangsta struts rounded the corner and moved up the sidewalk in our direction. Spotting Woolsey's car, one elbowed another, and the group formed a scrum. Seconds later, they performed handshake acrobatics, then continued in our direction.

Reaching us, two of the teens hopped onto the hood, leaned back on their elbows, and crossed ankles ending in designer Nikes. A third circled to Woolsey's door, a fourth to mine.

I noticed Woolsey's hands drop from the wheel. Her right arm stayed lightly cocked, hand tense beside her right hip.

I glanced at the gangsta who'd stationed himself on my side. He looked about fifteen and slightly larger than a pet ferret.

The ferret indicated I should lower my window. I ignored him.

The ferret spread his feet, folded his arms, and gave me a hard sunglasses stare. I held the stare a full five seconds, then turned away.

Ten minutes.

The ferret's counterpart was older and accessorized with enough gold to refinance WorldCom. He tapped the knuckle of an index finger on Woolsey's window.

"Wassup?" His voice sounded muted inside the closed-up car.

Woolsey and I ignored him.

The kid draped a forearm crossways on Woolsey's window, bent, and leaned his forehead on it.

"Yo, white sisters. You lookin' to do some bidness?"

When the kid spoke, only the right half of his face rode along, as though the left suffered from Bell's palsy, or had sustained an injury that deactivated the nerves on that side.

"You lookin' fine, pretty mamas. Lower the glass so's I can talk wit' chew."

Woolsey flipped him the bird.

The kid pushed upright with both palms.

Woolsey made a shooing motion with her left hand.

The kid took one step back and gave Woolsey the ghetto glare.

Woolsey glared back.

Eleven minutes.

Bracing his feet, the kid wrapped both hands around Woolsey's side mirror and turned to her. One half of his mouth smiled. His eyes did not.

I'll never know if Woolsey was reaching for a gun or reaching for a badge. At that moment Slidell's Taurus rounded the corner, pulled over, and lurched to a stop behind us.

Though not on the upper end of the IQ curve, the little creeps harassing us could make a cop car a hundred yards off. As the doors of the Taurus flew open, the point men slid from Woolsey's hood and started moving up the block. Throwing me one last up-yours glance, the ferret joined them.

The tough guy on the driver's side straightened, formed a pistol with his right hand, and pantomimed a shot at Woolsey. Then he drum-slapped the car's hood several times with his palms, and swaggered off after his buddies.

As Slidell stormed toward us two cruisers pulled in behind the Taurus. Woolsey and I got out of the car.

"Detective Slidell, I'd like you to meet Detective Woolsey," I said.

Woolsey stuck out a hand. Slidell ignored it.

Woolsey held the proffered hand in the air between them. In my peripheral vision I saw Rinaldi emerge from the Taurus and stick-walk toward us.

"This the detective you're talking about?" Slidell jammed a thumb toward Woolsey. His face was raspberry and a vein in his forehead was pumping a gusher.

"Calm down or you're going to blow a valve," I said.

"Since when do you give a rat's ass about my valves?"

Slidell turned his scowl on Woolsey.

"You're on the job?"

"Lancaster."

"You've got no jurisdiction here."

"Absolutely none."

That seemed to disarm him some. As Rinaldi joined us, Slidell gave Woolsey's hand a perfunctory shake. Then Rinaldi and Woolsey shook.

"What's your interest here?" Slidell yanked out a hanky and did one of his face mops.

"Dr. Brennan and I were having breakfast. You know. Catching up. She asked for transportation to this location."

"That's it?"

"That'll do for now."

"Uh-huh." Slidell swiveled to me. "Where's Tyree?"

I indicated the house behind the black Lexus.

"You're sure it's Tyree."

"It's Tyree. He went in about fifteen minutes ago."

"I'll send backup to the rear," Rinaldi said.

Slidell nodded. Rinaldi walked to the second cruiser. He and the driver exchanged words, then the cruiser reversed up the block and disappeared around the corner.

"Here's what you two are going to do." Slidell bunched the hanky and shoved it into a back pocket.

"You're going to get into this nice lady detective's Chevrolet, and you're going to drive away. Go to a nail salon. Go to a yoga class. Go to a bake sale at the Methodist church. I don't care. But I want plenty of geography between you and this place."

Woolsey folded her arms, the muscles in her face rigid with anger.

"Look, Slidell," I said. "I'm sorry if I bruised your delicate sense of propriety. But Darryl Tyree is in that house. Tamela Banks and her family may be with him. Or they may be dead. In either case, Tyree may be able to lead us to them. But only if we nail his ass."

"I never would have thought of that." Slidell's voice dripped sarcasm.

"Think about it," I snapped.

"Look, *Doctor* Brennan, I was busting scum while you were still changing pumps on your Barbies!"

"You didn't break any land-speed records finding Tyree!"

"We might want to keep our voices down," Woolsey said.

Slidell spun on her.

"Now *you're* offering tips on how I should do my job?"

Woolsey held Slidell's gaze. "There's no sense in giving your collar a heads-up."

Slidell looked at Woolsey like an Israeli might a Palestinian gunman. Woolsey didn't blink.

Rinaldi rejoined us. Over Woolsey's shoulder I noticed a curtain move in a front window of the house in front of which Tyree had parked.

"I think we're being watched," I said.

"Ready?" Slidell asked Rinaldi.

Unbuttoning his jacket, Rinaldi turned and waved a come-on to the uniforms in the remaining cruiser. Their doors swung out.

At that moment the front door of the house whipped open. A figure shot down the steps, sprinted across the street, and disappeared down a walkway on the opposite side.

29

Slidell didn't blow a valve. Nor did he take down Darryl Tyree. To the best of my recollection, what happened was this.

Slidell and Rinaldi started humping up the block, legs pumping, ties flying backward. The two uniforms blew past them in seconds.

As the four cut toward the houses on the opposite side of the street from the Lexus, Woolsey and I exchanged glances, then scrambled into the nice lady detective's Chevrolet.

Woolsey hammered up the block and took the corner in a tire-screaming turn. I braced between the door handle and dash. Another hard turn and we were boogying down an alley. Gravel flew from our tires and pinged off Dumpsters and rusting car chassis moored at angles to our right and left.

"There!" I could see Rinaldi, Slidell, and one of the cops about ten yards down.

Woolsey accelerated then hit the brake. Lurching forward then back, I did a quick read of the situation.

Rinaldi and one uniform stood with feet spread, guns trained on a rat pack of arms and legs on the ground. Slidell was doubled over, hands on knees, taking in long drafts of air. His face was now something in the violet family, Rinaldi's the color of morgue flesh.

"Police!" Rinaldi panted, gun aimed in a two-handed grip.

The two men on the ground flailed like a pinned spider, cop on top, quarry beneath. Both were grunting, their backs dark with sweat. I could see gravel and fragments of cellophane and plastic in cornrows below the cop's right shoulder.

"Freeze!" the standing cop yelled.

The thrashing ratcheted up.

"Freeze, asshole!" the standing cop elaborated.

Muffled protests. Appendages writhed on the pavement.

"Now! Or I blow your junkie balls off!"

Grabbing a wrist, the wrestling cop levered one of the prone man's arms backward. Another protest, then the thrashing diminished. The wrestling cop reached to unhook cuffs from his belt.

The cornrows jerked, and the body bucked wildly, catching the wrestling cop off guard. Rolling sideways, the man broke free, lurched to his feet, and reeled forward in a half-crouch.

Without hesitating, Woolsey jackhammered into reverse, gunned backward, then forward, slamming the Chevrolet across the alley.

Shutter fast, the wrestling cop was on his feet and across the alley. He and his partner hit the man at the same time, slamming him into the side of the Chevy.

"Freeze, you fucking freak show!"

The wrestling cop again cranked one of the man's arms upward behind his back. I heard a thunk as the man's head struck the car roof.

Woolsey and I got out and looked at the man draped over her car. His wrists were cuffed and the standing cop's gun was at his temple.

Breathing hard, the wrestling cop kicked the man's feet apart and frisked him. The search produced a Glock 9-millimeter semiautomatic and two Ziploc baggies, one filled with white powder, the other with small white tablets.

Tossing the Glock and drugs to his partner, the wrestling cop spun his collar. The standing cop caught the baggies and took a step back, keeping his gun barrel trained on the man's chest.

Darryl Tyree regarded us with all-pupil eyes. One lip was bleeding. The ghetto gold chains were knotted, and the cornrows looked like they'd mopped an arena.

Slidell and Rinaldi holstered their guns and approached Tyree. Slidell was still breathing hard.

Avoiding eye contact, Tyree shifted his weight, shifted back, then back again, as though he wasn't sure what to do with his feet.

Slidell and Rinaldi crossed their arms and regarded Tyree. Neither detective spoke. Neither moved.

Tyree kept his eyes on the ground.

Slidell dug out and tapped his Camels, extracted one with his lips, and offered the pack to Tyree.

"Smoke?" Slidell's face looked scalded, his eyes furious.

Tyree gave a tight head shake, wiggling the tiny pigtails at his neckline.

Slidell lit up, inhaled, placed hands on hips, and exhaled.

"Rock and E-bombs. Planning a two-for-one sale?"

"I don' deal." Mumbled.

"I'm sorry, Darryl. I didn't hear that." Slidell turned to his partner. "You get that, Eddie?"

Rinaldi wagged his head.

"What'd you say, Darryl?"

Tyree slid his eyes to Slidell, but what little sunlight entered the alley was at the detective's back. Squinting, Tyree turned his face to one side.

"Shit's not mine."

"I got just one problem with that, Darryl. The product was traveling in your pants."

"I been set up."

"Now who would do a thing like that?"

"I been around. Man makes enemies, you know what I'm sayin'?"

"Yeah, I know. You're a tough guy, Darryl."

"You got nothin' on me. I'm jus' goin' 'bout my bidness."

"What business would that be?" Slidell.

Tyree shrugged and kicked a heel at the gravel.

Slidell took a drag, dropped the butt, and gave it a twist with the ball of one foot.

"Who you serving for, Darryl?"

Another shrug.

"Know what I think, Darryl? I think you're into some double-breasted dealing."

Tyree wagged his head on his long, goose neck.

Slidell let loose a sigh, disappointed.

"These questions too tough for you, Darryl?"

Slidell turned to his partner. "What do you think, Eddie. Think maybe we're going over Darryl's head?"

"Could try a different approach," Rinaldi said. "Learned that in my interrogation workshop. Vary the approach."

Slidell nodded.

"How's this?" Slidell turned back to Tyree. "Why'd you do Tamela Banks and her little baby?"

Tyree's eyes showed the first hint of fear.

"I didn't do nothin' to Tamela. We was together."

"Together?"

"Axe anyone. Tamela and me, we was together. Why I gonna do her?"

"That's nice, isn't it, Eddie. I mean, being together's a great thing, don't you think?"

"All you need is love," Rinaldi agreed.

Slidell turned back to Tyree.

"But you know, Darryl, sometimes a woman gets wandering eyes, know what I mean?" Slidell gave an exaggerated boys' club wink. "My way of thinking, being together means being together. Sometimes a man's gotta bring his gal back into line. Hell, we've all been down that road."

Tyree flopped his head to one side. "Beatin' on a woman is messed up."

"Maybe one little slap? A punch to the kidneys?"

"No, man. I ain't into that shit."

"How about beating on a baby?"

Tyree kicked out with one heel, his head flopped to the other side, and his eyes dropped to the ground.

"Shi-i-t."

Slidell's brows shot up in mock surprise.

"We say something to offend you, Darryl?"

Slidell turned to his partner.

"Eddie, you think we offended Darryl? Or do you think Mr. Tough Guy's got a secret he don't want to share?"

"We all have skeletons," Rinaldi played along.

"Yeah. But Darryl's was a tiny one in a great big nasty woodstove." Directed at Tyree.

"I didn't do nothin' to Tamela."

"What happened to the baby?"

"Baby jus' dead."

"And the woodstove seemed like a touching memorial?"

Another heel kick.

"Man. Why you tryin' to do me like this?"

"We're real sorry, Darryl. We realize this little setback might delay your making Eagle Scout."

Tyree shifted his feet.

"Maybe I do a little bidness. That don't mean I know nothin' 'bout Tamela."

"A little business? We just nailed you with enough blow and E to send my three nephews through Harvard."

Slidell took two steps forward and put his face inches from Tyree's.

"You're going down hard, Tyree."

Tyree tried to back up but the Chevy kept him trapped within breath range of Slidell.

"Know how long baby killers last in the joint?"

Tyree twisted his face as far to the side as his neck would allow.

"I'd say about three months." Over his shoulder to Rinaldi. "That sound about right to you, Eddie?"

"Yeah. Maybe four if you're tough."

"Like Darryl."

"Like Darryl."

I could take it no longer.

"Please," I said. "Do you know where Tamela is?"

Tyree tipped his head and glanced over Slidell's shoulder. For a moment his eyes fixed on mine. It was only a moment, but it was enough. I felt like I was looking into the dark, empty void of hell.

Wordlessly, Tyree turned away.

"Please," I said to the side of his face. "It's not too late to help yourself."

Snorting air through his nose, Tyree shifted his feet and gave a who-gives-a-shit shrug.

A terrible thought kept recycling through my brain. Tamela and her family are dead. This man knows.

This man knows a lot.

As I watched Tyree being led off, a cold, sick feeling overcame me.

*   *   *

At the MCME, Tim Larabee's office door was open. I suspected he'd been lying in wait for me. He called out as I passed.

"Hear you're bucking for a spot on *NYPD Blue*."

I stepped into his office.

"Word is you wanted to do an orifice search on Tyree. Slidell had to restrain you."

"Slidell was in no shape to restrain anybody. I thought I'd have to do CPR on him."

"Tyree tell you anything useful?"

"He's innocent as the Little Flower."

"That the kid saw the Virgin at Lourdes?"

I nodded.

"Cute analogy."

"I was taught by nuns."

"Hard to break the habit."

Eye roll.

"Now what?" Larabee asked.

"Once they've completed intake, Rinaldi and Slidell are going to grill Tyree, play him off against Sonny Pounder. One or the other will roll over."

"My money's on Pounder."

"Good bet. The question is, how much does Sonny know?"

Larabee's face got the look of a kid bursting with a secret.

"Guess who's in storage?"

Larabee's way of referring to a decedent's sojourn to the morgue. Temporary storage.

"Ricky Don Dorton."

"Old news."

"Osama bin Laden."

"Better than that."

I gave him a come-on gesture with my fingers.

The name was the last I expected to hear.

30

"BRIAN AIKER."

I felt a plunging sensation like you get just before screaming downward toward terra firma on a roller coaster. One of my toothpick towers was collapsing.

"Are you sure?"

"Body was found in Aiker's car. Lots of ID on the body. A perfect match on the dentals."

"But the skull, the Lancaster bones . . . ," I sputtered.

"Not your boy. You already knew the skull wasn't his. Turns out the bones aren't either."

"How? Where?" I was too taken aback to ask meaningful questions.

"Hauled his car out of a small lake at Crowder's Mountain State Park."

"What was Aiker doing at Crowder's Mountain?"

"Not paying attention at the wheel."

"It took five years to find him?"

"Apparently it's not a popular lake."

"Why now?"

"The region's experiencing drought conditions, water levels are down. Kid slid down the embankment or fell off the jetty or some damn thing. Car was a couple yards off a boat landing, roof twenty inches below the surface."

It happens all the time. A couple leaves a restaurant, vanishes. Two years later their Acura is found at the bottom of their neighborhood pond. Grandpa drops the kids off, heads home. Next Christmas the old man's Honda is spotted in a culvert under the highway. Mama releases the brake and steers the family SUV into a reservoir, boys and all. Four months later a propeller hits metal, and vehicle and victims are hauled from the muck.

Thousands drive, golf, pedal, or walk by accident scenes every year. No one spots anything. Then someone does.

"Windows were up, car was sealed well enough to keep the crabs and fish out," Larabee continued. "Aiker doesn't look that bad, considering how long he was in the drink."

"Where?"

Larabee misunderstood my question.

"Backseat."

"Was the body sent to Chapel Hill?"

Larabee shook his head.

"They've got two pathologists on vacation and one out sick. Chief asked if I'd mind doing the post here."

I nodded absently, my mind on bones that were *not* Brian Aiker's. Larabee picked up on my mood.

"Guess that leaves you sucking wind with the privy skull and the Lancaster bones."

"Yeah."

"Ever get that report you were waiting for?"

"No."

Larabee waited while I sorted through my thoughts. He was still waiting when his phone rang. After hesitating a moment, he reached for it.

I withdrew to my office for more sorting. The process did not go well. I tried adding coffee. No improvement.

Opening my laptop, I tried organizing in cyber bytes what I'd learned in the last eleven days.

Category: **Places.** Foote farm. Airplane crash site. Lancaster County, South Carolina. Columbia, South Carolina. Crowder's Mountain State Park.

Weren't the Lancaster remains also found in a state park? I made a note.

Category: **People.** Tamela Banks. Harvey Pearce. Jason Jack Wyatt.

Ricky Don Dorton. Darryl Tyree. Sonny Pounder. Wally Cagle. Lawrence Looper. Murray Snow. James Park. Brian Aiker.

Too broad. I tried subdividing.

Bad Guys. Harvey Pearce (dead). Jason Jack Wyatt (dead). Ricky Don Dorton (dead). Darryl Tyree (under arrest). Sonny Pounder (under arrest).

Victims.

That didn't work. I was placing too many question marks after names. I bifurcated.

Definite Victims. Tamela Banks's baby. The owner of the privy skull and hand bones. The headless skeleton from Lancaster County.

Possible Victims. Tamela Banks and her family. Wally Cagle. Murray Snow. Brian Aiker.

Did Tamela Banks and her family belong in this category? Had they really come to harm, or had they simply been spooked into going underground?

Did Tamela Banks's baby belong *out* of this category? Was it possible the baby had died of natural causes? I knew from the bones that the baby had been full-term, but it could have been stillborn.

Was Cagle's collapse real, or had his coma been induced in some way? Was Cagle's unknown visitor at the university the same man with whom Looper had seen him at the coffee shop? Why hadn't Looper taken his partner to the nearest hospital? Where was Cagle's report on the Lancaster remains?

Had Murray Snow died of natural causes? Had the Lancaster County coroner been reopening the investigation of the headless, handless remains when he died? Why?

Did Dorton belong in this category? Dorton died of an overdose. Had it been self-administered? Had he been helped?

I was getting nowhere.

Grabbing pen and paper, I tried diagramming links. I drew a line from Dorton to Wyatt and wrote *Melungeon* over it. Then I extended the line to Pearce, and printed the word *Cessna* over all three names.

I connected Tyree to Pounder, marked the line *Foote farm,* extended the line to the words "privy skull," then to the name Tamela Banks.

Connecting Tyree to the Dorton-Pearce-Wyatt line, I jotted *cocaine.*

I made a triangle linking Cagle, Snow, and the Lancaster remains, then hooked that to the Foote farm privy skull. Shooting an extender from that, I added nodes for the bear bones and bird feathers, shot a line up to J. J. Wyatt, added another, and wrote the names Brian Aiker and Charlotte Grant Cobb at its terminus.

I stared at my handiwork, a spiderweb of names and intersecting lines.

Was I trying to link unrelated events? Disparate people and places? The more I thought, the more frustrated I became with how little I knew.

Back to the laptop.

Possible Victims. Brian Aiker.

Neither the privy skull nor the Lancaster skeletal remains could be assigned to the missing FWS agent. Aiker had driven his car off a boat landing and drowned. I was deleting his name from the possible-victim category when a troubling thought stopped my hand. Why was Aiker found in the back of his vehicle?

A manageable question. Shoving back my chair, I went in pursuit of an answer.

Larabee was working in the stinky room. I knew the reason as soon as I entered.

Aiker's skin was mottled olive and brown, and most of his flesh had been converted to grave wax. Exposure to the air was not improving him.

What remained of Aiker's lungs lay sliced and splayed on a corkboard at the foot of the autopsy table. Other decaying organs rested in a hanging scale.

"How's it going?" I asked, drawing shallow breaths.

"Extensive adipocere formation. Lungs are collapsed and putrefied. Liquid putrefaction in the airways." Larabee sounded as frustrated as I felt. "What air spaces remain look diluted, but that may be due to air bubbles."

I waited while Larabee squeezed Aiker's stomach contents into a jar and handed the specimen to Joe Hawkins.

"Accidental drowning?"

"I'm not finding anything to suggest otherwise. Fingernails are broken, looks like the hands may have been abraded. The poor bastard must have struggled to get out of the car, probably tried to break a window."

"Is there any way to determine absolutely that death was by drowning?"

"Pretty tough call after five years in the drink. Could test for diatoms, I suppose."

"Diatoms?"

"Microorganisms found in plankton and freshwater and marine sediments. Been around since shortly after the big bang. Exist by the zillions. In fact, some soils are formed entirely of the little buggers. Ever hear of diatomaceous earth?"

"My sister uses DE to filter her pool."

"Exactly. The stuff is mined commercially for use in abrasives and filtering aids."

Larabee continued talking as he opened and inspected Aiker's stomach.

"It's really a kick to look at diatoms under magnification. They're beautiful little silica shells in all sorts of shapes and configurations."

"Remind me what diatoms have to do with drowning."

"Theoretically, certain waters contain certain genera of diatoms. So, if you find diatoms in the organs, the victim has drowned. Some forensic pathologists even think you can tie a drowning victim to a specific body of water."

"You sound skeptical."

"Some of my colleagues hold a lot of stock in diatoms. I don't."

"Why?"

Larabee shrugged. "People swallow diatoms."

"If we could find diatoms in the marrow cavity of a long bone, couldn't we conclude they'd gotten there by cardiac action?"

Larabee thought about that.

"Yeah. We probably could." He pointed a scalpel at me. "We'll have a femur tested."

"We should also send a sample of the lake water. If they find diatoms in the femur they can compare the profiles."

"Good point."

I waited while Larabee cut lengthwise along Aiker's esophagus.

"Is it significant that he was found in the rear seat?"

"The weight of the engine would have pulled the front of the vehicle down, leaving the last bubble of air trapped against the roof in back. When victims can't get car doors open, they crawl back and up to keep breathing as long as possible. Or sometimes the corpse just floats to the rear."

I nodded.

KATHY REICHS

"We'll run a tox screen, of course. And crime scene's processing the car and boat ramp. But I'm not finding anything suspicious."

Aiker's clothing and personal effects were drying on the counter. I walked over for a look.

It was like telescoping the agent's last morning on earth into a few soggy, mud-coated items.

Jockeys. T. Blue-and-white-striped long sleeve shirt. Jeans. Athletic socks. Adidas cross trainers. Black Polarfleece hooded jacket.

Did Aiker put his socks on before his jeans? His pants before his shirt? I felt sadness for a life so suddenly ended.

Beside the clothing lay the contents of Aiker's pockets.

Comb. Keys. Miniature Swiss army knife. Twenty-three dollars in folding money. Seventy-four cents in coins. Wallet-sized billfold with FWS badge and ID. Leather cardholder.

In addition to a North Carolina driver's license, Hawkins had removed a long-distance calling card, a US Airways Frequent Flyer card, and Diners Club and Visa credit cards from the rectangular leather pouch.

Gloving my right hand, I ran a finger across the photo on the driver's license. The steady, brown eyes and sandy hair were a long way from the grotesque distortion lying on Larabee's table.

Leaning close, I studied the face, wondering what Aiker had been doing on a boat landing at Crowder's Mountain. I picked up the license and flipped it.

Another card was adhering to the back. I peeled it off with my thumbnail. A Harris-Teeter supermarket VIC card. I laid the card on the counter and glanced back at the license.

And caught my breath.

"There's something stuck to the back of this," I said.

Both men turned to look at me. Digging forceps from a drawer, I peeled a limp, flat sheet from the back of the license.

"Looks like folded paper."

Again using forceps, I teased free an edge and tugged back a layer. One more tug, and the paper lay unfolded on the counter. Though blotchy and diluted, lettering was visible.

"It's some sort of handwritten note," I said, easing the paper onto a tray to carry it to the fluorescent magnifier. "Maybe an address or phone number. Or road directions."

"Or a last will and testament," said Hawkins.

Larabee and I looked at him.

"More likely a shopping list," Larabee said.

"Guy could've scribbled something then shoved it in between his plastic thinking maybe it'd survive." Hawkins sounded defensive. "Hell, that's probably exactly what did happen. Paper was protected from the water because it was sealed between the cards."

Hawkins had a point about the mode of preservation.

As I clicked on the tube light surrounding the lens, Hawkins and Larabee joined me. Together we viewed the writing under illumination and magnification.

> *o question. C o ins dirty.*
>   *ding to lumbia.*
> *Be car*
> *See you in tte day.*

Even under ideal conditions, the scrawl would have been hard to decipher.

"The first part is probably 'No question,'" Larabee said.

Hawkins and I agreed.

"Something to Columbia?" I suggested.

"Sending?"

"Lending?"

"Heading?"

"Landing?"

"Something's dirty." Hawkins.

"Clowns?"

"Collins?"

"Maybe that's not a C. Maybe it's an O or a Q."

"Or a G."

I positioned the magnifier closer to the paper. We leaned in and stared, each of us trying to make sense of the blotches and smears.

It was no good. Parts of the message were illegible.

"See you somewhere on some day," I said.

"Good," Hawkins and Larabee said.

"Charlotte?" I said.

"Possible," Larabee said.

"How many places end in *tte*?"

"I'll check an atlas," Larabee said, straightening. "In the meantime, the Questioned Documents guys might be able to do something with this. Joe, call over to QD and ask if we should keep this thing wet or let it dry."

Hawkins removed gloves and apron, washed his hands, and headed for the door. I clicked off the lamp.

As Larabee proceeded with his autopsy, I told him about Cagle's coma, and about my discussion with Terry Woolsey. When I'd finished, he looked up at me over his mask.

"Think maybe you're working with a lot of what-ifs, Tempe?"

"Maybe," I said.

At the door I turned for one last comment.

"But what if I don't?"

31

And what if I'd missed something?

Instead of furthering my frustration with more computerized exercise, I went to the cooler, pulled out the privy skull and hand bones, and did a full reanalysis.

The remains still whistled the same tune: thirty-something white boy.

But it wasn't Brian Aiker.

Back to the laptop.

The privy skull and hand bones turned up at the Foote farm. Bear bones and macaw feathers turned up at the Foote farm. Coincidence?

The Lancaster skeleton turned up sans head and hands. Coincidence?

The Lancaster skeleton was found three years ago. Brian Aiker vanished five years ago. Coincidence?

Brian Aiker and Charlotte Grant Cobb disappeared around the same time. Coincidence?

Bear bones and feathers from endangered bird species. Missing FWS agents. Coincidence?

Think outside the box, Brennan.

I was prying off the lid when the phone rang.

"Yo." Slidell.

"What's up?"

"Pounder's singing like a canary on crack."

"I'm listening."

"Tyree was serving coke for Dorton."

"There's a surprise."

"Dorton got the blow from a South American connection, Harvey Pearce made pickups somewhere down east near Manteo, hauled the stuff up to Charlotte from the coast. From there it went to points north and west."

"Tyree paid Pounder to use Mama Foote's farm as a relay point," I guessed.

"Bingo."

"And Dorton's cousin J.J. made his living in the family business."

"Here's the part you're really going to like. Seems Pearce got talked into buying a bird from one of the South Americans some time back, sold the thing for a nice profit. Dorton got wind of it. Ever the entrepreneur, Mr. Strip Club and Drug Lord decided to branch out."

"Let me guess. Ricky Don took advantage of little J.J.'s hunting skills."

"Pearce also supplied product from the Low Country."

Product. Rare and special animals being slaughtered for profit. What noble creatures we hominids are.

"Dorton hooked himself up with an Asian connection, became the king of gall."

"Who?" I asked.

"Pounder didn't have a name. Said he thought the mutt was Korean. Had some kind of inside line."

"Inside line on what?"

"Dick-brain wasn't sure. Don't worry. We'll nail the guy's ass."

"What's Tyree saying?"

"I want a lawyer."

"How does Tyree explain the calls between his cell phone and J. J. Wyatt's?"

"Little ragnose says things ain't always what they seem. I'm paraphrasing."

I was almost afraid to ask the next question.

"What about Tamela Banks and her family?"

"Tyree claims to know zip."

"What about the baby?"

"DOA."

Slidell's callousness curled the fingers of my free hand into a ball.

"We're talking about a dead newborn, Detective."

"Excuse me." Singsong. "I missed my charm school class this week."

"Call me when you know more."

Slamming the receiver, I leaned back and closed my eyes.

Images skittered through my mind.

Eyes devoid of caring, irises swallowed by drug-dazed pupils.

Gideon Banks's tortured face, Geneva hovering silent in a doorway.

Charred and fragmented baby bones.

I thought of my daughter.

Infant Katy in soft, footed pj's. Toddler Katy in pink ruffled swim-suit, chubby feet splashing in a plastic pool. Young woman Katy in shorts and tank, long brown legs pushing a front porch swing.

Scenes of normalcy. Scenes in which Tamela's baby would never have a part.

Needing something, but unsure what, I reached for the phone and dialed my daughter. Her roommate answered.

Lija thought Katy had gone to Myrtle Beach with Palmer Cousins, wasn't sure because she'd been away herself.

Was Katy answering her cell phone?

No.

I hung up, feeling scared.

Wasn't Katy working as a temporary receptionist at Pete's firm? This was Tuesday.

Didn't Cousins have a job to go to?

Cousins. What was it about the guy that made me uneasy?

Thinking about Cousins brought me back to Aiker.

Back to the box.

Paw your way out.

I began typing random ideas onto the screen.

Premise: The Lancaster remains and the privy remains were one person.

Deduction: That person is not Brian Aiker.

Deduction: That person is not Charlotte Grant Cobb. DNA testing confirmed that the Lancaster remains were male.

Slidell's DOA comment had me angry and on edge. Was I being unfair to him? Maybe. Still, I kept losing my train of thought.

Or was it anxiety over my daughter?

It was Slidell. The man was a bigoted, homophobic cretin. I thought about his tactless treatment of Geneva and Gideon Banks. I thought about his insensitive digs at Lawrence Looper and Wally Cagle. What was that metaphoric quagmire about sleeping in tents and buying undies? Or his pearl concerning gender roles? Oh, yeah. Nature throws the dice, you stick with the toss. Embryonic brilliance.

Outside the cube.

What appeared to be coke turned out to be goldenseal.

What appeared to be leprosy turned out to be sarcoidosis.

Another Slidellism: Things ain't always what they seem. Or was that a Tyreeism?

Outside the four squares.

An idea. Improbable, but what the hell.

I went to my purse, pulled out the card I'd taken from under Cagle's blotter, and dialed.

"South Carolina Law Enforcement Division," a female voice answered.

I made my request.

"Hold, please."

"DNA." Another female voice.

I read the name from the card.

"He's out this week."

I thought for a moment.

"Ted Springer, please."

"Who's calling?"

I identified myself.

"Hold on."

Seconds passed. A minute.

"Madam Anthropologist. What can I do for you?"

"Hi, Ted. Listen, I've got a favor to ask."

"Shoot."

"Your section did a case for the Lancaster County coroner about three years ago, headless, handless skeleton." Again, I read the name from the card, explained that the man wasn't in. "Walter Cagle did the anthro."

"Do you have a file number?"

"No."

"Makes it tougher, but God bless computers, I can track it down. What do you need?"

"I wonder if you could take a look at the amelogenin profile in the case, see if anything looks odd."

"How soon do you need this?"

I hesitated.

"I know," Springer said. "Yesterday."

"I'll owe you," I said.

"I'll collect," he said.

"Margie and the kids might not approve."

"Point taken. Give me a few hours."

I gave him my cell phone number.

Next I called Hershey Zamzow at his FWS office in Raleigh.

"I'm curious. Do you know the whereabouts of any of Charlotte Grant Cobb's family?"

"Cobb grew up in Clover, South Carolina. Parents were still living there when Charlotte went missing. As I recall, they weren't too cooperative."

"Why?"

"Insisted Cobb would turn up."

"Denial?"

"Who knows. Hold on."

I twisted the phone cord as I waited.

"I think they were real active in some church group down there, so I suppose it's possible they're still at this address. I only heard Charlotte mention her folks once. Got the impression they didn't have much to do with each other."

As I jotted the number, a question occurred to me.

"How tall was Cobb?"

"She wasn't one of those petite, little things. But she wasn't what you'd call an Amazon, either. Guess you heard about Brian Aiker?"

"Tim Larabee did the autopsy here today," I said.

"Poor bastard."

"Was Aiker working on something at Crowder's Mountain?"

"Not that I knew of."

"Any idea why he might have gone there?"

"Not a clue."

I looked at my watch. Six-forty. I'd eaten nothing since breakfast at the Coffee Cup with Woolsey.

And Boyd hadn't been out in thirteen hours.

Oh, boy.

Boyd charged the lawn like the Allies hitting Normandy. After devouring the cheeseburger I'd bought him at Burger King, he spent ten minutes trying to stare me out of my Whopper, and another five licking both wrappers.

Showing somewhat more restraint and considerably more dignity, Birdie nibbled the corner of a French fry, then sat, extended one hind leg, and diligently cleaned between his toes.

Cat and dog were sleeping when Ted Springer called from Columbia at eight.

"Microbiologists put in a long day," I said.

"I was running some samples. Listen, I found the file on your Lancaster skeleton and there may be something."

"That was quick," I said.

"I got lucky. How much do you know about the amelogenin locus?"

"Girls show one band, boys show two, one the same size as the ladies, one slightly larger."

"B-plus answer."

"Thanks."

"Amelogenin appears as two bands on a gel, but there's one nifty little variation not everyone recognizes. With normal males, the two bands are of similar intensity. You with me?"

"I think 'normal' is going to be the operative word," I said.

"With Klinefelter's males, the band representing the X chromosome is twice as intense as that representing the Y chromosome."

"Klinefelter's males?" My brain was grinding, refusing to shift into gear.

"The XXY karyotype, where there are three sex chromosomes instead of two. My colleague didn't pick up on the intensity difference."

"The unknown had Klinefelter's syndrome?"

"The system's not one hundred percent."

"But KS is a good possibility in this case?"

"Yes. That help any?"

"It just might."

I sat motionless, like a hunting trophy that's been stuffed and mounted.

Klinefelter's syndrome.

XXY.

A bad roll of Slidell's embryonic dice.

Booting up the computer, I began surfing. I was working through the Klinefelter's Syndrome Association Web site when Boyd nudged my knee.

"Not now, boy."

Another nudge.

I looked down.

Boyd put a paw on my knee, raised his snout, and snapped at the air. Gotta go.

"Is this on the level?"

Boyd dashed across the room, spun, snapped, and twirled the eye hairs.

I checked the time. Ten-fifteen. Enough.

Killing the computer and lights, I headed for Boyd's leash.

The chow danced me out of the den, thrilled at the prospect of one last sortie before bedding back down.

The darkness in the annex was almost total, relieved only by heat lightning flickering through the trees. Inside, the mantel clock ticked. Outside, moths and June bugs fought the windows, their bodies making dull, thudding sounds against the screens.

When we entered the kitchen Boyd's demeanor changed. His body tensed, and his ears and tail shot up. A short growl, then he lunged forward and began barking at the door.

My hand flew to my chest.

"Boyd," I hissed. "Come here."

Boyd ignored me.

I shushed him. The dog kept barking.

Heart pounding, I crept to the door and pressed my back to the wall, listening.

A car horn. June bugs. Crickets. Nothing out of the ordinary.

Boyd's barking was becoming more urgent. His hackles were up now. His body was rigid.

Again I shushed him. Again he ignored me.

Over Boyd's barking, I heard a thunk, then a soft scraping just outside the door.

My insides turned to ice.

Someone was there!

Call 911! my brain cells screamed. Run to the neighbors! Escape through the front door!

Escape from what? Tell 911 what? A bogeyman is on my porch? The Grim Reaper is at my back door?

I reached for Boyd. The dog twisted from me and continued his protest.

Was the door locked? Usually I was good about security, but sometimes I slipped. Had I forgotten in my hurry to let Boyd out?

Fingers trembling, I felt for the lock.

The little oblong knob was horizontal. Locked? Unlocked? I couldn't remember!

Should I test the handle?

Don't make a sound! Don't let him know you're here!

Had I engaged the security system? I usually did that just before going upstairs to bed. My eyes slid to the panel.

No flashing red light!

Damn!

Hands shaking badly now, I lifted a corner of the window curtain.

Pitch-black.

My eyes struggled to adjust.

Nothing.

I leaned close to the glass, shot my eyes left, then right, peering through the tiny opening I'd created.

No go.

Turn on the porch light, one rational brain cell suggested.

My hand groped for the switch.

No! Don't tell him you're home!

My hand froze.

At that moment the sky flickered. Two silhouettes emerged from the darkness.

Adrenaline rocketed through my body.

The two silhouettes were standing on my back porch, less than two feet from my terrified face.

32

THE FIGURES STOOD FROZEN, TWO BLACK CUTOUTS AGAINST A pitch-black night.

I dropped the curtain and shrank back, heart pounding in my throat.

The Grim Reaper? With an accomplice?

Barely breathing, I stole another peek.

The space between the figures appeared to have shrunk.

The space between the figures and my door appeared to have shrunk.

What to do?

My terrified brain came up with variations on the same suggestions.

Phone 911! Throw on the porch light! Yell through the door!

Boyd's barking continued, steady but unfrenzied.

The sky flickered, went black.

Was my mind playing tricks, or did the larger silhouette look familiar?

I waited.

More lightning, longer. One, two, three seconds.

Sweet Jesus.

She looked even bulkier than my recollection.

My hand brushed the wall, found the switch. The overhead bulb bathed the porch in amber.

"Hush, Boyd."

I laid a hand on his head.

"Is that you, Geneva?"

"Don't be setting no dog on us."

Reaching down, I grasped Boyd's collar. Then I unlocked and opened the door.

Geneva had one arm around a young woman I immediately recognized as Tamela, the other thrown up across her face. Both sisters resembled frightened deer, their eyes blinded by the unexpected light.

"Come in." Still holding the chow's collar, I pushed open the screen.

Clearance having been granted the callers, Boyd's barking gave way to tail wagging.

The sisters didn't budge.

I stepped backward into the kitchen, dragging Boyd with me.

Geneva opened the screen door, nudged Tamela inside, followed.

"He won't hurt you," I said.

The sisters looked wary.

"Really."

I released Boyd and turned on the kitchen lights. The chow hopped forward and began sniffing Tamela's legs, his tail doing double time.

Geneva stiffened.

Tamela reached down and tentatively patted Boyd's head. The dog twisted and licked her fingers. They looked so delicate, the hand could have been that of a ten-year-old child. Except for the bloodred nails.

Boyd shifted to Geneva. She glared at him. Boyd shifted back to Tamela. She squatted, rested one knee on the floor, and ruffled his fur.

"A lot of folks have been searching for you," I said, looking from one sister to the other. I tried to mask my surprise. After all this time, Tamela was actually standing in my kitchen.

"We're OK." Geneva.

"Your father?"

"Daddy's fine."

"How did you find me?"

"You left your card."

My surprise must have broken through at that.

"Daddy knew how to find you."

I let it go, assuming Gideon Banks had obtained my home address through some university source.

"I'm very relieved to see you're safe. Can I get you a cup of tea?"

"Coke?" Tamela asked, rising.

"I have Diet."

"OK." Disappointed.

I gestured to the table. They sat. Boyd followed and put his chin on Tamela's knee.

I didn't want Coke, but popped three cans to be sociable. Returning to the table, I placed a soda in front of each sister and took a chair.

Geneva was dressed in a V-necked UNCC Forty-niners jersey and the same shorts she'd worn the day Slidell and I visited her father. Her limbs and belly looked bloated, the skin on her elbows and knees cracked and wrinkled.

Tamela wore a backless red halter that tied behind her neck and ribs, orange and red polyester skirt, and pink flip-flops with rhinestones on the plastic band. Her arms and legs were long and bony.

The contrast was striking. Geneva was hippo, Tamela pure gazelle.

I waited.

Geneva looked around the kitchen.

Tamela chewed gum, nervously scratched Boyd's muzzle. She seemed skittish, unable to remain still for more than a second.

I waited.

The refrigerator hummed.

I waited long enough for Geneva to collect her thoughts. Long enough for Tamela to settle her nerves.

Long enough for the entire five movements of Schubert's *Trout Quartet.*

Finally, Geneva broke the silence, eyes now on her Coke.

"Darryl off the street?"

"Yes."

"Why's he in jail?" Heat lightning pulsed in the window behind her.

"There's evidence Darryl's been dealing drugs."

"He gonna do jail time?"

"I'm not a lawyer, Geneva. But I would guess that he is."

"You guess." For some reason Tamela directed the comment to Geneva.

"Yes," I said.

"How do you know?" Tamela canted her head sideways, like Boyd studying a curiosity.

"I don't know for sure."

There was another long silence. Then, "Darryl didn't kill my baby."

"Tell me what happened."

"It weren't Darryl's baby. I was with him, but it weren't Darryl's baby."

"Who is the father?"

"White boy named Buck Harold. But it don't matter. What I'm sayin' is Darryl didn't do that baby no harm."

I nodded.

"Baby didn't belong to Darryl and I don't, like, belong to him, know what I'm sayin'?"

"Tell me what happened to your baby."

"I was staying at Darryl's place—well, it weren't his place but he was living there, like, in one of the rooms. So, one day, like, I start having pains and I figure my time come. But the pain just keeps getting worse and worse, and nothing happens. I knew something was wrong."

"No one got you medical care?"

She laughed, looked at me like I'd suggested she apply to Yale.

"After that night and the next day, finally the baby came out, but it was messed up."

"What do you mean?"

"It was blue and it wouldn't take no breath."

Her eyes glistened. Looking away, she swiped the heel of a palm across each cheek.

A steel shaft entered my chest. I believed her story. I felt pain for this young woman and for her unbearable loss. Pain for all the Tamelas of this world and their babies.

I reached out and laid my hand on hers. She pulled back, dropped both hands to her lap.

"You put the baby's body in the woodstove?" I asked gently.

She nodded.

"Darryl told you to do that?"

"No. Don't know why I did it, I jus' did it. Darryl still believin' it's his baby, getting off on the fatherhood trip."

"I see."

"Nobody did nothin' to that baby." Tears glistened on her face, and her bony chest heaved below the red halter top. "It was just born wantin' to be dead."

Tamela wiped her cheeks again, anger and sorrow betrayed by the roughness of the gesture. Then she curled her fingers and rested her forehead on her fists.

"You couldn't revive it?"

Tamela could only shake her head.

"Why did you go into hiding?"

Tamela looked over her knuckles at Geneva.

"Go on," Geneva said. "We're here. Now you tell her."

Tamela drew several unsteady breaths.

"One day Darryl gets to fighting with Buck. Buck tells him I been playin' him the fool and the baby was his. Darryl goes batshit, decides I killed my own baby to dis him. He say he gonna find me and mess me up bad."

"Where did you go?"

"Cousin's basement."

"Your father is there now?"

Two head shakes.

"Daddy's went over to his sister in Sumter. She drove up and got him, but she won't have nothin' to do with us. Say we the devil's own offspring, and we gonna burn in hell."

"Why have you come to see me?"

Neither sister would raise her eyes to mine.

"Geneva?"

Geneva kept her gaze on the fingers curled around her Coke.

"We gonna tell her," she said, her voice flat.

Tamela gave a suit-yourself shrug.

"This mornin' my cousin is poundin' on the door, yellin' her man looking at my sister too much, yellin' at us to get out. Daddy's mad at us, our own kin's mad at us, and Darryl's wantin' to kill us."

Geneva's head was down so I couldn't see her face, but the trembling in her ponytail revealed her desperation.

"We gotta leave where we was, we can't go home, case Darryl get out and come looking for us." Her voice trailed off. "We run out of places."

"I ain't—" Tamela started, but couldn't finish.

I reached over and placed one hand on each of theirs. This time she didn't pull away.

"You will stay with me until it's safe to go home."

"We won't take nothin'." Tamela's words were hushed. The voice of a frightened child.

I took Boyd for a five-minute walk. Then we spent half an hour digging out towels and bedding for the sleeper sofa. By the time the Banks sisters were settled, Boyd having been granted a place in the den over Geneva's objection, it was well past eleven.

Too agitated to sleep, I took my laptop to my bedroom, logged on, and resumed my Klinefelter's research. I'd been at it ten minutes when my cell phone rang.

"What's wrong?" Ryan sounded alarmed at the tenor of my voice.

I told him about Geneva and Tamela.

"You sure it's legit?"

"I think so."

"Well, be careful. They could be fronting for this mope Tyree."

"I'm always careful." No need to mention that moment of uncertainty concerning the lock. Or the unset alarm.

"You must be relieved that the Bankses are safe."

"Yes. And I think I've discovered something else."

"Does it have to do with fractals?"

"Ever heard of Klinefelter's syndrome?"

"No."

"How are you fixed for chromosomes?"

"Twenty-three pairs. Should hold me."

"That would suggest that something about you is normal."

"I have a feeling I'm about to learn about chromosomes."

I let him listen to the sound of me saying nothing.

"OK." I heard a match strike, then a deep inhalation. "Please?"

"As you so astutely point out, genetically normal individuals have twenty-three pairs of chromosomes, one per set coming from each parent. Twenty-two pairs are called autosomes, the other pair is made up of the sex chromosomes."

"XX gets you the pink booties, XY gets you the blue."

"You're a whiz, Ryan. Occasionally, something goes awry in the formation of an egg or sperm, and an individual is born with one chromosome too many or one chromosome too few."

"Down's syndrome."

"Exactly. People with mongolism, or Down's syndrome, have an extra chromosome in the twenty-first pair of autosomes. The condition is also called trisomy 21."

"I think we're getting to Mr. Klinefelter."

"Sometimes the abnormality involves a missing or an extra sex chromosome. XO women have a condition called Turner's syndrome. XXY men have Klinefelter's syndrome."

"What about YO men?"

"Not possible. No X, no survival."

"Tell me about Klinefelter's."

"Since there's a Y chromosome in the genome, XXY, Klinefelter's syndrome individuals are male. But they have small testes, and suffer from testosterone deficiency and infertility."

"Are they physically distinct?"

"KS men tend to be tall, with disproportionately long legs and little body or facial hair. Some are pear-shaped. Some exhibit breast development."

"How common is the condition?"

"I've read figures ranging from one in five hundred to one in eight hundred male conceptions. That makes KS the most common of the sex chromosome abnormalities."

"Any behavioral implications?"

"KS individuals have a high incidence of learning disabilities, sometimes decreased verbal IQ, but usually normal intelligence. Some studies report increased levels of aggression or antisocial behavior."

"I don't imagine these kids feel really good about themselves growing up."

"No," I agreed.

"Why are we interested in Klinefelter's syndrome?"

I told him about Brian Aiker, and recounted my conversations with Springer and Zamzow. Then I shared my boxless idea.

"So you think the privy skull goes with the Lancaster skeleton, and that the person could be Charlotte Grant Cobb."

"Yes." I told him why. "It's a long shot."

"Zamzow told you Cobb wasn't that tall," Ryan said.

"He said she wasn't an Amazon; if the leg bones were disproportionately long, that would have skewed the height estimate."

"What do you plan to do?"

"Track down Cobb's family, ask a few questions."

"Can't hurt," Ryan said.

I updated him on what I'd learned from Slidell and Woolsey.

"Curiouser and curiouser." Ryan liked saying that.

I hesitated.

What the hell.

"See you soon?" I asked.

"Sooner than you think," he said.

Yes!

After checking a map on Yahoo! I crawled into bed.

Can't hurt, I thought, echoing Ryan.

How wrong we both were.

33

NEXT MORNING, I WAS UP AT SEVEN-THIRTY. SILENCE IN THE DEN suggested Geneva and Tamela were still dead to the world. After spinning Boyd around the block, I filled pet bowls, set cornflakes and raisin bran on the kitchen table, jotted a note, and hopped into the car.

Clover lies just beyond the North Carolina–South Carolina border, halfway between a dammed-up stretch of the Catawba River, called Lake Wylie, and the Kings Mountain National Park, site of Ryan and Boyd's Revolutionary War excursion. My friend Anne calls the town Clo-vay, giving the name a je ne sais quoi panache.

During off-peak traffic hours the trip to Clo-vay takes less than thirty minutes. Unfortunately, every driver registered in either the Palmetto or the Old North State was on the road that morning. Others had joined them from Tennessee and Georgia. And Oklahoma. And Guam. I crept down I-77, alternately sipping my Starbucks and drumming the wheel.

Clover was incorporated in 1887 as a railway stopover, then boomed as a textile center in the early nineteen hundreds. Water seepage from the railroad tanks kept the place damp and carpeted with clover, earning it the name Cloverpatch. Aspiring to a more imposing image, or perhaps wanting to dissociate from the Yokums and the Scraggs, some citizens' committee later shortened the name to Clover.

The image polishing didn't help. Though Clover is still home to a few mills, and things like brake parts and surgical supplies are cranked out nearby, nothing much happens there. A perusal of chamber of commerce literature suggests that good times are had elsewhere: Lake Wylie, the Blue Ridge Mountains, the Carolina beaches, Charlotte Knights baseball games, Carolina Panthers football games.

There are a few antebellum homes hiding in the hills around Clover, but it's not a place for French country hand towels and stripy umbrellas. Though very Norman Rockwell, the town is strictly blue-collar, or, more correctly, no-collar.

By nine-forty I was at the point where US 321 crosses SC 55, the beating heart of downtown Clover. Two- and three-story redbrick buildings lined both blacktops forming the intersection. Predictably, Route 321 was called Main Street along this stretch.

Remembering the Yahoo! map, I went south on 321, then made a left onto Flat Rock Road. Three more rights and I found myself on a dead-end street lined with longleaf pines and scrub oaks. The address Zamzow had given me led to a double-wide on a cement slab eighty yards down at the far end.

A front stoop held two metal lawn chairs, one bare, the other with green floral cushions in place. To the right of the trailer I could see a vegetable garden. The front yard was filled with whirligigs.

A carport hung by suction cups to the trailer's left end, its interior filled with oddly shaped stacks covered with blue plastic sheeting. A stand of shagbark hickories threw shadows across a rusted swing set to the left of the carport.

I pulled onto the gravel drive, killed the engine, and crossed the yard to the front door. Among the whirligigs I recognized Little Bo Peep. Sleepy and Dopey. A mother duck leading four miniature versions of herself.

A skeletal woman with eyes that seemed too large for her face answered the bell. She wore a saggy, pill-covered cardigan over a faded polyester housedress. The garments draped her fleshless form like clothes hanging on a hanger.

The woman spoke to me through an aluminum and glass outer door.

"Got nothing this week." She stepped back to close the inner door.

"Mrs. Cobb?"

"You with the kidney people?"

"No, ma'am. I'm not. I'd like to talk to you about your daughter."

"Got no daughter."

Again the woman moved to close the door, then hesitated, vertical lines creasing the bone-tight flesh on her forehead.

"Who are you?"

I dug a card from my purse and held it to the glass. She read the card then looked up, eyes filled with thoughts that had nothing to do with me.

"Medical examiner?" she said.

"Yes, ma'am." Keep it simple.

The aluminum grillwork rattled when she pushed open the door. Cold seeped outward, like air from a recently unlocked tomb.

Wordlessly the woman led me to the kitchen and gestured toward a small table with antique green legs and a simulated wood top. The trailer's interior smelled of mothballs, pine disinfectant, and old cigarette smoke.

"Coffee?" she asked as I seated myself.

"Yes, please." The thermostat must have been set at fifty-eight. Goose bumps were forming on my neck and arms.

The woman took two mugs from an overhead cabinet and filled them from a coffeemaker on the counter.

"It is Mrs. Cobb, isn't it?"

"It is." Mrs. Cobb set the mugs on the simulated wood. "Milk?"

"No, thank you."

Sliding a pack of Kools from the top of the refrigerator, Mrs. Cobb took the chair opposite mine. Her skin looked waxy and gray. A growth protruded from a comma below her left eyelid, looking like a barnacle on the side of a pier.

"Got a light?"

I dug matches from my purse, struck one, and held it to her cigarette.

"Can't ever find the darned things when I need them."

She inhaled deeply, exhaled, flicked a finger at the matches.

"Put those away. I don't want to be smoking too many." She snorted a laugh. "Bad for my health."

I shoved the matches into my jeans pocket.

"You want to talk about my child."

"Yes, ma'am."

Mrs. Cobb fished a Kleenex from a sweater pocket, blew her nose, then took another drag.

"My husband's dead two years come November."

"I'm sorry for your loss."

"He was a good, Christian man. Headstrong, but a good man."

"I'm sure you miss him."

"Lord knows I do."

A cuckoo popped from its clock above the sink and sounded the hour. We both listened. Ten chirps.

"He gave me that clock for our twenty-fifth wedding anniversary."

"It must be very dear to you."

"Fool thing's kept working all these years."

Mrs. Cobb drew on her Kool, eyes fixed on a point midway between us. On a point years past. Then her chin cocked up as a sudden thought struck her.

Her gaze shifted to me.

"You find my child?"

"We might have."

Smoke curled from her cigarette and floated across her face.

"Dead?"

"It's a possibility, Mrs. Cobb. The ID is complicated."

She brought the cigarette to her lips, inhaled, exhaled through her nose. Then she flicked the ash and rotated the burning tip on a small metal saucer until the fire went out.

"I'll be joining Charlie Senior shortly. I believe it's time to set a few things right."

She rose from her chair and shuffled toward the back of the trailer, slippers swishing on the indoor-outdoor carpet. I heard rustling, what sounded like a door.

Minutes cuckooed by. Hours. A decade.

Finally, Mrs. Cobb returned with a bulky green album bound with black cording.

"I think the old goat will forgive me."

She laid the album in front of me and opened it to the first page. Her breathing sounded wheezy as she leaned over my shoulder to jab at a snapshot of a baby on a plaid blanket.

The finger moved to a baby in an old-fashioned bassinet. A baby in a stroller.

She flipped ahead several pages.

A toddler holding a plastic hammer. A toddler in blue denim coveralls and bicycle cap.

Two more pages.

A towheaded boy of about seven in cowboy hat and twin holsters. The same boy suited up for baseball, bat on one shoulder.

Three pages.

A teen with palm extended in protest, face twisted away from the lens. The teen was about sixteen, and wore an enormous golf shirt over baggy cutoffs.

It was the hammer-baseball-buckaroo boy, though his hair was darker now. The visible cheek was smooth and pink and dotted with acne. The boy's hips were wide, his body softly feminine, with a marked lack of muscle definition.

I looked up at Mrs. Cobb.

"My child. Charles Grant Cobb."

Circling the table, she sat and wrapped her fingers around her mug.

For sixty ticks we both listened to the cuckoo. I broke the silence.

"Your son must have had a difficult time during his teenage years."

"Charlie Junior just never went through the right changes. He never grew a beard. His voice never changed, and his—" Five ticks. "You know."

XXY. A Klinefelter's syndrome boy.

"I do know, Mrs. Cobb."

"Kids can be so cruel."

"Was your son ever examined or treated?"

"My husband refused to admit there was anything wrong with Charlie Junior. When puberty came, and nothing seemed to happen except for Charlie Junior getting heavier and heavier, I suspected something wasn't right. I suggested we have him looked at."

"What did the doctors say?"

"We never went." She shook her head. "There were two things Mr. Cobb hated with all his might. Doctors and fags. That's what he called, well, you know."

She dug for another Kleenex, blew her nose again.

"It was like arguing with a cinder block. To his dying day Charlie Senior believed Charlie Junior just needed to toughen up. That's what he was always telling him. Tough up, kid. Be a man. No one likes a girly boy. No one likes a pansy."

I looked at the boy in the photo, and thought of cool guys shoving geeks in the halls at school. Of kids taking lunch money from smaller kids. Of loudmouthed bullies picking at flaws and frailties, making others bleed like unhealed scabs. Of kids taunting, tormenting, persecuting until their victims finally give up on themselves.

I felt anger, frustration, and sadness.

"After Charlie Junior left home he decided to live as a female," I guessed.

She nodded.

"I'm not sure exactly when he switched, but that's just what he did. He"—she struggled for the proper pronoun—"*she* visited once, but Charlie Senior pitched a fit, told him not to come back until he'd straightened himself out. I hadn't seen Charlie in over ten years when he"—more pronoun confusion—"when he went missing."

Conspiratorial smile.

"I talked to him, though. Charlie Senior didn't know that."

"Often?"

"He'd call about once a month. He was a park ranger, you know."

"A Fish and Wildlife Service agent. That's a very demanding profession."

"Yes."

"When was the last time you spoke with Charlie Junior?"

"It was early December, five years ago. I got a call from a cop not long after, asking if I knew where *Charlotte* was. That's what Charlie Junior took to calling himself. Herself."

"Was your son working on anything in particular at the time of his disappearance?"

"Something to do with people killing bears. He was pretty fired up about it. Said people were slaughtering bears by the bushel just to make a few bucks. But, as I recall, he talked about it like it was something on the side, not an official assignment. Like it was something he just stumbled on. I think he was really supposed to be looking out for turtles."

"Did he mention any names?"

"I think he said something about a Chinese. But wait." She tapped a bony finger to her lips, raised it in the air. "He said there was a guy in Lancaster and a guy in Columbia. Don't know if that had to do with bears or turtles, but I remember wondering about it later, because Charlie Junior was working up in North Carolina, not down here."

The clock cuckooed once, marking the half hour.

"More coffee?"

"No, thanks."

She rose to refill her cup. I spoke to her back.

"Skeletal remains have been found, Mrs. Cobb. I believe they could be those of your son."

Her shoulders slumped visibly.

"Someone will be phoning?"

"I'll call you myself when we're sure."

She balled her fists, slipped them into the pockets of her sweater.

"Mrs. Cobb, may I ask one last question?"

She nodded.

"Why didn't you share this information with those investigating your son's disappearance?"

She turned and regarded me with melancholy eyes.

"Charlie Senior said Charlie Junior'd probably gone off to San Francisco or somewhere so's he could pursue his lifestyle. I believed him."

"Did your son ever say anything to suggest he was considering a move?"

"No."

She raised her mug to her lips, set it back down on the counter.

"Guess I believed what I wanted to believe."

I rose. "I should be going."

At the door, she asked one last question.

"You read much Scripture?"

"No, ma'am, I don't."

Her fingers bunched and rebunched the Kleenex.

"I can't figure the world out." Barely audible.

"Mrs. Cobb," I said, "on my best days, I can't figure myself out."

Weaving through the whirligigs, I felt eyes on my back. Eyes filled with loss and sadness and confusion.

As I walked toward my car, something on the windshield caught my attention.

What the hell?

Two paces more and the object grew focused.

I stopped in my tracks.

One hand flew to my mouth. My stomach rolled over.

Swallowing hard, I took two steps closer. Three. Four.

Dear God.

Revolted, I closed my eyes.

An image crawled through my mind. Crosshairs on my chest.

My heartbeat shot into the stratosphere. My eyes flew open.

Did the Grim Reaper have me in his sights? Had I been followed?

I had to force myself to look at the macabre little form scare-crowed against my windshield.

Propped between the wiper blade and the glass was a squirrel. Eyes glazed, belly slit, innards sprouting like mushrooms on a rotting log.

34

I WHIPPED AROUND.

The inner and aluminum doors were closed.

I scanned the block.

One jogger with a mongrel dog.

Had I been followed? I felt a chill spread through my gut.

Holding my breath, I lifted the wiper blade, took the squirrel by its tail, and tossed it into the trees. Though my hands were shaking, my mind was automatically taking notes.

Stiff. Not freshly dead.

Digging Bojangles' napkins from the glove compartment, I cleaned the glass and slid behind the wheel.

Use the adrenaline. Go with it.

Gunning the engine, I shot up the road.

The jogger and dog were rounding the corner. I turned with them.

The woman was thirtyish, and looked like she should jog more often. She wore a spandex bra and bicycle shorts, and headphones with a small antenna framed a blonde ponytail. The dog was attached to one of those blue plastic leash feeders.

I rolled down the window.

"Excuse me."

The dog turned, the jogger did not.

"Excuse me," I shouted, inching forward.

The dog cut to the car, nearly tripping its owner. She stopped, dropped the headphones around her neck, and regarded me warily.

The dog placed front paws on my door and sniffed. I reached out and patted its head.

The jogger appeared to relax a bit.

"Do you know Mrs. Cobb?" I asked, the calm in my voice belying my agitation.

"Uh-huh," she panted.

"While we were visiting, something was left on my windshield. I wondered if you'd noticed any other cars near her trailer."

"Actually, I did. That road is a dead end, so it doesn't get much traffic." She pointed a finger at the dog, then at the ground. "Gary, get down."

Gary?

"It was a Ford Explorer, black. Man at the wheel. Not very tall. Good hair. Sunglasses."

"Black hair?"

"Lots of it." She giggled. "My husband is bald. *Balding,* he'd say. I notice hair on men. Anyway, the Explorer was just parked there opposite Mrs. Cobb's driveway. I didn't recognize the car, but it had a South Carolina tag."

The woman called to Gary. Gary dropped to the pavement, hopped back up against my side panel.

"Is Mrs. Cobb doing all right? I try, but I don't get over to her place very often."

"I'm sure she'd appreciate company," I said, my thoughts on a black-haired stranger.

"Yeah."

Tugging Gary from my door, the woman repositioned her headphones and resumed her jog.

I sat a moment, debating my next move. Talking myself down.

Lancaster and Columbia.

Short with black hair. *Good* black hair.

That described Wally Cagle's coffee partner.

That described Palmer Cousins.

That described a million men in America.

Did it describe the Grim Reaper?

What the hell was going on?

Calm down.

I took a deep breath and tried Katy's cell phone.

No answer. I left a message on her voice mail.

Lancaster and Columbia.

I phoned Lawrence Looper to check on Wally Cagle.

Answering machine. Message.

I phoned Dolores at the USC anthropology department.

Wonderful news. Wally Cagle was coming around. No, he was not yet coherent. No, he'd had no other visitors at the university.

I thanked her and hung up.

What would another trip to Columbia accomplish? Spook Looper? Spook Palmer Cousins? Locate Katy? Thoroughly piss off Katy for trying to locate her? Thoroughly piss off Skinny Slidell?

A trip to Lancaster?

Clover was halfway there.

Wouldn't piss off Katy.

Skinny would get over it.

Cagle wasn't coherent yet, anyway.

I headed south on 321, then east on 9, eyes constantly clicking to the rearview mirror. Twice I spotted what I thought were black Explorers. Twice I slowed. Twice the vehicles passed me. Though outwardly composed, the chill stayed with me.

Five miles out of Lancaster, I phoned Terry Woolsey at the sheriff's department.

"Detective Woolsey isn't in today," a man's voice said.

"Can I call her at home?"

"Yes, ma'am, you can."

"But you're not allowed to give me the number."

"No, ma'am, I'm not."

Damn! Why hadn't I gotten Woolsey's home number?

I left Woolsey a message.

"How about a number for the county coroner?"

"That I can give you." He did. "Mr. Park might be in." He didn't sound like he believed it. "If not, you could try him at his funeral home."

I thanked him. Disconnecting, I spotted another black SUV. When I looked up from dialing the coroner's office, the vehicle was gone. The chill intensified.

The operator was right. Park wasn't in. I left my fourth message in ten minutes, then stopped at a gas station to ask directions to the funeral home.

The attendant conferred with his teenaged assistant, a lengthy discussion ensued, agreement was finally reached: Follow Highway 9 until it becomes West Meeting Street. Hang a right onto Memorial Park Drive, cross the tracks, hang another right about a quarter mile down, watch for the sign. If you pass the cemetery, you've gone too far.

Neither could remember the name of the road on which the funeral home was located.

Who needed Yahoo!? I had my own pair.

But their directions were accurate. Fifteen minutes and two turns later I spotted a wooden sign supported by two white pillars. Embossed white letters announced the Park Funeral Home and listed the services provided.

I turned in and followed a winding drive bordered by azaleas and boxwoods. Rounding my ninth or tenth curve, I spotted a gravel lot and a group of structures. I parked and surveyed the setup.

The Park Funeral Home was not a large operation. Its nerve center was a one-story brick affair with two wings and a central portion that stuck out in front, two sets of triple windows to either side of the main entrance, and a chimney on an asphalt tile roof above.

Behind the main building I could see a small brick chapel with a tiny steeple and double doors. Behind the chapel were two wooden structures, the larger probably a garage, the smaller probably a storage shed.

Ivy and periwinkle covered the ground around and between the buildings, and tangles of morning glories crawled up their foundations. Elms and live oaks kept the entire compound in perpetual shadow.

As I got out, the goose bumps did a curtain call. My mind made an addition to the services listed on the entrance sign. Funerals. Cremation. Grief support. Planning. Perpetual shadow.

Stop the melodrama, Brennan.

Good advice.

Nevertheless, the place creeped me out.

I walked to the large brick building and tried the door. Unlocked.

I let myself into a small foyer. White plastic letters on a gray board indicated the locations of reception, the arrangement room, the pallbearers' room, and parlors one and two.

Someone named Eldridge Maples was booked into parlor two.

I hesitated. Was "arrangement room" a euphemism for office? Was "reception" for the living? White plastic arrows indicated that both venues lay straight ahead.

I stepped through the foyer door into an ornately decorated hall with deep lavender carpet and pale rose walls. The doors and woodwork were glossy white, and white faux Corinthian columns, complete with rosettes and volutes at ceiling height, hugged the walls at intervals.

Or were they Doric? Didn't Corinthian columns have capitals at the top? No, Corinthian columns had rosettes.

Stop!

Queen Anne sofas and love seats filled every inter-columnar space. Beside each, mahogany tables held silk flowers and Kleenex boxes.

Potted palms flanked closed double doors to my right and left. A grandfather clock stood sentry at the far end of the corridor, its slow, steady ticking the only sound in the crushing stillness.

"Hello?" I called out softly.

No one answered. No one appeared.

I tried again, slightly louder.

Gramps tocked on.

"Anyone here?"

It was my morning for ticking clocks.

I was considering "arrangements" versus "reception" when my cell phone shrilled. I jumped and then looked around, hoping my skittishness hadn't been noticed. Seeing no one, I scurried out to the foyer, and clicked on.

"Yes," I hissed.

"Yo."

My eyes did a full orbital roll. Had the man never learned to say "hello"?

"Yes?" I hissed again.

"You in church or something?" Slidell sounded like he was working on one of his ubiquitous Snickers.

"Something."

"Where the hell are you?"

"At a funeral. Why are you calling?"

There was a pause while Slidell mulled that over.

"Doc Larabee asked me to give you a shout. Said he had feedback from the Questioned Documents section, figured you'd want to know."

For a moment my mind didn't link over.

"The note you and Doc found in Aiker's shorts?"

I didn't bother to point out the note's correct provenance.

"Doc said to tell you that you were right about Columbia," Slidell said.

Irrationally, I turned my back to the hallway entrance, as though dead Mr. Maples might pose an eavesdropping threat.

"The writer of the note was going to Columbia?"

"Looks that way. QD guys used some sort of voodoo light, managed to bring out a few of the missing letters."

"Anything else?"

A door slammed in the vicinity of the chapel or garage. I cracked the entrance door and peeked out. No one was in sight.

"The only other word they could make out was 'cousins.'"

My brain sparked like an electrical short.

No question. Cousins dirty. Heading to Columbia.

It was like being slapped awake.

A short, muscular man with thick black hair. A FWS agent who knew nothing about bear poaching.

Palmer Cousins.

Slidell was talking, but I didn't hear him. I was flashing back to a conversation with Ryan. The privy remains were found on Tuesday. The Grim Reaper began his photo stalking on Wednesday.

Palmer Cousins was at the Foote farm that Saturday. He knew what Boyd had found.

Had Cousins placed the squirrel on my car? Was it another Grim Reaper threat? Was he following me? Did he have Katy? Would he hurt her to get at me?

My heart was pounding, my palm sweaty against the phone.

"I'll call you later," I said.

Slidell sputtered.

I cut him off.

Hands trembling, I jammed the phone into my purse and pushed through the front door.

And slammed into a chest like concrete.

The man was about my height, dressed in ebony pinstripes and a dazzling white shirt.

I mumbled an apology, stepped sideways to pass.

An arm shot out. Steely fingers closed around my biceps.

I felt my body spin, saw thick black hair, my face reflected off metallic lenses, mouth wide with surprise.

Fingers splayed across my left ear. My head shot forward and cracked against the door.

Pain screamed through my skull.

I struggled to free myself. The hands held me like a vise.

Fingers clawed my hair. My head whipped back. I felt blood and tears on my cheeks.

Again, my head shot forward and slammed into wood.

My neck snapped back yet again.

Forward.

I felt an impact, heard a dull thud.

Then nothing.

I SMELLED MILDEW, MOSS, A FAINT SWEETNESS, LIKE LIVER FRYING
in a pan.

I heard geese overhead, or calling to one another on some distant lake.

Where was I? Lying prone on something hard, but where?

My brain offered only disconnected fragments. The Cobb trailer. A
gas station. A funeral home. Someone named Maples.

My fingers groped the ground around me.

Smooth. Cool. Flat.

I caressed the surface, breathed in the odor.

Cement.

I moved a hand over my face, felt crusted blood, a swollen eye, a
lump on my cheek the size of an apple.

Another mind flash.

Pin-striped black. Antiseptic white.

The attack!

Then what?

I felt panic start to rise in my chest. My tortured gray cells shot
orders, not answers.

Wake up!

Now!

Drawing both palms beneath me, I tried to push up to my knees.

My arms were rubber. Pain sluiced through my skull. A spasm
gripped my stomach.

I eased back down, the cold cement good against my cheek.

My heartbeat hammered in my ears.

Where? Where? Where?

Another barked command.

Move!

Rolling onto my back, I sat up slowly. White light fired through my brain. Tremors twitched the underbelly of my tongue.

I drew my ankles to my bum, lowered my chin, and breathed deeply.

Little by little, the nausea and dizziness subsided.

Slowly, I raised my head, opened my one good eye, and peered intently into my surroundings.

The darkness was like a solid thing.

I waited for my pupil to dilate. It didn't.

Gingerly, I rolled to my knees and stood, groping the darkness, crouching, hands extended. Blindman's buff and I was it.

Two steps and my palms hit vertical cement. I crab-walked sideways. Three steps to a corner. Turning ninety degrees, I followed the perpendicular wall, right hand in front of me, left hand Brailling the concrete.

Oh, dear God. How small was my prison? How small? I felt perspiration form on my face, my neck.

Four steps and my left toe jammed a solid object. I pitched forward. Both my hands shot out and downward into darkness, then slammed something rough and hard as my shin cracked against an edge of something on the floor.

I cried out from the pain and trembled from fear.

Again the tremors in my mouth, the bitter taste.

I had tripped over what felt like a stone slab. I was stretched across it, my hands and arms on the floor beyond, my feet back where they had made contact with the near edge.

I melted to the cement. A tear broke from my good eye and coursed down my cheek. Another oozed from the corner of my swollen eye, burning raw flesh as it slid across.

Cooling sweat. Burning tears. Racing heart.

More images, faster now.

A bulldog man with thick black hair.

Metallic lenses. A fun house reflection of my startled face.

A ricochet flashback. Forty-eight hours. An exchange between Slidell and a feisty deb.

"What *did* you see?"

"Myself!"

Dolores was referring to mirrored lenses!

Sweet Jesus! My attacker was the man who had visited Cagle!

Cagle, who'd spent the last week in a coma.

Think!

My cheek was on fire. My shin throbbed. Blood pounded in my swollen eye.

Think!

Kaleidoscope images.

A jogger in headphones. Mrs. Cobb. The cuckoo. The photos.

I caught my breath.

The matches!

I jammed my fingers into a back jeans pocket.

Empty.

I tried the other, broke a nail in my frenzy.

Both front pockets.

One tissue, a nickel, a penny.

But I put the matches there. I know I did. Mrs. Cobb asked me to. Maybe I wasn't remembering correctly. Think through the sequence more slowly.

I had a sensation of walls compressing around me. How tiny was the space in which I was trapped? Oh God! The claustrophobia goosed the fear and pain.

My hands trembled as I kept thrusting them from pocket to pocket.

The matches had to be there.

Please!

I tried the small square at the top of the right front pocket. My fingers closed around an oblong object, thick at one end, rough at the other.

A matchbook!

But how many?

I flipped the lid and felt with my finger and thumb.

Six.

Make them count!

Six. Only six!

Calm down! Take it by quadrants. Locate a light. Locate an exit.

Orienting toward what I hoped was the room's center, I spread my feet, detached a match, and dragged it across the striker.

The head tore off without igniting.

Damn! Down to five!

I detached and struck another, pressing the head against the friction strip with the ball of my thumb.

The match sputtered, flamed, illuminated my shirt but little else. Holding it high, I crept forward and took a mental snapshot. From what I could see the room seemed fairly large.

Crates and cardboard cartons along the wall I'd been following. Headstone that had taken a piece of my shin lay flat on the floor. Metal shelving, perforated strips holding the shelves in place. Gap between shelving and wall.

Fire burned my fingers. I dropped the match.

Darkness.

More Braille-walking. At the end of the shelving I struck my third match.

Wooden door in the middle of the far wall.

Angling the match downward so the flame rose, I searched for a light switch.

Nothing.

The flame went out. I dropped the match, strode toward the door, groped for the knob, and twisted.

Locked!

I flung my weight against the wood, banged my fists, kicked, called out.

No reply.

I felt like screaming in anger and frustration.

Stepping back, I turned toward three o'clock, took several steps, and lit my fourth match.

A table emerged from the inky black. Objects lined up on the tabletop. Bulky items stacked beside it.

The match died.

My visual recall centers pasted the three glimpses to form a composite sketch.

The room was about twenty by twelve feet.

OK. Manageable. My claustrophobia ratcheted down a notch. My fear did not.

Boxes and shelving along one wall, table or workbench opposite, storage beside that, door at the far end.

Recentered in the room, I turned my back to the door and inched forward, planning on a closer inspection of the back wall.

Trembling, I placed the next-to-last match head on the striker strip. Before I struck it, I sensed that this part of the room was more pewter than black.

I turned back. A small rectangle was visible high above the table.

I peered more intently.

The rectangle was a window covered with grillwork, grime, and dust.

Shoving the matchbook into my pocket, I climbed onto the table, stretched up on my toes, and looked out.

The window was half underground, surrounded by a vine-clogged well. Through the top portion I could see trees, a shed, moonlight oozing through a crack between eggplant clouds.

I heard more geese, realized their squawking was muffled by earth and concrete, not altitude or distance.

My pulse began to race again. My breath came even quicker.

I was trapped in an underground room, a basement or cellar of some sort. The only way out was probably a stairway beyond the locked door.

I closed my eyes, breathed deeply.

Move! Take action!

As I hopped from the table, a dozen filaments swayed in the moonlight, each glistening like spider silk. The sweet liver smell was stronger.

I stepped closer.

Each filament held a fleshy mass about the size of my fist. Each mass was suspended over a small shielded burner.

Bear galls! They must have been dried already because the burners weren't on.

Outrage and anger sent the last of my claustrophobia packing.

Act now! Do it fast! The break in the clouds won't last.

I struck match number five and moved to the far end of the table.

File cabinets. Parking signs. Flower stands with long spiky points. A baby casket. A miniature steel vault. Rolls of fake grass. A tent.

Unrolling a layer of canvas, I grabbed a tent stake, stuck it in my pocket, and crossed the room.

Find candles! Get light next to the door. Use the tent stake to try to break the lock or pry the handle.

Barely breathing, I struck the last match and scanned the cartons. Embalming fluids. Hardening compound.

I got to the shelves, squatted, peered into an open box.

Eye caps, trocar buttons, scalpels, drain tubes, hypodermic needles, syringes. Nothing that would break a door.

The room began to dim.

Could I move one of the burners? Could I light it?

I stood.

The upper shelves housed a theme park of urns in bronze and marble. An eagle with outstretched wings. Tutankhamen's death mask. A gnarled oak. A Greek god. A double crypt.

Sweet Jesus! Did the urns contain cremains? Were the uncollected dead staring down on my plight? Could a bronze eagle break a wooden door? Could I lift it?

The clouds closed. Darkness claimed the basement once again.

I felt my way back to the table, climbed up, and peered out. Could I attract anyone's attention? Did I want to? Would the dark-haired stranger return and finish me off?

My leg and face pulsated with pain. Tears burned the back of my lids. Clamping my teeth, I held them in check.

The landscape was a study in black.

Minutes passed. Hours. Millennia.

I fought feelings of helplessness. Surely someone would come. But who? What time was it?

I looked at my watch. The darkness was so thick I couldn't see my hand.

Who knew I was here? Despair clawed my brain. No one!

Suddenly, a light appeared, flickered as it moved through the trees.

I watched the light bob toward the small patch of denseness I knew to be the shed. It disappeared, reappeared, bobbed in my direction. As it neared, I started to yell out, then stopped myself. I began to make out the form of a man. He drew close, veered out of my field of vision.

A door banged overhead.

I dropped from the table, scuttled across the room, and shrank behind the far end of the shelving. The case wobbled as I pressed against it. Reaching into my pocket, I withdrew the tent stake, wrapped my fingers around it, and dropped it to my side, point down.

Moments later I heard movement outside the basement door. A key turned. The door opened.

Barely breathing, I peered between the urns.

The man paused in the doorway, lantern held above his right shoulder. He was short and muscular, with thick black hair and Asian eyes. His sleeves were rolled, revealing a tattoo above his right wrist.

SEMPER FI.

Hershey Zamzow had spoken of Asian middlemen in bear gall trafficking.

Sonny Pounder had spoken of a Korean dealer, someone with an inside line.

Ricky Don Dorton had worked his mortuary scheme with a Marine Corps buddy.

Terry Woolsey was suspicious about her lover's death, and about his replacement as coroner.

In a heartbeat my mind forged another composite.

My attacker was the man who had hastily embalmed Murray Snow's body. The man who had visited Wally Cagle. The man who smuggled drugs and bear galls with Ricky Don Dorton.

My attacker was the Lancaster County coroner, James Park! James Park was Korean.

Park stepped through the doorway and swept his lantern about. I heard a sharp intake of breath, saw his body stiffen.

Park moved to a point directly opposite the shelving and hefted a burlap bag in his left hand. The bag moved and changed shape like a living thing.

Adrenaline shot through every fiber in my body.

Park's circle of light darted through the basement's macabre assemblage, its jerky motion a barometer of its holder's anger. I could hear Park's breath, smell his sweat.

My grip tightened on the tent stake. Unconsciously, I tensed and pressed closer against the shelving.

The shelving wobbled, ticked the wall.

Park's light leapt in my direction. He took a step toward me.

Another. The glow lit my feet, my legs. Moving slowly, I slipped the hand with the tent stake behind my back.

I heard another gasp, then Park stopped and raised the lantern. Though not bright, the sudden illumination caused my good eye to squint. My head jerked to the side.

"So, Dr. Brennan. Finally we meet."

The voice was flat and silky, high like a child's. Park wasn't bothering to disguise it now, but I knew instantly. The Grim Reaper!

My grip tightened on the stake. Every muscle in me tensed.

Park smiled a smile that was pure ice.

"My associates and I are so appreciative of your battle on behalf of wildlife, we've decided to give you a small token of our gratitude."

Park raised the bag. Inside, something writhed, causing shadows to ripple and morph in the burlap.

I stood frozen, back pressed to the wall.

"Nothing to say, Dr. Brennan?"

How to play it? Reason? Cajole? Lash out? I chose to remain mute.

"All right, then. The gift."

Park took a step back, allowing shadow to swallow me once again. I watched him set the lantern on the ground and begin unknotting the tied ends of the bag.

Barely thinking, I slid the tent stake behind the shelving and levered with both hands. The top-heavy case swayed forward, settled back.

Engrossed in his task, Park didn't notice.

I dropped the stake.

Park's head came up.

I grabbed a metal upright with both hands and rocked the shelving away from the wall with all my strength.

Park straightened.

The shelving pitched forward. Urns flew through the air.

Park threw both hands up, twisted his upper body. The Karnak special caught him in the right temple. He dropped. I heard his skull crack against cement.

The lantern glass shattered and its light went out, leaving only the smell of kerosene.

For what seemed a lifetime, objects crashed and rolled on the floor.

When the noise finally ceased, there was eerie quiet.

Catacomb darkness.

Utter stillness.

One heartbeat. Two. Three.

Was Park unconscious? Dead? Lying in wait? Should I flee? Grope for the tent stake?

Burlap rustled, sounding like thunder in the silence.

I held my breath.

Was Park releasing his malicious present?

A whisper, like the soft brushing of scales on cement.

More silence.

Had I imagined the sound?

The tiny scraping started again, stopped, started.

Something was moving!

What to do?

Then a terrifying, stupefying rattling deadened my every response.

Snakes!

I pictured slithering bodies coiling to strike. Darting tongues. Lidless, gleaming eyes.

Glacial cold cramped my chest, then rolled outward through my heart, my veins, my stomach, my fingertips.

What kind of snakes? Moccasins? Copperheads? Did those snakes rattle? Diamondbacks? Something exotic from South America? Knowing Park's history, I was certain the snakes were venomous.

How many were out there, slithering toward me in the dark?

I felt totally alone. Totally abandoned.

Please, please let someone come!

But no one was coming. No one knew where I was. How could I have been so stupid?

Struggling to function, my mind flew in a million directions.

How does a snake locate its prey? Vision? Smell? Heat? Motion? Does it go on the attack or try to avoid contact?

Do I freeze? Bolt? Go for the tent stake?

More rattling.

Panic overcame reason. Good eye wide in the darkness, I shot toward the door.

My foot caught on the fallen shelving and I pitched headlong into the rubble. My hand hit flesh and bone, unconsciously jerked left.

Hair. Something warm and wet, puddled on the cement.

Park!

The rattling reached a crescendo.

Fighting back tears, I rolled to my right and felt a wooden leg.

Stand! Raise your head out of striking range!

As I tried to pull myself up I noticed lights rake the window.

Then white-hot fire shot up my ankle.

I screamed from pain and terror.

As I draped myself over a table, the burning moved up my leg, my groin. What little vision I had blurred.

My thoughts floated to a different place, a different time. I saw Katy, Harry, Pete, Ryan.

I heard pounding, scraping, felt my body lifted.

Then nothing.

36

It was a week before Ryan and I hauled our sand chairs across Anne's boardwalk and parked them on the beach. I wore the long-anticipated bikini and an elegant white sock. A large-brimmed straw hat and Sophia Loren shades hid the black eye and scabbing on my face. A cane kept the weight off my left foot.

Ryan was dressed in surfer shorts and enough blocker to protect Moby Dick. On our first beach day he'd turned Pepto pink. On our second he was moving toward tobacco-leaf gold.

While Ryan and I read and chatted, Boyd alternated between snapping at the surf and chasing seagulls.

"Hooch really likes it here," Ryan said.

"His name is Boyd."

"Too bad Birdie wouldn't change his mind."

During the past week Slidell, Ryan, and Woolsey had filled me in on the missing pieces. Ryan and I had zigzagged between discussing and avoiding the culminating events in Lancaster. Ryan could sense I was still subject to flashbacks of terror.

The snakes turned out to be timber rattlers captured in the Smoky Mountains. Park liked to work with natural ingredients. Thanks to Slidell and Rinaldi, I was bitten only twice. Thanks to Woolsey, I was at the ER before the venom spread.

Though I was violently ill for twenty-four hours, I improved quickly thereafter, and Ryan's daily visits hastened my recovery. Four days after my encounter in the funeral chapel basement, I was back home. Three days after that, Ryan and I split for Sullivan's Island, Boyd doing his saliva act in the backseat.

The sky was blue. The sand was white. Pink strips were glowing around the edges of my swimsuit. Though my left foot and ankle were still swollen and uncomfortable, I felt terrific.

My sudden epiphany about James Park had been correct. Park and Dorton had been drug-smuggling buddies since Vietnam. When Dorton returned Stateside he invested his profits in hunt camps and strip clubs. When Park got home he went into the family funeral business. Mama and Daddy Park, both born in Seoul, owned a parlor in Augusta, Georgia. After a few years, with a little help from the folks, James bought an operation of his own in Lancaster.

Park and Dorton stayed in touch, and Park booked into one of Dorton's wilderness camps. Ricky Don, having established himself in the import-export business, pointed out the prosperity to be had from franchises in drugs and wildlife, and Park allowed as how he could tap Asian markets for both the imports and the exports.

Jason Jack Wyatt supplied bears from the mountains. Harvey Pearce hunted on the coast and brought the bear parts to Dorton on his drug runs to Charlotte. Park prepared the galls and hawked them in Asia, often exchanging them for drugs to supplement Ricky Don's Latin American suppliers.

"Sunscreen?" Ryan waggled the tube.

"Thanks."

Ryan applied lotion to my shoulders.

"Lower?"

"Please."

His hands worked their way to the small of my back.

"Lower?"

"Um."

His fingertips slipped under the elastic of my bikini bottom.

"That'll be fine."

"Sure?"

"The sun's never shined that far down, Ryan."

As Ryan dropped into his chair, another question occurred to me.

"How do you suppose Cobb uncovered the bear gall operation?"

"Cobb was looking into turtle poaching in Tyrrell County and made the bear discovery by accident when he was shadowing Harvey Pearce."

Anger welled in me as I thought of Harvey Pearce.

"The son of a bitch baited bears with Honey Buns, then blew their brains out, cut off the paws, cut out the gallbladders, and dumped the rest."

"Maybe Pearce's particular circle in hell will be full of bears, and Harvey without so much as a peashooter."

I thought of something else.

"That note in Brian Aiker's wallet really threw me."

"Cobb's note to Aiker."

"Yeah. I assumed Cobb meant Columbia, South Carolina. I forgot Harvey Pearce lived in Columbia, North Carolina." I shook my head at my own stupidity. "I also thought Cobb was referring to Palmer Cousins as the person who was dirty."

"He meant plural not singular, the Dynamic Duo from Sneedville, Tennessee." After some grammatical stumbling, Ryan and I had agreed on the masculine pronoun for Charlotte Cobb.

"The Melungeon cousins."

I watched a pelican swoop over the water, tuck its wings, and plunge toward a wave. Seconds later it came up empty.

"Do you suppose the Spix's macaw and the goldenseal were just opportunistic sidelines?" I asked.

"Dorton may have asked Cousin J.J. to gather the goldenseal. He probably planned to persuade his regulars that the stuff was effective at masking drugs during urine tests."

"And Harvey Pearce probably got the macaw the same way he scored the bird Pounder mentioned."

"Probably," Ryan agreed. "Tyree sold coke on the street for Dorton. Tyree, Dorton, Pearce, and Park met periodically at the Foote farm. Pearce probably brought the bird to the farm on one of those trips. Sadly for all, it didn't survive its ordeal."

"But someone saved the feathers, thinking they might be good for a few bucks."

Exactly as Rachel Mendelson had suggested.

"That would be my guess," Ryan said.

Boyd spotted a kid on a bike, ran with him a few yards, then veered off after a sandpiper.

"Tamela had nothing to do with the drugs, just went to the farm with Tyree." I pictured the Banks sisters in my kitchen. "You should have seen her face, Ryan. I believe her account of the stillbirth."

"Couldn't prosecute anyway. No way to prove cause of death."

We both rolled that thought around. Then I had another.

"So Cobb alerted Brian Aiker, and the two began poking around. Dorton or Park found out."

"Dorton probably gave the order, but according to Tyree, Park killed Aiker," Ryan said. "Drugged him, took two cars to the boat ramp, and rolled Aiker's car into the water. Wouldn't surprise me if Tyree drove one of the cars."

"And Tyree killed Cobb."

"According to the innocent accused, he ain't no killer. He only does 'bidness.' Fills a human need. All Tyree admits to is hauling Cobb's head and hands to the Foote farm in a sack provided by Park, who wanted to make the body more difficult to identify."

"Two bullets in the head strike you as Park's style?" I asked.

"Not exactly," Ryan agreed. "Tyree claims to know nothing about bear parts, either. Claims that was entirely Jason Jack's and Harvey's enterprise. Claims he had to dig up and move some of the bears because the privy was becoming overfull and he was afraid the smell could draw attention to Cobb's remains."

"Only the moron dug up part of the very thing he was trying to hide." Another question skipped into my mind. "Did Park kill Dorton?"

"Very doubtful. No motive, and the tox screen showed Dorton was skyed to the eyeballs on coke and alcohol. We may never know if the cause of death was homicide or acute numerical ascension."

"OK, Ryan. I'll bite."

"His number was up."

The orbital roll caused moderate pain.

"But we do know Park made a trip to Charlotte two days after Sonny Pounder's arrest."

About the time I was analyzing Tamela's baby's bones.

"Why?" I asked.

"That's unclear. But Slidell discovered Park made a credit card charge at a gas station on Woodlawn and I-77."

"Think Park and Dorton were planning to take Pounder out if he talked?"

"Wouldn't surprise me. What is clear is that Park killed Murray Snow. Woolsey found a tin of Ma Huang in the chapel basement."

"I'm confident you're going to tell me what that is."

"Ma Huang is an Asian herbal poison, known on the streets as 'herbal ecstasy.'"

"Let me guess. Ma Huang contains ephedrine."

"Step to the head of the class."

"Park knew Snow had a bad heart."

"Probably gave him tea laced with Ma Huang. It's often administered that way. Wham-o. Cardiac arrest."

"Why?" I asked.

"Same reason he poisoned Cagle. He was becoming nervous over too much interest in the headless skeleton."

"*How* did he poison Cagle?"

"Not knowing Cagle's medical susceptibility, our hero had to step up to something more powerful. Something that would do in even a healthy man. Ever hear of tetrodotoxin?"

"It's a neurotoxin, called TTX for short, found in fugu."

Ryan looked at me like I'd spoken Romanian.

"Fugu is Japanese puffer fish," I explained. "Gram for gram, TTX is about ten thousand times more lethal than cyanide. Diners die from it every year in Asia. The terrifying thing about TTX is that it paralyzes the body but leaves the brain fully aware of what's happening."

"But Cagle survived."

"Is he talking yet?"

"No."

"So we don't know how Park administered the stuff."

Ryan shook his head.

"How do you know Park used TTX?" I asked.

"Tetrodotoxin looks like heroin. In addition to the Ma Huang, Park's pharmacopoeia included a packet of white crystalline powder. Woolsey had it tested."

A seagull circled, landed, bobbed at us like one of those breakfast table water toys.

"Why the snakes?" I asked.

"Your death had to look accidental." Ryan mimicked a TV newscaster. "While hiking in heavy forest in Lancaster County, an anthropologist was tragically nailed by a rattler today." Ryan's voice returned to normal. "Except Park was the one who got nailed."

I shuddered, remembering the sound of Park's head cracking on the cement. According to the police report, Park had suffered fatal skull fractures both from a falling object and from striking his head against the concrete floor.

Spotting a gull floating toward shore, Boyd charged across the beach. The bird took off. Boyd followed its flight path, then returned and shook himself, bombarding us with sand and salt water.

"Heineken?" I asked, covering my face with my arms.

"S'il vous plaît."

I opened the cooler and dug out a beer for Ryan, bottled water for Boyd, and a Diet Coke for myself.

"Why do you suppose Park sent me the Grim Reaper e-mails?" I asked, handing Ryan his beer. Boyd raised his snout and I dripped water into his mouth.

"Wanted you to back off from the privy skull."

"Think about your own reasoning, Ryan. The e-mails started on a Wednesday. How could Park have known who I was or what we'd found at that point?"

"Rinaldi sent out his query about the headless skeleton on Tuesday. It probably went to Lancaster and included the coroner. We'll find out eventually. Slidell's convinced Tyree will roll over."

"Slidell," I snorted.

"Skinny isn't so bad," Ryan said.

I didn't reply.

"He saved your life."

"Yes," I agreed.

Boyd flopped onto his side in the shade of my sand chair. Ryan went back to his Terry Pratchett. I went back to my *E* magazine.

I couldn't concentrate. My thoughts kept hopping to Skinny Slidell. Finally, I gave up.

"How did Slidell know where I was?"

Ryan stuck a finger in his book to mark the page.

"Rinaldi's background check on Dorton turned up the fact that Ricky Don's Marine Corps smuggling buddy all those years ago was none other than the current Lancaster County coroner. Slidell tried to warn you about Park when he phoned your cell with the news about Aiker's note."

"I cut him off."

"According to Rinaldi, Slidell fumed for a while, then agreed to drop by the annex. You weren't at home, but Geneva showed them your note."

"Which said I was going to South Carolina."

"Slidell put that together with your funeral wisecrack, and he and Rinaldi hauled ass to Lancaster. Got there right about the time the rattler was introducing himself to you. Woolsey was with them and she hauled you to the hospital, practically drove her patrol car through the ER doors, Skinny said."

"Hmm."

"He also phoned me from the hospital to fill me in."

"Hmm."

"And he's admitted he was wrong about Tamela."

"He has?"

"Took the family a chrysanthemum."

"Skinny did that?"

"Yellow one. Made a special trip to Wal-Mart for it."

Skinny took Gideon Banks a plant.

Hmm.

"I guess I've been pretty hard on Skinny. I hate to admit it, but the guy really is a good cop."

A smile tickled Ryan's mouth.

"How about Agent Cousins?"

"All right. Maybe I misjudged Cousins. Anyway, Katy never went to Myrtle Beach with him."

"Where was she?"

"Spending a few days in Asheville with Pete. She didn't bother to tell me because she was miffed over my pressing her about the Grim Reaper e-mails. But it doesn't matter, anyway. Katy called from Charlottesville this morning all agog over some premed student named Sheldon Seabourne."

"Ah, fickle youth."

Ryan and I settled back to our reading. With each page I was realizing how naïve my faith in the Green Movement had been. At moments my disgust boiled over. One such moment arrived shortly.

"Did you know that more than nine million turtles and snakes were exported from the United States in 1996?"

Ryan dropped his book to his chest. "Bet you can think of a couple you wish had been among them."

"Ever hear of the Captive Bred Wildlife Foundation in Arizona?"

"No."

"Their slogan is 'When turtles are outlawed, only outlaws will have turtles.'"

"That's idiocy that rings a bell."

"These kind citizens will be happy to sell you a pair of Galápagos tortoises for eight to ten thousand bucks. You could take a sparrow, put it on the endangered species list, and some asshole would pay two grand for it."

"There's CITES," Ryan said. "And the Endangered Species Act."

"Protection on paper," I said with disdain. "Too many loopholes, too little enforcement. Remember Rachel Mendelson's tale of the Spix's macaw?"

Ryan nodded.

"Listen to this." I quoted from the article I'd been reading. "'In 1996 Hector Ugalde pled guilty to federal conspiracy charges in Brazil for smuggling hyacinth's macaws.'" I looked up. "Ugalde got three years' probation and a ten-thousand-dollar fine. That'll really stop him."

Boyd came over and put his snout on my knee. I stroked his head.

"Everyone knows about whales, and pandas, and tigers, and rhinos. Those animals are sexy. They have foundations and sweatshirts and posters."

Boyd followed a sandpiper with his eyes, considered.

"Fifty thousand plants and animals become extinct each year, Ryan. Within half a century one-quarter of the world's species could be gone." I flapped a hand at the ocean. "And it's not just over there. One-third of all U.S. plants and animals are at risk of extinction."

"Take a breath."

I did.

"Listen to this." I resumed reading, selecting excerpts. "'At least four hundred and thirty medicines containing eighty endangered and threatened species have been documented in the United States alone.

At least one-third of all patented Oriental medicine items available in the United States contain protected species.'"

I looked up.

"The illegal trade in black bear galls in California alone is estimated at one hundred million a year. Think about that, Ryan. Ounce for ounce, bear gall is worth more than cocaine, and hairbags like Dorton and Park know that. They also know they'll get a slap on the wrist if they get caught."

I shook my head in disgust.

"Deer are killed for their antler velvet. Siberian tigers are hunted for their bones and penises. Sea horses are killed to help men grow hair."

"Sea horses?"

"Rhinos are shot, electrocuted, and driven into pits lined with sharpened bamboo stakes so men in Yemen can make dagger handles. There are only a few thousand rhinos left in the world, Ryan. Jesus, you can go on the Web and buy smoked gorilla paws."

Ryan got up, squatted by my chair.

"You feel very strongly about this."

"It sickens me." I let my eyes travel to Ryan's. "A cache of six metric tons of elephant ivory was seized in Singapore last June. Now a group of South African countries is talking about reversing the ban on ivory trading. Why? So people can make ornaments out of elephant tusks. Every year the Japanese take hundreds of whales for research. Yeah. Right. Research that ends up in the seafood market. Do you have any idea of the length of the evolutionary process that created the animals we have today, and the shortness of the time needed to kill them off?"

Ryan took my face in both his hands.

"We helped do something about it, Tempe. Park and Tyree are going down. No more bears or birds will be dying because of them. It's not much, but it's a start."

"It's a start," I agreed.

"Let's keep at it." Ryan's eyes were blue as the Atlantic and steady on mine. "You and me."

"Do you mean that, Ryan?"

"I do."

I kissed him, wrapped my arms around his neck, and pressed my cheek to his.

Pulling free, I wiped sand from his forehead and settled back to my reading, eager to find a place to begin.

Ryan took Boyd for a run on the beach.

That night we ate shrimp and crab on the docks at Shem Creek. We walked in the surf, made love, then fell asleep listening to Ryan's eternal ocean.

FROM THE FORENSIC FILES
OF DR. KATHY REICHS

For legal and ethical reasons I cannot discuss any of the real-life cases that may have inspired *Bare Bones*, but I can share with you some experiences that contributed to the plot.

Monsieur Orignal

Shakespeare spoke of "murder most foul" (*Hamlet*, 1.5), but not all forensic anthropology cases are the result of violence.

A variety of bones find their way to my lab: trophy skulls smuggled from foreign lands; teaching skeletons spirited from classrooms to fraternity houses; Confederate soldiers buried in unmarked graves; pets laid to rest in backyards or crawl spaces.

It happens all the time. Bones or body parts are discovered. Local authorities, unfamiliar with anatomy, send them to the coroner or medical examiner. Occasionally the "vic" turns out to be a reptile or bird, but most are members of the class Mammalia. I've examined spareribs, deer metapodia, ham bones, and elk horns. I've gotten kittens in gunnysacks and wood rats mixed in with murder victims. Bear paws, which particularly resemble human hands and feet, also sometimes show up at my lab.

The skeletal remains that found their way into *Bare Bones* actually entered my life during a blizzard in Montreal on a Thursday in November 1997. Driving as a Southerner versed in snowfall panic, edging my speed up to thirty only in the tunnel, I arrived late to the lab and thus missed the morning meeting at which the day's cases had been discussed and assigned. One document lay on my desk, a Demande d'Expertise en Anthropologie.

Wasting no time, I skimmed for critical information: case number, morgue number, coroner, pathologist. I was being asked to examine cut marks on leg and pelvic bones to determine the type of saw used for dismemberment. The summary of known facts included one French word unfamiliar to me: *orignal*. Guilty over my tardiness, I headed straight for the bones, opting for a vocabulary check at a later time.

Throwing on a lab coat, I crossed to the counter reserved for new cases. When I unzipped the pouch, my jaw dropped. Either this victim had a colossal pituitary disorder, or I was looking at Goliath himself.

About-face. Dictionary.

Orignal: élan, n. m. Au Canada on l'appelle orignal.

My dismemberment victim was a moose.

On more careful reading of the request-for-expertise form, I discovered that the analysis had been requested by the Société de la faune et des parcs, the Quebec equivalent of the U.S. Fish and Wildlife Service. A poacher had been killing moose for years with blatant disregard for the annual quota. Conservation agents had decided to prosecute and wanted an opinion. Could I tie the cut marks on the moose bones to a saw recovered from the suspect's garage?

I could.

Big bones. Big animal. Big lesson in proceeding rapidly while not fully cognizant of the mission.

No need for Shakespeare here.

Thoreau put it well: "Some circumstantial evidence is strong, as when you find a trout in the milk" (*Walden*).

Or Bullwinkle in a body bag.

ABOUT THE AUTHOR

Kathy Reichs is forensic anthropologist for the Office of the Chief Medical Examiner, State of North Carolina, and for the Laboratoire de Sciences Judiciaires et de Médecine Légale for the province of Quebec. She is one of only fifty forensic anthropologists certified by the American Board of Forensic Anthropology and is on the Executive Committee of the Board of Directors of the American Academy of Forensic Sciences. A professor of anthropology at the University of North Carolina–Charlotte, Dr. Reichs is a native of Chicago, where she received her Ph.D. at Northwestern. She now divides her time between Charlotte and Montreal and is a frequent expert witness at criminal trials. Her first novel, *Déjà Dead,* brought Dr. Reichs fame when it became a *New York Times* bestseller and won the 1997 Ellis Award for Best First Novel. *Death du Jour, Deadly Décisions, Fatal Voyage,* and *Grave Secrets* also became international and *New York Times* bestsellers. *Bare Bones* is her sixth novel featuring Temperance Brennan.